THE MECHANICS OF LUST

A MACKENZIE COUNTRY STORY
BOOK 2

JAY HOGAN

SOUTHERN LIGHTS PUBLISHING

Published by Southern Lights Publishing

Copyright © 2023 by Jay Hogan

This is a work of fiction. Names, characters, places, and incidents are either the product of the author's imagination or are used fictitiously, and any resemblance to actual persons, living or dead, business establishments, events, or locales is entirely coincidental.

All rights reserved.

This book is licensed to the original purchaser only. Duplication or distribution by any means is illegal and a violation of international copyright law, subject to criminal prosecution and upon conviction, fines and/or imprisonment. No part of this book may be reproduced in any form or by any electronic or mechanical means, including photocopying, recording, or by any information storage and retrieval systems, without written permission from the author, except for the use of brief quotations in a book review. Any ebook format cannot be legally loaned or given to others.

To request permission and all other enquiries contact the author through the website.

https://www.jayhoganauthor.com

Trade Paperback ISBN:978-1-99-110413-7

Digital ISBN: 978-1-99-110412-0

Digital Edition Published October 2023

Trade Paperback Published October 2023

First Edition

Editing by Boho Edits

Cover Art Copyright © 2023 Reese Dante

Cover content is for illustrative purposes only and any person depicted on the cover is a model.

Proofread by Lissa Given Proofing and L. Parks

Printed in the United States of America and Australia

For my family who read everything I write and keep on saying they love it all, blushes included.

THE REAL MACKENZIE COUNTRY AND ACKNOWLEDGMENTS

The Mackenzie Basin in the South Island of New Zealand is one of the most stunningly beautiful and scenic places in the world. Home to the Southern Alps that form the backbone of our small country, it is also the site of New Zealand's highest mountain, Aoraki Mount Cook. The region is riddled with glaciers, majestic lakes, braided rivers, and towering peaks. A dark sky reserve blankets the area making it one of the best places in the world to stargaze and maybe even catch a glimpse of the Southern Lights.

The high country sheep stations that call this spectacular land home are a farming legacy unique to New Zealand, and they take their role as custodians and guardians of the environment very seriously. The stations mostly farm the sturdy merino breed of sheep who spend their summers traversing back and forth over some of the highest ranges in this area, many only accessible by foot. Tourists from all over the world book to be part of an annual muster—a down under term similar in meaning to roundup—where the mobs of sheep are brought down from their high altitude summer grazing to lamb and to overwinter. It's a once in a lifetime experience.

In my research for this series I spent time at two South Island high country stations and I am grateful to the owners and shepherds who let me tag along as they worked, and who put up with an endless barrage of questions from this clueless townie not to mention all the follow up emails. I am also grateful to my expert beta reader Jill McCaw who made sure I got my high country farming terms right and everything in its place.

Any mistakes are completely my own.

In this series I have tried to stay true to the dominant landmarks, towns, and the general feel of the Mackenzie Basin, but for the purpose of the storyline itself I 'added' the fictional Glendale River and its glacial valley as home to Miller Station, while Lane Station is situated on the other side of a mountain range that lies between the two. In a map these fictional valleys would sit somewhere east of the Macauley River. I also created the fictional supply town of Oakwood, so please don't add it to your sightseeing list.

As always, I thank my husband for his patience and for keeping the dog walked and out of my hair when I needed to work, and my daughter for her incredible support.

Getting a book finessed for release is a huge challenge that includes the help of beta readers, editing, proofing, cover artists and a tireless PA. It's a team effort, and includes all those author support networks and reader fans who rally around when you're ready to pull your hair out and throw away every first draft. Thanks to all of you.

THE MECHANICS OF LUST

I broke the rules and fell in love with my best friend. Newsflash. He didn't feel the same. I had to stand by and watch him fall for someone else. Moving on hasn't been easy since we all live and work on the same high country sheep station, but I'm finally getting there.

I'm building a new life, a new set of dreams, planning a different future, just me and my dogs. The last thing I need is Luke Nichols, the sexy, enigmatic, ex-husband of my nemesis, filling my head with a laundry list of cravings. Talk about complicated.

Luke is only in Mackenzie Country for a few months and I'm not about to put my heart on the line again just for a little fun. But the more I'm around Luke, the harder it is to remember exactly why Luke and I are a bad idea, the *worst* idea.

Things between us are about to go nuclear.

Maybe I'm wrong.

Maybe we *can* keep it simple.
Maybe I can satisfy my cravings *and* hold on to my heart.
And maybe pigs can fly.

Trigger warning: This book contains references to the past death of a child.

AUTHOR NOTE

This book contains references to the past death of a child.

CHAPTER ONE

Zach

"Speech, speech!" A slow clap reverberated off the faded walls of the Oakwood pub's back bar, which locals had affectionately named The Fleece.

I put my back to the wooden bar and watched a furiously blushing Gil throw Holden a withering, you-are-in-so-much-trouble glare before stepping onto the small stage. He surveyed the crowd from under the *Happy Fortieth Birthday* banner, which had taken four of us an embarrassing amount of time and a few beers to finally get in place.

I was amazed we'd managed to keep the surprise party a secret, but somehow we'd done it, and Gil had been stunned, tearful, and touchingly overwhelmed when he'd walked into the packed bar to a loud chorus of happy birthday that rattled the rafters.

As I listened to his emotional thank you to everyone who'd turned up to celebrate, including some of his friends who'd flown in from Wellington, it was hard not to be charmed by the man. Not quite a year in the district and Gil's name was almost as synonymous with

Miller Station as Holden's. This was partly due to their gay-couple status, but also because of the run of free seminars Gil had begun offering locally on grief, stress management, and rural mental health. The result was a bar chocka with birthday well-wishers.

And I was one of them.

Cue the shocked gasps of disbelief.

Keeping my eyes on Gil, I shuffled sideways to let a man in at the bar behind me.

"We must stop meeting like this." The gravelly voice sent a shiver down my spine, and I turned to find a familiar pair of blue eyes dancing over my face.

Luke Nichols. Dammit.

Luke flashed that wicked smile that always made my dick sit up and pay attention and just, damn my bad luck. The man smelled of Tom Ford, summer, and trouble, and I cursed the familiar tingling sensation his proximity always managed to induce in my body. A fact that only strengthened my resolve to make sure he caught my eye roll. He did. But the amused smirk he returned my way didn't help matters.

"Well, look who the cat dragged in." I tried not to lean in for another waft of that expensive cologne. "Guess there's no show without Punch, right?"

Luke gave an amused snort. "I guess not." His gaze raked over me, head to foot, before he turned his attention to the small stage where Gil was winding up his speech. "Ah, the birthday boy."

I followed Luke's gaze, pretending to listen while shooting covert glances back his way because . . . well, because I was an idiot. And because he looked so fucking edible. Dressed in dark-wash jeans paired with a crisp white shirt—open at the neck and with the cuffs rolled up to reveal the green silicone wristband he always wore—Luke looked annoyingly cool as a cucumber in the late January heat that had the rest of us layering on the deodorant.

Smelling fresh from the shower, Luke brushed a stray lock of dirty blond hair back into place in a way that made me want to shove a hat over my own shaggy, auburn waves. A woven black leather cord hung around his neck and disappeared under his shirt, and a pair of trendy black loafers poked out from the bottom of his jeans. It pained me to admit it, but the man was effortlessly chic.

Enough already. I refocused on Gil who was gesturing to Holden to join him on the small stage.

"Get up here, baby." Gil drew Holden in for a long, slow kiss that had the birthday crowd whooping and wolf-whistling.

I waited for the once familiar knot of jealousy in my chest, but it never came. Wistful? Sure. Envious of what they had? Absolutely. But jealous still? I thought about it again. No. Maybe I was fooling myself, but I was going to take that for a win.

Luke leaned in close. "Does this feel as weird for you as it does for me?"

I glanced over my shoulder. "I've no idea what you mean," I lied.

His lips twitched in an almost smile that I chose to ignore. "Oh really?" he asked sardonically. "Because here we are, you and me, at a party celebrating *my* ex-husband's birthday, thrown by his *new* love who just happens to be *your* best friend slash ex. One could be forgiven for saying it's a bit of a mindfuck, right?"

When I didn't answer, he elbowed me gently. "Oh, come on. A little conversation won't kill you."

I huffed. "Says you." I was being a dick and we both knew it, but that was par for the course as far as things between us went.

To be fair, Luke had attempted to build a bridge many times since our inauspicious first meeting. He'd arrived uninvited at the station the year before in an attempt to force Gil to talk and I'd been . . . less than welcoming. I might not have liked Gil much at that time, and I still didn't know the whole story of what had happened between them, but to walk out on your husband six months after your daughter was killed in a car accident? The rest of Miller Station might have found a way to gloss over that fact and forgive him, even Gil. But as far as I was concerned, how much more did you really need to know about a guy?

Not to mention, getting all buddy-buddy with the man would've meant having . . . conversations and likely being paired up to work when he helped out on the station. The problem was that any proximity to Luke brought with it a minefield of potential disaster best avoided.

Luke was sexy as shit and his obvious interest in me might fizz in those wicked blue eyes. But he was trouble with a capital *T*, and I wanted no part of him for too many reasons to list. Although if I *did* happen to list them, right at the top would be the fact that my body lit up like a Christmas tree every time the man came within spitting distance.

Not since those first times with Holden had I felt anything like that.

Maybe not even then, and that fact just plain pissed me off.

Too bad I was done with complicated men.

DONE.

Luke gave a resigned sigh. "Have it your way." His gaze returned to Gil and Holden who had joined Holden's mother, her new fiancé, and a few others slow dancing to an Adele song. He remained quiet for a long time until he finally huffed, "Jesus, look at them."

Like I wasn't already glued to the sight. The whole damn bar was.

Luke added almost wistfully, "They're so in love it's sickening."

Now, that was something we could actually agree on.

"You know, I'm not sure Gil ever even looked at me in quite that same way," Luke said almost too softly to catch. Then he fell quiet, and I stole a sideways glance to find his expression shuttered.

Fighting the urge to say something reassuring because . . . I didn't even know why; I instead employed the time-honoured tradition of changing the subject. "I have to say I'm surprised to see you back this way so soon." Luke had visited the station just a couple of weeks beforehand to help build a storage and holding pen extension on the woolshed. I was hardly going to forget a week of watching him wearing not much more than cut-off jeans and a tempting tan while I tried to come up with other things, *anything*, that needed my urgent attention and would take me out of close proximity.

Luke took a mouthful of beer, and I absolutely did not watch the way he swallowed it down. "Gil and Holden didn't tell you then?"

I narrowed my eyes, my stomach sinking. "Tell me what?"

He caught my gaze. "I accepted a job with Wild Run. One of their regular helicopter pilots took a job in South Australia. I'll be flying his schedule until they can find someone more permanent for the position. Three to six months. Heli-skiing, sightseeing, airport meet and greet, that sort of thing. I moved down a couple of days ago."

I blinked as my brain did a fair impression of a hamster wheel before totally checking out. "What, here?" I practically squeaked, and heat blazed up my throat.

Luke bit back a smile. "I've always found it helpful to be in the same city or town as my job, so yes, here in Oakwood. I rented a house just off Main Street. It's costing me about a quarter of what I was paying in Wellington."

I dry swallowed, hard. Best mate or not, I was gonna kill Holden. Slowly. Very, *very* slowly. I turned and waved the bartender over. "A shot of tequila, please." I glanced sideways at Luke to find him watching me.

"That bad, huh?" His blue eyes danced merrily. "I can't say I was expecting a standing ovation, but a solid *congrats on the new job* wouldn't have gone amiss."

I kept my eyes on the barman as he filled my order. "Yeah, well, congrats on the new job."

"How kind of you." He turned and put his drink on the bar, his arm pressed hot against mine. "But don't worry. Autumn and winter are insanely busy with tourists, apparently, so you'll hardly see enough of me to offend your delicate sensibilities."

Yeah, I wasn't buying that for a second. For some reason, Luke loved helping out at the station, and the team inexplicably loved him in return. But right when I was about to make some quip I would undoubtedly regret, the tequila shot arrived and I slammed it back and ordered another.

Luke's eyes burned holes in the side of my face, but when I refused to meet them, he eventually shook his head and spun back to watch the couples on the tiny dance floor.

When the second shot arrived, I downed that one just as fast and then turned to go.

"Leaving already?" Luke studied me with the flicker of a smile that looked anything but real. "And here I was about to ask you to dance. I hope it's nothing I said."

Dance? I blinked, quashed the brief surge of excitement that rose traitorously in my belly, and kicked my brain back into gear. "Don't flatter yourself. No, I'm not leaving. But as one of the official party planners, I think I should mingle." It was a thin excuse at best and we both knew it.

"Did someone say dance?" Spencer Thompson sidled up to Luke, eyebrows waggling. The forty-something veterinarian was never far from the action, his easy charm and boyish good looks drawing plenty of attention from men and women alike. "I wouldn't say no to a little action on the dancefloor." He glanced between the two of us. "Ooh. Am I interrupting something perchance? Please say yes, because the idea of being the meat in this particular sandwich has hot as hell written all over it."

I rolled my eyes. "Jesus, Spencer, do you ever take a night off? I'm surprised there's any skin left on your dick."

He grinned. "I can't lie. The pressure is real." Then he eyed me up and down. "You're looking good tonight, Zach." He nudged Luke. "What do you think?"

Luke's gaze ran hot over my body, sending a thrill of electricity straight to my balls. Then he caught my gaze and held it for a long second. "Zach always looks good."

Spencer cast another glance between us and a smile stole over his face. "Oh yes, this is going to be good."

"Shut up, Spencer," I grumbled, not sure which was worse—my

dick doing a little happy dance in my jeans or the fire lighting up my cheeks. Not for the first time, I cursed my pale-skinned Irish genes.

Spencer's face lit up with a shit-eating grin. "Well, well, well. It seems I hit a nerve."

I fired him a withering glare and he raised both hands and backed up a step. "Fine, I'll shut up. I was only kidding."

Like hell he was. Ever since Spencer had found out I was gay and that my father had been a dick about it, he'd been determined to set me up with a boyfriend. I hadn't wanted one. Still didn't. I hadn't even had sex with a man in almost a year, not since Holden and I . . . well, whatever it is you do when you're fuck buddies and then stop because one of you went and fell in love and the other . . . didn't. No points for guessing who was on which side of that.

I liked Spencer and I appreciated his good-natured support, but I wasn't a guy who hooked up on a whim. When Holden and I had been doing our no-strings, *friends-with-benefits* thing, I was well aware that Holden occasionally hooked up with other people, and I knew he assumed I'd done too. But the truth was, I hadn't. He'd been it for me.

My list of conquests was depressingly short and uninteresting. After Holden and I had eliminated the benefits thing from our friendship, no one else had particularly floated my boat. I'd begun to wonder if maybe I was demisexual, or that Holden had simply been it for me and that I'd have to learn to live with the disappointment of no one else turning my crank ever again.

It made a weird kind of sense. Or it had until a year ago when Luke Nichols had driven onto Miller Station looking all gorgeous and dangerous, and my libido had shot to attention, waved a white flag, and mentally shouted in an embarrassingly needy voice, *pick me, pick me.*

The fucker had been screwing with my attention ever since.

I caught sight of Gil and Holden leaving the dance floor and grabbed my chance to escape. "As riveting as this conversation is, I should check in with the guest of honour. Be seeing you arseholes around."

They both laughed and Luke raised his beer in salute. "You can count on it now that we're almost neighbours, right?"

It was all I could do not to tip the bottle's contents all over that crisp white shirt. Instead, I spun on my heels and went in search of my best friend with culpable homicide on my mind.

Alongside the sound system, I found the man in question, canoodling with a very tipsy Gil. "Gentlemen."

"Zach! Just the man I wanted to see." Gil shoved his glass into Holden's hand and launched himself at me.

I gathered him in my arms a fraction before he veered into the crowded Miller Station table. Holden shot me an apologetic look, pointed to the glass in his hand, and I got the message. Just in case I'd missed it, the bourbon fumes that washed over my face sealed the deal.

"Thank you sooooo much." Gil kissed my cheek and I glanced helplessly at Holden who merely smiled indulgently at his boyfriend. "It was so sweet of you to help Holden with the surprise party. I can't believe you kept it secret."

Neither could I. "It was my pleasure." I wriggled free of Gil's bear hug and held him in place with my hands on his shoulders.

He grinned lazily and patted my cheek. "You're a good man, Zachariah Lane. And a good *friend*. I want you to know that."

Oh god. "Ah, thanks? You're a good friend too." I sent Holden a pleading look, which he dutifully ignored.

"Looking hot there, Zebedee." Charlie eyed me up and down and I smiled at the nickname. Then she got up from the table and grabbed Gil's hand. "Come on, Boss number two. Time to dance some of that alcohol off. Let's see what moves you've got."

Gil beamed. "Awesome! I haven't danced with a girl since high school. Just keep your hands above my waist."

Charlie laughed. "Like I'd be interested in your bits and bobs." She shuddered. "Ew. Just the thought. Come on."

"Wait." Holden stepped in, kissing Gil softly on the mouth. "Happy birthday, beautiful. Next dance is mine."

"*Every* dance is yours." Gil chased Holden's lips. "Every dance that matters."

Holden cradled Gil's face and something unspoken passed between them, something that tugged at my heart and all those hopes I'd carried around for more years than I could remember.

Jesus Christ, what's wrong with me? I blinked back the emotion and turned away, only to find Luke's bright blue gaze watching me from the dance floor where he and Spencer were swaying to Mariah Carey, Spencer's leg shoved determinedly between Luke's, not that Luke seemed to be paying attention. For some reason, the sight pissed me off. They were as bad as each other. From what Gil had let slip, Luke had been making the most of his single life in Wellington, as if I needed another reason to ignore my perplexing attraction to him.

"I'm cutting him off." Holden's declaration jolted me from my musings, and I left Luke and Spencer to their dance. Holden indicated Gil's empty glass before placing it on the station table. "He's pissed as a newt, and I know it's his birthday, but the alcohol fucks with his PTSD something shocking. I have standing orders not to let him go to bed like that."

Tom, Miller Station's senior shepherd, nodded and turned to Sam, our junior shepherd. "Go grab Gil a zero-alcohol beer. He won't have a clue what he's drinking anyway."

Sam shot to his feet and made a beeline for the bar.

Holden turned back to watch his boyfriend dancing and chuckled affectionately as Gil and Charlie deliberately banged into Luke and Spencer, sending them all flying.

I elbowed Holden. "This was a great idea. Did you see his face when he walked in?"

Holden grinned. "Yeah. Priceless." He caught my eye. "I couldn't have done it without you. And Gil meant what he said."

I raised a brow.

"That you're a good man. And that he thinks of you as a good friend."

I couldn't hold his gaze. "It goes both ways."

Holden tipped my chin up. "And you're *my best* mate. I'm so fucking glad we made it through."

There was no explanation needed, and I swallowed hard around the lump in my throat, around all the what-ifs and might-have-beens, because Holden was right. "Yeah, me too." The silence stretched for a few awkward seconds before I finally remembered why I'd come over. "But while we're on the subject of mates, I have a bone to pick with you." I poked him in the chest. "Did you forget to tell me something, *mate*?"

He frowned, then caught the flick of my head toward the dance floor, and bit back a smile. "Oh, you mean Luke moving to Oakwood?"

My glare said everything that was needed.

Holden rushed to explain. "Well, he did only accept the job a week ago. Plus we figured it was his business who he told and when. We haven't mentioned it to anyone." He hesitated. "Except Emily. Oh, and Tom." Holden's cheeks pinked. "And okay, so maybe I avoided telling you because Gil and I think the move is a great idea for Luke. He's been . . . struggling. And maybe also because you obviously don't like the guy."

Shit. "It's not that I don't like him—"

Holden eyeballed me and I huffed.

"I just don't click with him like the rest of you seem to."

Holden shook his head. "To be honest, I don't understand why. You generally get on with *everybody*. It's one of the most annoying things about you."

I wasn't about to explain that keeping Luke at a distance was mostly down to self-preservation, so I settled for, "I don't like what he did to Gil."

A roar went up from the dance floor and we jerked around just in time to see Charlie drop Gil into an impressive dip before hauling him back to his feet.

Holden chuckled, then sighed. "But what does any of that have to do with *you*? Gil and Luke have made their peace, and that's all that truly counts. And what happened wasn't all Luke's fault. You know that, right?"

I did know. *Have I mentioned the being-a-dick part?*

"You know it would be nice if we could support him. No matter what you think about what happened, Luke lost his child too, and he's had a rough ride of it lately."

I fired Holden a sceptical look and he returned his infamous puppy dog eyes. "Ugh. Don't look at me like that," I grumbled. "But okay, I'll try to be less of a dick. No promises though."

Holden clapped me on the back. "That's all I ask. Now, I'm gonna grab my boyfriend for a dance. Do you need a ride back to the station tonight?"

"With you two?" I almost choked. "God, no. You're nauseating enough to watch at a distance. I'll leave my ute and catch a lift with Tom and the others."

Holden grinned and planted a kiss on my cheek, and I caught myself in time before I covered the spot with my fingers. *Idiot.*

I headed for the bar and another shot of tequila . . . or six.

CHAPTER TWO

Zach

SEVERAL HOURS AND I HAVE NO IDEA HOW MANY SHOTS LATER—because who fucking counts that shit anyway—I was dancing, aka swaying slightly drunkenly, with Spencer to some rock-techno nobody band that neither of us was sober enough to keep up with, while at the same time lamenting the failure of the local rugby team to take away the previous season's regional trophy.

"I blame Happy George," I slurred, referring to a local station owner who'd produced a hat trick of towering muscle-bound jocks for sons. "He should never have let William go to Auckland University. Best flanker we ever had. Should've made him go to Christchurch." I slammed a pointed finger in the air, almost taking out Spencer's left eye. "Oops, sorry." I patted his cheek.

"There's no medical school in Christchurch," Spencer pointed out, tripping over my right foot and almost sending us both to the floor before stumbling into a miraculous recovery that set us both laughing.

"Pfft." My head lolled on Spencer's shoulder. "Doctors are a dime a dozen. William was the Best. Flanker. *Ever.* Players like that are as rare as chicken's teeth." I hesitated, then giggled. "*Hen's* teeth." I poked Spencer in the ribs. "It's a stupid saying anyway. And what about roosters? That's sexism right there."

Spencer nodded far too many times to make sense. "Yeah, of course."

"Of course . . . *what?*" I squinted to try and bring him into focus, failed, and whined, "You're not listening to me, Spennnnncerrrr. You're a vet. You *must* know about this stuff." I swayed a little on my feet and Spencer blinked.

"What stuff? What the hell are you talking about? I don't—" His face paled and he swallowed hard. "Oops, gotta go." He gave me a crooked grin and slapped me on the shoulder. "Thanks for the dance, Zach. Awesome night."

"No, don't go." I went to grab his hand but he was already lurching for the front door, so I sighed and sank into a seat. The music finished and the bar fell spookily quiet. *Huh. Where is everyone?* Nola generally kept the doors open until at least ten.

I checked my phone and blinked in disbelief. Almost midnight? What the hell? I glanced around. There were a couple of people at the bar watching the server clean and pack up, and two tables of four quietly chatting. One held a group of Gil's friends from Wellington who looked about as trashed as I felt. The other was a bunch of guys from the rural supply store. There was no sign of Holden and Gil or any of the station crowd, and a vague memory of Tom offering me a ride back to the station popped into my head, along with me calling them a bunch of pussies for leaving too early. *Shit.* Guess I'd be sleeping in my ute.

Wouldn't be the first time.

"You're embarrassing yourself."

I spun to find my father glaring at me from just a few feet away, his lip curled in disapproval. I stumbled back, trying to make sense of him even being there.

"Dad, don't." My brother stepped forward, his grey eyes full of apology. With his dark hair and tall, willowy frame, Julian took much more after our mother. He lowered his voice and angled his back to our father. "I'm sorry, Zee. I had no idea you'd be here. We just stopped in for a drink on our way back from the sales." He turned back around. "Come on, Dad. Let's head on home." He tugged at our father's arm, but Paddy Lane shrugged him off.

"Dancing with another man." My father looked scandalised. "Jesus, Zacharia."

I tried to come up with a clever comeback, but my alcohol-soaked brain couldn't work fast enough.

"Leave it, Dad," Julian tried again, but my father was having none of it.

His voice rose and he leaned forward, getting right up in my face. "Is this what you want, son? You want people laughing at you? At *our* family?"

My stomach roiled and I swallowed around the bile surging up my throat, trying to steel my emotions so my father wouldn't hear the tremble in my voice as I replied. "I don't see anyone laughing, *Dad*."

"Things okay here, Zach?" Luke's warm voice came over my shoulder and a hand pressed against the small of my back.

It was enough to break the mental rabbit hole I was tumbling down, and my spine straightened. "Thanks, but I'm fine." I leaned back just enough to feel the pressure of his palm solidify, telling me he wasn't going anywhere. I should've been pissed at his interference, but all I felt was . . . gratitude.

My father narrowed his gaze—forced to look up since Luke had a good ten or so centimetres on him. "And just who the hell are you?"

I winced at his tone, but Luke answered without hesitation. "Luke Nichols. Who the hell are you?"

I drew a sharp breath, knowing Luke must've known full well who he was talking to. He'd heard the story of my coming out and likely most of the conversation.

My father blinked. Almost nobody spoke to Paddy Lane in that tone of voice—the last person being Gil before he threw my father off

Miller Station the previous year. I couldn't help but smile, guessing that was more than likely exactly what Luke had been aiming for. To throw my father off his game.

But Paddy was made of stern stuff and rallied quickly. "So, *you're* Luke Nichols." He looked Luke up and down, clearly unimpressed, and I wondered how or what he knew about Luke. "Well, *I'm* Zach's father, and you're interrupting a private conversation."

"Dad, give it up." Jules pulled at our father's jacket. "Come on. It's late."

Luke's mouth set in a thin line as he coolly studied my father. "That wasn't a conversation," he said bluntly. "That was an insult."

My father reddened. "Just who the hell do you think you are?"

"I'm Zach's friend." Luke started forward and I immediately put out a hand to stop him.

"It's okay, Luke. He's leaving, aren't you, Dad?" I glared at my father, who looked about to say something we were all going to regret, when the publican stepped between us.

"Paddy, that's enough." Nola eyed my father sternly. "Julian, take your father home before I have to ban his sorry arse." She held my father's gaze, unblinking. "*Now*, Paddy."

My father chewed the inside of his cheek a moment longer, then grunted. "You belong back on Lane Station when you come to your senses, not with . . . *them*. Don't throw away your life for no reason." He held my gaze a moment longer, then made for the door.

Nola shot me an apologetic look, cast a curious glance at Luke, and then headed behind the bar, grumbling about ignorant, stubborn old men.

I rolled my eyes at Jules who pulled me into a quick hug. "I'm sorry, Zee." He glanced to where my father waited for him with a sour look on his face. "I forgot it was Gil's birthday bash or I wouldn't have stopped by."

I shrugged. "It's a small place. It's not like Dad and I can avoid each other forever."

"I know, but still . . ." His cheeks pinked. "So, how are you doing?"

"Okay, I guess." I glanced at my father who was still scowling, although this time at Luke whose hand hadn't moved from my back. I took a half step sideways and Luke's hand dropped away. "How's the station?"

Julian glanced between Luke and me with obvious interest. "Same as usual. Dad is determined to muster two weeks later this year and it's driving me crazy. He wants to use the new shearing board in the woolshed, and the contractors say it won't be finished until then. There's no reason we can't use the old board until we shear again in spring, but you know Dad. Same shit, different day." He paused. "We miss you. *I* miss you. Can we meet up again soon?"

I blinked hard. "I miss you guys too. And yes, please, let's do that. Come for dinner at the cottage and bring your guitar. I hate to admit it, but I miss listening to you play."

Julian's eyes went soft. "Yeah, I'd like that."

"Julian, let's go," my father grumbled. "You were the one in a hurry."

I shot him a filthy look and whispered, "Dickhead."

"Give me two minutes," he told our father and then turned back to me and lowered his voice. "You're right. He *is* a dickhead, but I'm working on him. We all are. Even Mum got shitty and snapped at him the other day when he refused to let us talk about you. He's so damn pig-headed."

My gaze jerked back to Julian. "She actually said something?" I tried not to feel hopeful. My mother generally followed whatever my father said without question, even when it came to him leaving me no choice but to leave home after I'd come out to them the previous year. If I was "going to be gay"—my father had almost spat the words like it was a choice—then I had to keep it out of their sight. I couldn't ever have a man stay over in my cottage or even raise the subject in conversation.

Given his ultimatum, it became the easiest and most difficult choice I'd ever made. I left the station that very day.

Jules snorted. "Well, don't get too excited, but yeah, she put him in his place. It shocked the hell out of him along with everyone else."

I chuckled. "Good for her. Tell her I . . . miss her."

Jules' smile turned sad and he nodded. "I will. She loves you; you know that. She's just not a strong person. But don't give up." His hand clasped my shoulder. "Anyway, I better go before he bursts a blood vessel. Lunch next week?"

"If I'm not still hungover from tonight."

He frowned. "You better not be planning to drive back to Miller's or I'm handing Nola your car keys right now."

I almost laughed. Jules had personified the protective older brother while we were growing up. "In this state?" I opened my arms incredulously, swaying slightly in the process. "I don't think so. I'll be sleeping in the ute."

Jules glanced over my shoulder to where Luke was still standing, and I realised Luke must've heard everything we'd said. Jules thanked Luke for having my back before adding, "And make sure he doesn't drive."

I was about to protest that Luke had absolutely no say in what I did or didn't do when Luke muttered, "Not a chance in hell."

I turned and fired Luke a killer glare, the impact no doubt tempered by the fact I over-balanced and Luke had to steady me. As soon as I had my feet again, I shoved him away none too gently.

Those spectacular blue eyes narrowed. "What was that for?"

"For being a dick. I don't need you keeping an eye on me. I don't need *anyone*."

Luke looked a lip twitch away from a smile, which only pissed me off further. Julian's curious gaze bounced between us, knowing he was missing something, but rather than ask, he pulled me into another quick hug and then headed back to my father.

I watched them leave, my hand lifting to cover that gnawing ache of grief and yearning in my heart. If only it was as easy to hate someone as it was to *want* to hate them. I'd once seen my whole life playing out on my family's station, or maybe Miller's—raising a family, training my dogs, working side by side with Julian or Holden.

It only went to prove how fucking badly you could get things wrong.

I scrubbed my palms over my eyes, shrugged off Luke's hand, and made a wobbly line for the front door. Outside, the warm summer air did nothing for my head, my brain spinning like a wonky top. I paused and sucked in a few deep breaths and let my head fall back. Over the Mackenzie Basin, a slightly blurry blanket of stars gleamed as far as the eye could see, the jagged peaks of the Southern Alps wrapped in black shadow against the midnight sky. As always, it set my heart to rest.

I gathered my wits and began to weave my way toward my ute, which I'd parked about as far away as you could get from the front door so that Gil wouldn't see it when he'd arrived. I'd got about halfway there when Luke's voice rang out behind me.

"Hey, wait up."

I didn't. I kept going, muttering over my shoulder, "Go away, Luke. I appreciate your concern back there with my dad, but I'm fine. Also, I'm tired."

He didn't go away, of course. Instead, he fell into step alongside. "I know you're not planning to drive home—"

"Hey—" I spun to face him a little too fast and had to give my brain a second to catch up. "Do I look like an idiot?"

He blinked and took a step back. "Not at all. That's why I said I knew you weren't. But you did leave this behind."

I scowled at the jacket in his hand and then grumbled, "Thank you." I went to take it from him, but he whipped it away, his eyes dancing.

"Only you could make thank you sound like a life sentence."

I narrowed my gaze, or at least I gave it my best shot, all things considered. "Now you're just pissing me off." I turned and kept walking. "Keep it. Whatever."

Footsteps ran after me. "Wait, Zach. I'm sorry. That was a stupid thing to do."

I hesitated, then held out my hand, and Luke handed the jacket over, saying, "I'm sorry about your dad—"

"I don't want to talk about it."

He sighed and gave a nod. "Fair enough. But the reason I followed you out was to tell you I have a spare bed if you want. You don't need to sleep in your damn car."

I blinked, then stared at him, surprised at the shy uncertainty I saw on his face. He almost looked . . . nervous? But no, that wasn't possible.

Luke shrugged. "The furniture came with the place, so it's ready to go. Has to be a better option than your back seat."

It was all I could do not to gape. "You're offering me a bed? For the night?"

A wry grin stole over his face. "I'm pretty sure that's what I just said."

"Don't be a smart-arse." I studied his face but saw nothing to suggest he was fucking with me. "And exactly how many beds are in this house of yours?"

He snorted. "Oh, right. Well, two, as it happens. One for me and one for—"

"Yeah, yeah, I get it." I squeezed my eyes shut for a second, then opened them again, but the irritating man was still there. I considered my ute and frowned. It had a pig of a rear seat.

Luke waited quietly, his expression one of obvious amusement. He raised both hands. "I promise your virtue is safe with me. Call me old-fashioned, but I prefer my bedmates conscious and consenting."

When I still said nothing, he sighed and took a step back. "Okay, do what you want. I'm at 47 Falcon Drive if you change your mind in the next half hour. It's a five-minute walk and I'll leave the porch light on. I was only trying to help." He walked away.

Before I could stop myself, I called out, "Why are you still here?"

He stopped walking and turned around. "What do you mean?"

I waved toward the bar. "You weren't with anybody, and you're clearly sober and everyone else has pretty much left, so why didn't you?"

He looked to the ground, then back up. "I was doing the rounds and talking with people. It's something you do when you're the new kid in town," he said pointedly, and okay, fair point. "Then I happened to hear you turn down Tom's offer to drive you home about an hour ago and I . . . well, I just wanted to make sure you were okay. You've, um . . . clearly had a bit to drink."

It took a minute for his words to sink in. He'd wanted to make sure that I was okay? I shook my head. "I don't need a minder, and that's creepy as shit, just so you know."

He shrugged. "I'll give you that, but it is what it is. You're a friend of Gil and Holden, and I wanted to see you safe. I'm not going to apologise. Have a good sleep, Zach. And lock your car doors."

Lock my doors? I frowned at his retreating back, cast another glance at my odorous ute, and then ignored every one of those warning bells in my head. "Okay, I'll come with you."

He spun on his heels, wearing one of those wide smirks that did funny things to my stomach. "Don't make it sound like you're doing *me* a favour. It's no skin off my nose."

He was right and I grumbled an apology. "Sorry. And thanks. I appreciate it."

He laughed. "Jesus, how did that feel coming out of your mouth?"

I fought a smile. "Like shit, if you must know. And just so we're crystal clear, it *is* separate beds, right?"

He nodded sagely and his hand lifted to his chest. "You have my word. I mean, one can't be too careful, right? Lord knows where you've been."

My brain was still a bit slow so it took me a minute to register the insult. In that time, Luke had walked over and taken the coat from my hands. He hung it over my shoulders and then headed out of the car park. "It's this way."

Incensed, I ran to catch up. "Hey, arsehole. What do you mean, where *I've* been? *I'm* not the one attempting to set the land-speed record on the number of dicks conquered in the province of Wellington, sleeper suburbs included."

Luke shot me a confused look over his shoulder as I tried to keep up with his Olympic pace. To be fair, I wasn't exactly pushing too hard, considering his arse looked spectacular in those jeans with every streetlight we crossed. "According to who?"

"According to your husband—"

"*Ex*-husband," he reminded me. "Who knows precisely zip about who I do and don't take to bed or any other aspect of my current sex life. Got it?"

Which was . . . fair. And the sooner we quit talking about Luke's sex life, the better for my unruly dick.

And so I did.

Quit talking.

Although the incendiary images flipping like a Rolodex in my brain proved less cooperative.

But that's what cold showers were for.

CHAPTER THREE

Luke

While I threw some sheets on the spare bed, Zach fumbled his way out of his clothes all the way down to his briefs. I deserved a fucking gold medal for not offering to help, and then another gold for keeping my gaze laser-focused on what I was doing and not on him standing there half-naked.

I figured his lack of concern was down to alcohol rather than the fact he trusted me, but I wasn't complaining. And it was impossible not to admire his gorgeous arse in those dark green briefs that matched his eyes, as he poured himself between the sheets and rolled to put his back to me. He drew the top sheet up to his waist and was lights out in minutes.

The warm night didn't require any blankets, but I popped one on the end of the bed, just in case. Then I put a mug of water and some ibuprofen on the bedside table within easy reach and a bucket on the floor. I had no idea whether Zach held his drink well or not, and I didn't particularly want to find out by having to clean the floors just a few days after I'd moved in.

All done, I stood at the door watching him sleep until I embarrassed even myself. The man was strikingly beautiful. *Pretty* seemed too juvenile, too . . . superficial, and Zach was anything but superficial. His lightly tanned arms and shoulders gave way to a back covered in acres of pale Irish skin dusted with groups of freckles like someone had thrown them at him in random handfuls.

I'd helped out enough at the station when shirts were shed in the heat to know exactly where every one of those delightful groups existed, especially the one that dipped under the waistband of his jeans—or the sheet around his waist—and drove my imagination crazy.

Zach muttered something in his sleep and rolled to face me, those auburn waves tumbling around his face, a lock or two catching in his lashes, those bright green eyes remaining shuttered in sleep.

Enough.

I left his door slightly ajar so the hall light would help if he woke in the night and headed to the bathroom for a shower. Zach Lane was doing my head in. What the hell was I doing crushing on this guy? Because there was no denying that's exactly what I was doing, had *been* doing ever since I'd first laid eyes on him the year before.

I stepped under the hot water, soaped, and rinsed, all the while stewing over why this guy was taking up far too much real estate in my brain. Why him? Why *anyone*?

Two and a half years since Gil and I had lost Callie and our marriage imploded, I was barely getting oxygen back into my brain. Crushing on the best mate of my *ex*-husband's new man was way too fucking complicated even for me. Not to mention the guy was a pain in the arse and made no bones about the fact he didn't like me, or at least the way I'd walked out on Gil.

I stepped out of the shower and towelled myself dry.

Nothing was ever easy with Zach, or at least it hadn't been for me. Everyone else got the easy-going, good-natured country boy. Me? Not so much. And true to form, he'd complained from the minute we'd set foot inside the house, right up until he fell between those sheets.

First, he'd insisted on simply crashing on my couch. When I won that argument, he started another about not needing any linen on his bed or any food to soak up the booze. I won both of those as well, forcing a peanut butter sandwich into his mouth before we hit the bedroom. I knew damn well he hadn't eaten a thing at the pub because I'd been watching him like the embarrassing stalker that I was. All. Night. Long.

The less said about that, the better.

I barely understood it myself. Zach had made his dislike for me clear from the moment we met. Back then he'd told me I had some balls just showing up at the station to see Gil like I had and then proceeded to watch my every move like I might steal the family jewels. It had been funny at first, but almost a year later, it was just plain frustrating. That ongoing censure was written in the disapproving frown he wore every time he looked my way. Well, all except for the times he looked like he might want to rip my clothes off and spread me over his plate for dinner.

So yeah, there was that conundrum to ponder as well.

Call it a balanced opinion, but it did give me a smidgen of hope. The question was, hope for what? And why I even gave a fuck about the answer was yet another troubling question.

It wasn't like I was ready for . . . well, anything, if I was being honest. Regardless of what I'd said to Zach about Gil not having a clue about my sex life, the honest truth was he hadn't been too far from the mark. It was a fact I wasn't too proud of and another excellent reason for me to have taken the job and moved away from all that.

Grief was a strange beast. The first year after Callie had been killed in a car accident, Gil seemed to have taken the hardest hit. Maybe because he'd been driving at the time, even though it hadn't been his fault. Two and a half years later and he was finally finding his way back to life with the help of Holden at his side, and I couldn't feel anything but happy for them.

My life, on the other hand, had held together marginally better that first year, but I'd faced a downward spiral ever since. And yes, I might've been using a few too many unhealthy ways to escape: self-medicating with alcohol and sex.

I pulled on a pair of boxers, cleaned my teeth, and wandered back down the hall to check on Zach one last time. I was greeted by soft snores and a face slack with sleep and free of care. A smile crossed my lips. He was too fucking cute for words.

I wasn't sure what it was about the prickly guy that he'd found a home under my skin, but he was undoubtedly there. Maybe it was because he'd had to watch the man he'd been in love with fall for someone else, someone who happened to be my ex-husband. Or maybe it was because of what he'd been through with his arsehole father. Or maybe because every time I watched Zach roughhousing with his dogs and any other dog that came within a country mile of Miller Station since all of them seemed to love him, I'd wished it were me who was the centre of his attention.

Yeah, mostly that last one.

Because although Zach had been through a tough time the previous year, it definitely wasn't sympathy I felt for the guy. Oh, no. It was something a whole lot less wholesome than that.

Leaving the hall light on, I headed for my bedroom, knowing one thing for sure: Zach Lane wasn't going to be at his best in the morning, which pretty much guaranteed I'd be in the firing line.

Happy days.

The first reminder that Zach was in my house and up and about was the thud of a box hitting the hall floor, followed by a grunt of pain and a whispered string of curses.

My eyes sprang open to find weak grey light pouring through the poorly fitted curtains. It striped my bed and crossed the floor leading out into the hall. But the hush of night still hung heavy in the house so I figured it couldn't be much after daybreak.

I lay still for a moment, wondering if it wouldn't be less trouble for everyone if I just let Zach sneak out, as he was no doubt planning to do. Then again, where would be the fun in that?

I kicked off the sheets and tiptoed toward the door. The air was thick with residual heat from the day before and the stale odour that houses developed when they hadn't been lived in for a while. I made a mental note to buy some scented oil and peeked around the doorjamb.

I had to quickly swallow a snort of laughter at the sight of Zach busily restacking my boxed linens while grumbling about the idiot who'd put them there.

Guess that was me.

"Going somewhere?"

He started and the box he was lifting slid from his grip. "Dammit." He jerked around with some no doubt snarky rebuttal at the ready and then froze as his red-rimmed gaze moved slowly up and down my half-naked body. When he got to my face, his expression hardened. "Jesus, can you not put some clothes on?"

"What do you think these are?" I tugged at my boxers.

"Underwear." His cheeks flared and his gaze shot away, but not before I'd caught a flare of heat in those eyes. "Please."

I snorted. "Last time I looked, this was my house, but let me check again." I peered up and down the hall. "Yep. Still is. But fine." I slipped back into the bedroom and pulled on a loose singlet before returning to the hallway. "Better?"

"Marginally." He righted the fallen box and set it by the wall, and then like he realised he couldn't avoid it, he added, "Thanks . . . for the bed last night."

I rolled my eyes and tried not to smile. I'd been right about his pissy morning mood. Didn't make him any less cute, standing there with his rumpled clothes, bedhead, and sour face.

I made my way to his bedroom and peeked inside. "Any clean-up required?"

He flushed red again. "No. It's . . . I was . . . No, it's fine. Clean."

I studied his dullish eyes and pained expression. "How's the head?"

He winced and waggled his hand between us. "I could do without the marching band currently in residence, but it's getting there. Thanks again . . . for the ibuprofen." His flush deepened. "Just so you know, I don't make a habit of drinking like . . ." He trailed off, clearly deciding he didn't owe me an explanation.

Which he didn't.

"Glad they helped. And don't worry about the boxes." I walked past him down the hall and toward the kitchen. "They only have linens and other unbreakables. Come on, I'll rustle us up some breakfast."

"Oh . . . no . . ." Footsteps followed me up the hall. "I need to get back to the station."

I took a left into the tastefully refurbished kitchen—with its clean modern lines and up-to-date appliances—switched on the coffee maker, and headed for the fridge. "I thought Holden gave everyone the morning off." I shot Zach a sideways glance, amused to see bright spots of pink flame on those lightly freckled cheeks.

"Yeah, well, I've got dogs to train," he answered too quickly.

I stared out the window over the sink and counted to five. "Look, Zach. If you don't want a coffee, I'm not going to hold you hostage and pour it down your throat. I just thought since I was already making one . . ." I trailed off, feeling his gaze hot on my back as I reached for the coffee pods and two mugs and put them on the countertop.

"You don't have to be nice to me," he grumbled.

"Who says I'm nice?" I kept my smile hidden. "Pretty sure that wouldn't be you."

Zach huffed and dragged a barstool along the floor. "Fine, I'll have a coffee then. Black. No sugar . . . please."

I shot a look over my shoulder to find him sitting at the small breakfast bar with its warm, autumn-toned granite top. "Coming right up." And while I set about making the coffee, I was aware of Zach's curious inspection of my rental, a carefully renovated 1920s two-bedroom bungalow.

"Isn't this the Halston home?" he finally asked.

I nodded and carried the coffees to the breakfast bar. "It is. They moved to Christchurch last year but didn't want to sell because they still have family in the area. They tried advertising it as an Airbnb but got fed up with the constant niggling damage and put it up for rental a month ago. Perfect timing for me."

Zach's eyes found mine, the previous night's trials written in the spiderweb of tired lines gathered at the corners. Those gorgeous eyes were the first thing I'd noticed as he'd been putting me in my place the year before, bright green and framed by all those dark auburn waves, even though all they'd been saying at the time was *watch yourself, mister. I've got your number.*

"I don't get it." He took a sip of his coffee and gave a soft grunt of appreciation. "Why would you move down here? Last I heard Air New Zealand had called wanting, according to Gil, one of their best pilots back."

I spooned some sugar into my coffee and thought about how to answer without sounding tragic, creepy, or just downright pathetic.

Zach waited quietly, which was another thing I'd noticed about him. When he wasn't giving me, and apparently only me, a hard time, there was a gentle, watchful quality to his presence, something that was undoubtedly part of the reason he was such a great dog trainer. Not that I saw a lot of that particular side, because the minute I appeared on his radar, the shields went up and the sharp-edged commentary began.

I set my spoon on the breakfast bar and met his watchful gaze. "They *did*, in fact, call with an offer, although they omitted that *one of their best pilots* line, an unfortunate miscalculation on their part." My brow arched and Zach's lips twitched. "But the truth is, I'm done with that part of my life. Don't ask me why because I'm not sure my answer makes any sense."

I took a swallow of the scalding hot coffee and considered how much I really wanted to say. Zach drank some of his own and as we put our mugs down, our eyes met, his as soft as I'd ever seen them, a glimpse of the man behind the walls.

It was enough.

"Since we lost Callie—" I hesitated, shifted the coffee mug from *A* to *B* on the granite top and then looked up again. "Well, not much of anything makes sense anymore. I figured maybe a change would help. Couldn't hurt, right? Not like I've been doing a grand job of getting my life back on track before now, as you so astutely pointed out last night. The change certainly helped Gil—"

"*Holden* helped Gil," Zach returned, then seemed to regret the interruption. "Or maybe they helped each other." He shrugged and his gaze slid sideways over my shoulder.

It let me study him for a second and wonder how much he still felt for his friend. "I'm sure their relationship helped," I agreed, and Zach's gaze returned. "But Gil said there was something about this place. The landscape. That you couldn't hide out here. Like it forces you to ask questions about yourself."

Zach nodded like he knew exactly what I was saying. "It's true. When you're alone on the hill or just you and your dogs walking the beats, it's like being in a freaking confessional. All sorts of shit bubbles to the surface. Emily used to say it's the Mackenzie's way of looking after its own. It's an isolated life and you need to let stuff out. Shouting it into the mountains generally works for me. You'd be surprised by the answers you get."

I held his gaze, feeling the first fragile threads of something like understanding begin to weave between us. "I can believe that. I felt it last year when we scattered Callie's ashes in the Havelock River. I'm not what you'd call a spiritual guy, but I sure was that day. It hit me hard and got me thinking. The next day I drove to River Hut and took a walk up to the tarn where I threw rocks over the edge and cried my fucking eyes out until I had no strength left. Then I walked down and slept in the ute."

Zach frowned. "I didn't know that. I thought you'd just left us all and gone into town for the night. I didn't understand why you would do that when Gil and Holden had worked so hard planning the weekend, and with your parents and cousin arriving—"

"I couldn't handle being around anyone that day," I blurted. "Gil and Holden both knew. Gil loaned me his ute." I swallowed hard. Was I really going to do this? I guessed I was. "They had each other, see? At the river, when we scattered Callie's ashes. Then at the meal after. And again that night. They were just down the fucking hall from me, and I lay there knowing they'd be talking about everything, sharing, wrapped in each other's arms, and I've never felt so fucking lonely in all my life."

"And you didn't have anyone," Zach offered with sudden realisation. Statement, not question. "I mean, I knew you didn't at the time, I guess. But because Gil was there, and all of us, I suppose I just wasn't thinking, and I should have."

I shrugged. "I wouldn't have let anyone know what I was feeling. Not back then. I didn't even tell Gil that part, just that I needed some time alone. Anyway, since that day, things haven't improved. I've been doing a lot of . . . hiding. Too much drinking and too many men; you were right about that." I shot Zach a sheepish smile, but his expression was unreadable. "Although to be fair, the men part stopped a while back. The job offer down here was just good timing and my therapist was in full support. It was Gil who gave me the heads-up about the opening. And since I've rediscovered my love of piloting choppers over this last year, it was a two-for-one deal."

Zach's surprise was obvious. "Gil *wanted* you to move here?"

I snorted. "I don't carry the plague, you know? Some people even like me."

Zach's cheeks brightened. "I didn't mean—" He hesitated. "You know, it doesn't matter. You and Gil were both dealt a shitty blow in life, and I hope this change works out for you. I mean that." He finished the last of his coffee and got to his feet.

"I wasn't looking for sympathy," I assured him, sliding off the bar stool to join him. "You asked me why I moved and I told you. Maybe I said more than I should have. I'm just looking to move forward."

Our eyes met and held, and there was a warmth in the exchange that had been missing earlier. "I can understand that." His words were followed by a silence that grew to fill the small space between us until finally, he broke it. "But I should be on my way. Thanks again for the bed *and* the coffee. It was surprisingly good."

I quirked an eyebrow at the back-handed compliment. "I'll take that as high praise from you."

He looked to be fighting a smile. "Yeah, well. Don't get all excited. I'm not exactly firing on all cylinders this morning."

I chuckled. "Noted."

His smile finally broke free, and the shock of having it directed my way stunned me speechless for a moment. And damn, I wanted a whole lot more of that. "Why not stay for breakfast?" The words were out before I could stop them. "My kitchen skills might not be as good as Gil's, but I *can* cook."

Zach hesitated, glanced behind me into the kitchen, and then shook his head. "Thanks, but no. I'll stop by Meg's café and grab something to eat on the drive."

Ouch. And that's why you shouldn't have asked, idiot. "Right, of course. Can't compete with that."

Zach frowned, and for a second I thought he might even change his mind, but instead, he broke eye contact and scanned the living room. "Have you seen my jacket anywhere?"

"Yes, it's hanging in the entrance." I followed him into the hall and down to the front door.

Zach grabbed his jacket and hung it over an arm before awkwardly meeting my gaze. "Thanks again."

"You're welcome." I reached around and opened the door for him to pass through.

He gave me an odd look like no one had ever done that for him, and before I could stop myself, I voiced the one question I'd promised myself I wouldn't. "Can I ask what your problem is with me?"

Zach froze halfway out the door and I hastily added, "I mean, I know I didn't give the best first impression arriving uninvited on the station last year, but I hoped we might be past that by now. I'd kind of like us to be friends."

His troubled look gave me pause. But when he remained silent, I added, "Don't you think I deserve a little wiggle room to prove I'm a better man than you obviously think?"

Zach huffed. "I'm not sure why you care what I think, but since you asked, leaving your husband six months after losing your child kind of says something about a person, at least it does to me. And I'm not sure providing a little wiggle room would be enough to change that."

Which only proved the old adage *be careful what you ask for*. I swallowed hard and quashed down the rising tide of guilt that it had taken me two years to get a handle on. I wasn't about to let Zach Lane undo months of hard work just because he made my dick twitch.

Not that his words were much of a surprise. I'd figured it had to be something like that, but that didn't mean they didn't sting or that he didn't have a point. But point or not, Zach Lane knew fuck all about what had really gone down between Gil and me, and although I might like the guy, I wasn't about to be judged by whatever stick he had shoved up his arse.

I took a step back and schooled my expression into stony neutrality. "Yeah, I imagine you're right. Silly me for thinking that maybe you had to be part of a relationship, a marriage, to truly understand why it broke. Sitting in judgement from the outside is hardly fair to either party, don't you think? I've beaten myself up enough about what happened. I sure as hell don't need anyone else wading in. And on that note, I won't hold you up. I'm sure you've got better people to spend your time with."

Zach stared at me with startled green eyes and bright red cheeks. "I'm sorry. I could've said that better. But . . . you asked."

I snorted. "I did. More fool me. You know, Zach, I've never denied that what I did hurt Gil. We hurt each other. And I'll always regret what happened. But there was a time we loved each other as well. Deeply. It's not as simple as pointing a finger. Relationships are complicated and I thought you, of all people, might understand that. But I get the message. You have a nice day. I'm sure we'll see each other around, and I'll make sure to keep my distance."

And with that, I closed the door on Zach Lane and relegated my ridiculous little crush to the bin. I had a life to put back together, and the last thing I needed was a reminder of how badly I'd fucked things up two years before. I could manage that particular reality check all on my own and did so with painful regularity, because no matter that Gil's and my marriage had been doomed long before Callie died, I could've done better in the aftermath, and nothing was ever going to change that.

CHAPTER FOUR

Three weeks later

Zach

"Hey, Zach, wake up." The bedroom window of Tussock Cottage rattled under Holden's knuckles.

"Go away." I pulled the bedclothes over my head. "It's my first sleep-in in months."

Holden's chuckle was far too cheerful for my liking. "Aw, sorry, no can do. Gary radioed. Your pickup time has been brought forward. That weather front that was supposed to skirt south is now expected to pass over the Mackenzie Basin early this evening, and Blue wants you guys done and dusted well before. You've got about half an hour to be up and at 'em, sleeping beauty."

"Fuck me. If it's going to screw up my sleep-in, then the least it can do is actually fucking rain this time. That last storm was just a piss in the wind." I levered myself up on one elbow, pulled back the curtains, and squinted against the daylight that flooded the room. Clear skies and another hot day, at least for now.

Man, we needed that rain.

The Glendale River was running as low as I'd ever seen it, its twisted braids thin as a wisp and almost lost amongst the fat fingers of gravel that punctuated their flow, while the large-scale pasture blocks had given up any pretence of green, sitting parched under a relentless sun and the dry winds that tunnelled through the valley. Winter feed-stocks were already impacted, and everyone was concerned how the mobs on the hill were faring and what we'd find when muster started.

Holden's face popped into view on the other side of the glass and I flipped him off before checking my phone. Eight o'clock. *Dammit*. "And you don't have to sound so happy about waking me up."

Holden pressed his lips and nose against the glass and waggled his brows. "Aw, don't be like that."

I slammed the curtains closed on his ridiculous face.

He laughed. "Why are you getting picked up anyway? They don't usually send the chopper?"

"I didn't ask," I called back. "Wasn't going to look a gift horse in the mouth."

Gil's voice popped up in the background. "By the way, there's a cheese toasted sandwich and two blueberry muffins outside your front door. And a lunch bag and energy bars. Don't say I never do anything for you."

Like I would ever do that. Gil spoiled all of the shepherds on the station, but he seemed to go out of his way when it came to me, something that had made it almost impossible to stay pissy with him when I'd first learned that he and Holden were a thing.

There was another rap of knuckles on the window. "I'm off to make sure Charlie is up as well. I can swing by the kennels if you want me to feed and fetch Nina and Jojo for you."

I smiled and swung my legs out of bed. "Yes, please. But just Jojo this time." Both my dogs were crack trackers, but Jojo was the best by a long shot. She usually led the chase while Nina swept the rear for anything we might've missed. It made them a super effective team and I was one of the few personnel to run two dogs. But today we only had room for me to fly one. "Don't you have Spencer coming to ultrasound those ewes?"

"Not until eleven," Holden called back. "And the others are working on smoothing the bumps and potholes on Dunwoody's beat after that last storm, so I'm fancy-free for a bit. But you better get moving. Time's a ticking. If you're ready in fifteen, I'll even give you and Charlie a lift to the airstrip. I've got to fuel the ute anyway."

"I'll be ready. I don't know about Charlie. And I'd keep my hands in my pockets if I was you. She can be a bit rabid in the mornings."

Holden's laughter trailed into the distance, and I threw back the sheet. Search and rescue dog-handler training days were the best. A chance to get off the station and work the dogs in the mountains? Hell yeah. It didn't get much better than that.

Stumbling toward the bathroom, I pushed away images of all those mornings I'd woken in the same room and headed for the same shower when Holden was living in Tussock Cottage and he and I were still doing our friends-with-benefits thing.

Jesus, was that only a year ago?

At the time, I'd been foolishly hoping for something more between us. The ill-thought-out decision to tell Holden that had not gone quite as planned. Newsflash, he didn't feel the same, and the benefit part of our friendship had come to an abrupt stop. Luckily, the best-mates part had survived. And then Holden met Gil and the rest was history. They proceeded to fall head over heels in love, with me relegated to observer status.

Go figure.

The universe could be a bitch that way.

I shook free of the memory and stepped into the shower, relishing the sting of the needles of scalding hot water pummelling my back.

The hurt and heartache of those early months had slowly softened into genuine happiness for my friend. It was hard *not* to feel glad for him considering how loved-up and contented he obviously was. Getting my own life back on track had become my focus from that point on.

Twenty-five minutes later and all four of us stood chatting at the airstrip while Charlie and I waited for our lift. Charlie was a newbie trainee for the local volunteer search and rescue, and she was working Hellboy—one of Holden's dogs. He was more suited to the work than her own dog, Elektra, and in addition to the LandSAR training, I'd spent many hours working with her as well. They made a good team, but it was only their third training exercise and Charlie looked nervous.

"You'll be fine," I reassured her. "Beats filling in holes on Dunwoody's, right?"

She smiled weakly. "Says the guy who has queues of people wanting him to help train their dogs. What if I fuck up? Hellboy and I are still getting to know each other."

I shrugged. "Then you fuck up. We've all done it. Me included."

She grimaced. "I don't want to look like an idiot out there."

"You won't." Holden rested a hand on her shoulder. "Jesus, Charlie, you've done amazing things with that dog already. And things are only going to improve now he's yours."

Her gaze jerked up in shock. "What?"

Holden smiled one of those smiles that used to melt my heart, and I almost had to look away. "You heard me," he said, gently squeezing her shoulder. "Hellboy is officially yours. He barely listens to me as it is. I tell him something and he immediately looks to you as if to say, 'Does this bozo know what he's talking about, Mum?'"

She snorted. "Well, that *is* true. The boy caught on fast that it pays to check all instructions with the best shepherd on the station, just in case."

Gil choked out a laugh just as Holden grumbled, "Fuck you."

Charlie chuckled. "You wouldn't be able to keep it up long enough."

"She's got you there." Gil held up his hand for a high five and Charlie obliged.

Then she shocked everyone by reaching up on her toes and pressing a kiss to Holden's cheek. "Thank you. I'll take good care of him."

Holden's expression was a picture of astonishment and he immediately pulled her into a hug. At thirty, Charlie was one of the best shepherds in the Mackenzie and a total badarse, but she rarely showed any vulnerability and watching the two of them embrace tugged on every one of my heartstrings.

"So where are they holding the training exercise?" Gil asked.

"Northwest of Gammack up into the Cass River valley," Charlie answered.

"Blue mapped a trail for Mel to lay," I added. "There's several indicator finds along the way and bragging rights and a bottle of tequila for the first team to hit the final cache. And that team will be us, right, girl?"

Jojo yipped and licked my nose as if in agreement, and Holden laughed. "Competitive much?"

"Hey, don't write me off just cos I'm green," Charlie protested.

"I'm competitive, not an idiot," I fired back. "You two have come a long way."

"Damn right." Charlie eyed Jojo who was busy circling our group, her senses on high alert, her border collie ears twitching in anticipation. "She knows, doesn't she?"

"Hell yeah, she does." I got to my knees and pulled Jojo in for a hug on her next pass.

Training days along with anything to do with mustering featured high on the collie's list of favourite ways to spend a day, and a trip to the station airfield was a dead giveaway that something awesome was about to happen. And since she'd been training with Hellboy more often, his equally excited presence only served to amp her up further. Being an isolated mountainous region with an abundance of tourists making dodgy decisions, we were called out more often than people thought, and Jojo knew the drill.

In contrast to our two bundles of trembling canine adrenaline, Holden's huntaway, Spider, lounged in the bed of Holden's ute, his gaze locked on Gil. I smiled and shook my head. The lazy dog had become more Gil's than Holden's, assuming the self-appointed role of protector, spookily sensitive to Gil's PTSD.

I was about to call him over for a head scratch when Jojo and Hellboy launched themselves across the airfield, barking madly. I scanned the southern sky, knowing full well that their keen ears had picked up what mine couldn't.

Our taxi was close.

Two seconds later the Wild Run chopper crested the sawtooth peaks at the southern end of the valley and made its way toward us. I called the dogs to heel and wiped the sweat from my brow. Not even nine in the morning and it was already hot as hell, the bluebird sky and warm breeze giving no indication of the weather front headed our way. With the dogs safely tucked behind, we watched in silence as the chopper drew near, turning away as the wash of the blades blasted our faces.

When the skids hit the grass and the rotor blades slowed, I reached for my backpack and high-vis safety gear while Jojo, Hellboy, and Spider all barked an excited welcome. The arrival of a helicopter usually meant an exciting day up the hill, a fact not lost on the dogs.

"Luke?" Gil's surprised call sent my heart knocking against my ribs.

Luke? Fuck, no. I spun around, and sure enough there he sat at the controls of the helicopter alongside Doug Carstairs, a lean, perpetually cheerful thirty-five-year-old wilderness guide from Oakwood who was part of our team.

Dammit to hell. It hadn't even occurred to me that Luke might be our pilot since it was usually Tommy who flew for our team. *Shit.* My happy mood went into freefall.

Apart from a countless number of unsolicited appearances in my shower fantasies, I'd managed to avoid Luke for an entire three weeks since our last . . . *discussion*. Even when he'd flown Gil and Holden to check the summering mobs and then stayed for lunch with the team at the homestead, I'd made sure I had plenty of work to do and taken a packed lunch with me—mostly because I was embarrassed.

I'd been a rude, unmitigated dick to him that morning, especially considering the man had given me a bed for the night. The trouble was, I didn't know how to make it right without launching into another conversation I'd rather avoid. And to be fair, the unmitigated dick part had been primarily to hide the fact that he'd almost busted me creeping on him while he'd been sleeping and I'd been trying to find the bathroom.

The memory still horrified me but also stirred my cock. Luke had been sprawled on his side facing the window, his lean-muscled leg hooked outside of the sheet, the waistband of his boxers pulled low enough to provide a tempting peek of the top of his crease, a few blond hairs across his arse, and miles of smooth, tanned skin all the way up that long, long back.

I'd been transfixed, not to mention semi-fucking-hard, and then Luke had jerked in his sleep as if he'd sensed I was there and I scrambled out of sight only to run into a stack of boxes and send them toppling. Seconds later, Luke had appeared in his boxers and my mouth ran dry. A smattering of fair curls fanned out across that wide chest and tight abs, coalescing into a thick happy trail that ran down into his boxers along with my imagination.

And just like that I'd felt myself stiffening . . . again. Whatever the hell was up with my dick, that fucker needed a leash and a muzzle pronto.

"Where's Tommy?" Holden shouted above the roar of the engine as he and Gil approached the cockpit.

"His wife went into labour last night and Rory's got a booking," Luke shouted back, his flat gaze landing on me. "Sorry, but you're stuck with me. I'll be taking Tommy's on-call days for the foreseeable future since Rory is only part-time. Today seemed a good opportunity to meet everyone and get to know the ropes."

Holden nodded, looking surprised. "That's good of you. It's a big commitment."

Luke shrugged. "It's no big deal. New fathers need time at home, right?" His gaze slid sideways to Gil who returned a knowing smile.

A niggle of guilt tugged at my belly. Holden and Gil were right. Offering to be on call for the local SAR was a big commitment, but since he'd first arrived in the Mackenzie, Luke had done nothing but try to get on with people, even me.

"Hey there, stranger." Holden looked past Luke to where Doug sat with a smile from ear to ear.

"Hey, yourself," Doug replied, then cast a sly smirk Charlie's way. "You too, gorgeous."

Charlie rolled her eyes. "Douggie, Douggie, Douggie. Do I have to box your bloody ears again? Cos I'm looking to release a bit of steam and you'd make a convenient target."

He grinned unashamedly. "Aw, you love me, admit it."

She bundled Hellboy into the carrier above the skid, threw her backpack into the chopper, and then shoved Doug's hat down over his eyes. "Arsehole."

"See." Doug hooted with laughter and pushed it back on his head. "Hey, Holden, you've been keeping secrets from me."

"What do you mean?"

"This guy." Doug gave Luke a gentle nudge. "Oakwood just got a whole lot more interesting."

Jesus Christ. Something coiled in my belly that had absolutely nothing to do with—nope, not going there. Doug was a nice enough guy, just an equal-opportunity flirt and shit-stirrer. No one took him seriously. So why did I suddenly want to wring his scrawny neck? Also not going there.

"Go easy on the poor guy. In another life, he used to be married to this guy." Holden indicated to Gil, and Doug blanched.

"Oops, I forgot about that. Sorry, mate."

Gil waved it off with a smile. "Luke's more than capable of looking after himself."

"Right here, dickheads," Luke reminded them, then turned to me. "You gonna get Jojo inside at some point or you just gonna stand there?"

And I suddenly realised I hadn't moved a jot since Luke had landed, completely fixated on the fact he was there at all. "Of course." I led an excited Jojo over to the chopper and lifted the lid on the carrier. Doug's huntaway, Carmine, immediately poked her head out in greeting and Jojo couldn't get in fast enough.

"All set?" I checked with Charlie who was already in her seat. When she nodded, I clambered inside and donned my headset. "Right, let's do this." I clapped Doug on the shoulder and he shot me a wide grin.

Luke kept his eyes forward and said nothing. Whether he was ignoring me or simply doing his job, I wasn't sure. And why the fuck it even mattered just plain pissed me off. I waved to Holden and Gil as we lifted off and tried not to think about how fucking awkward the whole thing was, focusing instead on the gorgeous day and the stunning landscape fanning out below us.

We swooped low over the homestead, drawing a wave from Emily standing on the front lawn. The house sat cradled at one end of a glacial valley, alongside the widely braided Glenmore River, and at the edge of a small crystalline blue lake. The valley was flanked by two towering ranges that rose steeply on either side, a kilometre between them at the widest point. A scattering of shepherd and tourist accommodation, shearing quarters, machinery sheds, and a single huge woolshed formed a kind of mosaic against the tawny tussock and patchwork pasture, the single patch of green in the entire landscape being the result of Gil's obsessive work in his market garden-sized vegetable patch at the back of the house.

As the others talked through their headsets, I blanked their conversation out and focused on the view out my window. Black dots signified the station's herd of Angus cattle moving slowly across the foothills, while much higher up on the barren-looking alpine slopes, the occasional cream specks of wandering merinos could be spotted if you knew what to look for.

It was farming on a knife edge in a complicated and inhospitable environment, politically and ecologically sensitive, and at the mercy of unforgiving weather extremes. It could suck the heart right out of you while filling you with joy at the exact same moment, and I loved every second of living right in the middle of it.

The ridgeline that marked the boundary between my family's land and Miller Station passed beneath us, and my mood took another dive. There'd been a Lane in charge of that station for three generations. Julian would be the fourth, and I swallowed hard thinking of him working it on his own while I would be . . . well, who knew what the fuck I'd be doing. One thing for sure, it wasn't going to include hanging around Miller Station forever and feeling sorry for myself. I needed a plan.

Luke, Charlie, and Doug talked and gossiped all the way to the fourth volunteer's farm by Lake Alexandrina. Once Kelsie and her mixed breed Pedro were loaded, the four of them continued to chat for the next ten minutes until we landed beside the Cass River. Charlie threw a few questioning looks my way, which I dutifully ignored. I made a couple of comments, but mostly I sat and stared out the window, stewing over Luke's obvious silence during any conversation that tried to include me. Well, that and Doug's equally obvious flirtations that were grating on my nerves big time.

Jesus fucking Christ. Was I twelve years old again?

Yes, apparently I was.

Blue strode over to meet us as we came in to land. A grizzled man with deep lines carved into his weathered face, he was a highly experienced fifty-something born-and-bred Mackenzie Basin legend who knew the mountains like the back of his hand. A heart attack a few years ago had seen him relegated to base camp team leader, but you couldn't wish for a better man to have your back.

Luke put the chopper down alongside the Cass River at the point it exited a steep gorge on its journey to Lake Tekapo. There was barely a bump as he laid the skids to rest on the flat bank of stones, and I begrudgingly admitted the man handled the machine like the pro that he was.

Blue was all smug smiles when he came over to greet us. "Are you ready to rumble? I've done you a doozy today."

We groaned loudly as one. Blue set the best and worst training trails. Super challenging and satisfying, but painful and lengthy if the dogs lost the scent and you got it wrong.

Kelsie grumbled, "I was hoping to be done by afternoon tea, throw a mud pack on, grab a beer, maybe even watch the cricket on the telly while Nev entertained the ankle-biter."

I snorted, wondering in what universe Kelsie would ever put her feet up. The embodiment of an energiser bunny, the woman was always busy fundraising for something.

"Then you better get your running shoes on," Blue fired back as he unlatched one of the equipment carriers.

Luke saw to the other, and I had to admit, the man looked mouth-wateringly good with his tall, rangy body poured into a slightly snug but flattering black flight suit with Wild Run's multi-coloured logo on the back. As he bent to re-secure the latches, the material stretched over the sumptuous curves of his arse and into the filthy recesses of my mind.

Good Lord. It was going to be a long day.

I tried not to stare, failed, and tried again with a little more success, although I couldn't help sneaking a sideways glance whenever I thought he wasn't watching, which gave me plenty of opportunity since he appeared to be ignoring me completely.

The second the dogs were released, Jojo began a mad sniff of the area before pouncing on Hellboy like they hadn't seen each other in years. Meanwhile, Carmine barked up a storm and, ignoring the others, he ran to greet Pedro as the two dogs were ridiculously besotted with each other.

"Do we get any clues?" Doug pressed Blue hopefully as he whistled for Carmine to slip the dog's harness on, and I did the same with Jojo.

"A clue?" Blue waggled his eyebrows. "Let me think." He touched his finger to his lip. "I know. How about the trail starts here?" He pointed to the ground at his feet and Doug rolled his eyes. "And I'll give you another for free. If you hit snow, you've gone too far." Which earned him another groan.

Luke approached Blue who was distributing the satphones. "I've got two tourist transfers after I leave here. One is just a short hop between stations, but the second is to ferry a couple from Tekapo up to Mairangi Station, adding a bit of a look-see on the way. There'll be little point heading back to the hangar when I'm done if your guys are close to finishing, so if you don't mind the company, I'd like to pick your brains about the volunteer search and rescue protocol."

Blue looked momentarily surprised, then pleased. "Sure. We appreciate Wild Run's support and you for giving up your time. Plus, it'll help pass the time while these bozos get lost."

I flipped Blue off. "No one's getting lost. Jojo's got her mojo on," I rhymed. "I can taste the margaritas already."

Kelsie laughed and planted a kiss on Pedro's head. "Good luck with that, sunshine. My boy's been in great form lately."

Charlie piped up, "And Hellboy says Doug smells like last month's dags. Carmine won't be able to get the stench out of his nose long enough to find *anything*."

Doug huffed, "You can both kiss my arse. Carmine for the win, hands down. None of you lot can handle your drink anyway."

"Says the man who tried to dance with Cooper's Angus bull at the last Christmas Party."

Doug's eyes danced. "In my defence, he was wearing a very fetching collar." He cast a wry glance at Luke. "I'm partial to a bit of leather."

Luke flushed a bright red not often seen in the Mackenzie and I tried not to deck Doug where he stood because . . . reasons . . . most that I refused to look at too closely. Noting my silence, Doug's curious gaze lingered on mine before his frown rapidly switched to a sly grin.

Dammit. I really needed to work on my poker face.

I got busy with my backpack and tried to ignore him. Life had been a lot simpler when everyone thought I was straight. When the word spread that I'd come out—read faster than a speeding bullet—I'd quickly found myself the centre of attention for a number of reasons, both good and bad. Those who wanted to gossip. Those who had opinions about my father's reaction. Those who stopped talking to me—well, fuck 'em. And those members of the LGBTQ+ community who wanted to bring me into the fold. Doug had been one of those, and although I was grateful, all these people trying to set me up were becoming a pain in my arse.

Throwing me a wink, Doug shouldered his pack and wandered over to Luke like butter wouldn't melt in his mouth. "So, how are you finding the social life in our tiny neck of the woods?" he asked, like I didn't know exactly what he was up to. "Must be slim pickings after what you're used to in Wellington?"

Luke blinked and glanced my way. Caught staring, I held his gaze, suddenly very interested in what the answer would be. He shrugged. "I, um, it's fine, I guess." His gaze bounced off mine again. "But I didn't come here for a social life, so you won't hear any complaints from me. To be honest, I'm enjoying the quiet. The club scene gets old pretty quickly."

Doug looked between us, nodding thoughtfully. "Oh, what it must feel like to be getting enough tail to get bored with it, right, *Zach?*"

I shot Doug a glare and said waspishly, "We'd have to drag you away from Cooper's bulls first, wouldn't we *Douggie?*"

Charlie hooted with laughter and everyone joined in, including Doug.

Blue clapped Luke on the back as he passed, saying, "We're an acquired taste, son." Then he checked his phone and opened his hands. "Okay, is everyone ready?"

We all nodded and Luke headed back toward the chopper without a word or another glance my way. *And why should he?* I reprimanded myself as I watched him go, a niggle of discontent rolling in my belly. It was exactly what I wanted, right? I wanted Luke to leave me alone. I wanted Luke to stop talking to me. Stop trying to be my friend. Stop . . . tempting me.

A hand on my shoulder put an end to my musings and I turned to find Doug following my gaze. He chuckled softly. "You're drooling. Then again, I don't blame you. The man has a fine arse."

I huffed unconvincingly and lied through my teeth. "He's not my type." Because he couldn't be. Because it made no sense. Because I'd been in love with Holden, and Luke was as far from Holden as you could get. Holden was steadfast, trustworthy, reliable. You knew where you stood with Holden. He had a solid plan for his life. He would never run when the going got tough.

Whereas Luke . . . well, Luke was annoyingly flippant and an unknown quantity in just about all of those other things, including a particularly poor performance record in the running-away category. There was enough uncertainty in my life without adding an unreliable man to the mix. I could admit to lusting over the man's looks and fantasising about . . . things, but that was as far as it went.

Doug was clearly unconvinced. "Yeah, well, I don't think your dick got the memo. But if you're not interested in tapping that beauty, then maybe I will."

The river fell silent, the voices of the others faded into white noise at my back, and I wasn't about to put a name to the surge of emotion that rolled through my gut as Doug's words dropped with a resounding clatter in my brain. Instead, I summoned my best eye roll and replied, "You couldn't tap a water main, arsehole, but be my guest."

Doug roared with laughter, but his eyes called me on the lie. Thankfully Blue interrupted before he could say anything more.

"Come on, folks. We've got a weather system to beat. Time to get serious."

We gathered around for our final instructions along with the scent packets, and it wasn't long before we were heading upriver with the dogs' noses to the ground. Somewhere behind me Luke's chopper lifted off and he flew a low pass over the river before banking left and heading to Tekapo.

And if I happened to stand there gaping unattractively as he flew overhead, it was nobody's business but my own . . . and apparently Doug's, at least judging by the shit-eating grin on his face when he caught me staring.

CHAPTER FIVE

Luke

THE FIRST TOURIST TRANSFER WENT WITHOUT A HITCH, AND the subsequent scenic flight involved a delightful German couple in their sixties who chatted the entire time like we were long-lost friends. It was their third visit to New Zealand but the first to the high country, and I quickly realised I needed to do a lot more research if their probing questions were any indicator of things to come.

I'd only been in the job a few weeks and I'd learned a lot from Holden and his team over the past ten months, but I felt woefully uninformed on many of the subjects the German couple had raised—the political climate around sustainability and protecting New Zealand's unique conservation areas like the high country being one.

You could've knocked me over with a feather when they came up with that one, and I was scrambling to find an answer. I might only be acting as a glorified and insanely expensive taxi driver, shuttling tourists to and from their accommodation, hiking, and heli-skiing adventures, but in my eyes, it didn't excuse ignorance about the spectacular region whose beauty funded my salary.

I wanted to learn everything I could. Three weeks into a new life and I was revelling in it.

Go figure.

Who'd have guessed I'd fall in love with my job all over again? Dipping and diving over the Southern Alps and around the myriad of lakes and rivers that made up the magnificent Mackenzie Basin had become my new favourite thing. It beat the hell out of cruising at thirty thousand feet. In the helicopter I felt in touch with the landscape, part of it, riding that thin line of safety that comes from a close connection with the terrain, and I wanted to learn everything I could about this region.

I foresaw a trip to the local library and some late nights of scrolling in my future. Still, nothing beat the knowledge buried deep in the brains of the people whose families had worked these stations for three, sometimes four generations. Stories handed down to people like Holden and Emily and . . . Zach.

Zach.

Just his name made my blood boil for two disparate but equally inflammatory reasons. First and by no means the least was his sheer irritation factor. Pig-headed didn't even come close to conveying the man's determination not to like me or even try. And okay, he didn't have to. Not everyone was going to, right? But he could at least maybe not be such an arsehole about it.

Second, and definitely the worst, the guy just fucking did it for me. Three weeks since he'd pretty much told me I sucked as a human being for walking out on Gil, and I still couldn't think of him without wanting him under, on, or in me—I didn't much give a damn which it was, as long as both of us were naked.

Fucking lust. It screwed you six ways till Sunday and left you wanting more. And contrary to my determination to walk away, Zach's pissy little attitude had done nothing to extinguish my almost obsessive desire to get all up close and personal in his business. Like *really* up close and personal.

And that wasn't why I'd come all this way. It was pretty much the opposite.

I might have enjoyed dipping my toes into the single life again as a win-win distraction from the massive holes in my life, especially after I found out about Gil and Holden, but I'd reined that in and even managed a little casual dating before I moved south.

But there'd been nothing like this thing I had for Zach. This thing that had lasted nigh on a year. Nothing that involved me constantly thinking about another guy. Nothing that was worth the inevitable messy conclusion. Which was why this little crush needed to end, not die the death of a thousand cuts like it was shaping into.

It was around one by the time I landed the chopper back alongside the Cass River and Blue wandered over to bring me up to speed.

"They hit pay dirt by eleven and are on their way back." He waved me to a camp chair set in a shady spot under the canvas gazebo. "Charlie and Hellboy made the first find, a woollen hat lodged under a pile of rocks about half a kilometre up. Then Zach made the next three, including the final backpack set well above the river at the top of a shingle scree. I swear that dog of his has radar antennae."

I smiled, imagining how much the win would have delighted my prickly nemesis. Zach was a good sport, but I knew his dogs meant a great deal to him, especially since he'd walked away from his family's land. His world had been turned upside down. The thought didn't sit well with me.

I reminded myself it was none of my business, accepted a coffee from Blue's thermos, and focused on picking Blue's brains about all things search and rescue as we waited for the team to arrive.

It was just after two when the first strains of laughter echoed down the valley. First into view were the four dogs who barrelled over for a scratch, a treat, and a well done. Then came Zach in the lead, singing "We Are the Champions" at the top of his voice. Before

I knew it, I was grinning and something burst in my chest that felt an awful lot like pride.

When everyone was safely ensconced under the shade of the portable gazebo and the congratulations and shit-talking was over, I left the team to their afternoon tea and debrief and took myself off to the river to soak my hot and tired feet. The icy glacial water did its thing within minutes and pretty soon I was yanking them back into the warm sunshine to pink up the dusky blue shade of my toenails.

"Is this seat taken?"

I looked up into the shadowed face of Zach and my heart did an embarrassing little jump. *What the hell did he want?* I shook my head. "Help yourself."

He did, leaving a good half metre between us as he stripped off his boots and socks to reveal crinkled, pale feet sporting a few blisters. I winced as he shoved them both into the water and let out a relieved groan that went straight to my balls.

Except it didn't. Because I was done with all that nonsense.

For what seemed an awfully long time, we sat in awkward silence against the background chatter from the gazebo fifty metres away. I fought the urge to make small talk. It was Zach's move. If he hadn't wanted to talk, then why leave the others to come and sit next to me?

Despite my determination not to, in the end, I couldn't stand the tension and said, "Congratulations on bringing home the win," at the exact same time that Zach said, "I'm sorry about what I said at your house."

Well, whaddya know? Our sideways gazes met and Zach snorted in amusement.

"You first," I said, curious to see where he was going.

His gaze slid to where the frigid water was swirling around his feet. He pulled them out to dry on the shingle bank alongside mine and said, "I'm saying you were right back then. It's not my place to judge what happened between you and Gil. I *don't* know all the facts, and I sure as hell don't know what it's like to lose a child, or anyone close to me in that way." He shot me an apologetic look. "I was way out of line."

I thought about what he wasn't saying. "But you still think it, right?"

He studied me for a few seconds, then grimaced. "Maybe? I'm trying to be more open."

I huffed out a laugh and began pulling my socks and boots back on. "I suppose I asked for that. Well, you know what, I'm okay with that. You're entitled to think what you like."

The line between Zach's brows deepened. "Fair enough. But while we're on the subject, you were also right about what you said in the pub that night."

My eyebrows hit my hairline. "Two things in one afternoon? Be still my heart. Do tell."

Zach rolled his eyes but there was a quirk to his lips. "I only meant that it *is* kind of weird . . . watching the two of them . . . being on the fringes when I'd once been . . ." he didn't finish, trailing off to study sparkling clear water clattering and clunking over the stony riverbed.

"Are you still in love with Holden?" The question was out before I knew it and Zach's surprised gaze slid sideways to meet mine.

He hesitated before answering, "No, I don't think I have been for a while now, although being around them all the time does tend to make things . . . confusing."

I frowned. "Confusing how?"

He thought again. "I suppose I want what they have, that . . . closeness. I've always imagined what it would feel like to have that constant support, that one person who was there just for me. And I've spent so long imagining, *hoping* that it might happen with Holden, that it's been hard to let that go. And now—" He shrugged. "—I don't think it's Holden I love, but maybe just the idea of what *they* represent. The funny thing is, it was always me who was the settle-down, white-picket-fence guy, while Holden was the love 'em and leave 'em sort." His cheeks reddened. "And I have no idea why I'm telling you any of this."

"Probably because of anyone here, I'm the one most likely to understand." I paused, then added with a wry grin, "Well, as much as a big bad marriage wrecker like me can possibly grasp those kinds of subtle associations." I shuddered for dramatic effect and Zach rolled his eyes.

"Fuck you."

I replied without thinking, "I'm not averse to that."

Zach shot me a startled side-eye and I quickly changed tack, admitting, "You don't think I watch the two of them and wonder where Gil and I went wrong? If things had worked out differently?"

Zach's brows knotted at the idea, but he said nothing, his gaze fixed on the tumbling water. After a long moment, he pulled on his socks and shoved his feet back into his boots. Then he stared up at the clouding sky and a pair of hawks circling over the river. The front was on its way, chasing the blue sky ahead of its steady northeast march and driving the temperature down. It looked like rain. It felt like rain. The humidity heavy in the air like a warm wet blanket.

"It might surprise you to know that I *do* sometimes wonder about all those things," I admitted, leaning back on my hands, hyperaware of the heat emanating from Zach's body, which suddenly seemed very close to mine. Somewhere along the way, between both of us pulling on our boots, we'd bridged the gap—a few centimetres to the right and our shoulders would touch.

"I'm not immune to how deeply they're in love, you know. And yes, at first it did hurt. Kind of ironic, right, since I was the one who eventually walked out. The failure of our marriage led Gil to the relationship he needed, leaving me on the outside. It was a sour pill to swallow for a long while."

Zach ran his palms down his thighs and turned his troubled green eyes to me. "Yeah, but you and Gil had been married, whereas Holden had *never* been in love with me." It sounded so matter of fact, but there was a wealth of emotion swirling in those green eyes. "So, the truth is, I have zero right to feel bitter about *anything*. Holden had been clear from the start, so it was my problem. But that's all beside the point—" He got to his feet and brushed the scraps of tussock from his clothes. "—I just wanted to apologise for what I said. And to say thanks for helping out today."

I nodded. "My pleasure." I caught his gaze and held it. "But just for the record, you don't need to justify what you feel, Zach. If I learned one thing being married to a psychologist, it's that you feel what you feel, full stop."

His gaze lingered on mine like he was maybe going to reply, but then he simply nodded and headed back to the gazebo, giving me the chance to admire that smooth country swagger I'd obsessed about from the first day we'd met. The man looked good coming *or* going and I wasn't above a little appreciation. It meant something that he'd apologised. That he'd made the effort.

But in the end, it changed little.

I needed to let Zach be and focus on carving out a new life for myself minus a marriage and the best daughter in the world. There were enough ways I could fuck that up without adding a poorly timed and ill-considered fling into the mix.

The trip back was a lot noisier than the morning flight, with everyone hyped up from the day's adventures. The volunteer team was a fun group that seemed to get on well, and I'd been smiling from the minute we'd loaded everyone on board. They were also completely different from the crowd I usually hung out with in Wellington—more relaxed and down-to-earth, throwing bullshit my way as readily as they did amongst themselves. It was a good feeling, I realised with a jolt. Not that I didn't have some good friends back home, but the majority continued to treat me with kid gloves, as they had ever since Callie had died.

I missed being just one of the crowd. Being the target of jokes and innuendo. Being just a regular guy. Not Gil's ex-husband. Not Callie's grieving dad. Not the man whose life was going nowhere.

Even if I was still all of those. With these people, I could also be just plain Luke, no bigger screw-up than anyone else.

Doug Carstairs had nabbed the front passenger seat again, turning a deaf ear to the grumblings of the others. There was no mistaking the less-than-PG interest in his eyes whenever they met mine, and I figured I wasn't going to have to wait long until he made a move. Deciding how I was going to handle it was the next problem.

Kelsie and Pedro were the first drop, and then I headed for Tekapo. Doug was having dinner with his sister's family and so I'd offered to drop him second, hoping to grab a few local history books from Holden before I beat the weather back to Oakwood. Doug's sister was waiting at the airfield and offered a cheery wave as we set down.

Doug slid the headset from his head, grabbed his pack, and climbed out. He set Carmine free and then caught my eye and leaned back through the open door.

I slid my headset to the side and waited.

Doug tilted his head and there was no mistaking the look he sent me. "Care to meet up for a drink at the Oakwood pub on Friday?"

And there it was. I fought back a smile and was about to say *thanks, but no thanks* when I caught sight of Zach's scowl in the mirror and my decision flipped on its head. "Um, yeah, sure."

Doug snorted. "No need to sound so excited."

I chuckled. "Sorry. You caught me by surprise. That would be nice."

He brightened. "Good. How about six? We could grab something to eat while we're at it."

Any chance to avoid cooking was fine by me, and I nodded. "Six it is."

Charlie whoop whooped in the back and when she chanted, "Douggie and Luke sitting up a tree. *K I S S I N G.*" I belatedly realised that my side of the conversation had carried through the microphone. *Dammit.*

I heard Zach mutter for Charlie to shut up, which only served to make her laugh louder.

Doug remained focused on me. "Cool, it's a date then."

I winced inwardly at the word and said, "A drink."

He grinned, acknowledging the clarification, and then turned to Zach who was sitting directly behind me and winked. "And *you* better be shouting drinks with that tequila you won, mate. Just saying."

Zach remained silent. But a quick glance in the mirror we used to check on our backseat tourists confirmed that scowl was still firmly in place. Doug grinned again, clearly finding something about the whole interaction amusing, and then he closed the door. And as the skids lifted off the ground and we headed out over the crystal blue waters of Lake Tekapo, I realised I was smiling.

For all that Doug came on a little strong for my tastes, there was no denying his raw, uncomplicated appeal, and the idea of meeting up with him was strangely growing on me. I'd been rattling around the rental on my own for a few weeks and had gotten into the habit of sinking a couple too many beers of an evening while staring at my favourite photo of Callie.

It wasn't rocket science to understand that wasn't high on the list of healthy grieving behaviours, and changing the geography of where I lived wasn't going to miraculously ease the pain that sank me to my knees more nights than not. Only time and my attention was going to do that. Widening my horizons and forgetting about a certain auburn-haired spitfire who'd spent way too many hours in my messy head was a safer option for everybody concerned.

"Very smooth, Mister Nichols." Charlie's teasing voice came through the headset and roused me from my musings. "Hooked and landed all in a day, you little hussy. Nice work."

I chuckled and started the climb to skirt the top of Champion's Peak, its deep green tarn looking dull under a ceiling of gathering clouds. "Get your mind out of the gutter. I'm just trying to get to know people, that's all."

"Yeah. Yeah." She laughed. "Pull the other one. It's got bells on." She gave my shoulder a light shove. "He's clearly hot for you. But you wanna watch yourself. He's left a trail of broken hearts, both men and women."

"Put a lid on it, will you?" Zach grumbled sharply enough to have me look up from the jagged terrain and check the mirror. He was staring out the side window, his jaw tight, his face set in a deep frown.

Interesting. My gaze flicked on and off the mirror, wondering if I could possibly be reading things right.

Charlie's smile slipped and she elbowed Zach gently. "Hey, are you okay?"

Zach shrugged. "Just tired. Sorry. I didn't mean to snap."

"'S okay." She patted his arm and I pulled my gaze back to where it belonged.

Other than me radioing Gil to tell him we were about six minutes out, the rest of the flight passed in silence until the skids touched down on the Miller Station airfield and Jojo and Hellboy set to whining their excitement at being home. How they knew from inside their tin can transport torpedo, I hadn't a clue.

Holden and Gil were already there to meet us, along with Spider who sat quietly at Gil's side. After the slightly weird conversation about them with Zach earlier in the day, seeing the two men with their arms wrapped around each other as they squinted into the residual wash of the chopper blades, I realised I didn't feel the familiar pang in my chest that I'd almost gotten used to.

I *was* happy for Gil, I realised. Happy for them both. I'd said the words so often in my head and aloud to friends and family, but it suddenly struck me that maybe I was only just beginning to mean them.

Self-preservation was a thing.

I powered down the chopper and ditched my headset. Then I spun in my seat just in time to catch Zach watching Gil and Holden in much the same way as I imagined I'd been doing. Our eyes met and he flushed a fetching shade of red before looking away.

Charlie glanced between us and a crease formed between her brows. "Jesus Christ, what the fuck is up with you two sour pusses?"

"Nothing," Zach muttered as he opened the side door and jumped out, taking his pack with him. He lifted the lid on the carrier and Jojo leapt free and made for Spider who was clearly up for a game and chased her into the open hangar. The minute he was released, Hellboy raced to join them.

As Zach walked over to Gil and Holden, Charlie touched my arm. "Jesus, what rat climbed up his arsehole?"

I laughed unconvincingly. "Your guess is as good as mine."

She stared at me for a moment, narrowed her gaze, and then shook her head. "Nope. I'm not buying it. But whatever. You gay boys are way too fucking complicated." She slammed shut the door and headed for the others.

Holden took one look at Zach's pissy expression and laughed. "Oh boy. Don't tell me you lost your number one spot."

"Shut up," Zach grumbled. "And no, I won, as it happened. But just for that, I won't be sharing my tequila with your sorry arse anytime soon, best mate or not. *Aaaand* it was actually Charlie who nailed the first find. Ta-da." He swept an arm Charlie's way and her cheeks pinked in pleasure.

Holden gave a low whistle. "Well done. That's two to Miller Station, then."

"And congrats to you." Gil slapped Zach on the shoulder. "Spider spent all day telling me just how much he wished he was there with you all."

As if summoned, Spider appeared from nowhere and Zach scratched the huntaway's head. "We all know your daddy is a lying liar who lies. Because coming today would mean exercise, and we all know exercise is the work of the devil, right, boy?"

Spider whined as if in agreement and shoved his head into Zach's hand for a harder rub. Everyone laughed, including Zach, and my heart lightened at the sound of it.

Charlie called Hellboy and then turned to us. "As much as I'd love to stay and chat with you boneheads, the minute I get this boy fed and put to bed, there's a bath with my name on it." She eyed Zach. "Do you want me to take Jojo as well?"

Relief swept his face. "Please. I'll owe you."

"I'll just add it to the list." Charlie whistled both dogs up into the bed of the ute and made her way to the driver's door.

But Zach got there first and opened it for her. "You did really, really well today. I'm super proud of you."

Charlie's eyes turned glassy and a tiny self-conscious smile tugged at her lips. "Thanks. But really, I'm just lucky you agreed to teach me."

"Hey." Zach dipped his head to catch her eye. "Teaching is only a small part of it. You have a natural talent, Charlie. It's a pleasure to help grow that."

She stared at him for a second, then blinked and wiped at her eyes. "Goddammit." She gave him a gentle shove. "Now look what you've done. I'm pissing off before I actually fucking cry and the world comes to an end." And with that she jumped in the ute and spat dust as she took off, leaving everyone smiling.

Gil caught my eye. "You got time for a coffee before you head back, or is that weather front too close?"

I glanced up at the grey sky. "If we make it a quick one. Gary's not expecting me back until four thirty, and I wanted to grab some of Holden's local history books if he doesn't mind?"

Holden's brows peaked. "Sure. Any particular reason?"

I grimaced. "I got hit with some gnarly questions from a couple of tourists today. Felt a bit of an idiot, if I'm honest."

Holden chuckled. "If you really want to impress people, then you should talk to Zach. He wrote a whole university paper on pioneering days in the Mackenzie Basin. He's got a ton of stories in that pretty head of his."

"Does he now?" I shot Zach a curious look.

He instantly turned away. "Doubt I'd be much help."

Holden frowned. "What are you on about? Of course you would.

Luke can pick your brains over coffee while I see what I can dredge up from Gran and Grandad's library."

If looks could kill, Holden's death would have been slow and painful based solely on the blistering glare Zach fired his way. Unperturbed or simply oblivious, Holden threw Zach's backpack on the bed of the ute and whistled Spider aboard.

"Maybe Luke could ask Doug since he's having a drink with him on Friday. His family's been in the Mackenzie as long as ours have."

That bombshell got Holden and Gil's immediate attention.

"What's all this?" Gil gave a sly grin. "You're going on a date? With Doug Carstairs?"

"Dashing Doug?" Holden chuckled. "Hoo-wee. You're just jumping right in there, aren't you?"

"We are *not* going on a date." I scowled at Zach, who suddenly looked a lot brighter for dropping me in it, the fucker. "We're just meeting up for a drink, that's all."

Holden countered, "Of course you are. But be warned, Doug *never* meets up *just* for a drink. Having said that, if you're after a bit of stress relief, you could do a lot worse. Doug's a nice guy and he's—" Holden shot Gil an apologetic look. "—energetic. Let's leave it at that."

Gil rolled his eyes. "Why am I not surprised?"

"It's just a drink," I insisted, but my protest fell on deaf ears and knowing chuckles from everyone except Zach who'd fallen noticeably silent once again, his face carved into deep don't-talk-to-me lines. "And just so we're clear, you two giving me hookup advice is way too creepy to ever happen again. Got it?"

They both said, "Yes," while energetically shaking their heads.

I flipped them off and left them to close the hangar while I opened the back door of the Hilux and waved Zach inside. He gave me another of those startled looks, then climbed in and scooted over to the middle since the far side was piled high with supplies for the guest cottages.

I slid in alongside and we shuffled for room, his thigh pushing hot against mine, our arms jostling for position. He smelled of the outdoors. Of lanolin and dry tussock, dogs, and the mineral scent of clear mountain streams all overlaid by a decent dose of clean sweat from the day's tough hike.

It was an interesting mix and oddly erotic. Mind you, there wasn't much about Zach that I didn't find erotic.

I angled my body onto one hip to give him a bit more room and in the process, the sides of our heads brushed and he jerked around, putting us almost within kissing distance.

He sucked in a sharp breath and his gaze dropped to my lips, the tip of his pink tongue showing for just a second. Then his eyes lifted back to mine, and it took all my strength not to close the gap and snag a taste of the intriguing man. He flushed red and looked away, his gaze fixed on the windscreen.

"Do you have enough room?" I checked more for something to say than anything else.

"I'm fine."

No arguing with that. With Gil and Holden almost back at the ute, I took the opportunity to whisper, "Just so you know, I don't expect you to stay and talk history with me."

Zach shot me a hard-to-read look. "It doesn't matter either way to me." Which was so obviously a lie I wasn't sure how either of us kept a straight face.

"Sorry about the squeeze." Holden slid into the driver's seat and put the ute in reverse. "Gil's upscaling the guest cottages' linen for this year's muster."

Gil turned in his seat. "We increased the—" He paused, his shrewd gaze landing on a still-flushed Zach, causing Zach to reach down and ferret in his bag for something he undoubtedly didn't need.

"Increased what?" I enquired, meeting Gil's questioning brow with a matching one of my own. The man was too fucking perceptive.

He held my gaze a moment longer, but I'd been married to him long enough to hold my own in the face of his ferreting manoeuvres.

Eventually, he gave up. "We increased the cost for the guest bookings during muster. And since they're going to be paying a frickin' fortune for the privilege of busting their arses for a week on the hill with thousands of smelly merinos, I figured the least we could do is provide a bit of luxury at the beginning and end. Million-thread-count sheets and towels thick enough to wipe even your sorry arses were a good start."

I snorted. "It's a far cry from the man who tried to survive university on three facecloths and a hand towel because he was too much of a Scrooge to replace the full towel he used to paint a pride flag on, which he then glued *and* nailed to the office door of his first-year history professor."

Holden glanced over at Gil. "You make me so proud."

Gil snorted. "The guy was the biggest fucking homophobe. Gave me a C+ on a paper because he felt I hadn't given adequate consideration to the validity of opposing views on the 1986 decriminalisation of homosexuality in New Zealand."

Even Zach gave a barely audible snort of amusement.

Holden slapped Gil's thigh. "From arguing homosexual law reform to spreading million-thread-count sheets for loaded guests. You've come a long way, baby. Are there any more stories of your misspent youth?"

Gil threw me a warning look, which I duly ignored.

"Oh, there's a ton more where that came from," I assured Holden, which earned me a dishtowel in the face from my darling ex.

CHAPTER SIX

Zach

"Not so fast, mister." Holden held me back as Gil and Luke made their way up the front path with Spider at their heels. "What's eating you? And don't say it's not. Did something happen today?"

"Nope. I'm just tired. I want a bath and a beer, and not in that order." I shrugged him free and started across the lawn toward Tussock Cottage.

"I don't believe you." He ran after me. "Come on. If you want a beer, then come in and grab it with us. You know way better stories about the Mackenzie than I do. You always have the guests in stitches. I know you don't like Luke much, but he's not as bad as you think."

I swallowed the urge to tell Holden exactly what I thought about Luke, starting with how badly I wanted to bend him over that king-sized bed of mine and fuck him senseless, but yeah . . . maybe not the best conversation starter. Instead, I sighed, reminded myself how Luke had helped us out today when he didn't have to, and dropped my bag on the deck of the cottage. "One beer. Are you happy now?"

Holden beamed and slung an arm over my shoulder. "Ecstatic."

The homestead's industrial-sized kitchen had wood and stainless countertops, a massive granite island, flagstone floors, and bright white cabinetry. It was made homely by soft furnishings done in a pale green and cream palette, masses of pot plants, and a wealth of copper pots hanging from the ceiling on a black metal frame.

There had been subtle changes since Gil had taken over from Emily and made it his domain, such as a couple of skylights over the kitchen island that flooded the space with light. But there were other changes too—a simpler crockery design, a clearer workspace, and the swapping out of the pale lemon small appliances for stainless steel versions had all added a more masculine touch while maintaining the welcoming feel of the place.

When we walked in, Gil was already frothing milk at the espresso machine and Luke was seated at one end of the long table that hosted the entire station team for lunch most days of the week. Luke had shrugged out of the top of his flight suit and tied the arms around his waist, leaving him sitting in a black sleeveless tank with far too much naked skin on display. My gaze fell to his nicely contoured forearms, tanned and dusted with a smattering of blond hair just like the rest of him. And how the fuck was that as sexy as it was?

At the sound of our footsteps, he looked up, and when he saw me, a small frown dipped between his brows.

"Sit and I'll get you that beer." Holden waved me to a seat at the table and headed for the fridge in the pantry saying, "I might even have one myself."

I took a seat at the opposite end of the table from Luke and his mouth turned up in a wry smile. "I can sit in the mudroom if you'd prefer?"

An amused snort came from the direction of the espresso machine but I chose to ignore it.

"Here you go." Holden returned and took a seat. He slid a local IPA across the table, one I knew he stocked just for me. "So, Douggie, huh?" Holden cast an amused gaze Luke's direction.

"For fuck's sake, can we just drop it?" Luke grumbled. "I don't get why everyone finds this so amusing?" His gaze landed on me. "I never claimed to be a monk."

"You're right." Holden took a swallow of his beer. "But hey, we live on a fucking sheep station. Any chatter from the outside world is solid gold to get us through the day. And I have to say, the dating life of my partner's ex-husband definitely qualifies."

"*Not* a date," Luke emphasised once again. "Not to mention, the divorce isn't actually final." He arched a brow and grinned. "Just saying."

Holden blinked. "Jesus, I forgot about that."

Gil laughed. "I assume you're not angling for a redo, Mister Nichols?" It was most definitely a joke, but Holden's horrified gaze jerked to Gil nonetheless.

I couldn't contain a snigger. There was nowhere Gil was going to be in the next fifty years that didn't include Holden at his side. Those two were fused at the heart.

"Hell, no." Luke squeezed his eyes shut and shuddered dramatically.

Gil chuckled. "Case closed."

Holden grew thoughtful and his gaze swept the room. He frowned and lifted a finger in the air, circling it as he said, "So, the four of us sitting here is really fucking weird, right?"

Gil walked a coffee over to Luke and gave Holden an affectionate peck on the cheek. "Aw, bless him, he finally got there."

Luke snorted while Holden held up his hands and griped, "You think you're all so funny, don't you?" We nodded almost as one and he grumbled and flipped us off. "I'm going to take my beer and see if I can round up those books while you lot chat."

"I'll come with you." Gil wiped his palms down his jeans.

Holden's brows dipped in confusion. "I can manage—"

"I'm coming." Gil eyeballed Holden. "I want to see what we have in case a guest asks."

As excuses went, it was pretty thin, and I could tell Holden had zero clue what was going on. I, on the other hand, knew exactly what Gil was up to and delivered a sharp toe to his calf to let him know I was onto him trying to build bridges between Luke and me. Meddling little psychologist fucker.

But Gil was good. He barely acknowledged my less-than-subtle warning and then sidestepped a second attempt by quickly dancing after Holden, leaving Luke and me alone in the kitchen. The room immediately fell into an awkward silence. Well, awkward on my part. Luke merely looked . . . amused.

"Like I said earlier, you don't have to stay," he repeated softly.

Ugh. Why is it when people say things like that, you feel even more obliged to do the thing you don't want to? "It's fine," I huffed, perfectly aware that I sounded like a put-upon teenager. "What is it you want to know?"

"Everything." He grinned. "But just a couple of local stories to start with will be fine. Something not on the tourist websites." He grabbed his mug of coffee and made his way to my end of the table, taking the chair right alongside, close enough so our knees touched.

The sizzle of that connection drowned every other sensation in my body.

"Much better." His eyes danced merrily over my face. "I almost needed glasses to see you from the other end."

"Personally, I don't see the problem," I argued, regretting the sulky words the second they left my mouth.

Luke stared at me for a moment then shook his head. "Jesus Christ, Zach." He scraped his chair back and got to his feet. "You know what, I don't need this. I don't deserve to feel like a fucking leper for whatever you think I've done or haven't done. Let's just go back to ignoring each other. Seems the best solution all around." He went to walk away but I grabbed his wrist.

"I'm sorry."

He turned slowly back around and waited.

"I . . . I just—" I fumbled, having no clue what I wanted to say. All I knew was the feel of his hot skin against my palm and the pounding of my heart in my throat.

Luke sighed but made no move to free his arm. "Just *what*, Zach? What do I have to do to earn your friendship?"

Not exist. Not look so tempting. Not fill my dreams and every fucking waking thought in my head. Not be nice. Not confuse me. Not make me wish for things I shouldn't. Not scare me.

"It's not you," I finally admitted. "It's me." It sounded ludicrous even as I said it, but for all intents and purposes, it was true. I might not be sure about Luke, but the fact I was absurdly attracted to him wasn't his fault.

He snorted. "Really? 'It's not me it's you.'" He made air quotes. "*That's* what you're going with?"

I shrugged. "It's all I've got. I'm working on it, okay? Can we leave it at that, please?"

He hesitated, scanning my face for . . . who the hell knew what. Eventually he sat back down again. "All right. But if you try and spray me with disinfectant, I'm out of here."

I couldn't help but smile and raise my hand, my thumb and forefinger barely apart. "Not even just a little—"

"No." He chuckled and batted my hand away, the tension between us dissolving for maybe the first time ever. "Come on then. Give me a couple of stories I can work with."

And so I did, sharing a few short accounts involving mustering misadventures, weather catastrophes, and the first female station owner in the Mackenzie. Luke listened raptly, asked a ton of questions, and I found myself slowly relaxing into his enthusiasm and obvious interest.

It wasn't . . . terrible. In fact, it was kind of nice, which was less reassuring than it sounded. Luke was quick-minded, interesting, and fun, exactly what the rest of the team had been telling me for months. He shared some of his own flying adventures but didn't hog the conversation, and he had the kind of dry, sardonic sense of humour that I loved, something I'd already known but refused to acknowledge, because . . . reasons, most revolving around the realisation that Luke wasn't just a pretty face. He was a lot more, a fact that made him particularly dangerous to my bruised heart.

Agreeing to talk had been a mistake, because slowly but surely Luke was wheedling his way under my skin and undermining my defences. I liked the man, no surprise there. But the already complicated history between Holden and Gil and myself notwithstanding, if Luke and I started fucking as well, the station would give any soap opera a run for its money.

By the time we were done talking, a half hour had passed. My beer was finished, Luke's cup was empty, the kitchen was dark under the clouded sky, a light rain was spattering on the window, and there was still no sign of Holden and Gil.

"I should go." I got to my feet and Luke quickly did the same. "Thanks for flying us today. It's good to know we still have a pilot."

"You're more than welcome." Luke's bright blue eyes found mine and lingered there for a beat or two. "I enjoyed talking with you, Zach."

Something fluttered in my chest, and I didn't trust myself to give any answer that didn't include shoving my tongue down his throat, so I simply nodded and turned to leave.

"But just so we're clear—" Luke's voice was so quiet I almost missed it. "—I'd rather it was you, on Friday."

I froze in place, keeping my back to him.

"I'd rather it was you and not Doug I was meeting for a drink."

I turned slowly to face him. "Me?"

A tiny smile tugged at his lips. "Yes, you. Call me a masochist, but I'd rather spend a few hours being put in my place by you than flattered by Doug."

I almost laughed. "Then you're crazy."

Luke's expression barely flickered. "It's been said before."

I folded my arms and studied him for a moment, the air between us electric with possibility. "I'm not interested in a hookup," I lied.

His smile broke free. "I don't recall asking, but good to know. However, the real reason behind me mentioning it is that I'm the new kid in town. I'm trying to meet people and make friends, and you seem like a nice guy to make friends with." He held my gaze. "When you give me a chance, that is. I'm *trying* to fit in. Trying to build a new life after . . . well, everything."

A nice guy to make friends with? I reeled in a surge of pleasure and sympathy because that fucked with the whole keeping Luke at a huge whopping distance thing, something that I was already doing a pretty shabby job of maintaining.

"And I wish you well with that," I finally offered. "I do mean that. But I'm sure Douggie will do a standout job for whatever it is you need."

Luke nodded. "Yeah, maybe you're right." His gaze burned into mine with enough heat to set every one of my lying protests alight. "Maybe I *am* imagining this." His finger waggled back and forth between us.

"This?" I sucked in a breath while berating myself for falling into the trap of asking the question.

His mouth curved up in a tiny smile and he took a step closer.

I took a couple back until my shoulders hit the wall.

Luke took another half step, and I was forced to look up and fall into those blue, blue eyes.

My mouth dried to dust, and it was almost painful to swallow, my heart taking up all the room in my throat, thundering loud enough that I thought for sure Luke couldn't miss it.

He was close. So close. Close enough to—

He leaned toward me, and for a hot terrifying second, I thought he might kiss me. Worse, I had to stop myself from rushing to meet him halfway. To feel the pressure of those soft lips. To get that first unique taste. My eyelids fluttered closed of their own volition and I braced for that first touch, my mind in freefall, my body frozen in place, ignoring every order from my brain to simply step aside since nothing was stopping me.

But I didn't, and instead of the kiss I was aching for, he bypassed my mouth to land only a soft puff of breath on my cheek as he whispered close to my ear, "I like you, Zach. I like you a lot." He pulled away just enough to look at me, his hot breath caressing my face, the spicy scent of his cologne mixed with a little sweat and a background hit of aviation fuel rising from all that bare skin to send my pulse soaring, along with another part of my traitorous anatomy. "It's a shame the feeling isn't mutual."

His gaze dipped to my mouth, his pupils flaring, and again I thought he might kiss me. Then his eyes crinkled at the corners, wistful and maybe even sad. He drew a ragged breath, and then another, and I heard my own reflected back at him.

"If that ever changes—" He ran a thumb over my cheek and I shivered to my toes. "You be sure to let me know, yeah?"

I didn't answer, hell I wasn't even sure I could speak. Luke had rattled my brain like it was a snow globe and the cells were still tumbling. Jesus fucking Christ, the man was potent.

And then without another word he was gone, leaving nothing but a draught of cool air and the sound of his footsteps on the polished wooden floor heading for the east wing.

My eyes shot open and I slumped against the wall, the residual warmth from Luke's body lingering on my skin as I waited for the oxygen to locate my lungs once again. I fingered dry untouched lips, and regret flooded my chest. Every part of my body had wanted that kiss and a whole fucking lot more.

I sucked in a breath and peered around the doorjamb. Voices floated in the distance, but the hallway was empty. Thank God. I fell back against the wall and replayed the scene in my head. *I like you, Zach.* Luke's words ran circles in my brain. *It's a shame it's not mutual.*

I huffed out an almost laugh. If only Luke knew exactly how much I liked him. How much he wasn't *imagining* anything. That I felt that zing between us too. How I lusted after him as well. Anything that got the two of us naked and sweaty. I ran my hand down my chest and over my belly to palm my semi-rigid cock, giving it a light squeeze before remembering where I was and dropping it like a hotcake.

What the hell's wrong with me?

I started at the sound of footsteps in the hall and lunged for the mudroom door. Call me a coward, but there was no way in hell I was locking eyes with Luke Nichols while sporting a semi and most likely the words *fuck me right the hell now* tattooed on my forehead.

I made it all the way around the house through the steadily increasing rain before my heart calmed and I got a grip on my head. The glacial blue lake had turned a dirty grey, its surface rippled, the ground beneath my feet growing slick and treacherous as the baked soil refused to soak up the water. Too bad I'd left my boots and coat at the front door. My socks were soaked, much like the rest of me.

Congrats on a solid job looking like a complete idiot.

When I finally reached the veranda of Tussock Cottage and shook myself off, I risked a glance toward the kitchen to find Luke watching me through the window, because of course he bloody was. I couldn't make out his face through the rain, but his hand lifted in some kind of acknowledgement.

I stood there for a few seconds, not believing the gall of the man to . . . to . . . *what?* I wasn't sure what he'd even done really, but whatever it was, it pissed me off. I set my lips in a thin line and flipped him off. Then I squelched up the stairs, peeled my muddy socks from my feet, and headed for the coldest shower known to humanity.

CHAPTER SEVEN

Zach

"Who's free to help with the River Hut re-roof?" Holden scoured the blank expressions of everyone seated at the kitchen table. Gil had outdone himself with lunch, serving up smoked chicken on buttered noodles with Irish soda bread and home-churned butter on the side. The carb coma was real. "Tom and I are gonna need another pair of hands this afternoon."

There was a prolonged and deafening silence in stark contrast to the rowdy banter that always accompanied a team lunch, which had helped distract me from my close encounter with Luke the afternoon before. Against that very wall to my right. That hard, familiar wall that I absolutely was not going to look at. Just like I wasn't going to think of the way he'd smelled, or the sense of his body so close to mine, or the way his nose had almost brushed my cheek, or—

Eventually, Sam huffed out a put-upon sigh and grumbled, "Yeah okay. I've finished the stock take, so I guess I can help. But I want to know when I get to lose the new-grad, everyone's-bitch status?" At twenty-two but looking like sixteen, Sam was the team's youngest shepherd and almost always landed the worst or extra jobs. It sucked, but it came with the territory.

"When another new grad comes along," Tom replied smoothly, and we all tried to keep a straight face.

Sam narrowed his gaze and shook his shaggy blond waves. "Oh, hell no! I am *not* doing *all* the four a.m. sweeps during muster this year." Then, as if hearing what he'd said, he swallowed hard and shot an uncertain look to Holden. "I mean . . . of course . . . I will if I have to, Boss, but—" He slumped in his chair. "Fuck it. I guess I'll be doing them."

Alek patted Sam's shoulder. "I'll help."

Charlie folded her arms and tried to look severe. "Hey, I did four years of that shit before Alek arrived. Newbies do the hard yards. Those are the rules."

"Four years!" Sam gaped. "But—" His gaze swept the group. "Really?"

"It was three years for me," I said sombrely, trying not to smile.

"Four for me," Tom piped up.

"Five here." Holden smiled. "It's like a badge of honour—boy-to-manhood kind of stuff. But if you want Alek to help you out, I won't stop him."

Sam said nothing for a minute, just sat there chewing the inside of his cheek with a troubled look on his face. "Well, okay. If it's a rite of passage, then I suppose I should do my part. I won't have anyone claiming I didn't earn my full-shepherd status."

I coughed into my napkin to hide the laugh threatening to explode up my throat, but Charlie didn't manage quite as well. She snorted, then gasped as I kicked her under the table.

Sam's gaze shot up. "What?"

"Nothing," Charlie practically squeaked, which almost sent me over the edge. "Just really proud of you."

A blush stole over Sam's cheeks and I almost lost it completely.

Holden's eyes lit with humour as he cleared his throat and asked Sam to fetch the ute.

"Me?" Sam stared bug-eyed. Holden never let anyone drive his ute except Gil.

"Sure." Holden threw him the keys and we all held our breath until he was well out of earshot before erupting into hoots of laughter.

"A badge of honour?" Emily threw Holden an are-you-kidding-me look. "That poor boy. When are you going to tell him you were only kidding and that if we don't have a grad or fresh team member, we draw straws and share the load?"

Tom snorted the dregs of his coffee down the front of his T-shirt and fumbled for a cloth to mop it up. The most experienced shepherd on the station, he'd come up through the ranks the hard way. "I was thinking maybe never," he said, and another peal of laughter circled the room.

Emily shook her head, supposedly in disappointment, but it was clear she was fighting a smile. "Some days I wonder about you lot. I truly do. But if you're going to have your fun, you better make sure that boy gets an extra two days off once muster is done. We don't play those power games on this station, remember?"

Holden stood and gave his mother a hug. "Don't worry. I promise we'll come clean after the first day."

"And I will help him out after that," Alek assured her.

"I can take a day or two as well," I found myself saying, and Holden shot me a grateful look.

Then he gave a double clap, which signalled lunch was done and we all pushed our seats back. "The station won't run itself, guys."

"More's the pity," Tom grumbled as everyone began moving toward the mudroom.

"Hang on." Charlie waved us to a stop. "You do realise it's Sam's birthday on Saturday, but since he's heading to his parents that morning, I was thinking we should shout him a round or two at The Fleece on Friday night. I'll even volunteer to drive your sorry arses."

Gil threw his hand in the air. "I can drive as well. I had enough alcohol on my own birthday to last a year. And don't forget the team cookout Saturday night, which everyone except Sam is expected to attend. No excuses. So, who's on for Friday?"

Everyone raised their hands. Everyone except Emily and me. The last thing I needed was to risk another encounter with Luke who was having his date... drink... whatever... with Doug that night.

"Harry and I already have plans, sorry," Emily announced.

Which left me.

Holden arched a brow. "Zach? Don't tell me you're gonna leave us hanging?"

I scrambled for an excuse. "Toby's coming to pick up Chester early Saturday morning and I want to work him again on Friday before he leaves."

Holden frowned. "Can't you work him earlier in the day?"

"I'm working the southern fence that day, remember?"

Holden studied me like he knew what I was doing, which he probably did, although not for the reasons he thought. "Don't recall that being a high priority. Shuffle things around. In fact, take all of Friday afternoon off. You're owed a ton of time, mate. That way, you can work Chester and still come celebrate with the team."

Team. A not-so-subtle reminder that Holden and Gil had worked hard to bring the Miller Station team closer by organising these kinds of celebrations on a regular basis, and I generally was first in line. They were good fun, something I needed more of in my life. I gave an inward sigh. "Well, I, um—sure." I managed a semblance of a smile.

"Great." Holden rubbed his hands together. "That's decided. But we won't all fit in Charlie's ute."

"I'll take my bike," I offered. "I'm not planning on drinking or staying long. Gil's birthday still haunts me."

In more ways than one. But the throwaway comment earned me a few chuckles and nodding heads. Mission accomplished. I'd be out of that hotel in under an hour.

Charlie slapped me on the shoulder. "You were so wasted. It was fucking epic."

"Shut up." I tried to noogie her head but she darted into the mudroom and out of reach and I followed.

"Hey, Zach," Gil called out to me. "Can I talk to you for a sec before you go?"

I swallowed a groan. Gil had tried to corner me twice since Luke had left the day before, but I'd seen him coming both times and skedaddled. I damn well knew he'd set me up when he'd left Luke and me together while he went with Holden to find those books, and I wasn't keen on whatever else he had to say. Had he seen us in the kitchen? I had no idea.

I wandered back into the kitchen and tried not to look worried. "You need something?"

Holden's curious gaze bounced between the two of us, and he looked about to say something when Gil kissed his cheek before patting his butt. "No need to wait. I'll bring *afternoon tea* out to you later." He winked and a flush rose up Holden's cheeks, and I really, really didn't want to know what that was all about.

As soon as Holden was gone, Gil waved me to a chair, but I remained standing, not sure what to expect. He sighed and leaned back against the granite worktop. "Okay, have it your way." He folded his arms, his blond hair almost gold in the slice of sun that fell through the new skylights above the kitchen island, his shrewd hazel eyes resting calmly on mine.

I returned his gaze with a cool one of my own. "Why do I feel like I'm fourteen and have been called to the principal's office?"

He snorted. "I don't know. Why *do* you feel like that?"

I wagged my finger at him. "Nope. I'm not playing any psychobabble games with you. I'd lose in a heartbeat. What do you want?"

He chewed on his lip for a second, then asked, "How are things with your family?"

I blinked, pretty sure that wasn't what he wanted to ask me, but whatever. "Dad's a blast, as usual," I answered a little sourly. "Whenever we run into each other, he mostly curses and pretends he hasn't seen me."

Gil winced in sympathy as I continued. "Mum has sent a couple of texts so that's something, I guess. And Jules is doing his best to keep in touch." The thought of my brother brought a smile to my face. "We meet up in Oakwood occasionally, but it's hard for both of us. With me gone, Dad's riding Jules hard and it's getting him down. Jules knows the station as well as Dad, but he's not allowed to make *any* decisions on his own. Still, things could be worse, right? Now ask me what you really want to know."

Gil forced a half-smile and relaxed his arms. "That obvious, huh?"

This time my smile was genuine. "Pretty much."

Gil gave me a measured look. "He's not a bad guy. You do know that, right?"

No points for guessing who *he* was. I sighed and dropped my head to consider the slate floors and exactly how to answer his question before looking up again. "I guess I'm beginning to see that."

"Good." Gil appeared relieved. "But to be honest, I don't care if you like him or not, but I do want *him* to feel welcome on the station without *you* feeling uncomfortable while he's here, and so I'm checking if there's anything I should know. Any reason for the animosity between you?"

My stomach sank. Considering I was Holden's best mate, his one-time friend with benefits, and the fact I was virtually living in both of their pockets, Gil had been incredibly understanding and kind to me. The last thing I wanted was to make things awkward between him and Luke. "No. I promise. There's nothing like that."

When I didn't offer anything more, he pressed. "Holden says I should apologise for leaving you guys alone yesterday, for forcing the issue. I suppose I hoped you might . . . I don't know, talk maybe? It seems whenever Luke walks in, you walk out."

A fair and accurate observation.

I studied the two rectangles of brilliant blue sky visible through the skylight while I got some kind of response together. Then I decided the truth would have to do. "It's stupid, I know, because it's none of my business, but I suppose I didn't like what he did to you. I know you guys have sorted things out, but it coloured my view of him from the start. It's my problem, and I'm working on it."

The relief in Gil's eyes was immediate and it occurred to me he'd been genuinely worried something had happened between Luke and me. He looked thoughtful for a moment and then gave me a long, level look. "I'm going to tell you this for no other reason than we're a family on this station, you included, understand?"

I nodded.

He drew a long breath and blew it out slowly. "I was as much to blame as Luke for our marriage imploding, in some ways, more."

I blinked, pretty sure the disbelief was etched deep upon my face.

"Now that—" He stabbed a finger my way. "That right there is what's tripping you up. I appreciate your loyalty, Zach, especially all things considered, but mark my words, I'm no angel. After Callie died, I made it almost impossible for Luke to stay. In his shoes, I'm not sure I wouldn't have done exactly the same thing and left him."

"But—" I snapped my mouth shut.

"We both wish we'd done things differently, but if *I* don't hold a grudge and *Luke* doesn't, then *nobody* else should. I'm in love with Holden, Zach, but Luke is one of the best men I've ever met, and he's been through hell, the same as I have. He made the move down here for much the same reasons I did, so think of him what you will, but don't base your opinion on half-truths and assumptions. I left you alone yesterday because I think you could be friends if you let yourselves."

I'm pretty sure I gaped, and Gil smiled wryly, adding, "Yeah, you might rub each other the wrong way, but that doesn't mean you can't get on."

I was tempted to blurt that there probably wasn't a wrong way that Luke could rub me . . . just saying, but thankfully the words stayed buried where they belonged.

Gil looked about to say something else, then shook his head. "That's it. I won't raise the subject again."

And I knew he wouldn't. That was Gil. He was nothing if not sincere and kind. And just like that, I realised he'd somehow miraculously become a friend, maybe even family. I crossed the distance between us and pulled him into a hug, something we rarely did. He tensed and then relaxed, chuckling, and gently slapped my back.

After a few seconds, I let him go. "Thank you. And I promise to try and do better with Luke." Which, I reminded myself, absolutely didn't include fucking the man senseless.

"That's all I ask." Gil regarded me with too-shiny eyes before adding, "I do have one more question though."

"Yes?" I waited.

"You and I are okay now, right? After everything that happened last year?" He didn't explain further. Didn't need to.

I found a smile that came from my heart. "Yeah, we're all good."

CHAPTER EIGHT

Luke

Doug Carstairs was a nice guy. He'd make a good friend. And that's exactly where I was going to keep him—firmly and plainly in the friendzone.

One thing that had crystallised in my brain in the short month I'd been living in Oakwood was that everything said about small towns and their lightning-fast gossip tree was abso-fucking-lutely true. One trip to the supermarket or the local hardware store, and I knew way more than I ever wanted to about the private lives of people I'd never even met. Add to that the somewhat limited opportunities if you were LGBTQ+ and looking for a hookup, and that rumour mill presented a very real dilemma.

The fact of Doug and I sharing a simple meal together in The Fleece had drawn more than a few curious looks from the other patrons. Doug wasn't exactly subtle about his sexuality, and most locals knew of my relationship with Gil. Hell, the first time Gil had ever taken me into Oakwood, half the people we met already knew my name.

Still, for a small rural community, the place seemed accepting enough of a bit of diversity in its ranks. Other than an occasional scowl, I'd had little pushback, people appearing more curious than anything else. Having said that, it was no wonder most of the non-straight population went out of the district to slake any thirst for a hookup. I was seriously considering it myself. I hadn't moved to Oakwood for its social life, true, but there was only so long a man could stroke his cock raw to images of a certain Zacharia Lane on his knees before said man needed to get a fucking life and find a real-life warm human being to get down and dirty with.

Trouble was, I didn't want to.

"Earth to Luke." Doug snapped his fingers in front of my face, startling me out of my musings and sending a wave of heat to my cheeks.

"I'm sorry," I flustered, meeting his amused grin. "That was rude. I have a flight tomorrow to a station I haven't visited before and I guess I was distracted."

Doug saw straight through me. "Yeah, I'm calling bullshit. But you can keep your secrets."

I offered him a warm apologetic smile but he simply snorted and wagged a finger at me. "Don't try and be cute. I know when I don't have a man's attention. How about another drink? You can tell me about it when I get back from the bar."

Never gonna happen. I glanced at the empty bottle sitting next to my plate, which held a few leftover fries and the juices of a surprisingly good venison cheeseburger and realised I had no memory of even drinking it. I was clearly rapturously good company.

"Thanks." I turned the label for him to see. "Another of these light beers. I've been cutting back." I rolled my eyes. "Believe me, I needed to."

Doug never even blinked. "Glad one of us is trying to be healthy."

It was another thing I liked about Doug. He was . . . uncomplicated. No judgement. No games. I watched him thread his way through the small crowd toward the bar and wondered why, despite his good looks and warm personality, I felt zero physical desire for the man. Doug was flirty and funny, but under all that swagger he was surprisingly open and honest. Our conversation had been easy and enjoyable. But the simple truth was, Doug wasn't Zach.

And there it was. It appeared my little crush wasn't giving up anytime soon.

I turned back to the window and watched three guys hanging a large sign above the door of the old stone bank. Two of the men were up ladders, affixing bolts or whatever was securing the sign in place while the third stood on a stool, taking most of the weight and clearly wilting in the sizzling heat. I recognised the third as Roz, the new owner of the place. The other two were strangers, or at least not local, I didn't think.

The fact Roz had been renovating the premises for almost a year made no difference to him being considered new to the area. He would likely stay that way for decades to come. That was simply how it was in the Mackenzie. According to local gossip, most had written him off as another townie wanting to start a business with zero idea of what made the region tick. I'd only met Roz once, but I suspected underestimating him was a big mistake.

Judging by the grimace on his face, I was pretty sure he had only a minute or two left in his tank supporting that sign when a shout went up and he was able to lurch free. The two laddermen immediately leapt down and all three grabbed each other in a group hug amid loads of laughter. Not your typical high-country red-neck behaviour and it made me smile.

"Here you go." Doug slid a fresh beer between my hands and retook his seat.

I nodded toward the old bank. "That looks promising."

Doug followed my gaze, and his face took on a pleased expression. "Well, well, well. The Barbecue Pit. So that's what he's been keeping under wraps. If it tastes as good as it sounds, Roz might be onto something. I can't think of a single restaurant between

Christchurch and Queenstown remotely similar, and if it's good enough, he might even get those tourist buses stopping after all."

We clinked bottles and I was about to take a long swallow of beer when the bar door swung open and the entire team from Miller Station strode in as a single pack led by a red-faced Sam. Gil caught my eye, glanced between Doug and me, and smiled. Then he nudged Holden who looked our way and did much the same thing, adding a wink at the end for good measure.

Dear God. Kill me now.

They swarmed around the bar and that's when I saw him hiding at the rear of the pack. None other than the elusive Zacharia Lane. Dressed in a fitted black T-shirt tucked into sinfully tight blue jeans that sported a large silver belt buckle, the man dripped sex appeal all over the pub's century-old floorboards. His auburn waves shone gold under the bright lights of the bar, and if I hadn't seen his face, I'd have known him from the sexy country-boy swagger he had down to a *T*.

Well, fuck me. Then he could do it all over again.

Tom slapped the wooden top on the bar to get everyone's attention and I almost jumped. "In honour of our youngest shepherd's fourteenth birthday—" Tom paused to hoots of laughter and Sam turned an even deeper shade of red. "—there's a round of drinks for everyone courtesy of Miller Station."

Everyone in the bar cheered and clapped.

Everyone except me.

Because I hadn't taken my eyes off Zach from the second I'd seen him. He was so fucking hot he sucked the air from the room. But not just hot. He was also beautiful in that way men had when they had no idea how truly lovely they were. When that innocence was unaffected and genuine. It knocked the socks off all the sophisticated bullshit games I'd spent the last year indulging in, in some misguided attempt to forget the pain of losing Callie and my marriage imploding. And as I watched Zach smile at something Charlie said and then casually reach out and ruffle Sam's hair, the straightforward, honest simplicity of the man stole the breath from my lungs.

But as I watched, I realised something else. There was a nervous quality to Zach I hadn't seen before, his gaze flitting around the bar like he expected to be set upon by thieves and vagabonds at any moment. I almost laughed, because there was no doubt in my mind as to the source of his discomfort and who the vagabond was. I didn't know whether to be flattered or plain pissed off that he clearly wasn't going to be happy to see me.

Either way, I didn't want to ruin his night. He deserved to enjoy downtime with his team without me cramping his style. I'd finish my beer and then leave him to his party and head home. But before I could look away, Zach's crystal green eyes finally found mine, and there was nowhere to run.

He blinked like he was processing the reality of me sitting there, then his gaze slid sideways to Doug, and I was pretty sure I caught an eye roll.

Well, shit. That stung a lot more than it should've. And also, hell no to leaving if that's the reaction I was going to get every time we ran into each other. I was kind of tired of the whole stale dance.

"Something I should know?" Doug's gaze flicked between Zach and me, a smile tugging at his lips. When I said nothing, he pressed. "Would he happen to be the reason this pleasant evening we've been having isn't going any further? Because it's not, is it?"

I ignored the bit about Zach and shook my head. "I'm sorry. I'm not looking for a rinse and repeat of my Wellington life. It wasn't helping me get back on track, if you know what I mean."

He shrugged. "Hey, you can't win 'em all."

I glanced over to where Zach was chatting with Tom and some other guy I didn't know and sighed, because for sure, you couldn't. Then I turned back to Doug. "I'd like to be friends though, if that works for you. I'm a little short of those right now. Besides, this is a small town."

"That it is." Doug's expression turned sympathetic. "Don't shit where you eat, right?"

I snorted. "Pretty much."

He lowered his voice. "And by 'back on track,' are you talking about recovering from the death of your daughter?"

I huffed dispiritedly. "I'm not sure anyone ever recovers from something like that, but feeling hopeful again would be a start. I have to stop running and start building something new that doesn't involve a merry-go-round of men and too much alcohol."

Doug nodded thoughtfully and raised his bottle. "Well, you can never have too many friends, right?"

I clinked mine to his and said, "Thanks."

We drank a toast to friendship and then Doug put his bottle down and tipped his head toward Zach. "So, are you saying it's nothing to do with a certain gorgeous young shepherd that keeps looking our way like he wants to punch me in the nose but eat you for dinner, and yes, he'll have fries with that?"

My gaze immediately shot sideways to Zach, and Doug huffed in amusement like I'd proved him right, which I supposed I had.

I levelled Doug with a half-hearted glare. "Arsehole."

"No doubt about that. But am I wrong?" His expression dared me to disagree, and I suddenly found myself tired of the whole fucking thing.

"No, you're not wrong," I admitted with a heavy sigh. "But don't ask me why cos I don't know."

"But you like him for maybe more than just a hookup." Statement, not question, and to my horror, I found myself nodding.

"Crazy, right? But nothing's going to happen. Zach's made that perfectly clear. He might wanna fuck me, but he doesn't *like* me, and although I might be a bit screwed in the head, I'm not interested in that kind of self-flagellation added to all my other issues."

"Amen to that." Doug chuckled, and we clinked bottles again.

And if I happened to notice Zach scowling at us from the bar, so be it.

We finished our beers and Doug pushed his chair back to stand. "Well, it's been nice getting to know you, *friend*." He offered his hand and we shook. "I'm up for a beer anytime, with or without the fries."

He winked and I found myself laughing again. After the week I'd had, it felt good, and I was pleased I'd agreed to the drink.

When Doug was gone, I debated the merits of getting sloshed in front of the telly while feeding my face with salty snacks and watching the last day of the Black Caps' cricket test in South Africa. The answer was a reluctant but healthy no to the first, but yes to the second and third, and I headed to the bar to buy a few packets of potato chips and save myself a trip to the supermarket.

On my way across the room, I stopped to wish Sam a happy birthday, say a quick hi to Holden and Gil while skirting their pointed questions about my *date*, and then made a beeline for the bar. I'd paid for my potato chips and was about to leave when I sensed Zach beside me. Freshly showered and lightly doused in the cologne he favoured, I'd have recognised him anywhere.

He leaned across the bar and raised a hand to get Nola's attention, brushing our shoulders in the process. It was all I could do not to turn my head and breathe him in.

"Just a minute, Zach," Nola called back as she disappeared into the kitchen.

Zach dropped his hand and rested his arms quietly on the bar, his gaze fixed on the mirrored wall of bottles that faced us. I was debating whether or not to say something and break the ice when he finally spoke, his eyes finding mine in the reflection.

"Did you have a nice date?"

I almost laughed. "You could probably tell *me* the answer to that."

He turned and leaned his elbow on the bar, green eyes blazing. And was it bad that I wanted nothing more than to kiss him and then fuck him senseless over the shiny surface? "What are you implying?"

I buried those images and shook my head. "Just teasing, sorry. And yes, I had a nice time, thank you for asking. Although, as I keep telling everyone, it *wasn't* a date." I gathered my bags of chips and made to leave. "You have a nice evening, Zach."

But Zach spoke before I could move. "He looked good . . . tonight. Doug, I mean."

Was he . . . fishing? Jealous? Was Doug right? I stared into those guarded green eyes lit with something more than curiosity, and thought, fuck it. In for a penny, in for a pound, right? "No one looks better than you did coming through those doors tonight, Zach." I let my gaze travel down his body and then back up, noting the fire blossom in his cheeks. "I couldn't take my eyes off you."

His pupils briefly flared and he swallowed hard, drawing my gaze down to that tempting dip at the base of his throat that I wanted to taste so bad. "So—" He cleared his throat and drew my attention back to his pretty face. "You didn't . . . I mean you're not going to . . . you two are just friends?" He glanced over my shoulder and I turned to find Gil watching us from a few metres away.

I raised a brow at my ex but all he did was grin. And when I turned back around, Zach was blushing again. Huh. *What was that all about?* "You were saying?"

Zach sighed. "I'm sorry, I had no right to ask."

I frowned at the apology, which was very un-Zach-like, and decided on that basis alone to answer. "Yes, we've decided to keep it to friends. I could do with a few, don't you think?" A little pointed but I was done treading lightly.

"Of course." Zach sighed and glanced toward the kitchen like he was mentally willing Nola to reappear.

I remained quiet and let him dangle. This was his show, after all.

He scratched his chin and said, "So, how's the new job going?"

I almost laughed. "Jesus, Zach, are we doing small talk now?"

He bristled. "It's a simple question."

It was, but it also wasn't, at least not from the man who'd spent a year shutting down every attempt at conversation initiated by me. I could pout and get all pissy about it, or I could take the unexpected turn of events for what it seemed—some kind of olive branch.

"Okay then, fine, I'll play along." I smiled at his eye roll. "Work is good. I like the flying. It's different from what I'm used to, and challenging, which I like. Gary Furlong is fun to work for. He's a straight shooter and I like that in a boss . . . and a man," I added simply to see that flush of Zach's deepen, which it did. Point to me.

"Right," he flustered, once again looking over my shoulder to where I supposed Gil was still standing, nosey bastard that he was. "The cute Irish accent doesn't hurt either."

"True," I agreed.

"It doesn't bother you being this close to Gil and Holden on a daily basis? It's a lot different from visiting."

It was a valid question and I considered my answer.

"Zach, here you go." Nola slid a beer along the bar.

Zach caught it with a "thank you," then turned back to me.

"I'm not following my *ex*-husband around, if that's what you mean," I answered. "I'm not quite that pathetic . . . yet."

"That's not what I meant." A flicker of apology flashed through Zach's eyes. "I'm just curious."

I wasn't so certain, but I let it go. "If you're asking do I like being close to my still-good friend? Then yes, I do. We lost a child together, Zach. That kind of thing fuses a bond that's hard to explain. It's good to be able to talk and share some of those feelings with someone who understands completely." I hesitated, then added, "But since Gil has Holden now, maybe I need him more than he needs me." I huffed in self-disgust. "Maybe I'm more pathetic than I think."

"I'm . . . shit." Zach looked like he was going to reach out a hand but then dropped it. "I wasn't implying that at all."

"Maybe not, but in truth, the real reason I came down this way is because the job offer came at the right time."

Zach muttered something that sounded like "lucky us," and I almost laughed.

He was trying to act cool but I definitely unsettled him, and it was no leap to assume that was because of my idiocy in Gil's kitchen earlier in the week. I'd chastised myself the entire flight back to Wild Run for crowding him against that wall. *Jesus. What the hell had I been thinking?* But at the time, he'd been so damn irresistible with his feathers all in a fluff and piss and vinegar in his eyes.

We stared at each other in silence, like we were taking stock of this new, awkward, not quite friendly but not quite so adversarial space we suddenly found ourselves in. Zach was beautiful, no doubt about it, and before I could stop myself, I leaned in and inhaled the fresh scent of his cologne.

He jerked away, his panicked gaze casting frantically around the bar to see if anyone was looking before landing back on me. "Don't do that again." He glared and I wanted to kiss him.

Instead, I simply smiled and said, "I apologise, but you are so fucking beautiful, it's almost impossible to stop myself."

His mouth dropped open and his cheeks flooded with red, all those cute-as-fuck freckles popping darker. "You're crazy."

I snorted. "Very likely. Enjoy the party, Zach." I breezed past and felt the burn of his eyes on the back of my head all the way to the door.

The short walk home—with a fresh breeze in my face and a violet-blue Mackenzie sky tinged pink with the beginning of sunset—cleared some of the Zach fog from my head and allowed me to see how reckless I'd been.

I didn't need Holden and Gil all up in my business, which they surely would've been if they'd caught that ill-considered performance of mine, and I was pretty sure it wouldn't have been from any concern about me. Holden was protective of Zach, and I got it. But whenever Zach was close, common sense seemed to take a back seat. The man short-circuited every thought in my head. Go straight to jail. Do not pass go. Do not collect any brain cells along the way.

At least my bungalow made me smile, and as I wandered up the front path, I took a moment to appreciate its sweet lines and cream and black paint scheme. Gil had always been the character property enthusiast, whereas I'd tended more toward minimalist concrete and glass. But the bungalow's careful renovation and the way the architecture fitted with the town and the landscape had won me over.

When I stepped through the front door, the gleaming polished floors and soft cream walls performed their usual magic, bringing calm to my restless mind. The whole space was . . . homely, something I'd sorely missed since moving out of the house Gil and I had shared what felt like a hundred years ago. The owners had rented it with most of the furnishing essentials intact, and although the style was surprisingly modern, the pastel colours and simple lines allowed character highlights to shine—the pretty floral tiled entrance, tall ceilings, and intricate plasterwork.

As I padded up the hall and into the kitchen, it occurred to me that I was probably nesting—for want of a better word—finding a safe space to lick my wounds and grow my wings again. Who the hell knew? Who the hell cared? It felt good. It felt right. And Lord knew there'd been little enough of either of those for too long.

Some days, I felt a long way from anywhere, maybe most days. Then there were days I caught a glimmer of a future. A future that included another family. Another chance at something more than simply existing. It was a fledgling thought, shocking when it first came, like the first spark that caught when you were trying to create fire. But it was a thought I'd never imagined possible only months before, and so I took it as a win.

I threw my keys and the packets of potato chips on the granite breakfast bar, opened some windows to let the day's heat escape, and grabbed a light beer from the fridge. The sun was beginning to skim the horizon and the far wall of the bungalow was painted in apricot, the rest draped in lengthening shadows.

I carried my beer and a packet of chips into the lounge, switched on a table lamp, and turned the television to the cricket. I'd barely stretched out on the oversized couch when the low rumble of a motorbike came to a stop somewhere close by. A rogue thought flickered through my mind, but I cast it aside and thought of what my

Wellington friends would say about my exciting new life as a single gay man on a Friday night in Oakwood.

I was still chuckling when a soft knock sounded at the front door. That rogue thought returned and my heart kicked up. *No way.* I sat my beer on the coffee table and headed down the hallway.

Through the stained-glass panel that ran down the centre of the door, I saw a figure waiting. I couldn't make out who it was, but I could guess.

I took a deep breath and opened the door. "Zach?"

CHAPTER NINE

Zach

"Not. A. Word." I shoved Luke back into the hall and up against the wall, kicking the door shut behind me. Then I did what he'd done to me back at the bar, only this time I made sure to touch him. I leaned in and ran my nose up the side of his face, inhaling his scent and drawing out a shudder that ran the length of his body.

He smelled so good. He felt so good. I drew back and ran my gaze over him, head to foot, trying for cool seduction and not like my heart was jumping out of my throat, which it so fucking was. He hadn't changed clothes, still wearing that white shirt with the black buttons hanging loose over a pair of painted-on black jeans, the outfit oozing just the right balance of casual but making an effort. The ever-present black leather cord hung around his neck along with the green band on his wrist. But for the date or meet-up or whatever he wanted to call it, Luke had donned a black leather cuff with silver rivets that added a bad boy element, which nearly melted my briefs the first time I'd laid eyes on him in the bar.

When he left me there after calling me beautiful, it was all I could do not to follow him out that door. But I'd made myself stay. Made myself wait. He and I had felt so fucking inevitable from the first time we'd met that I'd wanted to at least plan how it might go, how I could have Luke and then walk away at the end without feeling . . . vulnerable. Without wanting more. I wouldn't open myself up to be hurt like I had been with Holden.

This *thing*, whatever it turned out to be, had to go differently.

This time *I'd* be the one in charge.

But the second Luke's mouth turned up in that wolfish grin of his, I felt the vague stirrings of unease and knew it wasn't going to be that easy.

"And good evening to you too." He smiled down at me.

"Shut. Up." I pressed three fingers to his lips and he fell quiet. Then I kicked his legs apart to get that ten-centimetre height difference out of the way and he acquiesced readily, looking intrigued and more than a little turned on.

He licked his lips. "You want me, Zach?" He leaned forward until my fingers were sandwiched between his lips and mine, teasing his tongue along the pads, dipping between the spaces to flick on and off my lips. "I'm all yours. Any which way you want to do this. Tell me what you want."

I almost laughed, mostly because this wasn't how things usually went in my limited experience with men. Holden had mostly taken charge of things between us, which hadn't bothered me in the least. I was happy to tag along. But I wanted something different from Luke. He'd gotten under my skin in a way Holden never had. Holden was the safe and steady harbour. Luke was . . . well, not that. Luke felt uncomfortable and raw and far too dangerous to just hand myself over.

"Be careful what you ask for." I pressed our bodies flush together and there was no hiding how very, *very* on board Luke was with me being there, our two cocks plumping to do battle between us. A hand slid around my waist and under my shirt, trailing fire over my hot skin, while mine circled his throat, pressing his head to the side so I could run my tongue up his neck and across his cheek. Then I turned him to the other side and licked my way back down.

"Damn, that feels good." He groaned and thrust against me, his leg moving so he could grind more efficiently. His fingers found the waistband of my jeans, but the belt stopped him from dipping under and he grunted in frustration.

I smiled against his cheek and pulled back to look at him. "Going somewhere?"

"Get them off." He tugged at the large silver buckle, but I slapped his hand aside.

"Not so fast." And with my fingers still loosely closed around his throat and holding him against the wall, I studied his flushed cheeks and those pupils blown all to hell, his breathing ragged in my ears. Exactly how I'd pictured this going in my head.

"Kiss me." Luke pushed against my hold, but I kept my grip solid and he stilled. "I've waited a year to taste you. I'm dying here."

All I did was smile, even though I wanted nothing more than to do just that. To kiss him. To feel him under, over, and around me. I wasn't too picky. To run my tongue through his mouth and have him desperate for more. I loved kissing almost more than sex itself, and just the thought of how close I was to having that with *him* sent a river of nerves through my belly.

Because there'd be no going back.

One kiss and it was all on.

We both knew it.

I nudged our noses together, and he groaned. "Jesus, Zach."

I brushed my lips over his, whisper soft, and his eyelids fluttered closed.

The tip of my tongue traced across the seam of his lips, and he sighed and opened for me.

I hovered my open mouth over his, almost touching but not quite, and he drew my breath into his lungs, then released it on a long shuddering sigh.

And then I kissed him, his plush lips yielding to the pressure, so soft, so hungry, so fucking perfect.

His arm tightened around my waist and my tongue swept into his mouth, savouring the combined hit of beer and salt and a flavour uniquely his. Nothing had ever tasted better.

A groan barrelled up my throat as Luke deepened the kiss and crushed me to him. Our tongues tangled and his hands found their way up to cup either side of my head, his fingers threading through my hair and fisting to hold me in place. The slight sting went straight to my balls and I thrust against him.

He moaned and flipped our positions, pulling off my lips to kiss down my throat as he ground against me. I gasped and the back of my head hit the wall as I hooked a leg around his thigh to improve the angle, and every cell in my body lit up.

"Fucking hell," he huffed into my open mouth. "I can't believe we're finally doing this." He covered my mouth with his, that wicked tongue thrusting deep as he fumbled around my belt buckle once again before growling, "Jesus Christ, this thing is like fucking Fort Knox."

"Let me." I shoved him off and undid the buckle. He immediately yanked it free of the loops and made as if to throw it away. I grabbed his hand. "Hey. That's a Stef Hamilton original."

He snorted. "I don't care if it's a bloody Van Gogh."

I laughed and dropped the belt gently on the carpet runner while Luke set to unbuttoning my jeans. He shoved both them and my briefs down my legs, and I kicked off my shoes and stepped free.

He drew a sharp breath and ran a finger up the length of my rigid cock. "Hell yeah. Now we're talking." His eyes met mine and he grabbed the hem of my T-shirt and slipped it over my head, muttering, "I'm negative, by the way. I can show you if you want."

"Me too," I huffed impatiently. "And no, it's fine." It struck me how much trust that implied, but oddly, I did trust him, about that much at least.

"Good to go, then?" He paused, one eyebrow raised.

Naked, I coyly bit my lip and stepped forward, tipping my head back to look up into those blue eyes cast grey in the shadows of the hall. "Yeah, Luke, we're good to go."

His gaze ran over my naked body like melted butter, setting my skin on fire. "Damn, you're hot." He pushed me back against the wall, stepped in, and palmed my dick, giving it a solid squeeze that sparked stars behind my eyes.

The back of my head hit the wall as I gasped, "Impatient much?"

He chuckled and brought our faces so close that our lashes almost tangled. "Only this first time." He kissed me hard. "The second time, we're taking it slow."

I put a hand on his chest and shoved him back. "Second time? That's a little presumptuous, don't you think?"

"You reckon you'll be done after just one time?" He pushed against my hand and kissed me again, gentler that time. Then he put his lips next to my ear and stroked my aching cock. "Because I know I won't. Once we unleash whatever this thing is between us, there's no putting the cork back in the bottle, baby."

He added a twist to his stroke, his thumb brushing over the head of my cock with each upward drive as he nibbled his way down my neck to the slope of my shoulder and then bit down ... hard.

Lights out.

Holy fucking hell. I couldn't remember the question, let alone come up with an answer. I couldn't find any damn words at all as he pumped me hard, kissing and biting all the way down my chest to nibble and suck first one nipple, then the other. Then it was back up my throat to tongue-fuck my mouth while fingering my slit.

Filthy groans poured up my throat, sounds I'd never imagined I was capable of.

Luke chuckled. "Having fun?" His tongue dipped into my ear and then he suckled at the lobe.

I choked out some inane answer that sounded a lot like, "Fuck you," and he chuckled again.

It was at that point I realised things weren't exactly going to plan, beginning with the fact that I was completely naked and Luke . . . wasn't. Not that the situation wasn't without merit. All things considered, it was pretty fucking hot, but it hardly married with the idea of me staying in charge. Then again, who was I kidding? This was Luke. Luke would find a way to top from the bottom if he was the bloody Titanic.

A finger slid into my mouth for a quick sweep and Luke hoisted my leg around his hip. He slicked my hole with the wet finger, dipped the tip inside, withdrew it, and then did it again and again, sliding deeper with each attempt while my brain took the last bus out of town.

I'd never been so fucking turned on in all my life. Holden and I had always had fun, but this was next level. Luke was . . . unpredictable, with a slightly dangerous edge that was apparently a button I'd never known I had. I considered that for all of one second before he started to kiss down my chest and I was lost again to the thundering tide of sensations that were rocketing me to the edge in record time.

I tried for a little breathing room. "Why don't we take this to the bedroo—oh, Jesus, fuck!" I cried as Luke swallowed my cock down the back of his throat. Here against the wall was just dandy, thank you very much.

With the next swallow, I fisted his short, dirty blond hair as best I could and gave a small reflexive thrust.

He coughed a little, then pulled off and winked up at me. "Yeah, just like that. Bring it on." Then he wrapped his hands around the back of my thighs and sucked me back down, working my cock like a fucking pro. His pull on my thighs encouraged me to keep those thrusts going, rocking me forward each time until I got with the program and started truly fucking his mouth, something I'd never felt comfortable doing.

But Luke made it easy, making it clear it was exactly what he wanted. He opened his throat and lifted those almost black eyes to meet mine. I dropped a hand to tip his chin up a little more, my thumb running over those swollen lips, which were locked around my cock.

It was a complete mindfuck. *This* man, on his knees, for *me*. Giving himself up for me to play with. Trusting me. And with saliva pouring down his chin, his eyes watering as he choked on my dick, he'd never looked better. And always those midnight eyes on mine.

It was the hottest fucking thing I'd ever seen. So hot, I knew I wasn't going to last, the orgasm coming from nowhere to rush through my body like a tidal wave, turning my legs to jelly, and lighting up those endorphins in my brain.

I had no time to even warn Luke, not that it mattered. The second he felt me tense, his arms tightened around my thighs to hold me up and he gave a filthy wanton groan as I pumped everything I had down his throat and he sucked me dry to the last drop.

The minute I was done, he shot to his feet and kissed me, shoving his tongue deep into my mouth to share the taste. I'd barely processed the pleasure and got my balance when he was dragging me down the hall.

"*Now* we can shift this to the bedroom." He led me almost stumbling past the guest bedroom—was it only three weeks ago—and into his.

I blinked in the orange wash of sunset that painted the room, my brain still working through its post-orgasm reboot. Luke rummaged in a bedside drawer, and lube and a couple of condoms landed on the bed. Then his fingers trailed gently down my back, and I turned to find him staring at me like he didn't know where to start or even what he wanted. He looked startlingly . . . uncertain.

It was enough to kick the slush from my brain and get me moving. "Get those damn clothes off." The command seemed to break Luke free and earned me a broad smile as he shed his clothes in seconds.

And just . . . wow. His dick was definitely in proportion to his size. More broad than long but still . . . big. Flushed red, cut, and with a slight curve to the right, it was mouth-wateringly tempting, and yeah . . . impressive. At least in my limited experience.

I walked a circle around him, eyeing his body up and down, trailing my fingertips over his hot, flushed skin and drawing a shiver when I grazed his nipples. "Beautiful."

He chuckled. "I'm glad you approve."

I glanced at his cock and raised a brow. "That's some challenge you're laying down there."

His expression softened and he cupped my cheek. "I don't mind what we do or *don't* do. No expectations, no pressure."

I considered his fucking perfect answer and it was tempting, but there was no way I was leaving that house without at least giving it a go.

I stopped at his shoulder and went up on my toes to lick the shell of his ear. "Just take it slow. I'll bow to your experience in getting me ready."

"I'll get you there." He turned and snagged my mouth in a quick kiss. I let him, then tut-tutted and pushed his face back around to face the front.

He snorted in amusement but stayed put as I did another circle, stopping at his back to run both hands down and over his firm arse and those soft blond hairs I'd caught a glimpse of three weeks before. It was a surreal moment. I squeezed the two handfuls of arse and pressed a kiss between Luke's shoulders.

He groaned and asked in a gravel voice, "You gonna fuck me, Zach? Because I'd really like that."

I blinked. Surprised. In my fantasies, I'd maybe hoped, but the truth was I'd never imagined Luke not wanting to top, especially our first time together. And although I was generally comfortable with my preferred role as a bossy bottom—although, come to think of it, maybe not so bossy in the face of that impressive dick—Luke's offer still ignited something.

"Yes." I must have sounded slightly dazed because Luke laughed.

To shut him up, I dropped to my knees, spread his cheeks, and ran my tongue over his hole.

It worked.

"Hoooooly shit." He grunted and fell forward onto the mattress, spreading his legs in the process. "Maybe warn a guy next time."

In answer, I pushed a hand between his legs to stroke his cock while I licked and lapped and probed that tight little hole until Luke was mumbling incoherently into the sheets and shoving his arse back into my face to get me deeper. Mission accomplished.

Luke wasn't the only one with oral skills. Rimming was one of my all-time favourite things and I was determined to get my money's worth. By the time he pushed me aside, complaining I was going to make him come, my cock had recovered and was jutting in his direction.

Luke flipped to his back and shuffled up the bed, the sunset washing a shadowy umber over all that bare skin. He was tall and beautiful, and I crawled up the length of his body until we were eye to eye.

"Say it again." I nipped at his lip as I lowered my groin to his and settled our hard cocks together.

"Say what?"

I dropped my mouth to his nipple and nipped.

"Oh, fuck." His head slammed back into the pillow. "All right. All right." He lifted up to look me in the eye. "I want you to fuck me, Zacharia Lane. Fuck me until I can't walk. And then if you want, you can do it all over again."

A smile spread over my face. "You sure about that?"

Luke rolled his eyes. "What do you think?" Then he eyeballed me and, for a second, his expression was deadly serious. "There isn't anything you can do to me that I won't love. I guarantee that. So, let loose. I want everything you've got." He cupped my face. "I have a feeling that's gonna be something special to watch."

The comment startled me. *Special?* Luke had fucked more men than I wanted to think about. How could anything I offered him be special?

He must've seen my disbelief because he drew me down for a long, slow kiss and then kept me there, his lashes beating against my own. "Yes, Zach. Special."

I couldn't hold his gaze, so I kissed him again and then trailed my lips down his body, over the stiff buds of his nipples and the fair hair on his chest. I kissed the leather cord around his neck and the heart that hung from it. I tried not to think about what that heart might mean and kept going. Over his smooth abs—nothing carved or gym-toned. I smiled at the twitch of his belly as I kissed down his happy trail. I licked the slit on his cock and then down its length to his balls, which I sucked into my mouth one at a time as he writhed and moaned above me.

Then I knelt to the side of his body and rolled on the condom as Luke watched. His fingers found my crease, teasing my hole as I slicked up, cranking the desire already pounding in my balls.

I was about to fuck Luke Nichols, and yet somehow the world was still turning.

"How do you want it?" I rasped, and Luke spread his legs wide in answer.

"I wanna watch your face every second."

Well, all right then. I knelt between his legs and ran a slick finger up his crease to disappear into his already loose hole.

"Jesus fucking Christ." He groaned and arched up and I added a second finger, and then the tip of a third, until I was sure he was ready for me.

"Lift them high," I ordered, shuffling forward into position.

Luke grinned and wrapped his legs around my waist, but I lifted them to my shoulders instead. He raised an amused brow.

"Deal with it," I said. Luke had given me free rein and I was taking him at his word. "You wanted to feel me?" I shot him a pointed look. "Then you're gonna feel me. I'll make damn sure of that."

He laughed and it occurred to me that sex with Luke was turning out to be a whole lot more fun than I'd imagined. And I'd imagined a lot. I'd known things between us would be hot; we had enough chemistry to burn the fucking house down. And maybe even a little bit angry, which I wasn't opposed to either, just for the record. But lighthearted fun? Nope. I wouldn't have put a bet on that sucker in a million years.

But the position did bring our faces close, closer than I'd planned for, and as I leaned in and pressed the head of my dick against Luke's tight ring of muscle, his eyes met mine and something explosive passed between us.

I pressed again, feeling the pushback ease, the slight stretch as he opened, and then the sudden slide as the resistance gave way and I was surrounded by a furnace of heat.

"Oh god!" His head pressed back into the pillow as he blew breaths in and out of his mouth, bearing down, slowly, slowly letting me sink deeper into his body. His eyes squeezed shut and his neck muscles corded as he panted. "Holy Christ on a cracker," he ground out, still not opening his eyes.

"You okay?" I hesitated, not wanting to hurt him.

"Just p-peachy." He opened his eyes, slid a hand around my neck and tugged me forward, growling all the way until I was fully seated. "Been a while."

The comment gave me pause, but not for long. The feel of his hot arse clamped around my dick was too fucking delicious, and the second he gave me the okay, I lost myself in the incredible slip and slide as I started shuttling inside him.

He twisted his hips slightly and shouted, "There. Like that! Oh, fuck!"

I figured I was landing on his sweet spot, so I pushed his arms above his head, threaded our fingers together, and watched his face from above as I pounded into his arse. He stared back at me, eyes wild, his breathing choked, his body crunched under mine, that big dick caught in the friction between us.

"I'm close." He arched and his eyelids fluttered closed, and a few seconds later he came with a loud grunt, the hot rush of come spilling between us as he shuddered, and his hole clenched around my dick.

That was all it took to follow him over, two more thrusts to the edge, and then one final drive to break the dam and send waves of pleasure crashing through me for the second time in under an hour. And with our fingers still threaded together, I collapsed onto Luke's chest and waited for the universe to stop singing in my blood.

CHAPTER TEN

Zach

It felt like the longest time until Luke finally let go of my hand and wriggled free. I half expected him to leave me for the bathroom, but he surprised me once again by pushing me over onto my back and kissing his way down my chest. He cleaned my belly and then worked his way back up to my mouth for a lingering kiss that curled my toes and set warning bells off in my brain.

Stay in charge. The reminder filtered through the haze in my brain, and I ended the kiss and tucked Luke's much bigger frame into my side, holding him in place with an arm around his shoulder.

He frowned at the abrupt change but soon settled against me, his fingertip tracing the splash of freckles that ran down my neck and sternum. "Damn, Nichols," I huffed against his hair, my heart still pounding against my chest. "That was . . . I don't even know what that was."

He chuckled. "Yeah, I'm not sure what that was either other than fucking awesome." His finger drew some kind of a pattern on my shoulder. "It's the hottest sex I've had in . . . I don't know how long.

And in case you missed the finale—" He gave me jazz hands. "—I came with no fucking hands."

I snorted. "Yeah, I noticed. I'm that good."

He laughed and gave me a playful shove. "I'd argue except for the fact that you're absolutely right."

I almost did a double take, but Luke was still talking. "You looked amazing while you fucked me, just like I knew you would. All of this hair flying—" He ran his hand through my waves. "—looked like fire in the sunset. So fucking beautiful." He cupped my cheek and drew me down for a kiss. "What am I going to do with you?"

Everything. You can do everything and anything you want with me. But of course, I said nothing.

Luke grabbed my hand and kissed the tip of every finger. It was such a tender gesture, so intimate, so sweet, so . . . not what this was meant to be about, and suddenly I needed to be anywhere but in Luke Nichols' bed, hearing him say those words. Feeling . . . whatever make-believe idiocy he was making me feel. Ridiculous things like maybe this didn't have to be a one-time thing. Maybe we could do it again. Maybe even on a semi-regular basis while he was in town. Maybe . . . more than that.

My eyes jerked wide and I nearly fell backwards out of the bed. Fucking Luke had never been about any of that. Precisely the opposite. It had been about getting it done and over with and out of the way.

A frown made its way over Luke's brow. "Are you okay?"

I nodded, settling back between the sheets. "Just a cramp." I fingered the green silicone wristband and opted for changing the subject. "You never take this off."

Luke looked for a second like he wanted to call me out on my clumsy segue but didn't. He lifted his hand so I could read the inscription on the inside of the band. *Poppa.*

A lump formed in my throat. "From Callie."

He nodded. "She made Gil buy it for me one Christmas. Ghastly colour, but I've never taken it off."

"You wear the name on the inside?"

He shrugged and looked away. "It stops people from asking."

Shit. My heart squeezed and I pressed a kiss to his hair. "What about this one?" I lifted the leather band from where it nestled in the fair hair on his chest, and the silver heart spun in the fading light.

"Gil gave that to me the day we took Callie home from the newborn unit."

It was like a cold bucket of water to the face. The wristband I could understand. That was Callie. The heart seemed more about their marriage.

Like he'd read my mind, Luke fingered the heart and said, "To be honest, I'm not even sure why I still wear it."

But I thought I knew. Gil had a powerful effect on his men.

"Will you tell me about Callie?" I redirected again. "What she was like?"

Luke studied me for a moment, then wrapped his arm around my waist and began to talk, starting with how he and Gil first met. "I saw him at a party of a mutual friend. Gil was in his first year at uni and I was doing my pilot's training. I literally spotted him across the room, and that was it for me. I hounded the poor guy until he agreed to go out."

So, it was love at first sight and not too dissimilar from Holden's experience meeting Gil for the first time. What was it about that man? And yet Gil and Luke hadn't lasted. There was a lesson in that somewhere, I supposed.

Luke spoke about his cousin's offer to be their surrogate and the joy of those first few years with Callie when he didn't think life could have gotten any better. The years when he and Gil had been in synch, their marriage solid. He said nothing about what had happened to change that, and I didn't ask.

"She was a super kid," he said, keeping his head on my chest so I couldn't see his eyes. "Loved school. Had a nice set of friends. Laughed a lot. Desperately wanted a dog, which I now regret we didn't agree to. Loved anything to do with being outside. Trampolines, parks, the ocean, camping, all of that."

I twirled my fingers through his hair. "That's why you and Gil scattered her ashes in the Havelock River last year, right?"

He nodded. "Yeah. She'd have loved everything about the station. The scenery, the rivers, the sheep, the lake, but maybe especially the dogs." He glanced up, a broad grin in place. "Jojo in particular. There's something about that dog that's always made me think of Callie."

My fingers froze in his hair and I couldn't stop the smile from spreading over my face. "Really? Jojo loves kids, which has always surprised me since she's hardly had anything to do with them."

"But there's a softness about her, a kindness, right? Whereas Nina is more . . . brash. Not unkind, just more *here I come*, I guess, more self-contained." He nestled his head back on my chest and something flip-flopped in my belly at the idea this man knew my dogs well enough to pick those subtle differences up.

"Right." I tried to keep the surprise from my voice.

Luke reached up and pushed my hand through his hair again.

I chuckled and kept going. "You like that, huh?"

"It feels nice." He settled again. "Callie wasn't perfect, don't get me wrong. She was smart as a whip and that landed her in trouble more than once. With my job taking me away from home two or three nights a week, Callie wasn't above playing Gil and me off against each other to get what she wanted, and it could cause friction between us until we twigged to what was happening. Gil was the day-to-day presence in the house and mostly I followed his lead. But it still took a fair bit of communication to make sure we were on the same page with what was going on in Callie's life. We did everything together as a family. We had a lot of fun." He swallowed and took a deep breath. "She was pretty much our entire focus . . . maybe too much." He went quiet for a minute and it wasn't hard to put that equation together.

"It must've been hard to be away from her all those nights."

"I hated it. I was considering swapping jobs." He hesitated. "Well, for a lot of reasons that I am sure you can guess, and then Callie was killed and everything changed."

I pressed my lips to his hair but said nothing as he took a few short gulps of air.

"It felt like the world stopped turning," he finally managed, his voice wisp thin like it might break at any moment. "I was flying that day, and by the time I finally got to the hospital, Gil had just come back from surgery. When he woke up, he was like a stranger, his voice flat and unemotional, in complete shock. He kept repeating over and over that she was gone because of him. That it was his fault. That he was sorry."

His eyes lifted to mine, and what I saw there stole my breath. They were riddled with pain and so much regret that I found myself wriggling down until we were facing each other side by side so I could kiss him. "You don't have to talk about it."

"It's okay." He tucked a lock of hair behind my ears. "I knew what Gil was saying was all bullshit, but I still couldn't seem to stop that small part of me that wanted to blame him for forgetting the friend's birthday present that day. For having to take Callie home before the party so she could get it. For putting the two of them in that intersection in the first place." He paused, his breathing laboured, his eyes glassy, and I stroked his cheek with my fingers.

"It's only human to try and find something or someone to blame."

He smiled sadly. "Maybe. I never accused him directly, but I kept asking him the same questions that first day about how fast he was going, and why he hadn't seen the other car, and how he could have forgotten the present when I'd left it by the garage door that morning so he couldn't miss it, and so on. It was a fucking horrible thing to do to him even though I managed to stop myself after that first day and apologise. It was too late. Gil says he blamed himself anyway, and that what I said made no difference. He was asking himself all the same things. I'm not sure I believe him. And no matter that our marriage was well on the rocks by then, I should've been a better person that day and I failed."

"Losing Callie must've put a huge strain on you both," I conceded, beginning to fully appreciate what a total dick I'd been in the things I'd thought and said.

"You could say that." He cast me a wry look like he knew exactly what I was thinking, and then fell onto his back, moonlight washing across one side of his face, the other left in deep shadow making his expression hard to read. "Callie's death was like a huge black hole that sucked away everything good that was left between us and left nothing but anger and grief. And we got really good at taking both of those out on each other until it got to the point where I couldn't see a way out for either of us, other than leaving. Gil had moved out of our bedroom months before, and he refused to go for joint counselling, saying he needed to focus on his PTSD first. He pretty much shut me out and I was spiralling fast in my own way."

I reached for his hand and threaded our fingers together. "I can't imagine."

He glanced down and smiled. "It wasn't as simple as who was right or wrong, but with hindsight, I understand a lot more about what he was dealing with. In that way, maybe I had it easier."

The comment made me blink, but before I could call him on it, he moved on.

"It was the worst fucking time you can imagine, and it totally sucked that we couldn't find a way to be there for each other. That I couldn't be there for *him*, for her dad. That I . . . walked away. She'd have been so fucking disappointed in m—" He stopped on a stuttered intake of breath, his expression stricken, those blue eyes wracked with guilt.

Letting go of his hand, I cradled his face, my thumbs brushing his damp cheeks. "You'd both lost your child, the absolute worst thing that can happen to any parent."

Luke's eyes locked with mine, but I couldn't read what he was thinking, so I just fumbled on.

"No one can prepare for that or what it might do to you as a person, let alone a couple. I was an idiot blaming you for walking out, and I'm sorry. I have no idea what it must feel like to go through something like that." I paused. "But you and Gil are talking now. More than talking. You're still friends, and I'd think that's pretty much a fucking miracle, right? But I think it also reflects the type of men you both are."

Luke regarded me thoughtfully. "And what type would that be?"

Oh boy. How to answer that one? "Determined, for one."

He grinned. "You mean stubborn."

My turn to grin. "Honest."

He gave a surprised nod.

"And I'm going to go with loyal, even though it flies in the face of what I've thought about you in the past. But I was wrong. And if I'd taken the time to think with more than my dick, I might've worked it out for myself."

His brows popped. "How so?"

"Because you came back. You followed him here to talk about Callie and what happened, knowing he might've turned you away. Because you kept trying, kept that connection for both your sakes in the face of Holden, and your impending divorce, and your own grief. And Gil did the same."

Luke's gentle eyes studied me for a second, like I'd surprised him. Then he leaned in and took my mouth in the sweetest of kisses. "Thank you. If you'd asked me a year ago, I wouldn't have dreamed Gil and I would be where we are now . . . or *you* and I, for that matter." He ran a finger down my forehead and nose to linger on my lips.

I pulled back a little and asked the question hanging on my tongue. "Do you think there's a part of you that's still in love with him?"

He blinked. "Am I—" He hesitated, regarding me intently, then he finished, "No, Zach. No, I'm not in love with Gil anymore. I haven't been for a long time. When I see him with Holden, it feels . . . right, as crazy as that sounds. They suit each other. They're good for each other. Maybe I'm a little sad for myself at the fact we fucked up something that had potential, but I'm ready to find my own path."

The level of relief I felt at his words was . . . troubling. Luke and I had fucked, nothing more. His feelings about Gil were his to deal with. They had no bearing on me. I felt for his loss, for the pain he'd gone through, but that was only human, right?

I took a deep breath and backed my feelings way the hell out of trouble. "Okay, well, since you both annoyingly insist on taking equal responsibility for your marriage falling apart, I guess it's time for me to back the fuck out of other people's business."

He grinned. "Annoyingly?"

I rolled my eyes, figuring I owed him some kind of explanation. "I know I've hardly been the poster child for seeing your side of things."

Luke gave a tiny snort of amusement.

"*But* in my defence, the timing of our first meeting was pretty damn abysmal. I was still wrapping my head around Holden and Gil being . . . *together*. I wasn't exactly in a generous mood, and you were a convenient target. And then—" I waved a hand between us. "—there was all this."

He smirked. "All *this*?"

I leaned closer and cupped his soft dick. "Yes, *this*." I gave him a squeeze and he groaned and drew me flush.

"Can you be a little more specific?" He rubbed our noses together.

"*This*," I repeated, nipping at his lower lip. "*You. Us.*" I pressed my firming dick alongside his. "This thing between us. This weird energy."

"Oh." He kissed me long and slow; his hand sliding down to cup my arse and draw me even closer. "You mean the fact I've wanted to strip you naked and suck your brains out of your cock every time I've laid eyes on you this last year?"

I snorted and hooked his leg over my thigh so I could reach into his crease. "Yes, an excellent example. And also . . . I think you just did that, by the way."

He chuckled into my hair. "That barely scratches the surface of all the things I'm planning to do to you."

"Planning?" I pulled back and stared into his shadowed eyes. "As in future occasions?"

"Well, yeah." A deep frown cut across his brow. "I'm kind of hoping this isn't a one-time thing?"

My heart absolutely did not skip in my chest, and if it did, it was fucking panic. "I, um—" I blew out a long sigh. "I didn't come here to *start* something, Luke. I came to fuck. To finally satisfy this ridiculous craving I seem to have for you. That's . . . all."

He blinked and I was pretty sure it was to hide his disappointment. Then he ran a hand down my nose to my chest and all the way down to wrap around my cock. "And how is that whole being satisfied thing working out for you?" He nuzzled into my neck and my cock twitched traitorously in his hand.

"Swimmingly, thank you," I answered primly while thrusting into his grasp.

He snorted and then nibbled at my shoulder, and okay, I might've groaned, which only served to spur him on. The nipping turned to firmer biting and long sucking as he worked his way across my chest, drawing each nipple into his mouth to suckle and nip the bud until I squirmed and pleaded to be fucked, every sting sending little bursts of fire through my balls. At one point, I caught sight of my reflection in the wardrobe mirror and winced at the patchwork of red blotches and bite marks painting my body.

Fucking hell. I wasn't going to be able to wear a singlet for a week, maybe two. Not that I gave a damn.

His lips brushed my ear. "What time do you need to leave in the morning?"

I angled my neck so he could lick under my jaw. "An hour ago."

He pushed me onto my back and leaned over me. "Give me tonight, at least. I'm not nearly done with you."

Like I needed any convincing. If this was my one and only time with this man, I wasn't leaving Luke's bed without having his dick up my arse at least once.

"I suppose I can stretch it to five."

He gave a slow, sexy grin. "In that case . . ." He flung the bedclothes aside, stood, and drew me into his arms. "I suggest we take this to the shower for round two so we can freshen up for round three back here. There's a lot to get through in—" He looked at the clock on the nightstand. "—eight hours."

I summoned my best put-upon look but my rigid cock pointing directly his way was a dead giveaway.

CHAPTER ELEVEN

Luke

I knew Zach was gone before I even opened my eyes. Before I felt the empty cold emanating from the other side of the bed.

Of course, he'd skedaddled. The man was harder to pin down than a stray cat.

I blinked against the grey wash of light that flooded the room. Drawing the curtains hadn't exactly been high on my priority list the night before. Thank God for tall camellias. I glanced at the clock and winced. Five too-fucking-early thirty. Getting up at random hours of the night was one of the things I didn't miss from my old job. Guess I'd gotten lazy.

I rolled onto my back and listened to the soft morning silence that filled the old house. Zach and I had made it back to bed about midnight, give or take. First, there'd been a round of lazy blowjobs in the shower accompanied by lots of laughing and teasing. Then, dressed in only towels, we'd refuelled on cheese toasted sandwiches cooked by Zach and eaten around the breakfast bar. We'd chatted about the upcoming muster and my new job while Zach deftly sidestepped all enquiries about his family, as usual.

Around toasted sandwich number two and a half, I was done wasting time and had hoisted Zach, laughing, onto one of the stools. Then I'd stood between his knees and we'd made out for the longest time. Somewhere along the way we both shucked our towels so we could shamelessly explore each other's bodies and discover all the sweet spots that got the other trembling and begging for more.

That scenario quickly escalated when Zach slid off the stool and pulled me over to the couch so I could bury myself inside his tight, welcoming body. His nervousness about taking me showed, but I did as I'd promised, and by the time I'd licked and fingered him to oblivion and back, he took me with no problem, and it had been the ride of my life. And when I'd come and pulled free, he pushed me to my knees and unloaded onto my face. It was the best damn sex I'd had in as long as I could remember.

Both sated, we stumbled back to bed and made out some more. I couldn't get enough of him, and it seemed the feeling was mutual. Zach was a delight to fuck—responsive, uninhibited, and surprisingly bossy in ways that made my toes curl. And if I didn't get the chance to have him again, I would be epically disappointed.

At some point in the night, I'd dozed off, and when I woke around three, Zach was lying on his back and staring at the ceiling. I pulled him into my arms but he was less pliant, maybe even a little cool toward me. I half expected him to disappear to the guest room and I wouldn't have fought him on it.

But when he finally relaxed, I'd gone all in and spooned him from behind with my arms wrapped tight around his hard body in a poorly disguised attempt to prevent him from skipping out on me the minute I closed my eyes. We'd drifted off to sleep that way with both our dicks needing splints and past the point of resuscitation.

But I'd known it was too good to last, and the fact I hadn't heard Zach's Kawasaki fire up in my driveway meant he must've walked the bike to the end of the road to avoid waking me. That said pretty much all there was to say about where his head was. Zach clearly didn't want to talk about what had happened. He didn't want any conversations about a repeat, or maybe any conversation. At. All.

I didn't come here to start something, Luke . . . I came to fuck.

I ran my hand down the cool cotton sheet where Zach had rested not that long ago and thought about that. It wasn't like I didn't totally get it. I'd spent a fair amount of the last year doing exactly the same thing and it was one of the reasons I'd come down here. To change all that.

So, what the hell am I doing? Am I just getting back on that same roller coaster I wanted to leave behind? Is Zach any different from all those other men?

Yes.

I didn't even need to think about it. Doug would have fitted that sad pattern. But Zach? Not in a million years. For one thing, he was too much hard work. I could get laid for a lot less effort and considerably less bruising to my ego. Not to mention, I'd never practically begged a hookup to stay the night or walked away wanting a whole lot more, wanting more than they did. Hell, most of the time I barely remembered their names. Also, regardless of what Gil thought, I hadn't had a hookup in months. I *had* already broken that pattern.

And if I were totally honest, I'd have to admit that Zach had been one of the attractions to moving down in the first place. A chance to get to know him better and see if I could break through that steel wall he'd shoved in my face. But I hadn't expected . . . last night. I hadn't expected to . . . feel, not like that, although maybe I should have.

I turned my head and stared through the window at the blush of dawn beginning to reach up from the horizon. I imagined Zach on his big bike thundering along the tussock-lined dirt road toward Miller Station. There was no way he wasn't thinking about what had happened between us, just like me. I didn't care which way he looked at it or how he tried to rationalise it in his head, last night wasn't going to be as easily put aside as he wanted.

I'd caught the wild look in his eyes. And I'd watched him throw his head back and holler when he'd come. I'd marvelled at the want on his face and his laughter as we'd teased and fucked each other like it was the best party in town. I'd been around long enough to know that type of chemistry didn't come along every day.

Zach and I were tinder to fucking flame and we'd both known it before he'd set a single foot on my doorstep.

And then there was all this, he'd said. *This. You. Us.*

We'd lit a fire in our bellies that was meant to burn for a lot longer than one night. The question was, how did I get Zach to admit to it? Because one night with the sexy country man was never going to be enough.

I forced my aching body out of bed and was reminded I wasn't twenty anymore. Or even thirty. Hell, even thirty-five was looking pretty damn tiny in the rear-view mirror. It had been a while since I'd had such athletic sex. Volume was clearly no substitute for quality.

I pushed the window up and stretched the kinks from my spine. The last weather front had freshened the ground, but not nearly enough to slake the high country's thirst, and my lawn looked, well, not like any healthy lawn should—brown being the new green. A soft rose wash painted the horizon and a welcome cool breeze licked around my groin. The slight sting made me glance down to discover an angry stubble rash blazing on my inner thighs.

The sight sent a Rolodex of sexy images cascading through my brain, and I did a quick inventory of all the other tender spots, starting with a pretty solid throb in my arse.

And whose great idea was that? I smiled at the memory.

I hadn't bottomed in . . . Jesus, it had to be two years or more. *Note to self—add a dildo to the shopping list—mail order.*

I turned away from the window and blinked at the sight of a piece of note paper sitting on Zach's pillow. *Huh.* I stared at it for a moment, then half nervous, half hopeful, I wandered across and picked it up.

Thanks. Last night was fun.
Zach

He'd written something else but then scribbled over it and I couldn't help but chuckle. *Fun?* It was succinct, I guess. Zach was clearly a man of few words.

I reached for my phone and texted, ***I'm so glad you signed the note in case my memory failed me. Could've been embarrassing if I replied to the wrong person.***

I slid the phone onto the dresser, caught my reflection in the mirror, and paused. I stared at the silver heart that hung low on my chest and thought of my conversation with Zach. Before I could change my mind, I undid the clasp and popped the heart in my drawer, leaving only the cord around my neck. I took a deep breath and confronted myself in the mirror.

Well, whaddya know.

I looked the same. The world hadn't stopped turning. And there wasn't the well of grief I'd been expecting. Maybe just a trickle. The heart had always been about Gil and me, a reminder of a time I'd never regret but was no longer a part of my future.

My gaze slid sideways to the framed photo of Callie standing next to the mirror and my heart gave a tiny stutter. I picked it up and ran my fingertips over her face. "Oh, baby." My throat thickened and I fought the tears that still appeared every damn time I took a minute to acknowledge the fact she was gone . . . for good. "I miss you so fucking much."

I grabbed my phone and slumped down on the bed, swallowing that all-too-familiar wave of emotion. Scrolling through my saved voicemails, I hovered over her name. Then I pressed play and fell back onto the mattress.

Hi Poppa.
You'll never guess what happened! Crabby Mr Martin said I gave the best speech out of everyone, and I get to pick the next book for our class read. Daddy said you'll help me choose. Will you call as soon as you land in Christchurch? I wish you didn't have to be away tonight. Daddy said he'd make me meatballs and spaghetti after the party so we can celebrate, but we both know he's gonna sneak some vegetables in there somewhere.
Her clear laughter rang out from the phone.
I love you, Poppa, forever and always. See you tomorrow night.

But I hadn't called her back.

And we hadn't seen each other the next night, either.

Because by the time I'd landed, Callie was already gone; killed in the car accident that nearly took Gil's life as well. I'd opened my phone to a ton of calls and messages telling me to get back to Wellington on the next flight. I hadn't even found her voicemail until days later.

I drew a ragged breath and ran the back of my hands over my eyes, wondering if I'd ever stop crying, and deciding I wouldn't. Fuck getting over shit like that. No one ever *got over* it. You just survived and found a way to muddle through the burden of grief and guilt to some semblance of a life after. It didn't matter whether the guilt was logical or not, deserved or not. I'd long ago decided that every parent who lost a child found a way to feel guilty about *something*.

Had I been too hard on Callie for things that didn't matter? Should I have changed jobs when Gil and I first discussed it years before? Would it have made a difference? If I had, would it have been me driving that day? Or would I have been there that morning to remind Callie and Gil to take the present? Would Gil and I have not fallen out of love if my job hadn't taken me away so often? Jesus, the list went on and on until for a long time, all I could do was try to find some relief in alcohol and being buried balls deep in another man.

Surviving, not living.

And sometimes barely that.

I fingered the band on my wrist. "But I'm doing better, sweetheart. I'm here. Trying for something different. Let's see if your daddy had the right idea."

I slid to my feet and winced at the state of my bed. And okay, maybe this thing with Zach wasn't exactly what I'd had in mind, but he also wasn't anything like the long list of others that had gone before him.

"I really like him, Callie," I said out loud, surprised at how easily the words settled in my head. "He's a million miles from your daddy, but I still like him. And I kind of think you would too."

I lifted the green band to my lips and kissed the word *Poppa*.

I had a couple of hours to kill before I had to be at work and by the time I was showered and dressed, there was an answer waiting on my phone.

Memory failure? Don't kid yourself. My name is imprinted in your arse. But FYI I won't be riding a horse anytime soon, either. You could still park the Orient Express up there. Have a nice day, Luke.

I laughed because he wasn't wrong about my side of it, at least, the cheeky shit. Still, I had one more surprise up my sleeve. *You too. See you tonight.* By the time I got to the kitchen, my phone was blowing up.

What do you mean tonight?

There is no tonight. We talked about that.

Not really.

Luke!

I finally put him out of his misery. *Don't panic. I was invited to the station cookout, that's all. Mmm. I think I'll bring a . . . tossed salad. :) I've been having some success with those lately. What do you think?*

He never texted back.

Wild Run was based at a tiny airfield with grass runways just out of Oakwood. It operated seven days a week to meet the tourist trade, and it was my turn to cover the weekend.

I pulled in beside the hangar at eight thirty on the dot, and Gary strolled out to meet me. At fifty-two, he stood taller than me by a smidge, and wider by a few caramel donuts a week from Lizzie's Bakery half a kilometre away. He had a serious face with enough wrinkles at the corners to show he had a sense of humour and a gruff but friendly manner that made him a pleasure to work for.

"Your afternoon booking cancelled," Gary informed me. "That means there's only the one-hour sightseeing flight followed by a guest transfer to Lane Station."

It would be my first visit to the Lane family's land and I couldn't deny I was curious.

"You should be done by one thirty if nothing else comes up, so feel free to clock out early. I know you're heading to Miller's. The next booking is noon tomorrow."

"Thanks," I said gratefully. "If I don't hear from you, I might stay the night."

"Fine with me. Tommy checked in to say he'll cover me for any search and rescue calls. His wife's parents are visiting the baby." Gary grimaced. "If you've never met them, that's all you need to know. I told him he'll need to make do with the old Airbus cos you'll need the H125 tomorrow."

"How's the search for a replacement going? I know you're turning down bookings because you don't want to use the old one for tourists anymore."

Gary's gaze slid away. "How do you think it's going? Choppers cost a bloody fortune. I did find a 2016 model in Aussie with reasonably low flight hours, but the cost of getting it here was enough to make my eyes bleed. The business can't afford it."

"I hate to be negative, but can it really afford not to?" I asked the unnecessary. "You can't keep turning down business. Wait much longer and you won't be able to sell the one you have to help get a new one."

He sighed. "You're bang on about that, but knowing it doesn't mean I can conjure money from thin air. Anyway, I need to crack on. Have a safe flight and tell Holden and Gil hi for me."

The sightseeing trip was a big success. The American couple asked a ton of questions, and I was pleased I'd spent a bit of time with Holden's books. I even managed a couple of Zach's humorous tales, and the couple hadn't been gone thirty minutes when Gary called me into his office to show me the five-star review they'd added to our website. I couldn't keep the smile from my face.

An hour after that, I touched my skids down at Lane Station and hauled far too many heavy bags onto the grass for a couple who'd arrived from the UK on a three-week vacation. Zach's brother, Julian, was there to greet me, along with his father, Paddy Lane.

When the older man recognised me from our slight altercation in The Fleece, his look turned thunderous. "What the hell are you doing here?"

The tourist couple cast startled looks over their shoulders and Julian elbowed his father.

"Go with Mum. I'll see to Luke."

Paddy looked me up and down, grumbled something under his breath that I was glad I missed so I didn't have to respond, and then followed the others.

"Ignore him." Julian offered his hand and we shook. "The man surely can hold a grudge."

Julian was a quietly handsome man with dark hair cut in a surprisingly modern style and longish scruff, which gave him a slightly nefarious air. Taller than Zach, although not as tall as I was, he had a leaner frame than his brother but was just as hard-muscled. He wielded the firm grip of a man used to hard work and no bullshit, and shrewd flint-grey eyes that caught and held your attention.

"Thanks for getting them here on time. Dad wants to take them up for a look over the station before evening."

My brows shot up. "Your father's a pilot?"

Julian shook his head. "No, but our stock manager has his licence and we have a fixed-wing Cessna. We, um . . . bought it off Miller Station a couple of years ago." Spots of pink appeared on Julian's cheeks.

"Oh." I remembered Holden saying how they'd had to sell the Cessna when his grandfather's dementia put the station's finances in trouble. As a pilot himself, he'd hated letting it go. But he'd never mentioned who'd bought it, and I suddenly understood why. It would've killed Holden to take money from Zach's dad.

Jules winced like he'd read my mind. "Yeah. Not our finest hour. I tried to convince Dad to just lease it so Holden could get it back, but he wouldn't even consider it. Holden doesn't feature high on Dad's list of favourite people." He turned to watch the Range Rover head down the track toward the homestead, billowing dust in its wake. "He's an ornery fucker."

One way of putting it.

Julian faced me again, a curious expression on his face. "So, you and Zach are . . . friends?"

I snorted. "*Friends* might be pushing it, at least if you asked Zach."

Julian frowned. "The way you had his back says otherwise."

He had a point there. "I never said *I* didn't want to be friends, but Zach has always been a little unconvinced. Let's leave it at that."

"Oh." A smile tugged at Julian's lips. "My little brother is nothing if not stubborn."

"You got that right."

Julian's clear, bright laugh made me smile. He was so different from Zach in looks, but they shared the same blunt honesty and warm humour. "Zach had no idea I knew all about what he and Holden were up to all those years."

"You did?" That surprised me.

"Most everyone on the two stations did, except for Dad and a few old-timers. Not to mention, best mates don't come back from sleepovers with *that* look on their face."

I laughed. "I don't imagine. In the meantime, I better get going." I climbed back into my seat. "I'm heading to Miller Station for a cookout later."

Julian backed away from the rotor blades. "Tell everyone hi from me. And don't give up on my little brother. His bark is worse than his bite."

The marks on my back from Zach's teeth stung in disagreement.

CHAPTER TWELVE

Zach

I glanced through the bathroom window and scowled at the sight of Luke's SUV parked in the drive alongside the homestead.

See you tonight.

Cheeky bastard. How in the hell had I missed that vital piece of information?

I wiped the steam from the mirror and studied my reflection.

Jesus fucking George. I fingered the bite marks dancing across my chest and the bruises that ran up the side of my throat, across my jaw, circled my hips, painted patterns on my thighs, and—I turned sideways to check my back—yep, all over that sucker as well.

Damn you, Luke. I looked like I'd gone ten rounds in an MMA ring and lost. I quashed the smile that was starting to leak all over my face because I wasn't happy about it at all.

I *wasn't*.

I leaned on the vanity and blew out a sigh. Okay, so maybe I was. Best damn sex of my life. I thought about Holden and our many, many times burning up the sheets and . . . nope, still no contest. A revelation that gave me pause. Because it wasn't that Holden and I hadn't had great chemistry too. He'd been somewhat of a mentor to my decidedly inexperienced gay self and we'd had a lot of fun. But compared to what had happened in Luke's bed just hours before, well, nothing before even came close.

Sex with Luke had been everything I'd imagined. Explosive and hungry and aggressive. But what shocked me to the core was the fact it had been equally tender and affectionate and selfless. And *fun*.

Maybe it was the fact Luke seemed to like that pissy, toppy side of me, a side I hadn't been all that familiar with myself because I'd left that role to Holden. But Luke seemed to enjoy everything and anything I brought to the occasion. The door was open wide and it was a heady feeling. He was an attentive and generous lover, and I'd spent the entire day reliving every moment I'd spent in his arms, or against his shower wall, or in his bed, or on his sofa, or up his arse —and okay, yeah, I'd wasted a fair amount of the day on that last one.

Which brought me back to my current predicament. I studied the reflection in the mirror again and groaned. There was no way in hell I was going to be able to hide all of that. So far, I'd managed to fly under the radar. I'd spent the day training my dogs and then fixing the intake system on the troughs supplying the south pasture.

But if I turned up to the cookout in a high-necked shirt, I might as well wave a flag above my head that said, *yes, I got right royally fucked last night, thank you very much.* I lathered shaving foam selectively above and below my stubble, hoping the remaining shadow would hide some of the bruising along my jaw and neck. Looking at the less-than-satisfactory result, I seriously considered texting an excuse to Gil and simply going to bed. And I might've even followed through if it weren't for the real possibility that he'd appear at the cottage two minutes later bearing chicken soup and sympathy. The man was a bloody mother hen.

I was still debating my options when a knock at the door almost made me drop my razor. *Shit. Had I fucking summoned the guy?* I peeked through the window and breathed a sigh of relief. It was Emily.

"Hang on." I tugged on sweats and a T-shirt and then draped a towel around my neck and hoped the shaving foam did the rest.

As I opened the door, Emily turned from where she'd been watching Charlie and Sam's antics as they cooled off in the glistening lake. She raised a quizzical brow. "I'm surprised you're not in there with them."

Not the way I looked. I leaned on the doorjamb as casually as I could manage and followed her gaze. "Would've been nice, but I had a late night and a busy day." As explanations went, it was mighty thin considering I swam most days over summer, and everyone knew it.

"Late night, huh?" Her smirk was telling as she ran a shrewd gaze over me, head to toe. "I heard your bike come in around six."

No surprise there, since Emily's cottage stood less than fifty metres from mine. Heat bloomed in my cheeks. "Sorry if I woke you."

She waved off my apology. "I'm no prude, son. You deserve to have some fun. I'm just pleased to see you getting out again."

Oh boy. I'd known Holden's mother all my life, and *she'd* known about our *extra-curricular* activities for longer than I cared to think about, because . . . mortifying. But it meant Emily also understood, more than most people, how difficult it had been for me when Holden and Gil became a thing. In many ways, she was like a second mother, and I loved her dearly.

She considered me with serious eyes. "I came to pick your brains."

That made me frown. I couldn't remember the last time Emily had asked *anyone* for *anything*. Self-sufficient and capable were her middle names.

"Sure." I waited.

Her gaze slid off me and back to the lake, its glistening surface beginning to rough in a fresh breeze channelling up the valley. "A friend of mine has a son who is thinking about leaving his partner."

I straightened. "I'm sorry to hear that."

Emily shook her head. "Don't be. None of *us* are. They've only been together a year, and the guy is an arsehole. He's stuck around too long as it is."

"Okaaaay." I frowned. "But I'm not sure where I fit—"

"There's a dog that might need a temporary home until everything is sorted out. I wondered if you could help."

My heart sank. "Emily, we can't just bring any dog onto a sheep station, you know that."

Emily's cheeks reddened. "Of course. I only meant that you might know someone local there who could help?"

I thought for a minute. "Not in Christchurch. Most of the dog owners I know around there are on sheep farms, like us." Then it hit me. "What about Spencer?"

Emily's brows lifted. "*Our* Spencer? The vet?"

I nodded. "Sure. He lost Silo to cancer last year and he's a sucker for a sob story—you can tell him I said so. I realise it's a three-hour drive but it's a safe option."

She nodded thoughtfully. "It could work. I'll keep him in mind, thanks."

"You're welcome. But if you do end up asking Spencer, remind him he still owes me for that crappy blind date he set me up on with that shearer from Wanaka. The guy was a bloody nutcase."

She went up on her toes and kissed me on the cheek. "I will. And I owe *you*." Her lips curved up in a sly grin. "Which is why I'm going to let you borrow my best concealer for those teeth marks you're wearing before Charlie or anybody else sees them. Lordy, that must've been some night you had, Zacharia Lane."

The look on my face must've said it all because Emily hooted with laughter, tipped my gaping mouth closed, and headed back to her cottage with a jaunty spring in her step.

Thirty minutes later, short of a mud bath, I'd done the best I could to cover the evidence of Luke's and my antics the night before. Emily's makeup did a reasonable job on the most obvious ones, and I made a mental note to buy some for myself. The concealer, in addition to wearing jeans rather than shorts, and adding a brightly patterned button-down that didn't look too out of place for me and was certainly distracting, and I was praying for the best.

Not working in my favour was the fact everyone would be there other than Sam, who'd gone to his parents, which meant a lot of curious eyes to evade. *In* my favour, the cookout was happening in the backyard around a fire pit and I only needed to get through the first hour before the alcohol consumption and fading light would do the rest.

Yeah, right.

I should've known better. I'd barely grabbed a seat around the fire pit when Charlie put down her beer and walked over. She yanked my collar aside and her hand flew to her mouth. "Holy fucking shit. Somebody's been busy." Her eyes danced over my face. "So, who was he?"

Holden looked over from where he and Gil were busy with the barbecue. "Who was who?"

"Shut up." I shoved Charlie's hand aside and resettled my collar. "None of your damn business."

"Why you dirty dog." Holden walked over to investigate but I was on my feet in an instant.

"It's none of *your* business either," I warned him.

"Aw, go on. Just a peek." He feinted to his right, then lunged to the left and made a grab for the collar. "Holy mother of God. You look like someone's main course they couldn't quite finish."

He was closer to the truth than he realised, not that I was going to tell him that. "Piss off, all of you," I grumbled, clenching my collar in my fist and retaking my seat. "You're just jealous."

Holden was staring at me. "But I didn't see you leave the bar with anyone."

I was about to tell him to mind his own business again when Gil saved me the bother. "Leave the guy alone," he admonished with a quirk to his lips and laughter in his eyes.

Holden pouted dramatically. "Spoilsport." Then he wandered back to the barbecue and gave his boyfriend a kiss before glancing over his shoulder. "But I'd consider getting a rabies shot if I was you."

I snorted. "Fuck off."

"Who needs a rabies shot?"

I didn't need to look to put a name to that gravelly voice. Not that long ago it had been whispering lewd comments in my ear while its owner's dick had been shoved up my arse and halfway to Mars.

"Zach." Holden waved a finger my way. "He's been a naughty boy and he's got the teeth marks to prove it."

"Is that right?" Luke plonked himself in the chair next to Alek on the opposite side of the fire. He stretched those long, long legs out in front and crossed the ankles. And fuck if he didn't look as sexy as hell. "Glad to hear you had a fun night." With no one else on my side of the fire to see, Luke ran hungry eyes over me, head to foot, and my belly did a little flip-flop. But when he finished with a downright filthy wink, everything south of that decided to join the party as well.

The man was catnip to my dick.

"So, who's the lucky guy?" he asked in an innocent voice, and I hoped my answering glare said everything I couldn't.

"No one important," I replied, flipping him off.

Luke's eyes glittered with amusement at the lie, and careful not to be seen, he discreetly tugged down the corner of his shirt collar to reveal the edge of a technicolour bruise with an imprint of teeth that no doubt matched mine.

My dick thickened in my jeans at the memory. *Jesus, had I really done that?* There was only one answer to that question, and I was pretty sure I flushed to the roots of my hair. I dragged my gaze away and cleared my throat. "Can we please change the subject?"

"Yes," Emily said, arriving with Harry to take the last spare seats around the edge of the fire pit. "Give the poor boy a break."

I shot her a grateful look. "Finally, some respect."

Luke looked up from studying the beer he held in his hands. "In that case, I vote we should talk about where I can repair the couch that came with my rental."

I froze with my mouth full of beer. *Surely, he wouldn't.*

"Seems it wasn't as sturdy as it looked." His gaze landed on mine and his mouth tipped into a crooked smile. "The leg's broken."

I choked on the beer and it sprayed from my mouth in an impressive arc to splatter the front of my shirt.

Alek ran over to slap my back. "Are you okay?"

I managed, "Fine," between slaps and coughs, and when I could finally breathe again, I looked up to find Luke watching me with a knowing smirk.

He raised his beer in a tiny salute and took a long swallow, the fucker.

"You're a bit hard on your furniture, mate." Holden went back to turning the blackening corn cobs. "Try the joiner on Garibaldi Street. He's the best around these parts."

"He gets my vote too," Gil agreed, his curious gaze flitting between Luke and me like he was trying to solve a puzzle. "He did some work for us last year."

While Luke noted the name in his phone, I caught Gil's attention, hoping to distract the nosey psychologist. "Can I give you a hand with something?"

Gil's lips twitched like I amused him in some way. "If you can slice up the two loaves of bread on the kitchen island, I'd be grateful. They should be cool enough now. And maybe ferry some plates and serving dishes to the outside table."

"Consider it done." I headed inside and was halfway through the first loaf when my phone rang.

"Hey, little bro."

I smiled at Julian's voice. "Will you stop with the whole little bro thing? To what do I owe the pleasure?"

"Aw, but you'll always be my little bro," he whined sulkily.

"This is me rolling my eyes," I informed him.

He laughed. "Just thought I'd let you know that I ran into your knight in shining armour today."

I frowned. "My... what?"

"Luke Nichols. He flew some guests out to the station today."

Oh God. "He's not my knight in any way, shape, or form," I blustered. Although to be fair, the idea of Luke dressed in all that shiny silver didn't come without a certain appeal.

"You sure about that?" Julian teased. "He seems a nice guy."

"And?"

"And nothing. Just that he's gay and single and clearly interested in you, judging by that night in the bar. And you're gay and single and—"

"Not remotely interested in him," I finished on a lie. "And stop meddling."

Jules chuckled. "I'm not meddling. I'm simply pointing out a fact."

"Oh really. Look, much though I'd love to chat I—"

"Dad was his usual friendly, hospitable self," Jules interrupted.

I blinked, thinking of Luke taking shit from my father. "Jesus, what did he say?"

Jules sighed. "Considering he recognised Luke from the bar, nothing too bad once he got the predictable *what the hell are you doing here* out of the way."

Shit.

"It could've been worse," Jules continued. "But I got Dad out of the way pretty quick, and Luke was nothing but professional."

Relief coursed through me. "Thanks. I owe you."

Julian huffed. "You owe me nothing. And you might not want to hear it, but I know Dad misses you, even if he won't admit he's screwed up."

I snorted. "I find that hard to believe."

A long sigh made its way down the line. "Yeah, I don't blame you, but for the record, I overheard him give your number to a Lake

Dunstan farmer asking for help with his new dog. He even told the guy you were the best."

My heart jumped in my throat, not sure what to make of that. But the spark of hope was quickly quenched by a rising tide of grief at the thought he could say that to a stranger and yet not find it in himself to talk to me. There was nothing I could do to force change on my father. The ball was in his court.

Jules dropped his voice and I wondered if Paddy was somewhere close by. "Hang in there, Zee. That's all I'm saying."

"I won't back down on my end, Jules. You have to know that."

"I don't expect you to." He paused and took a breath. "Anyway, I just wanted to check in and say I like this guy who seems to like you."

I groaned, "Just stop, please."

There was a long silence before Jules finally spoke again. "You've got a whole life to live now, Zee. Not the partial, closeted one you suffocated in for too long. You gave up a lot for that freedom, and it's a big world out there. How about living it a little?"

"I *am* living it."

"Are you?"

The question caught me unawares, and I said nothing, too scared the truth might squirm its way out.

"I'm sorry, Zee. I didn't mean to go all serious on you. Enjoy the cookout. I miss you. We all miss you."

I'd just put my phone back in my pocket when a warm body pressed against me from behind and a voice whispered in my ear, "You're looking particularly gorgeous tonight."

Hands slid under my shirt and around my waist, sending goosebumps cascading down my spine. Luke Nichols was in the house, and my balls did a little happy dance in my jeans.

"I've been wanting to do this since the minute I saw you sitting there." He sucked the lobe of my ear into his mouth and hot breath fanned across my neck and cheek. I was about to lean back into his hold when common sense kicked in and my gaze shot to the mudroom door.

"Are you crazy?" I delivered a sharp elbow to his ribs and he immediately stepped back, grunting in pain. "Someone might see."

"You know, a simple *stop* would've sufficed," he said, groaning as he slowly straightened. "Besides, I can't be held responsible. You are too fucking tempting for words, standing there covered in my handiwork from last night."

I rounded on him. "Keep your voice down."

"It is," he hissed, and I realised he was right. We were both still whispering.

"Someone could come in at any moment," I pointed out, glancing wildly toward the mudroom door.

"Calm down." He raised a hand and tucked a wave of hair behind my ears. "Gil sent me to help. He's busy with the barbecue, and they're all listening to Alek's list of the latest bullshit immigration is putting him through regarding getting his little brother here. I figure we're safe for a bit."

"Safe?" I raised a brow. "Damn right we are, because *nothing* is going to happen, understand?"

"Absolutely." He added a cute-as-fuck salute and it was all I could do not to laugh.

I studied his smirk and then asked the one question that I knew that I shouldn't. "We, um, broke your couch?"

He nodded, and two seconds later, we both burst into muffled laughter.

"Oh my god." I covered my mouth and shook my head. "I thought I felt something give."

Luke cupped my cheek and drew me close, staring down at me with those beautiful bright blue eyes. "It was worth every second."

At least that was something we could agree on.

"Was that your brother on the phone?" Luke dropped his hand and I instantly missed the warmth.

I nodded. "He said he saw you today. Seems to like you for some reason."

Luke shrugged. "Hey, I'm a likeable guy."

I summoned an eye roll, and for a few seconds, we simply stood there, staring at each other. One step away from a kiss I was desperate to get, and a million miles from an answer about what was happening between the two of us that made any sense.

And then Luke's mouth was on mine, and any questions I had flew out the window along with every scrap of my common sense. I wanted him. Plain and simple. And nothing about the night before had slaked any of that driving thirst.

The taste of him back on my tongue made every mark he'd put on my body come alive and sizzle with need. "This is insane," I managed, although apparently, I was okay with that. I grabbed his hand and dragged him into the walk-in pantry. Then I shut the door and slammed him up against it.

"I know I'm going to regret this, but I wanna see." I stood back and waved a hand over his body. "Come on. Hurry up before someone comes."

Luke cocked an eyebrow and then slowly peeled the hem of his shirt up to reveal a tapestry of bruises and bite marks that rivalled mine. But it wasn't only the bruising that caught my attention. My gaze lingered for a few seconds on the empty leather cord. I reached out to finger it, and when I caught his eye, he simply smiled.

I dropped the cord and ran my fingers over his mottled skin, my dick stiffening in my jeans, my heart banging in my chest. "Jesus Christ," I marvelled. "You're a worse mess than I am." I leaned forward and pressed my lips to one of the colourful blotches and Luke's fingers threaded through my hair.

"I love them," he said huskily as I tongued my way up his chest to his throat. "Get up here." He tugged me up and kissed me thoroughly, tongue fucking my mouth until we were both swallowing moans. Then his hands circled my waist and pulled me tight against him. He was hard. So fucking hard.

"Jesus, what you do to me," he said as he shoved a knee between mine to add a little much-needed friction and, fuck, it felt good. Then he kissed down my throat and my head fell back. "Watching you sitting all prim and sour in that chair, telling me it's none of my damn business, and it was nobody important when *I* put those marks on you. *Me*."

I chuckled, angling my head to give him better access. "Aw, did it dent your ego?"

He nipped at my clavicle. "*My* teeth, *my* mouth—" He grabbed my butt. "—*my* dick in your arse." He licked up the side of my face and I shuddered. "It was *my* business all right. I wanted to strip you right then and there and fuck you in front of that fire."

"Would never have picked you for an exhibitionist," I said, then gasped as his hand cupped my dick and gave it a firm squeeze.

"I would never have picked you for a toppy son of a bitch." He squeezed again as he humped against my leg and grunted unsteadily into my ear. "I guess we've got a lot . . . ugh fuck . . . still to learn about . . . each other."

My cock definitely liked the sound of that as it strained painfully against the zip of my jeans. I was done. I took a half step back and started unbuttoning his fly. If I didn't get my mouth around his cock soon, things were going to get messy. He gave a grunt of approval, and it wasn't long before I had them halfway down his thighs when—

"Zach?" Gil's voice pierced the haze of lust fogging up my brain, but it took me a few seconds to shift focus.

Luke was quicker. He grabbed a tablecloth from a nearby shelf and shoved it into my hands, whispering, "Get out there before he comes looking."

"Me?" I asked, horrified.

His eyebrows shot up and he swept a hand to where his hard cock was jutting from his jeans.

Oh, right.

Luke straightened my shirt and pushed me toward the closed door, whispering, "Get rid of him."

Rid of him? This was *Gil's* bloody kitchen. How was I supposed to get rid of him? I fired him my best are-you-shitting-me look, but his only response was to give me another push and then flatten himself against the shelves behind the door.

"Luke?" Gil called again from what sounded like the hallway. "Anyone here?" Closer that time.

"Go on," Luke insisted. "Just . . . act natural."

My eyes bugged as I whispered back, "*Natural?* Are you fucking kidding me?"

A mischievous grin played over his lips and then he kissed me, hard. "Now, go."

I swore softly, opened the door, and almost walked straight into Gil. "Oh, were you looking for me? I was trying to decide on a tablecloth." I held the green-chequered material in front of my rapidly wilting hard-on. Having your friend almost catch you with your mouth around his ex-husband's dick will do that to a guy.

"A tablecloth?" Gil frowned at the messy bundle. "It's a cookout, Zach, not freaking MasterChef."

"I know, I know." I made a beeline for the kitchen island, hoping Gil would follow. "Making an effort to raise the bar is all. Bad idea?"

Gil glanced into the open pantry, his frown deepening. With a sinking heart, I thought for sure that he'd heard something. That he'd go inside to check. But instead, he walked away and joined me at the island. "Whatever floats your boat. Did Luke come through here? I sent him to help you."

I narrowed my gaze. "Why? Are you meddling again?"

"Of course not." But his sly smile gave him away. "Okay, maybe."

"Yeah, well, stop it." I had his attention now. "And yes, he passed through about five minutes ago. Didn't mention anything about helping though." I added a dramatic eye roll to the lie. "Typical, if you ask me."

Gil frowned. "Not rea—"

"Gil," Holden called from outside. "Bring some more beer when you come back, yeah?"

Gil glanced at the mudroom.

"Do you want me to get that?" I offered, knowing full well what his answer would be.

"No, I'll do it. And by the way—" He caught my gaze and smiled. "—I don't think I said thank you."

"For what?"

"For making the effort with Luke last night in the bar. I appreciate it."

It was all I could do not to look directly at the pantry, pretty sure my cheeks were blowing scarlet as I remembered exactly how much effort I'd expended on Luke last night and in ways that would blow Gil's brain clear out of the water. "No problem," I said somewhat huskily. "I guess he's not so bad."

Gil's eyes grew soft. "Glad you think so. Now, we're about five minutes away from serving, so if you can get those plates on the table, with or without a tablecloth, I'd appreciate it. And if you see Luke, light a fire under his arse, courtesy of me, will you?"

I bit back a smile, imagining Luke standing in the pantry with his ears flapping. "It'll be my pleasure."

The minute Gil was gone, Luke appeared from the pantry with a wicked gleam in his eye. He crowded me against the island and put his lips next to my ear. "You can light a fire under my arse anytime, baby. In it too, for that matter."

"You're ridiculous." I shoved him away. "And quit trying to kiss me."

"Didn't hear you complaining a minute ago. And also—" He arched a brow. "—typical?"

My cheeks bloomed. "I'm not supposed to like you, remember?"

Something flashed in his eyes that looked a lot like surprise. "Does that mean you *do* like me?"

"You're fishing. And no, I don't like you." I tried not to smile. Epic fail. "Okay, maybe a little. When you're not being a dick."

Instead of the smart comeback I'd expected, Luke's response was a thoughtful frown. "Gil asked you to be nice to me, didn't he?"

I huffed. "Yes, although he didn't quite put it that way. He wanted me to give you a chance. But in case you're wondering, I don't make a habit of fucking men I'm asked to be nice to. That regrettable decision was entirely my own."

His frown smoothed and he stepped in close once again, the fresh scent of him muddling my brain. "Regrettable, huh?"

I swallowed hard and stared up at him, every thought in my head fading into those blue, blue eyes, my stomach swooping. This close, Luke was so fucking potent. He filled the room and everything else paled beside him. "Maybe not *entirely* regrettable." My tongue dragged over my dry lips and Luke followed the movement, his pupils flaring. "I suppose there were one or two redeeming moments."

"Just one or two?" His voice dropped to a husky baritone and he ran his nose up the side of my face, turning my legs to jelly. "Do tell—"

"Zach, we need those plates," Gil called from outside.

Dammit. I shoved Luke away and glared at his smirking face. "Stop messing with me. Here." I reached for the stack of plates. "Make yourself useful and take these outside."

He accepted them with the sexiest fucking smile that curled my toes. "You're adorable when you're all prickly."

"I am not prick—"

He shut me up with a kiss and then headed for the mudroom, adding over his shoulder, "Yes, you are. And I'm pretty sure you like me more than a little."

I glared at his back. "I do not."

He laughed. "Do too."

I waited for the back screen to close and then leaned over and banged my forehead on the granite countertop . . . twice.

CHAPTER THIRTEEN

Luke

I STARTED AWAKE AND SQUINTED INTO THE UNFAMILIAR darkness. No streetlights shining through thin curtains. No clunk of the fan on my dresser. Just an all-pervading deep silence, a presence all in itself. Except for . . . that. The distant mournful bellow of cattle.

The homestead.

What the hell time is it?

I rolled over to pick up my phone and the screen flashed one thirty. *Ugh.* Then I saw two unread texts sent in the previous minute and there was no need to guess what had woken me. I pushed up on one elbow and stared bleary-eyed at the screen. Then I blinked and looked again, and a slow smile spread over my face.

You up for some fun? You have five minutes before this offer expires.

Then a few seconds later: **If you don't want Spider to sound the alarm, use the window and take the long way around.**

My phone shook in my hand as I texted back. **On mu wsy.** I corrected. ***my way***

I had the sheet off and my feet on the floor when my phone buzzed for a third time and an image appeared of Zach sprawled across his bed with his erect dick in his hand. The porn-worthy filthy look on his face sent my balls into overdrive, and I was pretty sure I broke the record for yanking on a pair of jeans and a shirt. My boots were in the mudroom so that was a no-go and to hell with anything else.

I crossed to the window and eased the sash up as far as I could, wincing at the high-pitched screech of wood on wood that slashed through the silence.

Frozen in place, I held my breath and waited.

Nothing. Not even a concerned bark from Spider who was no doubt familiar with all the house noises. I was in the clear.

I stepped through the window and was hit by the lingering aroma of barbecued lamb and the welcoming cool of the mountain air pebbling my skin. A three-quarter moon hung in an inky sky lit with a million stars. It provided enough light for me to pick my way around the house without needing to use the light on my phone, but not quite enough to stop me from stubbing my toe on the garden edging.

"Shit, shit, shit!" I hissed. Maybe at least socks would've been the smarter choice. Too late. I hopped about on one foot until the sting eased and then tiptoe-ran across the crunchy dry grass, past the untidy circle of chairs, the empty beer bottles littering the ground between them, and on to the far back corner of the house.

Gil and Holden's bedroom lay at the front with a window onto the lake. To avoid passing too close, I veered left through Gil's precious vegetable garden, which was a big mistake. Big. Mistake. With only the moon to light my way, I was forced to navigate barefoot through a field of overgrown zucchinis while trying to avoid pumpkin vines scratching at my legs, ankle-breaking trenches left from old potato beds, and a complicated bean trellis thingy with decidedly homicidal tendencies.

Finally free on the other side, I scooted down the edge of the front lawn, the lake a velvety black shadow in the distance, the moonlight catching the tips of its rippling surface. Halfway down, I veered left between two camellias and skulked toward Tussock Cottage where Zach was standing naked at an open window, waiting.

"Through here." He waved me over. "Watch out for—"

"Ow, fuck!" I came to an abrupt stop as a squillion prickles pierced the soles of my bare feet.

"The prickle weed," he finished with a snort of laughter. "Come on. Hurry up before someone sees you."

"I *am* hurrying." I hobbled my way the last couple of metres and Zach helped me through the window.

The minute I was inside, I made a dive for his bed. Zach slid the sash closed and was on me in an instant, crawling up my body to lick into my mouth with a desperation I could totally get on board with, except—

I clasped both hands around his head and lifted his face so I could look at him. "I have one word for you. Prickles."

He glanced down at my bare feet and shook his head. "Where are your damn shoes?"

I shrugged. "They're in the mudroom and I didn't want to risk waking Spider."

"Idiot." He grinned and wriggled back down my body—mouthing my cock through my jeans as he passed—until he was kneeling on the floor in front of my feet.

"Pass me your phone." He snapped his fingers and I slapped my phone into his hand. He switched on the flashlight, got it shining where he wanted, and set it against a pillow. "Now, hold still."

I did as I was told and Zach began painstakingly removing every single prickle, the tip of his tongue poking out of the side of his mouth, his gaze focused and intent. Wearing nothing but miles of bare skin, a ton of bruises and teeth marks, and those intriguing splashes of freckles all painted in shades of grey in the wash of moonlight that lit the room, Zach looked so young, so lovely, so . . . bewitching, and I was charmed in a hot second. Not to mention, there was something tender and ridiculously intimate about the whole process, as if the act of prickle removal somehow meant more than the sex I'd initially raced down for, and I was reminded that I was in real trouble with this man.

I dragged my eyes off Zach to take in the small bedroom. It was simply furnished, courtesy of Miller Station, no doubt. A small dresser stood at the end of the bed alongside a full-length mirror—the source of the pic he'd sent me, no doubt—and a dozen or so items hung in an otherwise glaringly empty closet. Then again, Zach had never struck me as a clothes horse.

Two towering stacks of books teetered against the wall beside the window. I couldn't read all their spines, but there was a mix of thriller fiction and historical non-fiction. On the bedside table, a weighty tome on the pyramids of Ancient Egypt was littered with bookmarks, and another on Scottish clan battles lay face down and open on top.

Colour me surprised. I glanced back at Zach who was still busy with my feet and tried to align this all-country boy with his choice of bedtime reading. Tried and failed. Which only intensified his allure. I was about to say something about the books when he looked up and caught me staring. He must've seen something in my expression because his smile stuttered for a second and a wariness crept into his eyes.

"Pretty sure that's the last of the buggers." He got to his feet with his half-hard cock bobbing enticingly and handed me back my phone.

"Now there's a sight." My gaze raked over his body and he relaxed, shooting me a filthy smile.

"Is that so?" He sauntered around the bed and stood beside me. "Let's even things up." He bent over to undo my jeans and my hand slid up the back of his thighs to cup his very naked, very warm arse. He hummed in approval and turned his hips in invitation, his cock plumping further.

I pushed up to lick across the slit, drawing a hiss of appreciation.

"Hold that thought." He pushed me back down and tugged at my jeans. "Lift up."

I did as I was told and in seconds, Zach deposited my jeans on the floor and then crawled onto the bed and straddled my thighs, working the buttons on my shirt until he could shove it off my shoulders. I wriggled free and then pulled him down on top of me.

"Mmm, much better." I nuzzled into his neck and he ground down into me.

"I promised myself I wouldn't text," he grumbled as he kissed up my throat.

"So, how's that working out for you?" I murmured against his lips as I slid a finger into his crease and over his hole.

He gasped. "Argh ... fuck ... how do you think it's working out?" He reached over me and into his bedside drawer, then dropped lube and a condom on the bed.

"Definitely in my favour." I grabbed the lube and slicked my fingers before returning them to his crease. When the tip of one slipped inside, he hoisted up his thigh to give me room and a filthy groan rumbled up his throat.

"I hate that you can do this to me," he grunted between my finger thrusts.

"Do what?" I added a second finger.

"Jesus fucking Christ." He clenched around me, then circled his hips and drew me deeper. "This," he hissed, arching his back, and slamming down until I was two knuckles deep. "Make me so hot for you that I can't think clear—oh god, right there!"

I crooked my finger again and he groaned and dropped his mouth to mine, plunging his tongue inside, once, twice and then he was back to watching me from above with those wild green eyes, his auburn waves tumbling in the weak moonlight as he rode my hand until I was so hard I thought I could come from the sight of him getting off on my fingers alone.

And then he pulled right off and my hand fell to the sheet. "Move up. We're almost off the bed." He slapped my hip and I scooted up the mattress until my head hit the wall.

I shoved a pillow under my head and Zach ripped the condom from its packet and rolled it down my aching length. Then he applied lube, lots and lots of lube.

I grinned. "You need another tube?"

He looked like he might be considering it, then flipped me off. "Fuck you."

I laughed and drew him up for a kiss. "Not by the look of it. Lucky me."

He huffed. "You bloody are, considering I'm still aching from last night."

"Nothing a little practice won't fix."

He snorted. "We'll soon find out."

I couldn't help but kiss him again. It was like being with Jekyll and Hyde in the best possible way. When Zach let loose in bed, that quiet, wary guy I'd first met took a back seat to a confident, sexy-as-fuck, take-charge spitfire that simply took my breath away.

He straddled my thighs and winked. "I take it this position works for you?" He drew his pouty lower lip between his teeth and eyed me saucily.

"What the hell do you think?" I wrapped both hands around his hips and guided him up and over my cock without any downward pressure. Then I took his dick in a firm stroke and he thrust forcefully into my hand, keeping his eyes locked on mine like he didn't want to miss a second. Jesus Christ, he was sexy.

I kept stroking, drawing small gasps as Zach wriggled his hole a little against the head until he had it exactly where he wanted. Then, he dropped down, centimetre by centimetre on an agonisingly slow slide, his jaw clenched, his face set in determination, the lines around his eyes tight with effort and edged with the sting of the stretch. Down and down, until the tight furnace of his arse engulfed me in a feeling that was pretty close to fucking magical.

Finally, fully seated, his balls nice and cosy against my groin,

Zach's eyelids fluttered closed, and he blew a few calming breaths as he waited for his body to relax. I counted every single one, desperate to thrust as I fought the rush to orgasm. It was way, way too soon. But by the time Zach looked up and smiled to let me know we were ready to go, I'd clawed back the control I needed, and all bets were off.

This was clearly Zach's show. He was in charge.

He leaned down and kissed me, licking into my mouth as his body slid up the length of my cock. Then he went back up on his knees and sank down once again, slowly, too fucking slowly, and with a coy smile plastered on his face.

The next time was faster, and then faster again, and then that smirk slipped as he found a position that worked and started shuttling up and down my cock. I took his hips in my hands and thrust as he sank, watching his face, checking he was okay. But he rode me hard, his skin slick with sweat, his gaze firmly locked on mine.

"Come here." I pulled him down to land a kiss on those swollen lips, the angle letting me thrust into him again and again as he groaned into my open mouth.

"Jesus, fuck. Do me like this." He pulled off and quickly switched to his hands and knees before backing to the edge of the bed.

"Oh, hell yes." I scrambled to my feet and steadied his hips in my hands while my cock slid back inside, the sweet bliss drawing a garbled run of nonsense from my lips.

"Fuuuuck." He thumped his closed fist on the mattress, then slammed back into me, forcing me even deeper. His head dropped to the mattress and he wriggled his arse against my groin, and I wasn't sure I'd ever seen anything so fucking delicious put on display for me to take.

I took the hint and the room fell silent except for grunts and groans and the sound of skin slapping on skin. It didn't get any better than watching my dick shuttling in and out of Zach's arse, or at least not until I caught sight of our reflection side-on in the mirror on the wall at the end of the bed.

"Damn . . . look at us," I managed to grunt between thrusts.

Zach gave a quick look over his shoulder. "Fuck, that's hot."

I repositioned us to improve the view and started up again. Zach's smile when he caught my eyes in the mirror was breathtaking, and as we both edged closer, I slipped a hand around his hip and took a firm grip of his cock.

"Oh god, yes." Zach's gaze left the mirror as his head fell forward.

"That's it, baby." I added a twist to my stroke and he jerked.

"Oh, fucking hell!" He dropped to his elbows and started working his hips in time with my thrusts, messing with the rhythm of my strokes. Not that it seemed to matter because a few seconds later, he tensed and his cock swelled and then erupted in my hand, come spilling through my fingers to the sheet as he jerked in my arms.

The sight of him going over and the tight grip of his arse on my cock was all I needed. I groaned and spilled into the condom, my arms tightening around his waist so I could haul him up and bury myself deeper until the waves of pleasure stuttered to a close.

Sated and spent, Zach fell forward onto the bed, dragging me with him until I was draped over his body like a sweaty cloak, my chin hanging over his shoulder. He drew a few gasping breaths and then his elbow caught me in the ribs. "Get off me before I melt."

I chuckled and gently eased free of his arse before rolling onto my back still panting.

"Oh, thank God." He took another couple of breaths through the slightly uncomfortable disconnection and then followed suit, starfishing across the bed, one arm covering my face.

"Let's not do that face in the mattress thing again until winter," he huffed.

I chuckled and shoved his arm off my mouth. "Pretty sure it wasn't my idea."

"Didn't see you complaining." He rolled to the side and traced a line down my chest before lifting the empty leather cord. "You took it off." His eyes found mine and there was an unexpected softness in their depths.

I ran my thumb down his cheek and over his lips. "I figured it was time." I cupped his face and brought our lips together. He melted into the languid kiss, taking it deeper but keeping it tender. And when he finally pulled away, neither of us voiced the unspoken question left hanging from my admission. Instead, Zach dropped his head to my chest and I slipped an arm around his waist and pulled him close.

He slung his leg over mine and played with the hair on my chest. "I like that you don't wax."

I snorted and kissed the top of his head. "I like that you like that I don't wax. I did try it once, but it seemed a hell of a lot of effort and pain just to have to turn around and do it all over again way too often to be worth it. Besides, I don't get what's wrong with a little hair. I happen to like hair on my men."

"*Your* men, huh?" He eyed me with amusement and I could've kicked myself. But it didn't seem Zach was too bothered. "Well, I guess you've had enough to know what you like and don't."

I knew he was teasing but there was an edge of enquiry there as well. One that I suddenly wanted to clarify. I caught his gaze and held it. "For the record, not that I need to explain myself, but I haven't been with a guy in over three months."

He blinked, clearly surprised, then he ducked his head sheepishly. "I shouldn't have said that. I'm sorry. What you do is your own business."

"It's fine." I captured his hand in mine and held it. "I pulled away from all that a while ago. You are not just another link in the chain, okay?"

He looked back up, but I couldn't name the expression in his eyes. "Thanks for saying that, but it's truly none of my business. I have no claim on you. That's not what we're doing here, is it?"

Isn't it? But I didn't say that. I let it go, and Zach seemed relieved to do the same.

"Anyway—" He reached up to nip me on the lips. "Just as well you like hairy men because I'll tell you right now, Holden always says I take better care of my dog's grooming than I do my own."

I laughed and ruffled his auburn locks. "That's fine with me. I'll let you know if I spot any fleas down . . . well, you know where."

"Fleas? Why you—" Zach's expression turned to outrage. He straddled my legs and smooshed the spare pillow into my face. "I'll have you know I have never *ever* had fleas, *anywhere*, but especially not there."

He tried to hold me down, but I had a height advantage and a fair few kilos on his lean tightly muscled body, and it didn't take much to reverse our positions and get his arms pinned above his head. He writhed and laughed between a string of threats, which he had zero chance of following through. And when he finally tired himself out, I released his arms and leaned down to take his mouth in a sweet, leisurely kiss that went on far too long for something that was supposed to be just about sex.

And when it seemed he was finally about to let me go, Zach instead pulled me down onto my side and we continued to make out, our hands moving gently over each other's bodies, still exploring, still getting used to the feel of each other. At different times our eyes met, his curious and a little uncertain. Who knew what he saw in mine? I hoped it was peace, because if I had to name it, that would've been it.

At times his eyes were softly closed. At times mine.

I kissed every inch of his face. He trailed his fingers all over mine, inspecting every line, every mark.

I drew slow circles on his back. He found my hand and kissed every knuckle.

I told him he was beautiful.

He blushed and told me I was crazy.

Our cocks awakened once or twice, only to soften again in response to the quiet mood and unhurried pace, and that was more than fine with me. I wasn't sure what was happening in that moment, but it sure as hell wasn't about sex or anything else that came with an uncomplicated explanation. Much better to leave it alone and just let myself feel. A pool of deep clear water at the end of a two-year desert.

At some point, we dozed off in each other's arms. I wasn't sure for how long, only that I was the first to wake, my eyelids fluttering open to find Zach still in my arms, silver moonlight falling over his face and chest all the way down to the sheet puddled around his waist. His skin was cool to the touch, so I carefully drew the bedcovers up over his narrow hips, pausing to run my gaze over his lean chest and the smattering of reddish curls that spanned his chest and belly before covering them too.

He muttered something I couldn't catch and burrowed closer. My stupid heart squeezed and I lifted the covers over his shoulders and pressed a kiss to his forehead. Zach pulled the blanket tighter under his chin and then his fingers found mine and curled around them.

My gaze shot up, but he was still asleep, breathing evenly, his face slack, free of all care and looking oh-so young. Something protective rallied in my heart and I lifted the hair from his eyes before falling back on my pillow so I could watch him sleep.

It wasn't for long. A few minutes later his eyes opened. When he saw me, his mouth tipped up in a contented smile and it was the best damn feeling in the whole world. Then as if he suddenly remembered what we were supposed to be to each other, a frown dipped between those brows and I immediately wanted to scrub it off his face.

"What's the time?" He stretched and reached over my shoulder to where his phone sat on the bedside table. "Damn. Three thirty. I'm gonna suck today. The dogs will run rings around me."

I kissed his neck because it was right there, and he glanced down with a half-smile that missed his eyes by a million miles. *Damn.* I traced his lips with my fingertip. "What are you guys up to?"

He shrugged. "The usual pre-muster planning. But I have a break this afternoon to do some training with Charlie and the dogs. I'll get Gil to lay a scent trail for us. He's always up for any excuse to get outside for a while."

I rolled onto my back and pulled him over with me. "You must miss working with your brother."

Zach didn't reply for a moment, and I wasn't sure he would. The subject had been glossed over but never properly discussed between us. All I knew was what I'd overheard or learned from others.

I pressed a little. "Julian mentioned you guys were close. It was clear he misses you."

I didn't miss the flash of pain in Zach's eyes or the sudden tension in his body as he answered, "I miss him too. *And* the station. Apart from university, I spent my entire life on that land. Jesus, I dream about merinos."

We both chuckled and he relaxed a little.

"It was no surprise how my dad reacted. In my heart, I think I always knew it would end this way. There was a reason I didn't tell anyone for so long."

He raised a hand and fingered my short hair, twirling it around and around before pushing it back off my face. "But it wasn't like he booted me off the place. Sometimes I wonder if I did the right thing by leaving. If I'd stayed, maybe I could've kept him talking. It's harder to ignore people who are right in your face."

I tipped his chin up, forcing him to look at me. "How much more time were you willing to give up? To keep your sexuality in the shadows. Not being able to bring anyone home. Knowing what he thought. Maybe he'd have come around. Maybe you'd still be waiting. You're a grown man, Zach. You have a right to a life not judged for who you take to your bed." I thought of Holden and added, "Or who you fall in love with."

He held my gaze, that small frown growing deeper. "You mean Holden?"

I nodded. "I know your feelings for him were a part of your decision to finally come out."

Zach rolled his eyes. "The drum beats loud across the station."

I smiled, adding, "They care about you."

He sighed. "I know. And I *was* in love with him."

I kissed him softly. "I know you were."

He studied my face, then breathed in and blew it out slowly.

"You know, as crazy as it sounds now, it never occurred to me that he'd say *no* that day. God, was it only a year ago?" He shook his head. "I thought he might need time to think, but a flat-out no? Nope. I never saw that coming."

"That must've been so hard." I tightened my hold and he leaned into it.

"It was, and I almost didn't come out at all after that. I'd convinced myself that Holden was the reason for finally taking that risk with Dad. But strangely enough, when Holden turned me down, that need to come out only became more of an imperative. If I couldn't have Holden, and I couldn't pretend anymore that we were headed for a real relationship, then I needed to take some action and get that side of my life in order, because if I didn't, I was going to end up alone."

I cupped his cheeks and rubbed our noses together. "It's a hell of a brave thing to do when you think you know the outcome isn't going to be great. My family was a breeze in comparison. Barely blinked an eye. Hell, my cousin offered to be our surrogate almost before the ink was dry on our wedding licence."

He smiled wistfully. "I'm glad you had that."

Something I knew only too well.

"Jules keeps saying he's working on Dad, but it's been almost a year, and to be honest, I think Dad's way too stubborn to ever admit he might've got things wrong. Two months after I left, he changed the station's trustee document so I'm not part of it anymore."

Anger burned low in my belly. "Jesus, Zach. Two months? That's a statement."

"Pretty much." His eyes shone suspiciously. "At the time, I thought he couldn't hurt me anymore, but he found a way."

"I'm so sorry." I pulled his head against my chest, wishing I could steal some of his pain. "And your mum?"

He sighed, his hot breath fanning my chest. "My mother is a lovely woman, don't get me wrong, and she does text now and then to keep in touch, but she's never stood up to him. She has bad rheumatoid arthritis and doesn't drive much anymore, so apart from a few video calls, I haven't seen her since I left. God, I sound like a broken fucking record. I should count myself lucky. Some people lose their whole families. I've at least kept contact with some of mine."

I released him and tipped his chin up once again, fighting to control the fury I felt for his arsehole of a father. "That isn't luck, Zach. That's the bare-minimum expectation of family who are supposed to love you. *No one* should have to lose their family because of their sexuality. No. One. You can't sacrifice yourself to keep other people happy, not even your parents."

He blinked at whatever he heard in my voice. Then lifted his lips to mine and whispered, "Thank you."

I kissed him back. "You're welcome. Have you got any plans for the future? Do you think you'll stay here?" *Please say yes.*

Zach shook his head. "Not long-term. I love the lifestyle, and I love working and living in these mountains, but my dream is to set up my own dog training business. That's where my heart lies."

I smiled. "Now why doesn't that surprise me? How is it shaping up?"

He rolled onto his back and I followed, drawing the sheet back over his shoulders. "Slowly, as in mostly non-existent. Shepherding is fine for training my own dogs, but it doesn't leave me enough time to work with others. I need to be doing a lot more of that along with starting a breeding program. A good sheepdog who has competition wins and a background to prove it can sell for eight to fifteen thousand dollars."

I gave a low whistle. "Holy shit. I had no idea."

He shrugged. "I'm talking the best of the best. But it takes a lot of training to get them to that level, a lot of investment. And there's a shortage of good working dogs, particularly in the South Island. Some dogs even go to Australia."

As he talked, his eyes brightened with a new excitement. This was Zach's passion and I found myself growing excited on his behalf. "Holden says your dogs are the best."

"He would, of course." Zach's gaze slid away, but he was smiling. "And they're right up there, I suppose. Miller Station's dog team is worth north of fifty thousand, but my two alone are probably worth close to twenty-five, so yeah, they're good."

Even on his back, I knew Zach was blushing. The pride he had for his dogs shone through every word.

"But it's not like I'm ever gonna sell those two," he said adamantly. "They mean everything to me and they're part of my future breeding and training program, along with the work I do with farmers and their existing dogs. But that means capital investment, which I don't have, not to mention time."

"How long does it take to train a pup?"

"Twelve to eighteen months for the basics, but if you hold on to them another year or so, that's where the price and the personal satisfaction skyrockets. It means a slower turnover and all the associated costs of that, but it's the way I want to go. I want to provide the best-trained dogs, not just numbers. I also need to be competing, something I haven't done much of since I was a teenager. And I need good quality kennelling if I want to breed and provide a live-in retraining service."

I took a moment to study him, unable to keep a silly grin from my face.

He frowned. "What?"

"Nothing. I'm impressed." I truly was. Talking about his dogs and the plans he had, Zach had come alive, vibrating with excitement and enthusiasm. "You've got this all planned out in your head. You know exactly what you need to do."

He gave a dismissive shrug. "It's hardly running a station or piloting a commercial airli—"

I smooshed his lips between my fingers. "Don't you fucking dare. I think you're amazing."

He gave a soft huff. "It's not that big of a deal, but it's all I've ever wanted to do. But to be successful, it's gonna take time and money I don't have."

"Maybe not right away," I agreed. "Do you have a business plan?"

He shook his head. "I did kind of have one, but that's when I thought I'd be able to use Lane Station as my base. Dad had even floated the idea of borrowing off him to finance the start-up. Clearly, that's no longer an option. It's my own fault. I shouldn't have relied on him *or* the station. On top of all that, I left with nothing much to show in the bank for ten years working there. Dad paid us the minimum because of our trustee standing. We were eligible for a percentage profit share through that, but I always left mine in there to accrue rather than risk spending it. God knows what'll happen to it now." He rolled his eyes.

"Aren't you still entitled to that?" I protested, outraged on his behalf. "Surely your dad can't simply refuse to pay you out?"

He shrugged. "I'm not sure. He's a canny bastard. I'm sure he has it covered."

"You need to get legal advice."

He stared at me, then nodded, like the thought hadn't occurred to him. "You know, you're right. Maybe I will. Either way, a year is long enough to be couch-surfing in Holden's cottage. I need to get myself sorted, although it's not like I've got a bunch of other skills to put to use."

I almost choked. "You don't . . . what? Zach, if there's one thing I've learned about shepherds over the last year, it's that you guys are like the fucking multi-tool of the farming world."

Zach huffed out a laugh. "A multi-tool?"

"Hear me out. There is nothing you guys can't put your minds and hands to. Every one of you is part mechanic, part veterinarian, part builder, part plumber, part engineer, part tourism operator, part nurse, part doctor, part athlete, part search and rescue heroes, and some of you are even part frickin' porn stars." I eyed him pointedly and he laughed. "How the hell do us mere mortals compete with that?"

He rolled over and planted a kiss on my mouth. "Porn star, huh? I'll take it. But you're nuts."

"No, I'm not," I said in my best don't-fuck-with-me tone. "I'm in awe of what you can do, Zach, and you need to start believing in yourself a bit more. That's also something I've noticed about shepherds. The life you guys lead is such a closed shop. It's solitary in lots of ways; even as part of a team you're all half-freaking hermit. But that means you stop seeing yourselves clearly. Seeing who you are and what you're capable of."

Zach had fallen quiet, his serious eyes intent on mine, his face pale in the moonlight.

I tapped my finger to his chest. "*You* are capable of doing anything you set your mind to with your dogs. Of that, I'm sure. And if your experiences with your dad and Holden taught you anything, I hope it was that you're a survivor, Zach. You're determined and self-reliant, and when you want something, I can't imagine you letting a bit of fear or disappointment or heartache get in your way. That puts you miles ahead of most people. If your old business plan has to be mothballed, so what? Draw yourself up a new one. It's clear this is your passion, Zach. So why not pull out all the stops and give yourself a chance of making it a reality? I—"

"Shh." Zach's fingers pressed against my lips. "Enough." The moonlight caught the glint of tears brimming in his eyes and my chest squeezed tight.

"Oh shit. I'm so sorry. I didn't mean to—"

"I said hush." Zach studied me from a heartbeat away, a deep frown on his brow and those shiny eyes. "Who are you, Luke Nichols?" He leaned in and ran his nose along my jawline and then up into my hair. "Every time I think I have a handle on you, I find another angle, another layer."

He paused in front of my face, his lashes beating once, twice. Then he smiled and warmth lit up my chest. "Maybe the things you said are true. Maybe some are more wishful than anything else. But you're right about a couple of things. I've been wallowing in my sad story—"

"I *never* said that."

"I know." He held up a hand. "But I think maybe that's what I've been doing. And you're right about another thing. I've always looked at Holden and seen this incredibly capable guy. Someone I admire and aspire to be like. I just never thought that maybe I'm that guy too."

I smiled and brushed my nose against his. "Down to your cute little toes."

He swallowed another smile and nodded. "Well, all right then. Maybe I *can* do more than I think. Maybe it's only me who's been stopping me. Maybe, *probably,* I'll have to start slower than I want. But I could at least start, right? If I don't, nobody else is going to."

I didn't have any words, and even if I did, they wouldn't have made it past the lump in my throat.

Zach cradled my face and kissed me soundly. "Thank you. I've got a lot to think about."

I stared into those earnest eyes and felt myself falling.

CHAPTER FOURTEEN

Zach

I TUCKED MY HEAD AGAINST LUKE'S CHEST, UNABLE TO HOLD ON to the intense emotion in those penetrating blue eyes, like I might disappear under their scrutiny and lose myself completely. There was something raw and acutely painful about his insights—like he'd peeled the skin from my bones and taken a peek at the parts of me I worked so hard to hide, even from myself.

The excuses I'd made over the last year.

The reasons to keep waiting, but for what? *Why* was I waiting? For my father to change his mind? For that reversal to somehow rescue me from the hard decisions?

Well, fuck that.

I wasn't sure I'd even want it to. *Nothing* could undo what had happened the previous year. It could be patched, maybe. But there was something irrevocable in what had occurred. Something that forever changed things in my relationship with my family, with my parents.

I hated every part of what had happened, everything except

knowing I had a safe haven to retreat to in Miller Station. But I'd been licking my wounds for long enough.

And Luke had seen that in me. Seen it and been brave enough to lift it into the light. Maybe he recognised things from his own experience after losing Callie.

Half of me wanted to fuck him into the mattress for being that perceptive, and for having that level of faith that I could achieve what I hoped to. The other half of me wanted to run as fast as I could in the opposite direction because I didn't *want* to be seen. Not by a man again. Particularly a man I liked. A man whose opinion, for some reason, seemed to matter. Like Holden's had. But especially I didn't want to be *seen* by Luke—a man who was blithely crossing every line I'd drawn in the sand to protect my heart like they weren't even there.

The room became suddenly small, my bed even smaller. I couldn't breathe.

"Anyway." I slid quickly from between the sheets. "You need to get going before anyone misses you."

He blinked in surprise but I ignored it, thrusting his clothes toward him as he swung his feet onto the floor. He stared at them for a second like he couldn't quite believe what was happening, and I didn't blame him.

"Thanks for *coming*," I teased. "I had a good time." For some regretful reason, I decided to add a saucy wink, which surely put the *i* in ridiculous, and then shot him a sunny smile I didn't feel and opened the window. I then stood alongside, making it clear the timing wasn't negotiable.

He looked a little stunned but then took the clothes from my hands and started to dress. Watching him, I fought the urge to simply rip them off his body once again. Tell him to get back in that bed and maybe cuddle me a little longer. Because that would be such a smart thing to do, right?

Finally dressed, he blocked my attempt to sidestep his approach, cupped my face in his hands, and kissed me . . . thoroughly . . . the zing threading all the way down my spine and into my balls, adding a little peppery oomph to my dick along the way. "And yes—" He ran his thumbs over my hot cheeks. "—that was indeed a *good* time."

I'd have said he was taking the piss, but his expression was deadly serious.

"Can I maybe call you or text?"

I jumped to answer, "I don't think that's a good idea. Last night was fun, but it didn't change anything." *Liar.*

He gave a slow nod, but I didn't miss the slight sting that registered in his eyes at my words. "Of course," he said evenly. "It's your call."

"Not that I don't appreciate your help—I mean . . ." I fumbled. "You know, helping me to see . . . well, encouraging me, I guess. Because I do. Appreciate it. But that doesn't mean we should . . . that I want . . ." I hesitated, and Luke waited, his expression a mask. We both knew what happened from here on would be down to my next few words.

So, what the fuck did I want? I wanted Luke to go. To not be a complication in my life. I wanted him to stay. I wanted this to be it between us. I wanted as much of him as I could get.

What eventually came out of my mouth was as much of a surprise to me as to Luke, judging by his crooked smile. "Maybe we could, you know, play things by ear?" It sounded so sensible and solved absolutely nothing. "Like if we happen to randomly run into each other and we're, I don't know . . ."

"In the mood?" he offered.

I pointed a finger at him. "Exactly."

"Or maybe you find yourself in town one evening and you want to . . . drop by?"

I nodded. "Or maybe you're dropping some guests at the station?"

"Excellent point." A sly smile stole over his face. "So, *if* we happen to find ourselves in that kind of handy proximity, then, I don't know, maybe one of us could text?"

I made a fair impression of a nodding bobblehead. "Precisely. Just check in and see how the other one is fixed, right? No pressure. No plans. Keep it . . . casual."

"Casual." He seemed to be running the word through his brain, but there was a quirk to his lips that I couldn't read. "Right."

Relief and something like eager anticipation coursed through me and then I remembered. "What about other people?"

He frowned. "Other people?"

I winced. "*Seeing* other people? What if you meet someone else . . . what if you and Doug—"

"I'm not *seeing* Doug," Luke clarified. "At least not as anything other than a friend. Would it be a problem if I was?"

Hell, yeah, it would. "I—" I hesitated, considering him for a moment. "Probably," I admitted. "I'm not . . . I mean, I don't . . . I guess it didn't occur to me that you might—"

"I'm not and I won't," he assured me. "Not while you and I are doing whatever it is we're doing. You?"

I nodded. "The same. Although for me, that's kind of a given. My social calendar has been kind of non-existent for a while."

He grinned. "Lucky me."

I flipped him off. "So, we're agreed then?"

"Agreed. I'll definitely be looking forward to our future . . . liaisons." He winked, and that was most definitely not a flutter that ran through my belly.

I leaned in and whispered against his lips, "You make it sound so dirty."

He whispered back, "I try."

I pulled away without kissing him. "You need to go." I glanced down at his still bare feet. "But let's risk the front door where there's no prickle weed."

He winced. "My feet will be forever indebted." And he followed me out of the bedroom, getting all kinds of handsy with my bare arse in the process.

I unlocked the cottage door and peered up toward the homestead. My deck had an unobstructed view of the front door, the wraparound veranda, and Holden and Gil's bedroom window. There was no one in sight.

I turned back around. "All cle—"

Luke's hard kiss stole the rest and all my good intentions flew out the window with it. I fell into his arms and kissed him back, swallowing his hum of pleasure as our bodies slotted together like puzzle pieces. Two nights together and we were already in sync, running like a well-oiled machine. Go figure.

The kiss lingered and grew tender, too tender. I wriggled free and locked eyes. "Luke, I can't . . ." I drew a deep breath and stepped away. He didn't try to stop me. "I like you. But I need to keep this simple."

He studied me for a moment and then nodded. "Understood."

"Thank you." I heard my words and huffed in disbelief. "I seem to be saying that a lot lately."

He chuckled. "Well, there's a lot about me to be thankful for, right?"

"I hadn't noticed," I shot back, but appreciated his attempt to lighten the mood as I checked the homestead once again and then gave him a gentle shove through the open door.

As I watched him leave in stealth mode, I had to smile. For a tall guy, Luke's loping gait had the elegant quality of a big cat stalking its prey, much like the experience of the man in bed.

I thought of our agreement and sighed.

Casual, huh?

Six letters that spelled nothing but regret.

Three days later

"Jojo, come away. *Come away.*" I whistled and watched Jojo move to the right, then turned my attention to Nina. "Nina, come bye," I called up the steep face of the range that ran all the way up to the newly named Holden's Castle—the rock fort with its amazing views across the glacial valley that housed Miller Station. Nina immediately swung left, and the three merinos straightened course and headed for the pen where I stood holding the gate open.

Holden had insisted I set up a competition-style circuit in the large holding paddock close to the woolshed. In a heading trial, a shepherd had to move three stock through a variety of obstacles, and the best dogs were sensitive to the smallest nuance of their owner's command. To have any chance of winning, the stock needed to be worked with a delicate touch. Three sheep provided the most challenging combination for the dogs because three tended to split off into a two-and-one scenario, making them hard to move as one unit.

In addition to the pens, I'd cobbled together a couple of gates: Two short sections of fence stood in a line with a gap between them that the sheep had to pass through. A bridge constructed from a raised dirt platform with ramps on both approaches and fences on the side. A pegged lane they had to pass along. A shedding ring where the dog had to separate one or two sheep from the rest. And a pen or yard.

All I had at my disposal to get the sheep successfully through all the obstacles and penned in a time-limited run was my heading dog Jojo, my voice, my whistle, and my shepherd's stick. But for Nina, the huntaway competitions were all about driving the stock up a hill in either as straight a line as possible or in a set zig-zag hunt.

And I'd had a ton of success with both forms, although I hadn't done much the last few years. Jojo had several South Island titles and two back-to-back National Championships, and Nina had four South Island and one national title. I didn't usually train them together, but occasionally I liked to test them as a unit the same way they worked on the station.

With Jojo coming up behind them, the approaching merinos clocked me standing with my hand on the open gate of the pen and veered off course.

"Jojo, stand. Nina, speak."

Jojo froze while the huntaway's deep bark echoed through the valley and the merinos hesitated, eyed up the source of all the noise, debated the nuisance factor, and then corrected course.

"Nina, quiet."

The huntaway fell silent.

"Jojo, walk up."

Jojo slowly crept forward and the sheep moved closer to the open pen. Almost there. But when the lead ewe reached the open gate, she saw something she didn't like—who knew what—and came to an abrupt halt with a look on her prissy little face that clearly said, *Oh, hell no.* She immediately turned to stare down Jojo who responded in kind, freezing position with one paw in the air.

"Nina, stand," I warned, as the huntaway looked ready to offer her kennel mate some assistance.

Nina dropped to the ground.

Meanwhile, back at the O.K. Corral, the front merino was stamping her foot at my border collie. Jojo eased her paw to the ground and took another excruciatingly slow step forward.

The merino stamped her foot again—and if sheep could narrow their gaze, she did an admirable job—and the two animals eyeballed each other.

Jojo took another step and the merino snorted dismissively, then turned and gave me the stink eye.

With one hand fixed on the gate as per rules, and the other holding my shepherd's stick out to the side in an attempt to discourage any of them from bolting past, all I could do was rely on Jojo to finish the job.

She crept forward another step, and then another. The lead ewe studied the challenge, calculated the odds, and opted to fight another day, leading the other two sheep nonchalantly into the pen as if that had been her plan all along.

I swung the gate closed, stopped the timer on my phone, and released the dogs. Seconds later I was being circled and set upon with much enthusiasm and wagging of tails. But it was the slow clap from the direction of the gate at the bottom of the hill that drew all my attention.

Luke.

An unexpected thrill ran up my spine at the sight of him dressed in that sexy damn flight suit. I'd heard the chopper but hadn't expected to see him in person. He was leaning on the gate, his boot resting on the bottom rail, and wearing a broad smile that was all mine.

I offered a casual wave—there was that word again—as if I'd known he was there all along, and he waved back. Meanwhile, the dogs were already halfway down the hill to greet him like some long-lost friend. Which in some ways, he was.

Luke visited the station often enough for all the dogs to know he was welcome, and I couldn't stop the smile on my face as he opened the gate, and then immediately got down on his knees so they could slobber their delight all over his fancy flight suit, and generally make a nuisance of themselves.

I called to both of them, "Get in."

They ran back and tucked behind my legs.

"Sorry about that." I set the sheep free and watched them scurry down the hill, bleating their indignance.

"It was me who opened the gate," Luke replied, clearly unbothered by the doggy mauling he'd received. "I know the drill."

The comment brought a smile to my face. Gotta like a man who gets silly with your dogs.

I made my way down the hill toward Luke, all the while trying to suck my tongue back into my mouth from where it dangled in the dust somewhere around my feet, because damn, the man looked good. Too good. Almost better than I remembered, and I remembered a fair bit, having beaten off in my shower to his image most mornings and nights since he'd left my bed three days ago.

Standing there, leaning on my gate, looking more delicious than anyone had a right to, that cheeky-as-shit smile promised a hundred dirty ways to get me off without breaking a sweat. Not that I was going to tell him that. Or accept the unspoken offer that twinkled in his eyes.

I wasn't.

"What are you doing here?" I eyed him up and down like he was taking up too much space on this thirty-five thousand-acre station.

"Delivering guests. I saw you as I flew in." He glanced up the hill. "That was pretty impressive, not to mention fascinating. Maybe you can explain it to me one day."

"I'll add it to the list of all the other things I don't have time for." I ignored his answering frown and watched as Jojo and Nina began circling his legs looking for attention, the traitors.

"Aw, now you've hurt my feelings." Luke dropped both hands and began absently scratching their ears. Dammit, but he was a nice guy.

"I highly doubt that." I passed through the gate and locked it, turning to find his heated gaze roaming my shirtless chest, all the way down to the old training jeans that hung off my hips. He looked up with a wolfish grin in place. "I hope you've got sun cream on."

I rolled my eyes. "About a litre, give or take." I pushed back the wide-brimmed cowboy-style hat that I favoured for training and took a long draught of water from the bottle sitting in the shade of the gatepost.

"Good. Gotta protect all that pale, beautiful Irish skin." He ran a finger down the slope of my shoulder, drawing goosebumps. "Yes, very . . . slick."

I arched an unimpressed brow and clumsily recapped the water bottle. The man had a way of unsettling me every goddammed time. "What do you want, Luke?" I leaned against the gate and his gaze licked fire down my body. "In case you haven't noticed, I'm busy."

"So, I see." Those blue eyes darkened. "And can I just say I love the hat? It's very . . . cowboy." He licked his lips. "Do you have any idea how fucking sexy you look right now?"

My heart banged in my throat and heat raced into my cheeks. I tugged off the offending hat and ran the back of the water bottle over my forehead before squinting at the sun and returning the hat reluctantly to my head. "Very fucking practical is what it is," I countered, grabbing my blue-check shirt from the gate and slinging it over my shoulder. "And in case you missed it the first time, what do you want, Luke?" I gathered the dogs and started walking toward the kennels.

After a few seconds and a whistle of approval for my arse, which I absolutely did not smile or blush at, Luke ran to catch up. "What I don't want is to upset you."

And damn if that wasn't the perfect thing to say.

"I was *checking in*." He ran in front of me and started walking backwards so we were face to face about a metre apart. "Remember? As per our agreement about finding ourselves geographically . . . available." He added a lick of his lips that I absolutely did not pay any attention to as I tried to sidestep him and failed because he parried too well.

"You're an idiot." But it was hard not to smile, and Luke immediately grinned in return.

"Aw, come on. Tell me you're not pleased to see me." He slid back alongside and tipped my hat back to look into my eyes.

I jammed it back in place and muttered, "I'm not pleased to see you." Shame about the smile.

Luke laughed and elbowed me gently. "You're a godawful liar."

Truth.

We wandered the rest of the way along the dusty track in a comfortable silence until Hellboy and Thor picked up our scent and started howling. They were the only two dogs left behind, while the others shifted the three hundred head of Angus the station ran alongside the merinos. Cattle were not on Hellboy or Thor's favourites list, and the feeling was mutual. Sometimes it was easier to leave them behind, and Holden had clearly decided it was one of those days.

"Anyone else around?" Luke's gaze swept the buildings and pens.

"No. They're all out on the south field, except for Gil."

"You're not with them?" Luke enquired as the kennel roofs came into view and the barking intensified. Set back against the shelter belt, the tall trees offered day-long shade and wind protection, and the raised kennels allowed for good air circulation.

I shook my head. "I took the afternoon off so I could get some training done before muster. I've, um . . ." I hesitated about telling him and then kicked myself for thinking it mattered. "So, I might've entered a dog competition in a couple of months." I started through the door of the shed housing the dog supplies, but Luke pulled me back around to face him.

"A competition?" He arched a brow.

I sighed. "Yes. Don't make a big deal of it. I talked to Holden and he's happy for me to squeeze in a few when I can. Said it's good for the station's rep as well."

A slow smile spread over Luke's face. "Wow. That's great."

I pulled free and went inside. "Yeah, well, you can take that smug look off your face. It'll likely be a disaster. I haven't competed for years." I whistled for Hellboy and Thor to shut up and they obliged, kind of. Then I grabbed a few biscuits and headed back out to the kennels with Luke following like an annoying puppy.

"You won't know until you try, right?" he said, and I almost jumped when his finger trailed down the bare skin of my back, goosebumps popping in its wake.

Jojo and Nina were already waiting inside their kennels. I threw them both a couple of biscuits and refilled their water before shutting them in. Then I chucked a biscuit each to the other two and turned to find Luke right there, leaning against the kennels, watching me.

"Maybe you'll let me watch you compete one day." His face was serious but the incredulity on mine must've been obvious because he winced. "But only if that's okay. I wouldn't want to upset your routine or anything. Maybe we could *all* watch?"

"All?" I croaked, staring at him in horror. No one except my father and Julian had ever watched me compete, and my father's purpose was solely so he could set me right on all my mistakes.

He frowned. "Is there a reason why not?"

I swallowed hard, unable to come up with any better reason than *not over my dead body*, and so I settled for, "Maybe . . . one day."

"I'll look forward to it." Luke's gaze swept over my body once again and he stepped in close, reaching for my shirt and pulling it gently from where it still hung over my shoulder.

The look in his eyes sent a shiver the length of my body, but he didn't come any closer.

"Tell me to stop." He leaned in and put his lips next to my ear. "Tell me to stop and I'll leave right now." He pulled back to watch my face.

Stop. My mind framed the word, but my lips remained closed, except for that part where they opened to let an embarrassing murmur float between us that sounded an awful lot like yes.

Okay. Just call me cheap and be done with it.

Luke smiled and then leaned back in to suckle on the soft lobe of my ear. "You are the sexiest fucking man I've seen for days." He kissed down my throat and his warm lips on my hot dry skin lit a fire in my balls. "At least since Saturday night in your cottage."

I huffed softly and angled my neck so he could kiss down the slope to my shoulder tip. "Fuck. Me. That feels good."

He chuckled. "I feel obliged to point out that bears no resemblance at all to stop." He kissed across my dusty clavicle to the other shoulder, his fingers working the buttons of my jeans.

Somewhere at my back, Jojo whined, and I opened my eyes to find all four dogs staring at us with cocked heads, clearly curious about these strange happenings in their domain.

I grabbed Luke's hand. "Not here." I tilted my head toward our audience, and he snorted with laughter.

"I think I just wilted."

I groped him through his flight suit and felt his cock jerk in my hand. "I think I can resuscitate you." I grabbed my shirt and tugged him toward the woolshed. "Hurry up. Gil's a sneaky shit." He nuzzled into my neck and I shrugged him off. "Quit that. Someone might see."

"He's busy with the new guests," Luke rightly pointed out.

But I didn't trust the psychologist for a second. He had a sixth sense when it came to ferreting out trouble.

I dragged open the weighty door to the woolshed and bundled Luke inside. The second the door closed on us, he walked me back against Gil's freshly painted walls and removed my hat before pinning my hands above my head and bringing our bodies flush, his cock solid alongside mine.

"See." He wriggled his hips to highlight the fact. "It's a miracle."

I laughed and he ran his nose up the side of my face and whispered, "Jesus, you smell good."

I huffed in disbelief. "I smell of sweat, eau de canine, sunscreen, dust, and sheep dags. But hey, whatever turns you on."

"*You* turn me on, Zach." He brought those warm lips to mine and kissed me. "Any which way you happen to come. And speaking of coming . . ." A wicked smile played on his lips as he finished unbuttoning my jeans. He had them down around my ankles in seconds, with my briefs following right behind. "You have such a pretty cock." He gave said cock a firm tug and my head fell back against the wall.

"Not pretty," I grumbled into his mouth as he kissed me once again. "Substantial, enormous, hefty."

He snort-laughed and pressed his forehead to mine. "Luscious, delicious, succulent, and the prettiest cock I've ever seen." He stared intently into my eyes. "Perfect, in fact." Then he smiled at my blush and kissed it all the way from the dip at the base of my throat up to my cheeks. "So pretty in pink."

I was about to roll my eyes when suddenly he was gone, dropping to his knees and taking my aching cock all the way to the back of his throat before swallowing around it.

"Oh my god." I dropped my shirt and slammed my flat hand against the wall, trying not to thrust. "How do you do that?" The man had some serious skills, and it wasn't long before I was gritting my teeth and fighting off an orgasm. I wanted more of his hot, sweet mouth on me before I came. But Luke wasn't playing around, and I remembered where we were and how at any second Gil could barge in, maybe even with guests in tow on a tour.

The idea sparked a curious surge of anticipation that shocked me. It was quickly followed by another of mild panic, but that strange excitement remained and my cock jerked in Luke's mouth.

He looked up and the lewd sight of his swollen lips around my shaft was almost enough to send me over. He must've seen something in my expression because he pulled off with a pop and the filthiest look I'd ever seen. With his eyes still locked on mine, he ran his fingers around the head of my cock until they were glistening. When he pulled them away, a thin glimmering thread stretched between the two until it snapped. He licked a stripe up the slick pads, slid them behind my balls, and pressed a single fingertip into my hole.

"Argh . . . f-fuck." I banged my head against the wall and thrust my cock somewhere in the direction of Luke's face.

He met it with his open mouth, and I was again engulfed in tight, wet heat. A few thrusts of his fingers and long tight sucks later, and it was all over. I wrapped my hands around Luke's head and thrust into his mouth. He gagged but yanked my thighs closer for more, and on the next thrust, I emptied everything I had into his hot, clever mouth, shuddering with the waves of pleasure that barrelled through me.

It seemed to go on forever until Luke finally pulled off and I slid down the wall, my jelly legs splayed out in front of me.

Once I was down, Luke scrambled to his feet, unbuttoned his flight suit, and started jacking himself off.

"On me," I managed between gasps, and he moved to straddle my thighs, still working his cock. I wrapped my hand around his and watched transfixed as he quickly stroked himself, faster and faster, his hand flying. Then his rhythm stuttered, and he tensed for a second before leaning one hand against the wall and shooting his load over my face with a muffled grunt of satisfaction. And as the warm fluid dripped down my chin and onto my chest, I scooped it up and licked my fingers clean.

He grabbed my hand and sucked my fingers deep. Then he

pulled me to my feet and kissed me, his tongue darting through my mouth, lips swollen and slick with come, his and mine. That done, he pulled away, although still cradling my face, both of us a mess, and grinning like the idiots that we were.

"Well, damn, Mister Lane." He put on an awful cowboy drawl as he leaned in to lick my face clean. "I might just be able to get into this farming gig after all."

I chuckled and pushed him off, reaching for my shirt to dry my face. "That's a big call based on a blowjob in the woolshed. Albeit an excellent blowjob."

He tipped an imaginary hat. "Why, thank you."

"Mind you, it's not the first time this building has played host to similar shenanigans. Holden and Gil have supplies stashed all over the station. Ask me how I know. How we *all* know."

His eyes flew wide. "Nope. I don't want to know. That's too weird."

I snorted. "Right? Although I have to say, I feel like I got a little of my own back this afternoon."

His smile faded. "Is that part of what this is for you? Evening the score?"

I blinked. "What? No. Of course not. I only meant that I'll be able to swap disturbing images of them for sexy ones of us. Way more interesting."

"Oh." Luke's shoulders relaxed. "In that case, you're welcome."

I thought about what he'd asked and couldn't pretend I hadn't wondered the same thing at times. "What about you?" I waited, feeling absurdly uneasy about his answer.

"Absolutely not." He hoisted my jeans and briefs back into place and carefully buttoned me in. Then he cupped my cheek. "You are definitely nothing to do with payback. The furthest thing from it."

His words relieved me in a way I didn't want to think about too much. "Good to know." I helped him back into his flight suit and dusted him off. "Thanks for *checking in* with me, geographically speaking."

He put my hat back on my head, then tipped it back to kiss me. "Until next time, then."

I returned his happy smile. "Until next time." *Lord, help me.*

The minute the door closed behind him, I sank onto a bench a few metres away and reminded myself that this thing between us was all about sex, nothing more.

Admittedly, great sex.

No denying that.

But in the end, just sex.

Luke was a good man and an outstanding fuck.

Didn't mean I was getting feelings for him.

CHAPTER FIFTEEN

Four weeks later

Luke

"Harder!" Zach's heels dug into my butt to emphasise his point.

After a month of regular sex with the feisty man, my body had more bruises than an MMA fighter. Not that I was complaining. I changed my angle and slammed into him exactly as ordered.

"Oh fuck, yes!" He grabbed me around the neck and dragged me down for a kiss, grunting into my mouth with every thrust I made while his other hand sneaked between our slick bodies to wrap around his cock.

A few thrusts later and his lips left mine, his head slamming back into the pillow as he arched and came with a jerk and a shout, clutching me to him like a life preserver. Didn't matter to me. I was already there, following him over just seconds later, the orgasm roaring through me like a truck, my eyes locked on Zach's face as he watched me fly with soft eyes, a sated smile, and a thousand unspoken questions dangling between us.

I shuddered with a final wave of intense pleasure and then collapsed on top of Zach's slick body, both of us drenched in sweat and gasping for air. The heat of late summer might've slipped rapidly into a cool mountain autumn, but whatever bed Zach and I came together in, we tore up the sheets until they smoked with scorching no-strings-attached sex that was anything but no-strings, at least on my part.

Because I *wanted* strings.

Too many strings.

I wanted *all* the fucking strings.

And therein lay a big problem.

Almost five weeks fucking each other's brains out and I still couldn't get enough of him. Five weeks of talking and laughing and learning about this complicated, beautiful enigma of a man. Five weeks of texting and planning and sneaking around to get as much time with each other as we possibly could. Five frustrating weeks of wanting more than sex with him but being too scared to ask. Five weeks of pretending that I wasn't falling for the man who'd wormed his way under my skin and was taking up far too much real estate in my head.

Five weeks of some of the best sex of my life.

Cue the highlight reel.

Having my arse owned by Zach in Miller Station's impressive haybarn after discreetly slipping away from Gil's one-year-anniversary party of arriving at the station. Our fucking had been accompanied by the bellowing of two curious Angus bulls who'd been penned outside. We were lucky not to have been discovered by Holden who went looking to see why the creatures were making such a fuss.

If it hadn't been for Zach's hand over my mouth as he kept fucking me with renewed gusto into my prickly and decidedly uncomfortable makeshift mattress, my laughter would've been a dead giveaway. As it was, when we were done, we had to check each other carefully for incriminating hay-based evidence before we could safely return to the house five minutes apart.

I'd spent the rest of the night mulling what appeared to be a change in Zach's earlier fear of being discovered, to what could only be described as excitement at the possibility. Who knew I had a budding exhibitionist on my hands? Not me. Not that I was complaining. I just needed to figure out how to fan that little flame safely.

Then there was the evening I owned Zach's arse in return at midnight in the bed of his ute, in a park alongside a rippling Lake Tekapo with moonlight washing over every curve of his body as he keened and cried out into the night.

Then we'd fucked for two hours in a motel room in Tekapo. The bathroom of a pub in Twizel. The back of the Wild Run hangar one Sunday when he'd dropped by, knowing I was alone and catching up on paperwork.

And on nearly every surface in my bungalow, in every manner imaginable. There was no room I could walk into that didn't have a memory of something Zach and I had done there, even if it had only been kissing and making out, because those were quickly becoming some of my favourite times in his arms. The times I got to have him, not simply his body, the strings almost visible between us if you looked hard enough.

"Another stellar encounter," Zach huffed into my ear, wincing as I eased my cock free of his arse and rolled off him and into a warm patch of sunlight bathing the sheets. Autumn had the Mackenzie in its grip and the sweat on our bodies would rapidly cool. "Man, I hate that part," he grumbled.

I stretched over to kiss him, then fell back, dealt with the condom, and blew out a long sigh. "I reckon your arse has worn a good centimetre off my dick in the last month."

He chuckled and turned onto his side, grabbing my cock and stretching it out like he was measuring it. "Mmm, you could be right. Another few months and there might only be a stub left. You better hope it lasts until you leave, or I might have to consider my options."

I knew he was only joking, but the reminder that my time in Oakwood had an expiry date and that he would likely move his attentions elsewhere dealt a sharp blow to my heart.

Seemingly oblivious, Zach stretched out beside me and slung an arm over my still-heaving chest. "You need to up your gym time, old man. Just as well you're not coming on muster. You'd never make it up Widow's Walk without a tailwind. Even then I'm not sure—"

"Shut up." I hit him with a pillow and then kissed him. "*You're* the reason I can't get to the damn gym more often. I've been too busy up your arse, or you in mine. Who knew a guy could have so many appointments in Oakwood in a month?"

Zach grimaced. "Yeah, Holden gave me a long sideways look yesterday when I said I was coming into Oakwood again to meet with the bank and then a 'client.'" He made air quotes and set about cleaning us both up. "Imagine his reaction if he found out the *client* was actually you."

I pulled him on top of me and kissed him soundly. "Or the nature of the truly excellent service that you provide said client. Finest in the Mackenzie Basin."

That made him laugh. "Well, it helps that you pay promptly."

"I always pay my debts." I kissed him again, softer, longer, until the sweet taste of him coated my tongue. "Now tell me what the bank thought of your new business plan?"

Zach groaned and rolled onto his back. "Pretty much what we expected. They liked the plan and the fact I'm only asking for enough to sort out some better kennelling and to invest in a couple of good dogs to start my own line. But neither of those come cheap, especially the dogs. The bank wants more evidence that I can produce the quality of training necessary to fetch those prices I bandied around their office before they'll commit to anything."

I rolled onto my stomach and perched on my elbows. "But you knew that was coming, right? We talked about it. But at least they liked your plan, and that's a huge step forward. Now, you have to do what you do best and prove you can deliver what you said you could. Have you talked to Holden yet?"

Zach pulled a face. "I wanted to talk to the bank first and see if I had a real shot. Going ahead means attending more competition trials *and* doing well in them, *plus* buying and retraining a couple of dogs to sell on at a good price while still working for Holden. I didn't want to raise the subject if it didn't have a chance of getting off the ground. I'll be tied to the station for at least another year, probably two. And that's if I can even find a couple of promising dogs whose owners will let me buy them. Oh, and pay for those dogs somehow as well. And they won't be cheap. It also doesn't solve my problem of not having enough time."

"Is that all?" I teased, which probably wasn't the best response, and Zach rolled his eyes. I leaned down and kissed him. "I get that it's going to be hard, so why not talk to Holden? Maybe you can negotiate something."

He shook his head and stared up at the ceiling. "I can't. He needs me."

I turned his face back to mine. "Does he? Think about it. He might've been stretched before you arrived last year, but the station was managing, and it still would be if you hadn't come. From what I understand, the station hasn't employed more than four shepherds for a while and owing to how hard it is to find one who can just slot in, Holden had no plans to change that. You were a welcome surprise."

Zach's green eyes turned flinty and his demeanour cooled. "Are you saying he's only doing me a favour?"

I bit back a smile, guessing it wouldn't go down well. "Smooth your hackles, gorgeous. I know Holden considers himself lucky to have you and relies on your experience. All I'm saying is that maybe there's some wiggle room there."

Zach looked . . . thoughtful.

I risked pressing a little more. "Are you sure your reluctance isn't simply because you feel you owe it to Holden and Emily after what they did for you?"

Zach huffed. "Of course I do. They gave me a home, Luke. I can never repay that."

I took his hand and brushed my lips over his knuckles. "Yes, they did. But Holden would also understand how important this is to you. He's your best friend, Zach."

"I know he is," Zach murmured, running his fingers through my hair. "He'd do anything to help me out, and that's part of why I don't want to ask. I won't put him in that position." His hand dropped and his eyelids fluttered shut. "Goddamn my father. This is such a mess."

I stroked his cheek. "Two things. One, at what point do you start claiming something for yourself and stop worrying about making other people happy?"

"But—"

"And two." I put a finger to his lips. "How about you let Holden make his own decisions?"

"Ugh." Zach screwed his eyes tightly shut. "I hate it when you're right."

I snorted. "What a surprise."

"Okay." He kept his eyes closed, and with a frown on his face, he looked like he was thinking it through. "But even if Holden agrees to negotiate my hours down, I'll need to start paying rent on the cottage. I can't stay for free if I'm only part-time. And I still have to buy dogs and sort kennelling. Doing all that on practically zero savings is going to be hard. I can sell my bike, I guess, but still."

I pried one of his eyes open with my fingers. "Methinks you're trying to find all the reasons why you can't do it."

He flicked the other eye open and rolled to face me. "I know. It just seems like . . . a lot."

I cradled his face and stared into those beautiful green eyes. "I have every faith that you'll find a way. But maybe you don't have to come up with all the answers on your own. Talk to Holden. Trust him, and maybe trust yourself. It doesn't have to happen tomorrow. One foot after the other, right?"

His gaze narrowed and he tapped the end of my nose. "Well, *methinks* you should take some of your own advice, mister. Have faith? Trust yourself? You don't have to do it alone? One foot after the other?" He pulled me down beside him and kissed me. "Stop finding all the reasons you can't have a life again. You've made a start, Luke. You came down here to stop putting obstacles in your own path, like booze, and bars, and men, and . . . well, men." He shrugged. "It was worth saying again."

I almost smiled but I was too blown away by him calling me on my shit. It wasn't something he'd ever done before, like it was part of his act of keeping me at a distance. But he was right. So fucking right.

"Callie's not going anywhere," he continued, shooting a quick glance at her photo on the dresser. "She's always here, right?" He tapped my chest and I nodded. "So that must mean she's waiting for you to take her on the next stage of your journey." He hesitated, those clear eyes searching my face, glinting like emeralds in the sunlight. "You know, Gil talks a lot about Callie." He fingered the band around my wrist. "About things she'd have loved to see or do on the station. But I've noticed you hardly mention her at all."

His words hit me like a gut punch, not because he was wrong, but because I hadn't considered anyone would care. I'd discovered early on in my grief that most people, even good friends, were happy for the awkward subject to be raised as little as possible. The fact that Zach had noticed and called me on it sent a wave of guilt through my chest.

I studied Zach's face, the soft concern in his eyes, the gentle set to his lips, the quiet way he waited, and something in my heart gave way. "I don't know how Gil does it," I admitted. "He's so much stronger than me. Every time I talk about her—*Callie*—I remember how badly I failed her."

Zach scooted across, bringing us eye to eye, but said nothing, just watched and waited.

I stroked his hair, feeling the run of tears on my cheeks. "I failed my own daughter, Zach. I missed out on so much. I wasn't there when she needed me. When they both needed me. And without Gil to talk to, someone who really understood, it was easier not to talk about her at all. I guess it became a habit." I sucked in a shaky breath and for once didn't shove all those messy feelings aside.

Zach ran his thumb under my eyes and brushed my lips with his. On and off. Just a reminder he was there.

I glanced over his shoulder at Callie's photo. *I'm sorry, baby. I'll do better.* "It's almost impossible to think about *her* and *not* immediately think about the day she died, like that's all she was," I choked out. "I know she was so much more than that one dreadful moment, but for a long time, I couldn't seem to hold her without holding that as well. It was too hard."

Zach's eyes softened and his voice dropped almost to a whisper. "I'm not religious in any way, and I sure as hell know nothing about losing a child, but I'm thinking Callie's larger spirit or essence or whatever you call it isn't tied to that one moment either. Watching you and Gil, it's clear there's no shortcut through grief. And if I had to guess, I'd say that maybe Callie's been waiting for you to be ready to find her again in more than just the day she died." He paused and colour flooded his cheeks, and when I didn't answer immediately, he quickly looked away. "Then again, what the fuck would I know?"

I yanked him back around and kissed him, hard. "More than you think." I warmed at the shy pleasure in his eyes. "And thank you."

His flush deepened. "For what?"

"For being you."

"Oh." He straightened, a half-smile on his lips. "Well, in that case, you're welcome."

We stared at each other until the silence thickened awkwardly and the room began to cool. So many questions remained unspoken between us. Feelings floating unnamed and ignored. I was sure Zach felt them too. I was equally sure he'd run like a rabbit if I gave voice to any one of them.

As if to prove me right, his eyes darted away and he threw the bed covers back. "I need to get the dogs back before they decide your sofa is a way better alternative to their kennel." He stood and held his hand out for me to take. "But I've got time for a shower first."

I let him help me to my feet but then tugged him into my arms. "Here's a thought. Why don't you stay the night instead? It's your day off tomorrow so you wouldn't have to leave early and we could . . . do something?" I grinned and nuzzled his neck. "Other than fuck, I mean, although I'm not averse to another round or two of that."

At my suggestion, that all-too-familiar skittishness appeared in Zach's eyes. It wasn't like he never stayed the night, but it was always reluctantly, a fact that was beginning to irritate me. Mostly he was armed with good excuses why he needed to go back to the station.

The first few times after our woolshed rendezvous, we'd simply fucked and said goodbye, although to be fair, no sex with Zach was ever *just* fucking. But the frequent return trips were exhausting, and Zach had started to stay over and leave early, like he'd done that very first time. It wasn't exactly terrible waking up with Zach in my arms and our legs tangled together, but he was always businesslike once he woke, and quickly on his way, not stopping for breakfast.

The sleepovers bothered Zach. That was clear. They blurred the lines and I got it. But I was beginning to dislike those early morning departures more and more. I hated how he changed from the sexy, chatty bundle of mischief in my arms when he arrived, and became this skittish, wary man who left my front door the next day.

I'd fallen for Zach in a big way, and I was pretty sure he'd guessed something was up. But the sheer depth of my feelings had caught me on the hop, a sign that my heart hadn't been scattered in the Havelock River along with Callie's ashes the year before, after all. Reassuring but scary as hell.

Because it created a very real problem. I desperately wanted to raise the possibility of exploring something more with Zach, but I wasn't at all sure he'd welcome the idea. I was almost positive he wouldn't. Still, if Zach didn't want to pursue anything more, then maybe it was time to call it a day before I risked getting hurt . . . *more* hurt. Because I wasn't at all sure my heart could take another hit after Callie.

Zach hedged, his gaze sliding off me to the window behind. "You don't have any dog food and I was going to train tomorrow."

I arched a brow. "You can't tell me that you don't carry some dog food in that Tardis of a ute you drive."

Zach's flush said it all.

"I thought so. And you'd still have the afternoon to train. But if you don't want to stay, that's up to you. I understand." *Only too well.*

He studied me for a moment, his expression unreadable, his gaze bouncing between me and the door like he was calculating the odds of his making it out before he did something he'd regret. Finally, he faced me, his expression resigned. "I'm not sure that spending more time together is a good idea. That's not what we were supposed to be about, Luke."

And there it was. My stomach dropped and I schooled my expression. "You're right." I released him and took a step back. "I crossed a line. Why don't you take the bathroom? I'll shower later." I made to leave the room, but he grabbed my wrist and pulled me back around.

"What *exactly* do you see us doing tomorrow?" He was studying me intently, chewing on that bottom lip like he did every time something was needling him—a tell I was pretty sure he didn't know he had.

My heart beat a little happy dance in my chest, but I kept my expression carefully neutral since there was no hiding the lingering wariness in Zach's eyes. "Whatever we feel like, I guess. A lazy morning, then maybe grab a coffee and go for a drive somewhere."

He arched a brow, a half-smile playing on his lips. "A drive?"

I huffed out a laugh. Like we both didn't spend half our lives in a vehicle of some description. "Okay, so I admit I haven't fully thought it out. I kind of figured you'd turn me down anyway."

The second eyebrow lifted to meet the first.

"But—" I held up a finger. "There is *one* thing I've been wanting to do ever since Doug recommended it, although that would have to be tonight, not tomorrow."

Zach's gaze narrowed and his tone was doubtful. "Doug?"

I grinned at the barest hint of jealousy. I knew Zach didn't like me talking about my friendship with Doug, but I never called him on it, taking it as a promising sign instead. "Yes, Doug."

Zach grunted something, which I ignored.

"He highly recommended I do the Mount John Observatory stargazing experience. World's biggest Dark Sky Reserve, right? Have you been?"

Zach blinked. "I live here, remember? I hardly need to pay for the privilege of looking at what I can see every night for free. Some nights on the tops of those mountains, the aurora can blow your fucking mind."

Oh. "Okay. I guess I didn't think that through." I tried not to let my disappointment show.

His eyes grew soft. "But no, I've never been to the observatory. Maybe I should, at least once in my life."

I brightened. "So, is that a yes? I'll give them a call."

He blinked. "You mean tonight?"

"Sure. Why not? It's not dark for a bit. We've got time." I saw the minute he gave in.

"Okay. But on one condition."

"Name it."

He threw me a crooked smile. "When we're done at the observatory, I get to show you *my* version of the night sky."

I cocked my head. "How could I possibly say no to that?"

I checked there was room on the tour, and then we both showered and dressed to ward off the much cooler—read bloody freezing—clear autumn night. Zach fed the dogs from a large container of food that magically appeared from his vehicle along with a decidedly red face, while I rustled us up some snacks and drinks from my meagre pantry. After that, we let the dogs out for a few rounds of the backyard before locking them in the laundry and throwing everything into the back of Zach's ute along with a heavy blanket and some cushions, which I thought were promising additions.

I'd organised to meet the tour at the observatory itself, rather than join the twenty-minute van trip from Tekapo. It meant Zach and I could begin phase two of the evening as soon as the tour was done.

As we pulled into the observatory car park, Zach chuckled. "You look as excited as a kid on a school trip."

"I am." I lifted my hand from where it had been resting on his thigh and took his hand instead. Surprisingly, he let me. "I love this kind of thing."

He grinned and shook his head. "You're a pilot. You must've seen some amazing skies."

I shrugged. "Not through a telescope. Besides—" I squeezed his hand. "—the company is everything."

He didn't look away, but he didn't say anything either, the burgeoning silence broken by the arrival of the tour company van that parked alongside. A half-dozen people climbed out and Zach cast a keen eye over every one of them before relaxing back in his seat. "No one local," he muttered, sounding relieved.

I felt a twinge of disappointment at his determination to keep us a secret, while at the same time acknowledging the whole evening could've been ruined if anyone had recognised him. You win some you lose some.

"Come on." I got out of the ute and beckoned him to follow. "Let's get this done so I can see what you have planned for later."

"Don't get too excited." He locked the ute and walked around to join me, looking like a wet dream in his soft-as-butter faded blue jeans, a long-sleeved black Henley, black beanie and scarf, black biker boots, and a black puffer jacket zipped to his chin. The outfit made his bright eyes pop and shine whenever the light caught them.

To say the air was crisp at the top of Mount John was putting it mildly. But at least the skies were clear. I rubbed my hands together to warm them up and then held one out for him to take. "No one here you know, right?"

He frowned at my hand, then up at me. I raised a brow, and after a few seconds, he shook his head and slid his hand into mine, threading our fingers together.

I tugged him close to my side. "Thank you."

He gave a soft huff. "You're an idiot." Then he shot me an almost-shy smile and if I hadn't been a goner for him before, that pretty much did it.

CHAPTER SIXTEEN

Luke

WE SPENT A LITTLE UNDER TWO HOURS OBSERVING SATELLITES, tracking a shooting star, listening to Māori legends, discovering new things about the Milky Way, the Southern Cross, and watching colours normally hidden from the naked eye come alive in long-exposure photographs taken through the massive telescopes.

I have to admit I spent more time watching Zach than looking at the stars, his uncensored expressions of wonder and delight had me wanting to bundle him into a dark corner and kiss him silly. I kept hold of his hand as much as humanly possible without handcuffing him to me. But perhaps more importantly, he hadn't tried to pull away, his attention fixed on our guide, his warm body pressed against my side. At one point, I'd slid an arm around his waist and for a short time, he even leaned into me.

To my surprise, he asked a ton of questions, and after the tour was finished, he and the guide had a long conversation about mustering, local cloud formations, weather, and a whole lot of things I had no clue about while I watched from a short distance away.

It didn't matter what they were talking about, I could've listened to Zach for hours. And it was then I realised that sex was never going to be enough for me again. Not with Zach. I wanted every part of him.

In the car park afterward, we held hands and stared at the sky, chatting as we waited for the tour van to finally leave. The minute they were gone, Zach turned and crowded me against the ute before taking my mouth in a hard kiss that quickly softened into something enticingly tender, something very boyfriend-like, very heart-stoppingly wonderful.

He licked into my mouth and hummed his pleasure, and it was hard not to hope it meant something more. My hands stole under his Henley and around his waist until I had an armful of the man I was failing to keep any distance from my heart.

When he finally pulled away, Zach cradled my face and pressed our foreheads together. "Thank you. That . . . that was amazing. I should've done it years ago." His eyes gleamed in the light from the observatory reception room. He looked so damn happy that for a mortifying moment, I was at risk of blurting something that would get me into all kinds of fucking trouble.

"Come on." He pushed me toward the passenger door. "It's my turn now."

We drove in comfortable silence. My hand found its way back onto Zach's thigh, and the fact he didn't protest made me ridiculously happy. Fifteen minutes later he made a left off the main road onto a dirt track and the ute made its way up one of the few low hills in the area.

I shot Zach a dubious look. "I hope we're not going to end a great night in a police cell for trespassing."

He chuckled. "Don't worry, I know the family. I came here a bit as a teenager." He hesitated, then shrugged. "I dated their daughter back in high school."

I choked on a surprised laugh. "I take it that was a passing phase."

He shot me an amused look. "It wasn't a phase at all, not really.

But it did a good job of keeping my dad's suspicions at bay. Not to mention, Cyndi's older brother was hot as hell, so there was that."

"Always a bonus." I almost bit my tongue as the ute lurched in and out of a decent-sized pothole. "So, you dated the daughter to drool over the son?"

Zach shrugged uncomfortably. "It wasn't quite like that. Cyndi was quick to pick up on my . . . preferences, shall we say."

That made me laugh. "Say it isn't so."

Zach rolled his eyes. "Kind of hard to hide the truth when things don't *happen* when they should."

"Oh." I grinned. "Enough said."

"Anyhoo—" Zach looked my way. "—Cyndi let me keep up the pretence for a while and we stayed good friends. I got to know her family quite well, and for the record, I don't think they were fooled one bit. Anyway, long story short, they don't mind me coming up here now and then if I'm in the area."

Zach wrestled the ute up the final section of the hill and onto the flattish top, the headlights revealing the black waters of a sizeable tarn with no more than a few ripples disturbing its surface. He brought the ute to a stop and jumped out. "Come on. Bring the goodies."

I grabbed the food and drink while Zach ferreted in the bed of the ute, pulling out a tarp and the blanket and cushions.

"This way." He led me toward a slight rise on the far side of the tarn, the looming black depths providing a watery reflection of the sparkling wonder above. Happy with his spot, he spread the tarp, positioned the cushions, and opened up the blanket. Then he made himself comfortable.

"Get down here." He patted the tarp, and I slid under the blanket and alongside his warm body with a canopy of stars over our head. His arm slipped around my shoulders and tucked me into his side, keeping the chilly edge of the night at bay.

Tekapo township glowed in the distance, while the lake in front bore a silvery sheen in the limited moonlight. But above us was where the action was taking place, a sky chock-full of starlight and galactic wonder. One look and my heart rate kicked up, or maybe it was simply the effect of being there with Zach, being in *his* orbit, his pull on my heart as strong as any planet to star up there.

"Wow." There really was nothing else to say.

"You're welcome." Zach pressed a kiss to my hair. "Technically, it might not be as good as what we saw at the observatory, or maybe even what we can see from the mountains behind the station, but I love it here."

I studied the sky and tried to remember what the guide had taught us. "Those are the Magellanic clouds we looked at through the scope, right?" I pointed to two small cloudy galaxies off to one side of the Milky Way.

"I think so," Zach agreed. "But I do know that's the Southern Cross." He pointed out the constellation, and from there we went turn and turn about identifying as many things as we could from what we'd learned that night. And when we were done, the mantle of silence that fell over the glistening tarn felt heavy enough to press our bodies into the earth and fuse our hearts with the stony soil.

After what seemed like forever, Zach's fingers threaded through my hair and his whispered voice came over my shoulder. "The sky feels bigger here than on the station with no mountains crowding the spaces. I've been here when the lake is this ethereal silver, like liquid mercury, like some kind of sci-fi portal to the stars. Like maybe you could dive in and swim with the galaxies."

I listened with my heart in my throat, not daring to move in case he stopped talking, thanking God when he didn't.

"Sometimes these mountains feel like they're alive, like they're watching me, waiting for me to click to what they're trying to tell me. Frustrated when I don't seem to get it. I feel part of something huge and important, and I never want to leave. But other times they feel like sentinels watching my life take one step at a time into oblivion, and it feels like the loneliest place in the world to live, and all I want to do is turn my back and run."

I let his words settle in my heart. Then I levered up on one elbow and stared down at him, brushing a lock of hair from his forehead. "You're such a romantic. I have to admit that it surprised me when I first realised that about you." I ran a finger between his brows to smooth the frown that appeared. "I guess I expected a practical country boy through and through."

He grinned. "Your stereotypes are showing. So, tell me, what did you find instead?"

I leaned in and kissed him long and slow, my mouth swallowing his soft murmurs of pleasure. "I found a man who reads about Egyptian pharaohs and Scottish clan wars, and who knows the difference between an IPA and APA."

Zach chuckled. "No one messes with my beer."

I grinned and cupped his face. "And I found a complicated, patient man with a soft heart and a strong will. Someone who has been through more than his fair share of heartache in life, and someone I admire."

He swallowed hard, his eyes shining in the starlight. "That's a big call, considering we hardly know each other."

The comment caught me off guard. "Do you truly believe we don't know each other? Jesus, Zach, I've been watching you for a year, thinking about you, listening to what people say about you, learning everything I can. But even if I hadn't, I wouldn't need to look past the way you love and treat your dogs and the fierce way they love you in return—the way *all* dogs love you. That tells me a ton about your heart and who you are as a man. And your reaction to everything that happened with Holden and then with your dad and family only goes to show how generous and resilient you are. Then there's the way you are . . . with me."

"With you?" His brows peaked. "We hardly got off on the right foot."

He was right about that. "True, but in this last month, I've learned so much more. I've learned that you're a generous lover, a kind man, and a loyal friend. There's a lot to like about all of that."

Zach scrutinised my face like he was looking for the lie that wasn't there. I waited for him to change the subject, or shut me down, or look away. But he didn't do any of those.

Instead, he said, "I think I know you pretty well too."

A tingle ran down my back. "Is that so?"

Zach traced a fingertip down my nose. "You are also a good man and a loyal friend. I know that from watching you with Gil, much as I admit that does tend to run against the tide of my earlier opinions. I think that I maybe needed a bad guy at the time, and you got the most votes . . . sorry."

I held his gaze. "No need. I think it was that stubborn, pissy attitude of yours that first drew me to you, as it happens."

Zach rolled his eyes. "I'll have to add that to my Grindr profile."

My heart skipped a beat. "You have a Grindr profile?"

Zach laughed. "As if."

I fought the urge to punch the air. "Okay, so what else do you think you know about me?"

"You really want to hear?" He raised a brow. "Even if it's about Callie?"

The notion gave me pause, but my answer didn't need much thought. "Yeah. I do. I trust your instincts." And I did. Go fucking figure.

Zach's eyes widened in surprise. "Okay then." He fell onto his back and I stayed propped up on my elbows, watching him. "Well, I think there's a lot more going on inside that head of yours than you let on. No surprise there. I think you hide your pain behind jokes and work and sex, and this little warm bubble of guilt you've created for yourself." He shot me an apologetic look. "Not so different to what you thought I was doing, right? You feel guilty that you couldn't stop any of what happened, just like Gil does. You might not have been in the car, but you still think you could've stopped it, somehow. You both struggle putting the blame where it belongs—with the other driver—you just deal with it differently."

I couldn't have moved if I tried, my gaze riveted to Zach's as he calmly and gently laid my soul out under the Mackenzie sky.

He eyeballed me. "And I don't believe either of you had it easier or harder. According to Gil, grief works its way through each person uniquely. There *is* no comparison. And that got me thinking about my dad and wondering if it's the same for everyone. That maybe it's not grief that does you in, but the guilt that seems to accompany it no matter what you're grieving for. All the could-haves and should-haves and wonderings that fuck you up. And I think that if you can't find a way to put that aside or at least not let it eat you up quite so much, then you can't move on." He reached up a hand and cupped my face. "And maybe that's why Callie's memories are stuck in that last day. Maybe she's waiting for you to let go of it."

I tried to swallow past the squeeze in my throat, but it was too tight, a sourness building at its back. "I—" But the words wouldn't come and I spun away, blinking back the tears that filled my eyes at an alarming rate. I wrapped my arms around my legs and dropped my chin to my knees, fighting for control.

Callie was gone. Still gone. *Always* fucking gone.

Another change of season without her. Another autumn. Another winter. Another list of the things she loved and hated and all the ways she'd filled my life, *our* lives.

How many more seasons until it didn't hurt? Until I didn't feel buried in the hole she'd left behind.

Please, no more tears. I was so done with fucking tears.

The lake rippled from a fresh lick of a wind, its silver surface now gloomy under a clouding sky. My eyes locked on the small shadow of Motuariki Island as I fingered the band around my wrist and tried to breathe. In and out. In and out. It was nothing I hadn't heard before, hadn't talked about with Gil, hadn't thought about myself, didn't already know. But Zach's tender words had hit home in a way nothing else had before and I felt stripped raw.

"Hey." Zach's arm slid around my waist as he sat beside me and drew me close, his head resting against mine. "I'm sorry. Maybe I shouldn't have said all that. Don't listen to me. What do I know?"

All I could manage was a shudder.

"Damn." Zach kissed the side of my head. "Me and my big mouth."

I almost laughed. "I happen to like your big mouth." And as I said it, somewhere in the back of my brain, a wall crumbled, and two and a half years of pain washed through the jagged rent and ripped through my heart to come out in a gulped cry.

"Oh, fuck." Zach pulled me back down onto the tarp and crushed me against him. "Hey, it's okay." His leg hooked over my thigh, his smaller frame enveloping mine in a tight hold that left me nowhere to go.

Nowhere except into that place I'd spent two and half years running away from. The place where I should've been home that day. Where I blamed Gil. Where I should've stayed with him so that we could help each other. Where I didn't walk away and leave him to cope with what had happened on his own. Where I was a better man, a better father, a stronger person. Someone who would've known what to do. Who wouldn't have run like a coward. Who might've been able to offer Gil a firm footing when things went scary in his head.

I thought I'd come to peace with a lot of it, sorted the truth from the wallowing, undeserved guilt, but it didn't seem to matter. Understanding it and living it were two different things, and Zach had seen through my glass house when no one else had in a long while.

Zach rocked us together while I trembled in his arms, my body wracked by choked sobs and soft cries. He kissed the tears from my cheeks. "It's just us here, sweetheart. It's only us."

Which was just as well since I couldn't seem to stop. "Jesus, I'm s-so s-sorry," I said brokenly between gulps of air. "I don't even know why—"

"Of course, you know why," he shot back, surprising me. "So shut the hell up and let it out. Besides, it's not your fault. Making grown men cry like babies is clearly my superpower, although I have to say I'd imagined it being mostly in bed."

I choked out a half laugh, which was kind of a miracle, all things considered. But it did the trick, and I was able to pull away and scrub my eyes with the heels of my hands. "Jesus, look at me. I'm such a fucking mess. I've cried enough bloody tears the last couple of years to sink a damn ship."

Zach lifted a damp flop of hair from my eyes, letting me see his beautiful smile. "So, there's like a law or something that says you only have an allocated number of tears deemed suitable for losing a child and then you're done? I must've missed that memo."

I gave an amused snort that was a little more productive than I'd expected, and Zach chuckled.

"Can't take you anywhere." He handed me the blanket we'd abandoned, and I wiped my nose and dried my face.

Feeling somewhat respectable again, I sat up. "I know you're right. I'll always cry." I blew out a long, slow breath. "I just hadn't expected . . . *that*, I suppose. And I haven't cried in front of anyone other than Gil in a long time." I shot him a rueful look. "People don't know what to do with it after a while, friends included."

Zach moved to sit cross-legged in front of me and took both my hands. "Yeah, well, most people are idiots. And if your friends get tired of it, then maybe you should raise the bar a little."

I huffed out a laugh. "That's pretty cutthroat."

He shrugged. "Hey, I'm a high-country lad. We don't have time for all the social niceties. If you're a friend, you show up when you're needed for as long as you're needed. It's not a difficult concept. Around this way, we don't have time to come looking for you."

I thought about my Wellington friends and how few had bothered keeping contact since I'd moved down. "Point taken. And I appreciate what you said about me not having it easier than Gil, although I'm not sure I agree. Gil couldn't run away. He couldn't leave it behind. He was in the car with her. He saw it happen. He heard her scream. And he had to deal with the PTSD on top of everything else. Plus, he had to do it on his own because I left him."

Zach's lips set in a thin line. He glanced down at our joined hands and then squeezed them . . . hard.

"Ow." I shot him a disgruntled look.

"That's for being an idiot," he said simply. "You *both* loved Callie. You *both* lost her. You both have the same giant fucking hole in your life, you suffered the same devastation. Tell me it isn't true."

I couldn't.

"Exactly." He tipped my chin up so our gazes met. "Then why should it have been easier for you to crawl out of that hole you were drowning in to save Gil who was drowning in his own hole? Newsflash. You aren't a superhero. So what? Neither is Gil. But you both made it through, give or take, and that's saying something considering what you lost. I'm a total mess when one of my dogs dies, let alone a child." His voice dropped to a hush. "You lost your daughter, Luke. I don't think it gets much worse than that. And there is no right way, no easier or worse way to grieve. It must fucking destroy you, no matter how you look at it, and I was an arsehole not to see that straight away."

"You had your own shit going on," I reminded him.

"True, but still." He squeezed my hands again. "Can I tell you something?"

My brows shot up. "This should be interesting."

He gave me a look that needed no interpretation. "When you and Gil sprinkled Callie's ashes in the Havelock River last year, it almost broke my fucking heart. I still don't know how you made it through. You were so strong. Gil, at least, had Holden. But you looked so damn lonely standing there watching them float down the river. I desperately wanted to go to you, but I didn't because—" He winced. "—see aforementioned arsehole clause. I'm sorry I didn't." He cradled my face and pressed his lips to mine in the gentlest of kisses. Then he kissed my damp cheeks and both of my eyes before pulling me down on top of him and wrapping his legs around my body in the best of hugs.

We lay like that for a long while, no words, nothing but the gentle thrum of some tune Zach must've decided needed humming. I liked it, just as I liked him, just as I . . . I rolled the words around in my head, feeling their rightness in my heart.

And when Zach figured we were done, he bundled me into the ute and we drove back to my place in silence, his hand around mine, his grip determined. I felt too shattered to do anything more than follow his lead, grateful for his presence, and fearful about what the future held, knowing I couldn't, *wouldn't* hide these feelings from him for much longer.

Back in the bungalow, Zach had me wait in the lounge while he let Jojo and Nina into the yard. When they were done chasing shadows, he walked me down to the bathroom, stripped and led me into the shower, pressing gentle kisses over my shoulders and anywhere else he could reach. He washed and dried me head to foot before pouring me into bed like the jelly-legged, empty shell of a man that I'd thought I'd left behind with the worst of my grief over a year ago.

So much for that.

I half expected Zach to see me into bed and then return to the station. I wouldn't have blamed him if he did. I was no company for anyone.

Instead, he crawled in behind me and whispered in my ear, "Let me make you feel good."

I looked over my shoulder to find his green eyes full of concern and gleaming in the light from the table lamp.

His lips pressed against my shoulder. "Let me bring you back just a little."

My mouth opened but nothing came out. The way I felt, it sounded impossible. It sounded like . . . a miracle. But I couldn't find the words to say no. Didn't want to.

"Is that a yes?" He pressed a questioning kiss to my lips and all I could do was nod.

"Okay." He shifted to his knees and loomed over me, a small smile painting his lips. "You don't move unless I say so, got it?"

Wasn't sure I could anyway. "Would you fuck me . . . please?"

He gave another of those beautiful smiles that sent his freckles dancing on his cheeks. And with that, Zacharia Lane proceeded to take me apart, one kiss, one touch, one stroke of pleasure at a time—making me feel something more than loss, more than pain, numbing the guilt, and planting warm seeds of hope.

And boneless as it was, my body responded like it always did when Zach touched me. But whereas we usually met on an equal footing, this time I was in Zach's arms, in Zach's care. And I trusted him to do as he'd promised, like I trusted him with pretty much everything else, and his firm direction and low rumbling growls of appreciation sang to my tragically hopeful heart. In that moment, after the evening we'd shared, one thing was crystal fucking clear—Zach felt a lot more for me than he was letting on, but the knowledge gave me zero reassurance. Because when I told him and he walked away as he most likely would, I was going to be in a world of pain.

And when he pushed my knees up to my chest and whispered, "Let me in, baby," I almost laughed at the irony, wanting to shout that he was already so far inside me, I'd never get him out.

He entered me slowly, gently, like I was some fragile, precious thing, and it was so unlike our standard fiery coupling that it pulled a soft cry of almost sad delight from a place I'd kept carefully locked away for a long time.

At the sound, Zach appeared over me, his face hovering above mine as he waited for me to adjust, our gazes locked, our bodies connected. And as I lost myself in his brilliant green eyes, a deep sense of peace rolled through me.

His mouth turned up in a soft smile and he kissed me once, twice, and then a third time before he finally started to move, rocking slowly into my body while keeping his eyes on mine, every molten stroke of his cock carrying me closer and closer until I teetered on the edge, tears coursing down my cheeks.

He kissed them away and gave two more gentle thrusts. Then he added a slight change of angle and that was enough. I arched in his arms and tumbled into the maelstrom of pleasure mixed with every other emotion that had raised its head that night.

It was almost too much, too raw, and I clung to his body as he tensed and followed me over with a soft grunt, cradling my head as he thrust a final time and then crushed me to him, my cheek buried against his chest, his lips in my hair, his skin hot and slick against my face.

If there was conversation after, I didn't remember. I didn't remember him pulling free of my body. I didn't remember him cleaning me up or tucking me in. I didn't remember where the glass of water came from or the extra blanket to keep out the cold.

All I remembered was Zach crawling into bed and pulling me into his arms. I remembered him hooking a finger into my wristband as he rocked me back and forth. I remembered feeling safe and somehow hollow and full all at the same time. And I remembered Zach's heartbeat against my ear, slow and steady, like a drumbeat calling me home.

And I remembered thinking, *I'm in love.*

CHAPTER SEVENTEEN

Zach

I LEANED AGAINST THE DOORJAMB, SIPPED MY COFFEE, AND watched Luke sleep. He was on his side, facing me, the grey light of dawn accenting all the dips and curves of his long body. The sheet was puddled over his hips and belly, his messy blond hair curled around his ears, those bright blue eyes that cut through my guard like a knife through hot butter now hidden safely behind shuttered lids. Which would be fine, except for the fact that nothing about me was safe around this man.

The night before had been . . . Well, shit, what the hell did you say about what had happened between us? Things had been so much simpler when I didn't like the guy. Lusted after him? Yes. But liked? Well, let's say I'd managed to convince myself otherwise for too long.

I'd safely categorised Luke as a sad, adrift guy who'd suffered a devastating loss and then skipped out on his husband when Gil needed him the most. Such a selfish thing to do, right? And I'd done a stellar job of keeping him in that role. After the emotional shitshow I'd gone through with Holden, and then my dad, the last thing I needed was a selfish man like Luke in my life, and the cautionary stance I took certainly kept my attraction to him under lock and key.

Until it didn't.

Until he came to live in Oakwood.

Until I got to know him.

Because then . . .

I watched the soft rise and fall of his chest, the way the sheet wrapped around the sweet swell of his arse and all that smooth tanned skin that rode his body invitingly.

Damn. I sighed and took another sip of my coffee, because not only had Luke turned out to be a nice guy, he'd proved to be a lot more, and it was that *a lot more* part that was doing my head in.

Because I liked Luke.

I liked him a lot.

I'd gone and gotten . . . *feelings* for the guy.

And I simply didn't know what the fuck to do about that.

I walked to the bed and carefully drew the duvet up over his cool skin, my shadow falling across his frame like my body had the night before. The sex between us was . . . well . . . spectacular came to mind. An excellent adjective, all things considered. But what I'd done with and to Luke last night had been nothing to do with straightforward sex.

I'd made love to Luke. In his bed. In his house. And in my head.

I might not be *in* love with him but hell if I wasn't heading that way.

I could try to convince myself otherwise with a whole lot of bullshit terms like compassion, and kindness, and even friends with benefits simply doing the decent friendship stuff for someone in pain, but I'd have been lying to myself.

I couldn't get my head around it. How could it be true when a year ago I'd been in love with Holden?

Hadn't I?

Dammit, I sucked at this casual shit. I should've learned my lesson after Holden. Then again, maybe I was the pathetic type who fell in love with every fucking man he slept with.

I stood at the end of the bed and studied Luke's face, the calm of sleep smoothing the lines of grief that had consumed his expression the night before. I glanced at the photo of Callie on the dresser and my heart squeezed. How did a parent survive that kind of loss? Two grieving fathers. Two very different paths travelled. Paths that had no end.

Any relationship Luke had in the future would always come with Callie and the pain of her loss. How did two people navigate that? How did Gil and Holden? How did you know you were ready to take that on, to love again? How did you not fuck that up? How did you know you loved someone enough to try?

Luke muttered something in his sleep and rolled onto his back. I waited until he settled again and then tiptoed back to the door. I was in way over my head, and the most sensible course of action was to leave Luke to sleep, grab the dogs, and head home.

At the station, I could think.

At the station, everything was less complicated.

At the station, I was Zach Lane, shepherd, dog trainer, and good mate.

At the station, I could imagine a life that didn't put my fucking heart at risk ... again.

I'd watched the man I'd been in love with fall for another man and then watched my arsehole father turn his back on me. I wasn't sure I could take another hit so soon.

After one final look, I pulled Luke's door closed, tiptoed back into the kitchen, and watched the dogs scoot around the chilly backyard. The sudden drop in temperature was a sober reminder of the icy mornings coming, and I hoped we weren't in for an early winter storm before we got the mobs down from the hill. Wouldn't be the first time.

I glanced back toward Luke's bedroom and sighed. I needed to leave but I couldn't seem to get my feet moving. I pulled out my phone and Jules picked up on the second ring.

"Isn't this your day off?" Jules breathed heavily into the phone, and I could imagine him already busy in the woolshed.

"It is." I watched Jojo ambush Nina from behind the lemon tree, their paw marks creating a crazy pattern in the light frost.

"And your first thought was to call me?" Jules laughed and the clear sound of it made me smile.

"I'm in trouble."

"Shit. Hang on." Jules issued muffled instructions to someone and then came the sound of a door closing. "Okay, I'm all ears," he said as he came back on the line. "Do I have to kill someone or hide a body? Cos I have to tell you, I'm a bit short on time today."

I snorted. "Nothing like that. But if I tell you I'm currently standing half-naked in Luke Nichols' kitchen with him asleep in his bedroom, and it's not the first time I've been here, does that give you some idea?"

Silence.

"Jules?"

"Yeah, yeah, I'm here. I'm just trying to get past the half-naked bit. I thought you didn't like Luke?"

"Yeah, well, I might've possibly overplayed that card. I *didn't* like him. But since he moved here, I've got to know him a little better."

Jules laughed. "I'd say that's putting it mildly."

"Shut up. He's a good guy."

"You don't have to convince me." Jules took a second, then added, "So, you're lighting up the sheets with Luke and having some fun. I've yet to see the problem."

I sucked in a breath. "The problem *is*, I think I really like him."

Jules chuckled. "Jesus, Zach. You make it sound like the damn plague. He's nice. You're nice. You're getting a few nice feelings and having nice sex—" He hesitated. "Aren't you?"

I groaned. "Best sex of my life."

More laughter. "TMI bro. TMI. But if that's true, then I still fail to see the problem."

"It's *Luke*."

"Yes, I got that part. So?"

"He's Gil's ex-husband, and I'm Holden's . . . whatever. If I think too hard about it, my mind explodes."

Jules hooted. "For fuck's sake, Zach. You're both adults. And I'm pretty sure neither Holden nor Gil will care if you two are banging. Honestly, you're just not that important."

"Fuck you." I rapped on the kitchen window to quiet the dogs from waking up the neighbours.

"You're running scared, aren't you?" Jules asked with a smile in his voice.

I snorted. "No shit, Sherlock. Can you blame me? It's like a damn soap opera around this place. People have only just stopped looking at me sideways after shit went down with Dad. And if things get awkward between Luke and Gil and Holden and me, the gossips will have a fucking field day. I can hear it now. Gay-love quadrouple or whatever the fuck the equivalent is to a love triangle."

Jules almost choked. "Yeah, I'm not touching that. But Luke's gone in a few months, which means you two can simply stay friends and cool the other part if it bothers you that much. I don't get what . . .?" Jules trailed off. "Oh, fuck me. You mean you really like him, as in *like* like him. As in having *those* types of feelings."

I huffed in frustration. "Just so you know, this is me rolling my eyes. Took you long enough."

Jules went quiet for a moment before saying, "Like you said, Luke is a nice guy, and the sex is apparently good. Is it really such a surprise that you're having feelings for him?"

"I had feelings for Holden," I pointed out. "I was *in love* with Holden. How is it possible to feel things for someone else so fast?"

He laughed. "And you think *I* have the answer? My dating history isn't exactly stellar. I can't even remember the last time I got laid."

My mouth turned up in a smile. "True. Although I thought you got pretty close to Laura before she headed north all those years ago. You guys were together six months. You seemed pretty smitten."

Jules went quiet for a moment. "Maybe. Not sure that was love though. Although the sex was amazing."

"Ew. Stop. The idea of men's and ladies' bits bumping together is so gross."

Jules laughed.

I took a deep breath and blew it out slowly. "I guess I don't want to make another mistake. It's hard to trust what I feel anymore. I got things so fucking wrong with Holden. And this thing with Luke seems . . . well, you couldn't write a book about it. And like you said, he's not staying."

"Then why not simply enjoy the ride? Pun fully intended. If he's not staying and you're not leaving, which I know you're not, then there's no real decision to make, is there? You can see what happens with an easy exit option."

"I guess." I opened the back door and whistled for the dogs, my nipples pebbling in the wash of frigid air. "Fuck, it's cold out there." I quickly shut the door and put my phone on speaker while I dried the dogs' feet.

"Just think about it, Zee. The Mackenzie dating pool is rather small, for both of us, but you especially."

"Don't remind me. But *you* could make it larger for yourself if you chose to," I suggested carefully.

He said nothing for a minute, then replied, "Maybe. But that's a question for another day. And yes, it's fucking cold. Look, I have to go. Dad's on the warpath. We didn't get the first frost around the house before April last year, but it's white as fucking snow today. If this keeps up, we're in trouble."

I frowned. "Are you guys still mustering late? I thought you talked him around."

"For about half a day. Don't even ask. And now look at it. Hence Dad's pissy mood. You know how much he hates being wrong."

Did I ever. "Okay, well, let me know if I can help out. We'll be almost finished by the time you start."

Jules huffed. "We both know he won't accept any help from you or Miller Station, but thanks."

He ended the call, and I opened the laundry door and let the dogs into the house.

Jojo skidded to a stop on the polished floors and quickly sat to attention in front of the breakfast bar, her eyes trained on the container of dog biscuits. Nina plonked down beside her kennelmate and I'd have sworn her gold eyebrows waggled as she scooted Jojo sideways into the fridge.

"Nope." I eyed the two dogs. "I'll feed you when we get home." It was still the best decision, no matter what Jules thought.

The dogs stared back like they could read my mind, and I threw another glance to Luke's bedroom door. "It's the worst idea ever," I grumbled.

Jojo gave a soft whine and Nina raised one golden eyebrow, or at least I'm pretty sure she did.

"You only like him because he lets you sleep on the sofa."

They continued to stare.

"Yes, I'm well aware that's a good indication of character," I answered their pleading eyes. "I never said he wasn't a nice guy, but we're leaving, and that's my last word on the subject so you can stop your begging."

And with that, I filled their two bowls with kibble and switched the coffee machine on for a second round.

Because that's how I rolled.

Half an hour later, as I was once again staring out the kitchen window and contemplating my idiocy, warm hands snaked around my waist, a pair of lips found that spot at the join of my neck and shoulder that drove me crazy, and I was pulled back against a furnace of hot, bare skin.

"Good morning." Luke nuzzled my neck, sending shivers down my spine. "I could get used to finding a man standing in just his jeans at my kitchen sink every morning."

"Which appears to be more than you're wearing." I shoved my arse back, feeling his very interested cock and not much else.

"I'm wearing briefs," he argued with a smirk in his voice. "And you look goddamn delicious." He kissed his way up to that sensitive spot behind my ear and I figured there were a lot worse ways to start the day than wrapped in the arms of a tall sexy man straight from bed and smelling of . . . us.

Jojo and Nina clearly agreed, circling Luke in an excited welcome.

He dropped one hand to pet them while keeping the other firmly around my waist. "I half expected you to be gone already," he murmured against my throat in an impressive display of multi-tasking. "I thought my brain explosion last night might've scared you off."

I tilted my head so he could nuzzle a little higher and he obliged. "Hey, I'm a country boy," I reminded him as he nibbled the base of my throat. "It takes more than a few tears to scare me off."

Luke turned me in his arms. "Doesn't make me any less sorry that I ruined the evening. I haven't broken down like that for a long time."

My hands slid around his neck. "You didn't ruin anything." I pressed a soft kiss to his lips. "And you're allowed to break down as often as you need. I told you that place was special."

"Hmmm, maybe." He let me go and took a seat at the breakfast bar, followed eagerly by Jojo and Nina who then stretched out on the floor at his feet as if they did it every day of their damn lives, the little hussies.

"I can put them outside." I eyed the mutts who were busy ignoring me.

Luke blinked. "Why would you do that?"

"Because right now it's the kitchen floor. Tomorrow, it's your bed."

He shot me a wicked grin. "If that means you stay another night, I wouldn't say no."

I wasn't about to touch that with a barge pole, so I wandered over to join him at the breakfast bar. He pulled me close and his kiss was hungry, greedy, almost desperate. It had me aching to be lost inside him again. He simply had that effect, that ability to switch off all the emptiness in my life, all the unanswered questions, unfulfilled plans, and aching holes. Everything fading in his presence, at his touch. Not gone, just . . . gentled.

When he pulled away, I chased his lips, but his hands on my hips kept me in place. "I want today to be about you. Tell me what you'd like to do."

I waggled my eyebrows and he rolled his eyes and said, "Anything except that. Something out of bed for a change."

I pouted. "Spoilsport."

He hooked a finger through my belt loop and tugged me close. "I never said we couldn't do that as well. But *after*. If you're still in the mood."

I cupped his dick and balls. "Oh, I'll be in the mood. But whatever we do, I have to leave by two. I still need to get some training in."

"We better get moving then." He spun me around. "You've got fifteen minutes to get ready to go. We'll take your ute for the dogs." He slapped me on the butt and gave me a shove toward the bathroom.

I stopped and spun back around. "Go where? And also, the dogs?"

He shot me a confused look. "They're coming, right?"

I couldn't hide my smile. "Right. But what happened to the day being about what *I* wanted to do?"

His mouth turned up in a slow grin. "That was before you introduced a time limit. Now you've only got twelve minutes left, so you better hop to it." He gave me another shove but I resisted.

"You could always come with me?" I tugged my bottom lip between my teeth and shot him a saucy wink.

He stabbed a finger my way. "And that right there is why you don't get to decide anymore." He manhandled me all the way down the hall and into the bathroom. "And don't use all the shampoo, you little minx."

I dropped my jeans, gave my cock a firm stroke, and smiled at Luke's sharp intake of breath. "Not too late to change your mind."

His gaze travelled my bare skin, his eyes hot and hungry, and for a second, I thought I'd won. Then the door slammed shut in my face and the words, "Nine minutes," faded up the hall.

CHAPTER EIGHTEEN

Zach

TWENTY MINUTES LATER, WE WHISTLED THE DOGS INTO THE ute, along with some seriously warm outerwear, and headed for the main street. First stop was Meg's café for coffee and breakfast buns, then I drove us out to a spot along the Tekapo Canal where the dogs could run free while we ate.

Unbeknownst to me, Luke had added an extra bacon sandwich to our order, which he proceeded to share with the two dogs who sat adoringly at his feet. Every now and then, one of them would shoot me a sidelong look as if to say, *I hope you're taking notes.*

"You're spoiling them," I chided Luke, only half joking. He looked so fucking cute in his puffer jacket with the Wild Run logo on the back, thick scarf pulled up to his ears and rainbow woollen hat sitting low on his forehead. I had to fight the urge to tackle him to the ground and kiss him silly.

"I am." He shot me a brilliant smile, which melted my toes in my socks and brought my brother's words back to mind.

Enjoy the ride ... it has an end date ... what's the problem?

Trouble was, that end date wasn't likely to come soon enough to stop a ton of hurt heading my way, and I also couldn't seem to put a halt to my feelings before they went too far. Or rather, *way* too far, because I'd sure as hell passed the *too far* signpost a long time ago at well above the recommended speed limit. Luke was an unexpected, irresistible, and dangerous kink in my plan to keep my bruised heart safe.

I had to create some space before it was too late.

Case in point—me smiling at him like an idiot while he fed the girls the last morsels of bacon, their ears twitching at his every word, eyes glued hopefully to his face, hearts no doubt a pitter-patter, and me knowing just how they felt. Like we were boyfriends, for fuck's sake. Like we did this every day. Like the girls were . . . ours.

We finished our coffees, and Luke walked our rubbish to the bins while I didn't watch the way his glorious arse bunched and moved in those threadbare jeans he wore just to fuck with me since it was too damn cold to justify them otherwise. The bastard knew I loved them, and my theory was proven correct when he paused at the bin and did a little shimmy for me before turning with a massive grin on his face. I flipped him off and all the fucker did was laugh.

"You think you're so damn funny," I groused, which only made him laugh louder. "I'd take you up on that offer if it didn't risk my nuts freezing and rolling like marbles into the canal."

"An image I could've done well without." He started ambling away from me, towards the canal, and Jojo immediately began circling him.

I chuckled at my idiot of a dog. "She's herding you."

"She's what?" Luke took another couple of steps and Jojo swept to her right until he stopped again.

Nina, who'd been stretched out at my feet watching her kennel-mate, decided to get in on the act and gave a deep bellowing bark before loping over.

Luke laughed. "Oh my god. Come on then, hotshot." He fired me a challenging look. "Let's see what you can do."

I bit back a smile. "Are you sure about that?"

He narrowed his gaze. "Why not? I'm game to see how you do with a creature a little further up the food chain."

Little did he know, the girls and I trained for this as well. More than once during a search and rescue job, I'd needed to encourage a confused hiker away from a dangerous situation. "Okay then. Don't say I didn't warn you, but you need to give them a fighting chance. No sneaky tactics. I don't want my training fucked with."

Luke saluted and I told my cock to settle down. Then he slid a few steps to the left and I whistled Jojo and Nina into action. Jojo whipped across to cut Luke off while Nina took a stand behind him.

"Speak."

Nina let loose a peace-shattering bay and Luke jumped, his hand flying to his chest. "Jesus Christ, she's loud," he grumbled and took a few steps back.

"Keep out."

Jojo flew in a wide circle to cut off Luke's escape, while Nina continued to slowly walk forward, her booming bark echoing the length of the canal.

Luke immediately switched direction and Jojo cut him off again while Nina kept walking forward. He tried the other way and got the same result.

"Come bye," I called. The trap was closing, and I couldn't help but laugh at Luke's increasingly desperate attempts to solve his predicament. "Any last requests?" I asked cheekily.

"Fuck off," he griped before shooting me a wide smile, his complexion beet red in the frosty air.

My heart did a little stutter.

A few minutes later, it was all over. Between Nina's relentless pursuit and Jojo's effortless switchbacks, they had Luke's number and soon had him backed against the canal.

"Hey!" he shouted, standing a metre from the edge. "You wouldn't dare."

All I did was waggle my brows and call, "Move on."

Luke cast an anxious look my way as Jojo crept forward on her belly and Nina gave another booming bark. Luke took one more step back, then checked nervously over his shoulder. "Any time now would be good."

I chuckled and called, "Get in behind."

The two dogs immediately circled away and back to where I sat.

Luke reached me in a dozen strides and straddled my lap on the bench. "You're a cheeky little fucker." He cradled my face, crushed his mouth to mine, and I drowned in everything Luke. All my concerns, my determination to walk away, everything lost to the sweet taste of his mouth and his deep rumbling laugh. "I guess I asked for that." He planted kisses all over my face.

"You did." I pushed him away so I could see those beautiful blue eyes. "I doubt they would've backed you in, though."

He cocked a brow. "You doubt?"

I shrugged. "You never know. They *are* very obedient, after all."

He stared at me until I laughed. "I'm just kidding." Although since I'd never actually tested them, I couldn't be entirely sure. They did have absolute trust in me, so maybe next time the team swam at the lake . . .

"Come on." Luke scrambled back onto his feet and held out his gloved hand for me to take. "Let's take a walk so the girls can stretch their legs a little more."

I stared at his hand for precisely 0.1 seconds before my fingers wrapped around his and he tugged me to my feet and threw an arm around my shoulder. I snuggled into his side like the space had been carved just for me, and as I glanced sideways at his arm hanging down around my shoulder, I couldn't erase the smile from my face.

Oh yeah, I'm clearly acing this creating-a-little-distance lark.

With the morning sun slowly thawing our bones one lick at a time, we took our time strolling along the canal, watching the dogs play silly buggers. We laughed at their antics, threw the occasional stick, and got regularly mobbed by wet feet and wetter tongues. The whole experience felt warm, domestic, and scary as hell.

"Can I ask what you did after you and Gil split?" I asked the question I'd often wondered about.

"You mean after I walked out?" Luke corrected and I rolled my eyes.

"You know what I mean."

His blue eyes softened, and he pressed his lips to my beanie. "Pretty much nothing, except fall apart, that is. I stayed with my parents for a while, pulled the curtains in my old bedroom and didn't come out for what felt like months."

Since his arm was still around my shoulders, I reached up and grabbed onto his hand.

"Mum and Dad eventually dragged me to the doctor who told me to go back to my therapist, which I did. He put me on some kind of anti-depressant, which I didn't like, but it helped me to at least get out of bed in the morning, so that was a win. After a few months, I rented an apartment, chucked in my job, pulled the curtains in my *new* bedroom, and cried my way through the next few months." He shot me a look. "Do you want me to keep going?"

"Yes." I squeezed his hand and he gave a resigned sigh.

"My, *our* friends didn't know how to take me leaving Gil, so mostly they simply stopped calling. Gil didn't respond to any of my attempts to get in touch, the new apartment grew smaller and lonelier by the day, and I started becoming overly familiar with the top shelf of my bar."

I lifted his knuckles to my lips, and he watched me kiss them with an incredibly tender look that punched me in the heart.

"Anyway," he finally continued, "One day, I decided enough was enough and got dressed and went out dancing."

I blinked and stared up at him. "Dancing?"

He chuckled. "Yeah. Stupid, right? But then I met a guy in the club who made me laugh and fucked my brains out, and I was able to forget for a while. I started smiling again, since people invite you out more if you do that, and we met up a few more times before he cottoned on that I was a sandwich short of anything resembling stable and suggested we call it quits and that I get some help. Wise man. And so, I stopped trying to date and just . . . escaped if you catch my drift."

My heart tumbled a little, remembering how I'd judged him so unfairly.

"It was maybe not the healthiest choice, but it got me through, at least for a while. But on my therapist's advice, I also started flying again at the local aero club, and that was the best thing I ever did. Being back in the air was the only place I felt like myself again."

I watched the dark water ripple in the chilly breeze sliding off the Alps and sympathised. "I totally get that. I know it's not the same, but after everything that went down for me last year, my dogs were my only refuge." *Until you.*

"I think it's *exactly* the same," he said softly, kissing me again as the dogs hurtled around us before taking off back to the canal. "Anyway, my life slowly settled and I began to think that maybe I had turned a corner. But when I found out Gil had moved down here, it felt a little scary, like I might lose something important: the chance to talk about the part of our lives we shared with Callie. And so, I followed him here to try and salvage what I could."

I turned in front of Luke and slid my hands around his neck. "And you did."

He enveloped me in his arms and brushed his lips over mine. "And here we are."

I couldn't stop from smiling. "And here we are."

We walked for almost an hour and then drove back to Luke's where we made out and then exchanged a couple lazy blowjobs on his sofa while the dogs lay curled up in front of the open fire and pretended they weren't disgusted by the whole affair.

More coffee, and two chocolate croissants later, we each took one end of the sofa and spent some time reading—Luke with his David

Baldacci thriller, while I grabbed a photographic account of World War II from his bookcase.

His lips quirked at my choice. "A bit of light reading, then?"

"Hey, those who don't learn from their mistakes are forever doomed to repeat them," I said loftily.

He chuckled. "You don't need to remind me. I've got a few I don't plan on repeating anytime soon. Where did your love of history come from?"

I settled myself against the cushions and dragged his feet onto my lap. "My grandad was a big fan and I loved listening to his stories about my great-grandfather in the war and his father before him. If I hadn't loved dogs and station life so much, I might've been a history teacher. Now shut up, you're cutting into my reading time and I don't get much these days."

"You're cute when you're grumpy." Luke wiggled his toes against my stomach until I groaned and shoved his feet to the side.

"You're a pain in the butt."

"I do my best." He shot me a wink and went back to his book.

I chuckled and did the same, sneaking the occasional glance his way to watch him as he read, the vertical crease between his brows deepening with concentration. He caught me looking more than once and returned a soft, almost-shy smile that only added to all those worrying feelings squirming in my belly.

We read for a good hour, broken only by a couple of short breaks of conversation and when the dogs pushed their snouts in for some attention. In his inimitable way, Luke solved that latter problem by ignoring my protests and inviting both dogs onto the couch. They promptly curled up between us, neither daring to look my way for fear of being ousted.

It was . . . nice. More than nice. The cosy room, the crackling fire, the smell of coffee and baking, the crisp blue sky out the window, the sun striping the floor, the dogs curled up between us and . . . Luke. It filled a hole I'd carried with me for as long as I could remember.

I gave up pretending to read, closed my book on my knees, and settled for watching Luke instead. He was chewing on his bottom lip and flipping pages at speed.

"Getting exciting, huh?"

"Shh!" He held up a hand.

I put my book on the coffee table and whistled the dogs off the couch. Then I got on my hands and knees and crawled toward him.

"Don't. You. Dare." He raised a finger without even glancing up.

"Dare what?" I leaned in and nuzzled the soft lobe of his ear.

"That." He groaned softly, then shrugged his shoulder in some pretence of rejection. "They've just found the cop's body."

"Mmm, is that right?" I cupped his dick through his jeans and kissed up his neck. "Well . . . since I have to leave soon . . . I was wondering if . . . maybe . . ." I squeezed him again.

"Dammit." He thrust up into my hand. "You're such a fucking tease." He threw me a stink eye. "You can't possibly be ready to go again."

"Aw . . . that's what youth does for you, old man." I took his book and dropped it to the floor. Then I put his hand on my hardening dick. "I definitely think I can manage . . . *something*."

He drew me down for a kiss while simultaneously undoing my jeans to free my cock, which he proceeded to stroke. "You lost my place in my book."

I grunted and thrust into his hand. "Sorry, not sorry. You can punish me later."

He nibbled at my neck. "I'll hold you to that. But age does have its advantages."

"Oh yeah?" I kissed along his jaw until I found his lips. "Tell me more."

"Well—" He angled his neck so I could continue kissing under his chin, one of his hot buttons. "For one, I'm far too old and tired to fuck you."

Huh? I pulled back and eyed him dubiously.

He gave a wry smile. "So you'll have to get out of those jeans and fuck *yourself* . . . on my cock . . . right here on this couch . . . and you better make a show of it. Us old guys need all the stimulation we can get." He unzipped his jeans and that gorgeous dick sprang free to greet me.

I licked my lips, lost my jeans in record time, and proceeded to do exactly what the man ordered.

I parked the ute alongside the cottage and groaned when I caught sight of Holden making his way down the front lawn toward me with Spider at his side.

"Thought you lot were working on the fences up Dunwoody's beat? The track's a mess, I hear." I climbed from behind the wheel and made my way around the back of the ute to release the dogs. They barrelled up to Holden who immediately dropped to his knees so they could inspect every centimetre of him and cast judgement on whatever they found he'd been up to while they were away.

"We are." He chuckled as Nina ran her nose through his dark waves. "Made for a late lunch."

"Aw, and you left the table just to come and say hi to me. I'm touched," I teased.

"They're still eating, in case you're hungry," he offered.

I cast a glance toward the homestead and shook my head. "No, thanks. I grabbed something in town."

"Is that right?"

I ignored the comment as the dogs moved on to Spider who got the same diligent once-over before they all headed off toward the lake for a little doggie catchup. I grabbed my duffle from the back seat and turned to find Holden sitting on the top stair, clearly going nowhere.

Oh boy.

"You've been spending a fair bit of time in town lately." Holden patted the decking beside him. "Anyone I know?" His eyes were twinkling but there was something else in his expression that I couldn't place.

But since I could hardly walk past and ignore him, I dropped my duffle on the deck and took a seat. "I'm over thirty, Holden. You're really going there?"

He spread his hands. "I'd be breaking every rule in the best-mate's handbook if I didn't. I've barely seen you in weeks and not being all up in your business makes me antsy."

I shot a glance to the homestead in time to catch Gil's face dart away from the window. "Did your boyfriend send you down here?"

Holden grimaced and glanced over his shoulder. "Why would you ask that?"

I stared at him until his cheeks pinked.

"Okay, so he might've suggested I check on you, but that's all."

I kept staring and he grunted.

"So, we've both been curious and a bit worried. There's no law against that, is there?"

I studied him for a second, not sure whether to be pissed or touched by the oddly parental concern. "Why on earth would you be worried?"

He leaned forward on his knees, those dark brown eyes soft. "You've hardly left the station in a year for anything other than Miller business, and then all of a sudden, you're gone several nights a week, including your day off, which you normally keep sacrosanct for training your dogs. I just wanna make sure you're okay." He looked genuinely troubled, and my irritation eased.

"I'm fine," I reassured him. "I've been a bit . . . pre-occupied." A smile found my lips before I could censor it.

Of course, Holden didn't miss it. "So, there *is* a guy." He chuckled. "I knew it. Come on, who's the lucky fella?"

"Oh, hell no." I raised my palms. "There is no way I'm throwing anyone to the wolves. Besides, it's just a bit of fun. Nothing serious." I swallowed around what was absolutely a big old fat lie.

Holden studied me for a second, then said, "Nah, I'm not buying it. You've never been the bit-of-fun type."

I held his gaze, my irritation rising once again, and said coolly, "Things change, Holden. People change. People . . . learn."

Holden flushed red, then gave a nod. "Yeah, I guess I deserved that. It's just . . ."

When he didn't continue, I sighed. "Go on, you may as well say what you came to."

His frown deepened and his gaze slid from me to the lake, its mirrored surface reflecting a cool blue sky. "It's just that I know you don't throw your affection around lightly." He turned back to face me. "You're cautious, Zach. And that's a good thing. And I'm sorry if what happened between us changed that for you in any way. I was so fucking oblivious to your feelings back then, and there's no excuse. I should've known."

"Why?" I scoffed. "I never said a word. You had no reason to believe anything had changed. Jesus, Holden, you don't have superpowers even though you might think you do. And you're not responsible for my feelings. I'm a grown man, like you. So how about you back off a bit."

He caught my eye and winced. "Okay, fair comment. But before we leave the subject, I'd like the opportunity to say something that's been eating at me, if that's okay with you?"

I answered warily. "Okaaay."

"That last year that you and I—" He shrugged. "—well, you know."

"Were fucking?" I offered with a smile that felt genuine and without any hurt attached, without anything much at all other than a kind of fond wistfulness.

Holden snorted. "Yeah, that. Well, I know we agreed not to be exclusive . . ." He flushed again. "But looking back now, I'm sorry if I did anything to hurt you. I knew you weren't out much with other guys, since you weren't out at all, but when you told me how you felt, well, I started thinking—"

"Jesus Christ, enough, Holden, please. I get it and thank you. But to be honest, it almost feels like a lifetime ago." *And damn if that wasn't true.* "Besides, it was all on me back then, not you. You did nothing wrong. And I don't want to hurt your feelings or anything, but I'm kind of over it."

He looked a little taken aback, and then when I chuckled, a deep frown cut his brow.

"Jesus, you should see your face." I cupped his cheek. "You're cute, and yes, I was in love with you. But sometimes when I look back, it feels more like a fantasy, like I wanted it to be true so badly because of all the other shit I was dealing with. You, or maybe the possibility of there being an *us*, was like this light at the end of the tunnel, you know?" I dropped my hand and his expression grew wry, maybe even a little relieved.

"Yeah, I can see that."

"I might have been hurt and jealous when you fell head over heels for Gil, but it was also so damned easy to see that you were made for each other."

He took my hand. "I want that for you too."

Luke's face flashed into my brain and I pushed it away. "Maybe, one day. For now, I want to get my own life back on track. So, please, stop worrying about me. I don't need anyone's sympathy or pity. I'm not pining for you, Holden. I'm not wasting away. I'm perfectly fine." *Kind of.* But that had nothing to do with him.

Holden rolled his eyes. "I guess that tells me."

"You know I don't mean it that way." I squeezed his hand and let it go. "Just be my best friend. That's all I need."

His shoulders relaxed and a weighty sigh fell from his lips, and for the first time in years, I felt like we were back on an equal footing. "So . . ." A sly smile stole over his face. "Does that mean you *are* seeing someone?"

I groaned, and answered, "I'm *fucking* someone, yes."

Something flickered in his eyes. "Is he treating you well?"

The image of Luke's blissed-out face as I was riding his cock only an hour before sprang to mind. "Yes, Dad. He's treating me well."

Holden huffed. "Good. You're special, Zach, and you deserve the best that's out there. The guy who lands you will have won the jackpot."

His words lodged like concrete in my throat. "Thanks. Now it's my turn to ask a question."

Holden grinned but didn't call me on the obvious change of subject. "Fire away."

And so I did, taking Luke's advice and explaining all my plans for building a business around training dogs, including my takeaway from the bank visit and whether Holden thought there was any wiggle room around my work hours.

"Of course there fucking is," he proclaimed like it was the most obvious thing in the world. "Come for dinner tonight. Bring your business plan with you and we'll talk. I'd like Gil to hear it as well if that's okay with you. He's great with strategies and we pretty much work as a team now."

I had zero problem with that and I told him so.

"Great. But what I can tell you right now is that until you can afford your own place, I'm happy for you to use that training paddock long-term. Do with it what you want, and if you make the new kennels transportable, there's nothing to stop you building them here using station discounts on materials and then relocating them when you leave."

"But—" My heart leapt in my throat. With a couple of broad strokes, Holden had dealt with two of my biggest issues. "Are you sure?"

Holden's brows knotted. "Why wouldn't I be? You're an asset to the station, Zach. If we get to keep you for another year or two, even at reduced hours, we'd be counting ourselves lucky."

I shook my head. "I don't want charity. If I'm not working full-time, we need to discuss rent on the cottage, and food, and fuel, and all the other stuff—"

"Pfft." Holden waved his hand dismissively. "I'll tell you what. Thor and Elektra aren't getting any younger. You know how Elektra struggled through last muster after that joint infection? If I grab a couple of pups, under your recommendation of course, and you agree to train them as replacements, we'll call it even. I'm sure I'll be getting the better deal out of that considering what they go for fully trained."

My mouth opened but nothing came out.

Holden smirked. "I'll take that as a yes. And not that I know anything about what it involves, but have you considered expanding your training focus?"

Still gobsmacked from Holden's offer, I struggled to catch up. "What? Um, no? How do you mean?"

He smiled. "Don't search and rescue dogs and owners need training opportunities? You already do it with Charlie, *and* we have accommodation on site. We could easily convert some of the old shearer's quarters as a more basic option, if you prefer, and then negotiate a suitable overnight cost for you to pass on."

"I—" I didn't know what to say. "Yes, I could absolutely do something like that. Damn, Holden, I always knew you had a good head for business."

He grinned. "But talk to Gil, as well. He's looking at a service dog training program with Spider. Maybe you could reach out and see what they do there. Apparently, there's a long waitlist for those dogs." He rubbed his palms down the front of his jeans and got to his feet. "I should go."

I leapt up and grabbed him in a hug. "Thank you. You have no idea what this means to me."

He gave me a strange look and smiled. "Yeah, I think maybe I do. And you deserve it."

He began walking away and then stopped and turned back, his eyes dancing. "Just so you know, whoever this guy is, if he hurts you, I'm gonna be taking names and tracking the bastard down, and I won't be denied. That is totally best-mate territory. We'll see you up at the house for supper."

And as he headed up the lawn, I swallowed hard, thinking I'd pay good money to see the look on Holden's face if he ever found out it was Luke. I grabbed my duffle and headed for my tiny kitchen. I needed a solid hit of caffeine and some thinking time to digest everything that had happened, from the bank visit, to what had gone down between Luke and me, to Holden's generous offer.

I took my mug to the deck and stretched out in the old lounger I'd rescued from the station recycling bin when Gil had upgraded the guest cottages. I blew on the steaming coffee and watched a falcon circle above the glistening lake before it headed for the ridgeline above Holden's Castle, its impressive wingspan silhouetted against the bluebird autumn sky.

The irony that Luke was the first person I wanted to tell wasn't lost on me. But I didn't fight it. **Talked to Holden about the business. He's all for it. Offered ideas and help. Going up for dinner tonight to talk more.**

I didn't have to wait long.

That's amazing! Holden's a smart man. And it has to be to his advantage having the best trainer in the Mackenzie on his payroll. Good luck for tonight. XX

The best trainer in the Mackenzie. They were sweet words, and the two kisses at the end had me smiling. But when I thought of all the work that lay ahead if I wanted this business to succeed, the gnawing uneasiness put a quick end to any sentimentality.

I rolled my eyes and pocketed my phone. What the hell was I doing mooning about a man who had his shit together about as much as I did, meaning not at all? I'd been given an opportunity I'd been waiting for all my life, one that would need my A game over the next couple of years to have any chance at success.

When my phone buzzed again, I fully expected it to be Luke, but instead, my mother's name stared back at me from the screen.

"Mum?" I answered warily.

"Zacharia, it's so nice to hear your voice." The slight scolding note to her tone made me bristle.

"Last time I called, you hung up on me when Dad walked in," I reminded her. "Left a sour taste."

She went quiet for a moment and when I pictured her sitting in her favourite armchair staring out toward Mount Sibbald, my heart ached. A year down the track and the gut punch of her failure to stand up for me still stung.

"You're right. I'm sorry. That's on me. But I've told your father I'll call whenever I like and he can deal with it."

I tried not to let the shock show in my voice or ask more about how that defiance had gone down, because I couldn't imagine it went well. My dad wasn't violent or even particularly argumentative; he was simply an immovable rock when it came to his views and silence was his weapon of choice. I remembered what Luke had said about the bare-minimum expectations from people who were meant to love you, and I thought about how my mother had left me hanging. I kept my response checked. "Good for you, Mum. What can I do for you?"

"Can't I just call to talk to my son?" Hurt had crept into her voice and I knew she'd expected more from me. I just . . . couldn't.

"Of course you can call. What's up?"

She proceeded to tell me, in a happier tone, about her latest doctor appointment and how the colder weather was playing havoc with her arthritis. She talked about her baking and the new shepherd the station had hired out of Australia and how the woolshed extension was going to make life easier for everyone. "We'd love for you to come visit and see the changes."

I said nothing, running her words through my head a second time while my heart thumped against my chest. "Who's *we*, Mum?" I took a breath. "Has Dad asked for me to visit?"

Her hesitation said everything I needed to know, and my stomach dropped in my boots as she answered. "Not exactly. But I'm sure if you come, he'll want to talk, you can *both* talk. He's a stubborn old man, you know that, but there has to be a solution to this . . . standoff between the two of you."

I shook my head and sighed. "There is, Mum." I winced at the hurt in my voice, not wanting her to hear. "And it starts with an apology, or at least with Dad approaching me *himself* if he wants to talk. I've heard nothing since Dad dropped Jojo and Nina off here last year, and that was hardly pleasant. He insulted me, Mum. And he insulted Holden and Gil *and* Miller Station. He doesn't get to do that and then think he can just keep calling the shots. I don't live on Lane Station anymore. Dad made sure of that. And he made it crystal clear that he didn't *approve* of me being gay."

"He never threw you off the station," she protested weakly. "You left."

Anger bit at my words. "I *left* because he told me that if I wanted to stay, I wasn't allowed to *be gay* on the station. No boyfriends, no mentioning my sexuality, nothing, so that *he* can pretend it doesn't exist. The *real* me doesn't exist."

"I know, I know," she relented. "And *you* know that I didn't agree with him. I should've said something at the time."

"Yes, you should have." My voice shook. "And I'm still not prepared to be anything other than who I am. So, unless Dad's changed his mind about those *rules*, we still have nothing to say to each other. Has he . . . reconsidered?" I couldn't tame the hope in my voice and hated myself for it.

"I . . . don't know," she admitted on a rush of air. "Some days, I think he has. He does talk about you and your dog training, and I know he pays attention to everything that's said about Miller Station, but beyond that, I'm not sure. But he's changed since you left. He's . . . harder, somehow, and I don't like it. I know he misses you. I don't think he ever believed that you'd actually leave. And now he doesn't know how to change things."

"Yes, he does," I corrected her. "And he wrote me out of the Station Trust, Mum. That doesn't sound like he wants to change things."

"That was right back when it first happened. He was only lashing out."

I grunted in disgust. The whole conversation was doing my head in, and I started second-guessing whether I was doing the right thing all over again. Was I expecting too much? Luke's voice sounded in my brain once again. *You can't sacrifice yourself to keep other people happy, not even your parents.*

It was enough to steel my resolve. "It's not my job to rescue him, Mum." The words leapt from my tongue. "Dad hurt me. Badly. You *both* did, but him in particular. For the sake of our family, I'm willing to meet him halfway, but I'm not going to offer myself up on a sacrificial plate. I won't walk onto Lane Station without Dad wanting and agreeing to talk ahead of time. And I mean *talk*, as in a discussion, not him ranting or lecturing me. I won't expose myself to that again, and he needs to know that's a hard line. I'll walk away. But if *you* want to meet up, then I'd love that. We could arrange something in Oakwood. Jules will bring you. But I won't come to the station without Dad asking."

The line fell silent, and I wondered for a second if she'd hung up. Then I caught a small grunt of acceptance. "Okay. I'll talk to Jules, and he can set up a time to meet for coffee in Oakwood."

A sigh of relief ripped through me. I hadn't lost her. "Sounds like a plan. Does Jules know about this call? About your plan?" I really, really hoped not.

"No," she answered quickly. "And I'd appreciate you not mentioning it. He's not exactly happy with me as it is."

That made me smile. *Good for him.* I had no doubt my brother had made his feelings patently clear to them both. Dad wouldn't have liked it, but he couldn't run the station without Jules, and he wouldn't dare risk losing him as well. "Don't worry. I won't mention it."

"Thank you. I do love you, Zach. I hope you know that?"

I made a sound of assent that I wasn't sure I felt, and I was still thinking about it when she hung up. After a few moments, it struck me that I did believe she loved me. She was trying to change, after all, and that had to mean something. But as for my father? For a second, I'd let myself hope. Lesson learned. I wouldn't be wasting any more energy wishing for that miracle.

Or for any miracle, for that matter.

Not even for the miracle of Luke Nichols. Maybe especially not for that one.

Luke was a great guy. He was more than that. But it was crazy to think he and I were going anywhere. I had nothing to offer and he had about the same. Our time together had been nice, really nice, too fucking nice. But I didn't have the luxury of Holden's tight-knit family and team behind me. I didn't own a station or live on my family's. I didn't have Gil's training, or a business to sell, or land on which to start another.

I was on my own.

And I needed to stay focused.

Who knew where Luke was headed? Not even Luke had much idea about that. But one thing seemed certain. It wasn't into *my* future, which was firmly locked in the Mackenzie Basin. A point worth remembering before things between us got even more tangled and I did something stupid that I'd live to regret later.

I winced at the voice in my head shouting that those things . . . *feelings* . . . between us were already impossibly tangled. It only served to underscore my determination to do what needed to be done to secure my future and get my life back on track.

A life where, as much as it hurt, Luke Nichols had only ever had a walk-on bit-part.

CHAPTER NINETEEN

Three days later

Luke

I SET THE SKIDS DOWN GENTLY BUT LEFT THE ROTORS SLOWLY turning—half of me desperate to turn around and leave as fast as I could, the other half knowing there was no running from this. It was time. Time to stand once again in the icy waters of the Havelock.

The wide river rushed past in a thunderous roar, its interconnected braids dirty brown and choked with water from an overnight storm—a far cry from the crystal clear, gentle flow the last time I'd been there. The day we'd scattered Callie's ashes. I hadn't been back since, though I knew Gil and Holden came often. I hadn't been able to find the courage.

"I've landed," I spoke into the headset as I gazed across the broad sweep of water and stones to the other side.

"Good. Be careful coming back, boyo. Those winds are getting up and it's apparently lashing down out west." Gary's voice fell softly in my ears. "Don't leave it too long, yeah?"

"I won't," I assured him. "And thanks for letting me do this."

"My pleasure. See you back at the hangar."

I shut off the engine and climbed out of the cockpit, zipping my jacket against the cold wind that roared down through the gorge from the towering Alps above. Low-hanging cloud cloaked the valley in a dismal grey. I shivered and tugged my beanie over my ears, then picked my way over the stones to the water's edge where a single boulder sat in the shallows like it was waiting for me.

I removed my socks and shoes and left them safely on a pile of stones, then rolled the legs of my flight suit and jeans to my knees and waded across. The shock of the icy water made me gasp, and bolts of cramping pain shot up my calves. But I kept going, my feet scrambling for purchase in the stiff current and less than stable shingle bed, until finally I reached the boulder and grabbed a seat on top with my legs hanging over the side.

I could've been days from civilisation and not just a twenty-minute drive to the homestead on Miller Station. Out here, there was nothing except wilderness as far as the eye could see—a maze of glacial valleys hidden amongst snow-tipped peaks that punched through the slate sky. Treacherous scree slopes tumbled from razor-back ridges, down, down to rivers like this, criss-crossing the valley floors like macrame on their passage to the sea. A place where thorny matagouri rubbed shoulders with pillowy soft brown tussock, the odd symbiosis a metaphor for the landscape itself—intimidating yet strangely inviting. And through it all, the unrelenting tread of thousands upon thousands of merinos who called this inhospitable country home.

I reached into my jacket and retrieved Callie's photo, staring between it and the river, remembering that day and the wrenching pain of watching her ashes tumble and swirl down this mighty river toward the sea. Gil and I stood side by side, a quiet peace between us, the Miller team at our backs.

I remembered the agonising loneliness of watching Holden comforting Gil. Remembered Zach's expression when I caught him watching and then having him tell me days ago what he'd been thinking and feeling. And I remembered how I'd thought I was coming out of the hole that day, only to realise I'd barely even glimpsed the light from the bottom. That it had taken many more months for that to change.

"So, hey, I'm finally back," I spoke over the rush of water that churned and waterfalled over rocks and ribs of gravel. "I'm sorry, Callie. I'm so sorry."

I dropped my voice and stared at the photo in my hand. "I'm sorry that it took me so long to get here." I ran my finger over her laughing face. "I . . . I don't know why it did, but I let you down," I choked around a sob. "I guess I wasn't as ready to let you go as I thought, even though it felt like it was time. In lots of ways, I'm still not. Maybe I never will be."

I rocked back and forward on the cold stone seat. "But I think now that maybe that's okay. Maybe I don't have to let you go. Maybe I have to learn how to take you forward with me. You weren't in those ashes anyway, you never were. Not that it made it any easier."

The churning current blurred at my feet and I scrubbed the back of my hands over my eyes.

"Zach believes you're waiting in my future for when I can see past all this stupid guilt, and maybe he's right. Some days I think I'm almost there. When the first memory of you isn't of that phone call. Isn't some imagined snapshot of you in that car. But instead, it's you waking in the morning, or laughing at me cooking dinner, or the two of us working on your homework, or dancing in the kitchen to Cher. Sometimes when I think about you not coming back, I can't breathe. My heart stops and going forward feels impossible. And then some days I have to reach to try and remember your voice, and that kills me. I know that's part of finding a new place for you in my life, but it hurts so much. How can I forget something like that? I'm your Poppa."

I threw my head back and shouted into the wind. "I'm your Poppa, Callie! You were the best thing to ever happen to me and I miss you so damn much. I'll always love you. Always."

I tore my hat off my head and buried my face in it, weeping until there were no tears left. Then I jammed it back in place and took a deep, cleansing breath.

"I love you, Poppa. Forever and always."

I spun at the words, almost toppling off the boulder as I strained for more, my gaze sweeping over the riverbank. Then it came again, a whip of wind through the chopper blades, a child's voice in the making. I closed my eyes and tipped my head up to the sky, smiling as the high-pitched hum vibrated through my heart. A trick of the wind that should've made me sad but didn't. Who knew in this strange life.

"I love you too, baby." I floated the words out across the river and then lifted my phone to my ear and pushed play.

Hi Poppa.
You'll never guess what happened! Crabby Mr Martin said I gave the best speech out of everyone, and I get to pick the next book for our class read. Daddy said you'll help me choose. Will you call as soon as you land in Christchurch? I wish you didn't have to be away tonight. Daddy said he'd make me meatballs and spaghetti after the party so we can celebrate, but we both know he's gonna sneak some vegetables in there somewhere.
Her clear laughter rang out from the phone.
I love you, Poppa, forever and always. See you tomorrow night.

I pocketed the phone and stared again at the photo. "Well, baby girl, I think maybe I'm ready to choose that next book with you now. A new adventure, right? Or maybe the second act of the same one I started with you. Who knows? I have a few ideas about the storyline, but I'm pretty sure I'm gonna need your help. The love interest is . . . reluctant at best."

CHAPTER TWENTY

Seven days later

Luke

You're avoiding me. I pushed send and slid my phone face down on the oak table.

Doug glanced at it, then back up at me, and his lips quirked. "So, how're things going with our mutual friend?"

Sam shot us a curious glance, and I kicked Doug under the table. "Keep your voice down. And I have no idea what you're talking about."

"Oops. Sorry." His smile said he wasn't.

I ignored him and reached for another slice of garlic bread. A cheer erupted from the other end of the huge table Miller Station had commandeered for their pre-muster party, and I glanced down to see Roz and his maître d' sliding platters of steaming barbecued meat onto the table, along with grilled lettuce drizzled in a white herby dressing, fire-roasted corn, jalapeño poppers, jam-glazed and charred beetroot, and a few other things I didn't recognise that smelled awesome.

The pre-muster party was usually little more than a beer or two at the Oakwood pub, but Gil had decided to fancy things up and make it a team event paid for by the station. We were instructed to bring a plus-one, and so I'd invited Doug. Sam had brought his brother. Charlie had turned up with a guy from Christchurch none of us had ever heard about. Tom ignored the edict and came alone—no surprise there. And Alek brought another recent Russian immigrant who was working on a dairy farm south of the Mackenzie. Extras included Spencer, the vet, and his colleague, Freddie; my boss Gary, and his wife; Emily and Harry; and then Jules who'd been invited by Zach.

No one needed their arms twisted to try Roz's newly opened Barbecue Pit. It was still finding its feet, but locals were already giving it rave reviews. Siting a barbecue restaurant in the middle of sheep country, and on a prime tourist route, was inspired, and the huge sign on the main road was already drawing a trickle of visitors into town who would otherwise have passed right on by.

Doug helped himself to a plateful of lamb and barbecue ribs and then landed a sharp elbow into my ribs. "You can't lie for shit. But if you want to play that game, then I'm talking about the green-eyed beauty at the other end of the table who keeps pretending he's not looking this way every chance he gets. And just so you know, the green-eyed part has nothing to do with their colour, although fuck me, they're gorgeous, and everything to do with the fact that if looks could kill, I'd have been a dead man the minute I sat down next to you."

Leaving my decision about which corn cob to choose, my gaze shot down the table to where Zach sat between Holden and Tom.

Thankfully, he was too busy studying his phone—a frown notched between those pretty auburn brows—to notice me staring. He typed something, put his phone down, and mine buzzed almost immediately. He gave me a sideways glance and our gazes locked. His green eyes widened for a second, then he looked away.

Doug gave a soft snort of amusement. "I rest my case."

"Shut up and eat," I grumbled, sliding my phone to the edge of the table so I could take a peek.

Sorry. Been busy with muster prep. Only two days left.

On the surface, it seemed fair enough, but it made zero sense after what had happened between us only ten days before. Ten days that felt like a lifetime.

Since then, we'd met up only once, at my place, and I'd seen him in passing when I'd flown to Miller Station for their pre-muster reconnaissance flight. He'd been waiting with Gil and Holden at the station hangar and my heart had jumped at the thought that maybe he was coming along for the ride. Any time I got to spend with Zach was a bonus, even if I had to share him with the others. But he'd taken off in his ute before my skids had even hit the ground, and I was left frustrated and even a little hurt.

The get-together at my place hadn't been any more satisfying. It had been a quick and dirty fuck—a million miles from the last time we'd been together—and Zach was there and gone in just over an hour. To be honest, it hadn't felt like he was there at all, like he wasn't even sure why he'd come, like he was holding back.

We'd talked a little, but he'd kept the conversation to the upcoming muster and his discussions with Holden about the training business and a couple of puppies Zach was sourcing for the station. All in all, it had been a wholly unsatisfactory experience, and an unwelcome reminder about how my feelings for Zach had changed so much since I'd arrived in Oakwood in January.

Back then, I'd have been fine with a quick hookup—any chance to get the sexy man in my bed. Since then? Not so much. Because now that I knew Zach, I wanted more. A lot more. I'd grown to love his quirky sense of humour and the way his eyes softened every time he looked at his dogs. I craved that bossy side of his nature that was hot as hell in bed, and I marvelled at his curious love of all things history and his preference for spending his evenings reading or watching a movie rather than going out. I loved watching him move about my kitchen like he belonged there, like I wanted him to. And I loved the extra toothbrush on my vanity, his shampoo in my shower, his favourite lube in my bedside drawer, the smell of him on my sheets, and the way his eyes seemed to light up whenever he saw me.

Or at least they had.

Then I'd fucked up and pushed too hard, too soon, taking him to the observatory that night, a date in everything but name, and then the whole domestic scene the next day. I'd scared him off, and I had no idea how to fix that or even if I could. But the ache in my heart and the need to be with him in every way I could was killing me.

Keeping quiet about my feelings was no longer an option.

Doug leaned closer. "Problems then, I take it?"

I loaded my fork with a piece of lamb and glanced his way. "Am I . . . are *we* that obvious?"

Doug looked at me sideways. "Only to people who know the two of you have wanted to rip each other's clothes off since day one."

I huffed softly. "A slight exaggeration."

"Is it?" He raised a brow. "Because I needed a shower just watching the two of you eye each other up that night in the bar when *we* were supposed to be on a date."

"It wasn't a date," I reminded him. "Now eat your damn food. It's fucking amazing."

He took a mouthful of the charred ribeye and hummed appreciatively. "Damn, you're right about that. I think Roz has got a hit on his hands." He took a couple more bites before leaning in once again. "Are you sure you're okay?"

I ignored the question, too tempted to blurt out that no, I fucking wasn't.

When I didn't answer, Doug turned in his seat to face me. "Hey, I'm sorry. I hadn't realised things between the two of you were getting serious."

"They aren't," I lied, then laid my fork down with a heavy sigh. "At least not on his part."

"Oh." Doug shot a quick look to the other end of the table. "Shit. I'm sorry."

I followed his gaze to where Zach and his brother were sharing a laugh about something. It brought a smile to my face and a simultaneous surge of anger directed toward his arsehole of a father. "Yeah, me too."

I was still watching when Zach happened to look up and catch me. I smiled, and after a moment's hesitation, he smiled back and everything was right in the world. Then he glanced at Doug, frowned, and turned back to his brother. And I felt like the loneliest man in the room.

Doug looked between us and snorted. "Fucking hell. You know, for a guy who's not serious, Zach's pretty fucking upset with the fact I'm sitting next to you."

Before I could reply, the chink of metal on glass caught everyone's attention and Charlie called out, "Speech, speech!"

The dining space grew quiet except for Holden's pained groan. "Oh, for fuck's sake." He got to his feet and shot daggers at his shepherd. "Why thank you so much, Charlotte."

Charlie winced at her full name and everyone laughed, but all I could do was stare at Zach who was busily ignoring me.

"First off, I want to thank you all for coming this evening," Holden began. "And let's hear it for Gil who organised it all."

A cheer went around the room and Gil flushed a pretty pink under the lights.

Holden went on to welcome and thank the three extra shepherds from other stations, who'd come to help with the muster, and their guests. Then he welcomed and thanked all the other plus-ones and finally Roz and the restaurant staff. The latter was greeted by another round of cheering and applause.

While all this was happening, I sent another text to Zach. **Can you meet me outside after?**

I watched as he picked up his phone and read the text. His gaze shot to me, then back at the screen, where he stared at my text for far too long for it to mean anything but bad news. No real surprise considering my unanswered text earlier in the day inviting him to stay the night.

After a long minute, he typed something in reply and my phone buzzed in my hand. **Okay, but I can't stay. I'm parked by the café. See you there.**

As in, *won't* stay, I read between the lines. Well, it didn't get much clearer than that. I replied with a thumbs up, because what the fuck else could I do, and the room grew smaller and smaller until all that was left was the weight of the pit in my stomach and the slow beat of my pessimistic heart.

I left before Zach, a little after eleven, making my exit with Doug who'd spent most of the latter part of the evening trying to buoy my spirits with cheerful banter. He was still trying to convince me to join him for a drink at the pub after I'd met with Zach, but I wasn't in the mood. There was a sour taste to the evening that I couldn't shake, and I figured it was only going to get worse.

I sent him off with a promise to call and then waited outside the café, hidden in the shadow of an old oak, and watched as the Miller Station crew exited the restaurant in dribs and drabs like Brown's cows.

It was a longer wait than I expected, and I zipped my jacket up to my chin and shoved my hands in my pockets. April was just around the corner and although daytime temperatures remained balmy, they dropped like a stone the minute the sun dipped below the horizon. Welcome to early autumn in the high country.

Tom and Sam wandered out, along with Sam's brother, Alek, and Alek's Russian friend. They chatted for a moment, then split up to head to their respective vehicles.

Holden and Gil were the next to leave, their arms wrapped around each other's waists. Holden pressed his lips into Gil's hair and Gil tilted his head up for a kiss. Holden whispered something and they laughed and ran for their ute, Holden tossing his keys to Gil before they tumbled inside, still laughing. I watched their taillights until they turned at the top of the street, and a wave of longing surged through me. Only it wasn't Gil I wanted to be driving home with. That role belonged to only one person.

"Hey."

I spun around at the sound of Zach's voice, my heart thumping in my chest. "Oh, hey." I closed the few feet between us and, hidden by the oak's trunk, I cupped his neck and drew him in for a kiss.

He came without hesitation, his lips warm and soft, his tongue eager as it tangled with mine, a soft hum of pleasure rising in his throat. Hope rallied in my chest. Maybe we were going to be all right, after all.

I pulled off and cradled his face. "I've missed you."

That crease I'd grown to hate returned between his brows. He pressed his lips to mine again, but this second kiss felt excruciatingly restrained.

He pulled away and took a step back. "You wanted to talk?" He looked nervous, his tone wary, and my heart sank once again.

"You sure you're okay to drive home tonight?" I checked, hoping for a reason to change his mind about staying.

"I'm fine," he said smoothly. "I stuck to light beer."

"I won't see you for ten days over muster. I suppose I was kind of hoping you might reconsider staying," I tried.

"I . . . can't." Shadows hid most of Zach's expression but as the oak branches moved with the wind, I caught a glimpse of bleak green eyes. "It's crazy before muster."

Right. I knew a brush-off when I heard it, which left close to zero chance that the conversation I wanted to have was headed anywhere good.

Which meant I had nothing to lose.

In the restaurant, the closed sign was hanging in the window, but the lights still blazed, and I could see Charlie and her man, plus Jules, and Roz, and the server, all talking at a table with drinks in hand. I reached for Zach's hands and drew him further behind the tree.

His eyes met mine and I caught the soft edge of something before it flickered and was gone. "Luke—"

"Zach—"

We spoke at the same time, then stopped and stared at each other.

"You first," he offered.

I nodded. This was it. I sent out a silent prayer. *Anytime now would be good, baby girl.* But as the words formed in my head, the weight of rejection was already building.

Still, fuck if that was going to stop me from actually saying them.

"I like you, Zach," I began. "But you already know that. You maybe even suspect that I *way more* than like you."

His sigh was accompanied by a gentle nod of the head. "I know."

"But what you might not know is that I'm falling in love with you. No, scratch that. I'm *in* love with you." There, I'd said it.

Zach froze. Like literally froze. Not a muscle moved. He didn't even blink an eye for what felt like the longest time. "You—" He licked his lips. "But you—" He squeezed his eyes shut, and when he opened them again, there was nothing but confusion there. "You can't *love* me, Luke."

I almost laughed, he looked so stunned. "And why not?"

"Because . . ." He paused, taking a deep breath. "Because it's too fast."

"According to who?" I countered. "I fell for Gil almost overnight, a month tops. There's no timetable for this stuff."

He was fervently shaking his head. "And look what happened to you and Gil."

Ouch. My hackles rose. "Hey. Just because Gil and I didn't make it doesn't mean we weren't in love. And Holden and Gil fell pretty fast."

Zach blanched. "I'm sorry. You're right. I only meant—" His shoulders slumped. "It was years before I knew I was in love with Holden. And you've got a ton of stuff going on with Callie and a new job. Not to mention you're only here because, in your own words, you're looking to find a way forward. What we've been doing is just . . . enjoyable and . . . convenient . . . for both of us, right?"

Whoa. I drew a sharp breath and gathered the shreds of my dignity as best I could. "Well, damn, I guess that tells me," I replied mirthlessly and Zach flushed under the streetlight, his pale skin turning a shadowy grey. "But you're wrong. You were *never* simply convenient, Zach. I haven't been able to get you out of my head since the first day we met. If anything, you've been the most *in*convenient thing to ever happen to me."

Zach's eyes widened. "But—" His gaze slid off my face, but I wasn't letting him off that easily. I cupped his cheek and turned him back to face me.

"Did I want you? Of course I bloody did. You're gorgeous. Were you a distraction? Only in that you made me feel for the first time in fucking forever. But were you convenient? Hell no, you weren't. I knew I was in trouble that first night you stayed, when we hadn't even slept together. You're smart and funny and sexy and kind, and I want as much of you as I can get, for as long as I can get it."

He shot me a pained look. "But you're not staying, Luke."

I swallowed hard and eyeballed him. *Here goes nothing.* "I have one or two ideas about how to change that."

His eyes narrowed. "But you were only supposed to be here for a few months. That was the plan. That was the only reason I agreed to this. You and I having some fun for a bit and then you go home." He sounded almost betrayed. "I can't have you staying just because of me. We aren't . . . *that*."

Not . . . that? His words landed like a punch to my gut, but I schooled my expression. "It's not *just* because of you. I've been—" I stopped and ran my thumbs over the backs of his hands. *Dammit to hell.* This was going nowhere fast. I took a deep breath and tried again. "Look, all I'm saying is that I'd like to try for something more between us. Maybe it'll work, maybe it won't, but can't we at least try? We're good together, Zach, and I know you feel it too. We might've started as one thing but that doesn't mean it can't change. You, of all people, should understand that." I knew it was the wrong thing to say even before his eyes hardened.

"Me, of all people? Don't use what happened with Holden against me, Luke." His gaze narrowed, and I wondered how the hell we'd found ourselves here.

I took a breath and tried to calm my racing heart. "I'm sorry. I shouldn't have said that. Look, I know I'm a mess. I'm still grieving, and I still don't have a solid direction in place. But I also know I'm in love with you, and I can't pretend that what we're doing is enough anymore. The rest is up to you."

Zach stared at me for a long moment, but I couldn't read anything in his expression. Then he turned away and ran a hand back and forth over his mouth like he was at war in his head, and I supposed he was. I hoped for the best, but when he finally turned back, I saw the answer in those beautiful sad eyes before a word was said.

"I'm sorry, Luke. I . . . can't be that for you. I more than like you too, but I'm only beginning to see a future for myself, and it's going to take all of my focus to make it happen. Part of that is thanks to you, but it didn't ever *include* you."

I swallowed around the gritty taste in my mouth. *It was clearly a night for home truths.*

But Zach wasn't done. "Between you and me, and Holden and Gil, there's a ton of ways that whole idea could go sideways. I owe them more than I can ever repay. I need that job. I need the station. And right now, I need to focus on getting my business running, otherwise, I have nothing to fall back on. I don't have time for a proper relationship, especially with someone who is so—"

"Broken?" I offered with a sad shake of my head.

"No." He cupped my cheek. "Not broken. Just . . . uncertain." He smiled softly. "I can't afford to risk my future on maybes, and I don't think you're ready either, Luke."

I shot him a long, level look. "Are you sure it's not *you* who isn't ready? Because there's nothing *maybe* about *my* feelings, Zach. I'm very clear on those. If there's one thing I've learned, it's that you don't regret putting the people you love first. The rest will follow, although I'm not sure what more I can do to prove it to you."

He leaned in and kissed me lightly on the lips. "Then maybe you shouldn't try." His warm breath condensed in the cool air and then dissipated, taking my hopes along with it. "I've enjoyed our time together. You've given me more encouragement and hope than I've had in a long time. But I have to focus on getting a life for myself again. I'd like to stay friends if you think that's possible. I'm just not sure it can ever be more than that."

Oh God. Oh God. As much as I'd guessed this was coming, it still hit me like a freight train, almost taking my legs from under me. *How the hell did I get it so wrong?*

How the hell was I going to get through this too? Callie. Gil. And now Zach.

I needed to say something, right? To ask him one last time? To . . . what . . . beg?

No.

He'd been crystal clear.

And so, I said nothing. Instead, I lost myself in those green eyes for the final time, feeling my own fill in reply. *I am not going to fucking cry.*

I held my breath as Zach cupped my cheek and stepped forward to kiss me one last time, his face in shadow, a slight hitch to his breath as he pulled away.

"Take care, Luke." His hand lingered on my cheek for a second, and then he turned and walked away.

I swallowed the cry that almost broke free as I tracked every step of his departure, willing him to turn around, to say he'd made a mistake, that he did want to try, that he felt the same way.

But Zach did none of those things. He silently climbed into his ute, threw it into gear, and drove away.

I continued to watch in disbelief as he barely paused at the top of the street before turning left, his taillights fading along with any hope I had that he might change his mind.

I fell against the gnarly trunk of the oak and tried to make sense of what had just happened.

Had I really read things so wrong between us?

Maybe Zach hadn't been ready to jump into anything more serious, but to end it like that? *Jesus, that hurt.*

Ten days before, we'd been walking hand in hand along the canal after an emotional night where I could've sworn he felt the same as I did. There was no way I'd simply imagined the change in our relationship over that weekend. It wasn't possible. *Was it?*

I scrubbed at my eyes and started walking, my breath fogging around my face. Yellow light from the streetlamps plunged through the thinning oak canopy to paint crazy patterns on the sidewalk, the cold westerly swirling the fallen leaves in slow circles that crunched underfoot and gathered in soft mounds in doorways and gutters.

The memory came from nowhere. Callie squealing and jumping into a pile of leaves I'd raked in our backyard. Giggling with delight when I gave up and joined her. Helping me scoop leaves to cover us both to our chins so only our heads poked free. Gil telling us not to move and running for his camera.

Oh God. Pain lanced through my chest, and I fell against the pharmacy wall, hands on my knees, dry retching time and again with nothing but the sour taste of bile in my throat to show for it.

Lifting my head, I swept the back of my hand across my mouth and stared at the cloud-muted night sky. Jesus Christ, this needed to stop. I'd guessed it was coming, so what the hell?

I pushed off the wall, pulled my icy hands up into my sleeves, and kept walking. Past the old Oakwood pub humming with muted conversation and the sound of someone singing "Yellow Brick Road" slightly off-key. Past the old church with its quaint graveyard and a hodgepodge of community announcements pinned to its noticeboard. Along streets packed with houses, darkened windows, and the occasional flicker of television screens. Heading home. Home, where an unopened bottle of rum sat in the cupboard above the fridge.

Home.

I thought about the word as the neighbour's Pekinese stared at me through a gap in the curtains, its tiny eyes glowing in the streetlight.

Home.

It felt right. Maybe not this house. But this place. Mackenzie Country.

Zach or no Zach.

I huffed out a half laugh. I guess I had my answer to that last bit, already.

I stepped through my front door, threw the keys on the hall table, and made a beeline for the kitchen, walking straight past the large bag of dog biscuits I'd bought to keep on hand for Jojo and Nina. So much for that.

The bottle of rum was exactly where I'd left it when I first moved in. I grabbed a glass from the cupboard, debated whether to just down a couple of shots straight, remembered I had to work the next day, and opened the fridge for a Coke to go with it. But when I reached for the can, the harsh light landed on Callie's green silicone band and my knees buckled.

I fell against the countertop and the bottle of rum exploded on the polished wood floor, its contents shooting from one side of the kitchen to the other.

"Jesus Christ." Doug burst into the kitchen and I barely even blinked. "What the hell happened here?" He surveyed the mess with a shake of his head.

I turned and studied him for a second, like his presence had only just registered in my brain. "What are you doing here?"

He looked me up and down and sighed. "I saw you pass the pub looking like . . . well, like that—" He waved a hand over me. "—and figured that was my cue to do the whole being-a-friend thing, although you owe me the beer I left on the bar. And you didn't even close the front door, you muppet." He picked his way across the floor and crouched at my side. "Are you cut anywhere?" He checked me out and pronounced me a lucky, bloody idiot. "Come on, let's get you in the shower while I clean this mess up. Then you can tell me what the fuck's going on."

"I'm not drunk." I accepted his help to stand, mostly so I didn't jag myself on any broken glass. "It's been a night, that's all."

He let me go and patted my cheek. "I know you're not, sunshine. Let me guess. Wonder boy said no to whatever you asked him?"

I rolled my eyes but didn't have the energy to deny it. "I thought maybe . . . I hoped . . . fuck, I don't know what I hoped. I was an idiot to expect anything. I'm hardly going through a lucky patch."

Doug shook his head grimly. "He's the idiot, not you." He tipped his head to the side and studied me for a second. "What else is going on?"

"Nothing new." I grimaced and stared up at the ceiling. "I just miss her, Doug. I miss her so fucking much."

"Oh, Jesus." He snapped me into a hug and I sagged against him, wanting the arms around me to be Zach's. Wanting it more than I'd have ever thought possible.

Eventually, he let me go and steered me toward the bathroom. "Get yourself in that shower. You smell like a distillery. I'll deal with all this. But man, the next time *I* fuck up my love life, I'm calling in a favour."

"I'll be there," I promised. "I'm pretty much an expert now."

CHAPTER TWENTY-ONE

Zach

SEVEN DAYS INTO MUSTER AND WE FINALLY HAD THE LAST stragglers off the hill and safely mobbed at River Hut ready for Tom to drive them down to the homestead the next day. While he did that, the rest of us would shift camp to Folly Hut to start on the second mob.

To celebrate a successful first stage of muster, we decided on an early dinner so we'd be done before dark and could enjoy a few beers and relax with the paying guests who were happily exhausted and barely standing upright. They'd proved to be a nice bunch of people, enthusiastic, and keen to get their hands dirty rather than just tag along.

Genuine extra hands were always a bonus, considering the station was one of the largest in the Mackenzie Basin—about thirty-five thousand acres and change—and stocked around ten thousand merinos and three hundred head of cattle. Summer grazing pushed sky-high into the Southern Alps over land too steep for horses, and bringing down all those thousands of merinos was the job of a bunch of crazy shepherds and their dogs. Walk in, walk out, just as it had always been done.

Happy tourists made life a lot more pleasant for everyone else, which was just as well considering we'd been dogged from day one by damp weather and bone-chilling low cloud—mountain fog, as we called it. The annoying stuff hung around until mid-morning and then returned at dusk. And the weather was set to get worse with a chance of sleet or even snow over the next twenty-four hours. It wasn't common in April, but it happened.

Not that the weather had dampened anyone's spirits, not even those of the guests. They seemed to relish every muscle-burning minute of the roller-coaster climbs and scrambles through treacherous valleys, proclaiming the spectacular views all the more appreciated because of it. Go figure. Some people were born to smile.

Charlie and I had been allocated clean-up along with making conversation with the paying guests, except the latter were holed up in their bunks resting their aching bodies, and Charlie was seeing to the dogs. Which meant I had some rare time to myself.

I'd commandeered a seat by the fire where I could keep an eye on the happenings in the hut's tiny kitchen while the rest of the team were busy following Holden's—*read Gil's*—detailed instructions regarding that night's dinner—a gigantic lamb pie, mashed potatoes, minted peas, creamed fennel, roast pumpkin, and a chocolate mud cake for dessert. Gil delivered meals to the hut on a daily basis, and most only needed a minimum of prep, but Holden was an autocratic arsehole when it came to making sure we got the final steps right so everything hit the table exactly as Gil intended. We gave him shit about how whipped he was, but we wouldn't change a thing. Gil spoiled the pants off us all.

With the noise of laughter and piss-taking in the background, I pulled my phone from my pocket and stared at the screen like I had a million times in the week since I'd left Luke standing in Main Street. Not that I'd made it very far—around the corner and into the supermarket car park had been as far as I could manage before something caved inside.

Hidden from view, I'd come to a screeching halt and slammed my palms against the wheel, choking back tears like a fucking idiot while second-guessing everything I'd just done—something that had become a bit of a recurring theme.

It had all seemed so clear at the time. But the more time that passed without seeing Luke, the less important all those concerns I'd had about the two of us together seemed to become.

Maybe because I'd lied to Luke that night. I'd lied when I'd said that my future plans had never included him. The truth was, I'd done nothing *but* imagine Luke there with me, alongside me. I'd fantasised about us lying in bed on the weekends with the dogs between us and taking more of those walks along the canal. About competing at trials with Luke watching. And having him fly us to my favourite remote places in the Mackenzie—to picnic in the mountains or ski on glaciers.

I'd fantasised a hundred ridiculously romantic scenarios that had my heart craving for something my head didn't seem to want to believe in anymore. Between me and Jules, I'd always been the dreamer. When had I become so cynical? I squashed the voice in my head that screamed, *a year ago*.

You're not cynical, I kept telling myself. You're being practical.

I sighed and read the text again, the one Luke had sent the night I'd left him standing on Oakwood.

These last couple of months with you have meant more to me than you'll ever know. I haven't felt happiness in a long time. I haven't felt much of anything at all. But you've given me hope that even though it won't be with you, maybe love's not done with me yet. I won't make things awkward. This is my last text on the subject. Yes, I'd like to stay friends. Take care of your-

self, Zach. You're a talented, beautiful man, and you're going places. Don't ever settle for second best.

Dammit to hell. Why did he have to be so . . . so . . . fucking perfect?

I'd fully expected . . . *deserved* to be ghosted. In fact, to have Luke avoid me for a year or two would've been just dandy.

It would've been . . . safe.

It would've given *him* time to leave.

It would've given *me* time to reset my brain, my heart, and my dick, and not necessarily in that order. Time to get busy with my business with no chance of being distracted by a man who had the potential to throw me right off track. Because no matter how much I liked him or where Luke's life might lead him, *I* wasn't leaving the Mackenzie, and I didn't have the stomach for any more heartbreak.

I read the text again.

But no, Luke was clearly going to be a gentleman about the whole thing. It was such an arsehole move. Because it made me feel guilty. Because it reminded me why I liked him so much, and yes, more than liked him—something I'd been thinking a lot about over the previous week. Not that it changed anything.

Except that maybe it changed everything.

Charlie appeared, dragging a chair behind her. She dropped it alongside mine and sank into it with a groan, stretching her legs to wriggle her feet by the crackling fire. I shoved my phone back in my pocket and handed her a beer from the chillybin.

"Thanks." She pulled the tab and we clinked cans.

After a minute of both of us staring at the fire and sucking on our beers, she elbowed me gently. "So, exactly what rat crawled up your arse and died, Mister Glumface?"

I elbowed her back. "No rats here. And good evening to you, too."

She snorted. "Good try, but not a chance in hell. Seriously, Zebedee, you've been moping around all week looking like someone shot your dog. Muster is the best fucking ten days of the year, man, and I don't need your sad-arse pouty face messing with my good vibes."

I almost choked on my mouthful of beer. "Wow, I appreciate the heartfelt concern."

She grinned. "You're welcome. It can be a burden always putting others before myself, but I wear the mantle lightly."

"Oh my god." I laughed and gave her a playful shove. "You're the worst."

"I try. Come on, Zach, spill."

"There's nothing to spill."

"Riiiight." Charlie knocked her foot against mine. "That's why you almost fell arse over kite down that scree today. In all our years of mustering together, I've never once seen you come even close to doing that."

"It's this bloody mountain fog. Everything's damp. I just lost my footing. I don't know why everyone's making such a big deal about it."

Charlie rolled her eyes. "Yes, I'm sure it had nothing to do with the fact you've been so distracted you practically needed an arrow pointing downhill every ten steps just so you could find your way back this afternoon."

I bit back a smile because she was right. I was a veritable legend on muster for my ability to navigate the trickiest slopes and rocky climbs. Tom even referred to me as the team goat. But instead of my usual panache on the hill, I'd spent most of the week patching up scrapes and bruises and cursing my stupidity. Even Jojo and Nina had taken to giving me a wide berth after I tripped over Jojo from not watching where I was going and stomping on Nina's paw. It kind of said it all.

"I'm having an off week." I stared at the flames dancing in the firepit and followed the tendrils of smoke as they wove their way upward into the misty gloom. A few more hours and the damn cloud would engulf half the mountain again.

"Rubbish," Charlie declared. "You forget, I know you too well. Something's eating at your normally chilled, good old country soul.

And if it has something to do with Holden, even better. He's had his bossy boots on all muster, and I could do with the leverage." A wicked smile crossed her lips. "Then again maybe it has nothing to do with our fair leader. So, tell me, what's our handsome pilot done now?"

I shot her a startled glance, which only served to broaden her smile.

"What? You think I didn't know?" She shook her head. "Tsk, tsk. It's like you don't even know me."

I chanced a worried look at the others who were still busy inside the hut.

Charlie followed my gaze. "Don't worry. I only picked up the vibe between the two of you that day at Cass River. You could hardly keep your eyes off each other, which was kind of a surprise since I thought you didn't like him much, but hey, things change, right? Same thing at the cookout, and again at Roz's restaurant. Put all of those together, along with the mauling your body's been getting lately, and it was kind of obvious."

I groaned. "It was just a bit of fun." And if I lied about that one more time, I was pretty sure I'd be going straight to hell.

She frowned. "Was? You mean it's over?"

I nodded and went back to studying the fire. "Yeah. We've both got a lot going on."

"Mmm." She sounded unconvinced. "Can I say something?"

I shot her a sideways glance. "Depends on what it is. If it's about Luke being Gil's ex, then don't bother. I already know it was a stupid thing to do."

Her gaze narrowed. "Why should I give a shit if he's Gil's ex?"

I looked up as Tom left the hut, balancing a pile of plates and knives and forks and putting them on the table. "Well, you have to admit, it's pretty *out there*. Two sets of exes hooking up?"

Charlie shrugged. "Luke's a good guy. You're a good guy. Holden and Gil are good guys. You all seem to like each other and get on.

Who gives a shit about what used to be? Unless one of you doesn't like the idea?" She eyeballed me. "Is that what's going on?"

"No." I took another swallow of beer. "Gil and Holden don't know. I thought *nobody* knew."

She huffed and nudged my shoulder with hers. "Yeah, well, sorry, not sorry. And I wouldn't bank on keeping that secret too long. Gil's a crafty fox. Not much slips past him."

The memory of Gil trying to persuade me to give Luke a chance came to mind, and I lifted my beer to my lips. "Nah, I think I'm safe."

A squeal broke the hushed quiet of the valley and Sam shot out of the hut with Holden in hot pursuit, a tea towel spinning in his hand. We laughed as Holden chased Sam around the back of the hut and the thwack of a strike was accompanied by a yowl from Sam and a hurried reappearance by Holden who disappeared back into the hut with Sam on his heels, baying for blood.

"My money's on Sam," Charlie declared.

I watched the two men circling the kitchen table and said, "I'll take that bet."

Charlie sank down in her chair, her eyes sparkling in the firelight. "So, is our friend any good in bed?"

I spluttered beer down the front of my sweatshirt and rocked forward on my chair. "Jesus, Charlie." When I'd flicked the worst of it off, I settled back. "That's none of your damn business."

She shrugged disappointedly. "Well, I guess you can't have everything."

I shot her a look. "I never said that."

Her eyes danced. "I knew it! Tall, gorgeous, and funny, he has to be a firecracker between the sheets, right?"

My blush must've been enough of an answer because she unexpectedly kissed me on the cheek. "Good for you, Zebedee. You deserve some fun."

"What is it with people?" I grumbled. "If one more person says I deserve to have some fun or to be treated well or to get back on the horse, whatever the hell that means, I swear I'm gonna throttle them,"

I grumbled. "I don't *need* a man to be okay or to be happy. I don't *need* my arsehole father. I don't *need* anyone. What I *need* is to get my shit together. I *need* to get some money in the bank. I *need* to start planning my future. I *need* a life."

"Wow." Charlie stared at me, wide-eyed. "That clearly struck a chord. Of course, you don't *need* a man to be okay. I never said that. Our happiness doesn't rely on some other person. But who says you can't have *all* of it or at least some of it?"

"Because that's not how life works, Charlie. At least it's not how *my* life works. I didn't get to keep the *guy*, *and* the family, *and* the farm, *and* what I thought was a lifetime home and a job. I lost pretty much all of it. What's to stop that happening all over again?"

Her mouth dropped open. "Jesus, Zach. When did you become such a pessimist? You *can* plan a future *and* have a life at the same time. It's called multi-tasking. Oh, but that's right. You're a man. I forgot. Multi-tasking is the work of the devil."

I couldn't stop the smile. "Yeah, yeah. Laugh it up. But in my experience, it doesn't pay to be greedy, because the universe likes to fuck over your plans and stomp on your heart like they mean nothing."

She scrutinised me for a long minute, and then her lips twitched and she raised both hands, rubbing her thumbs and forefingers together, giving me the whole orchestra. "Aw, poor baby."

And just like that, I was laughing. *God, I loved her.* "You're a terrible person," I scolded, and she chuckled.

"I know. And I'm sorry. You've had a shit year, but no matter what you think, nobody has to do it all on their own. Look at Holden and Gil—"

"Something else I wish people would stop saying," I interrupted grumpily. "I mean, I get it. They're wonderful and made for each other and blah blah blah, excuse me while I vomit, but I'd rather not have their relationship shoved down my throat on a regular basis as some kind of example to aspire to, you know? Who says I even want that?"

Charlie glanced to where Holden was carrying two loaded serving dishes to the table and gave a sympathetic sigh. "This is true. They are prone to curdle the stomach a bit, for sure."

"Right?" I shot her a look. "So, then why—"

"Because for all of their differences," she broke in, "they somehow make it work. Did you know Gil almost walked out on Holden after an argument last year?"

I blinked, shocked. "What? No."

She smiled. "He packed his bag and was halfway to Tekapo before he decided he was being an idiot."

It was hard to believe. "I . . . wow." I shook my head. "Just wow."

"Yep, so there's no magic dust, sunshine. You obviously like Luke, and I'm not talking about you bumping uglies with the guy. To be honest, I can see the two of you working."

I gaped. "But . . . why would you think that?"

She shrugged. "You're a gentle guy and you're a bit of an old soul. You've been hurt by people who should know better, people you trusted. You have tender places inside, and I expect Luke knows a lot about tender places. We've all got to know him this last year, all except *you*, since you were too busy trying to hate him and pretend you didn't want to fuck him silly."

I groaned . . . again.

She laughed and slipped her arm through mine as she continued. "Luke is easy-going, and kind, and the fact he's hot as hell doesn't hurt either."

"I'll give you that," I agreed. "But he's still working through Callie and a shitload of grief. He has no idea what his future holds. The whole thing is too . . . loose."

"Are you sure about that?"

"Jesus, you sound just like him."

She arched a brow but said nothing.

I slumped in my seat. "Okay, so he might've asked if I wanted us to be more serious. Said he was considering hanging around longer."

Charlie's eyes widened, then narrowed again. "And let me guess, you said no, because of course you bloody did, you nincompoop." Charlie whacked me on the bicep. "Because, after Holden, you're running scared."

I bristled. "I am *not* running scared." *Am I?* "Luke won't stay in Oakwood."

She blinked in disbelief. "Says who? You? Why not let *him* decide what he can and can't do? Or what he does and doesn't want?"

"Because... because... I don't know why," I flustered.

Her eyes blazed and she lowered her voice. "Because you're scared to open your heart again in case he throws it away," she hissed. "In case he's another Holden who ends up not wanting you the same way. If you don't give him a chance at your heart, then you can't get hurt."

"Jesus, Charlie." I scrubbed a hand down my face. The woman was relentless. "I'm not saying you're completely wrong, but Luke can't stay here just because of me. It's too much... pressure. What if we don't work?"

"What if you do?"

"Are you crazy?" I scoffed. "What are the chances?"

"What are the chances of any couple working at the start?"

"Stop doing that," I growled. "I don't know, all right?"

She took a breath and blew out a long sigh. "How do you recognise a potential match with a dog?"

I choked out a laugh. "Now, I know you're not comparing boyfriends to choosing a damn dog, right?"

She shrugged. "Just answer the question."

"Whatever. Well, there's breeding, obviously."

She chuckled. "Let's pretend Luke passes the hip-dysplasia test and other hereditary issues."

"All right. Well, there's temperament. For me, I like bold but not stubborn. Intelligent. Quick thinking. A dog that anticipates what I need but who can pivot. Who has the potential to work as part of a team. Who wants to work. Who bonds with me. Trusts me." I rolled my eyes at Charlie. "You think you're so clever, don't you? But this has nothing to do with real human relationships."

"No, you're right," she agreed far too readily, and I steeled myself. "Human relationships are way more complex because the roles can shift. There's give and take, stepping in when the other needs you to lead for a while, and vice versa. Encouraging the other to grow and take chances, all of that."

I thought about how Luke enjoyed me bringing it both in bed and out of it. And how when I was with him, I felt more fully . . . me, like that made any sense. It wasn't like I hadn't been *me* with Holden, but with Luke, it felt . . . more.

Sam appeared and headed for the kennels, while Tom called out to let the guests know dinner was almost ready and Holden started walking our way.

Charlie leaned in close and whispered, "All I'm saying is—and I can't believe I'm having to remind a gay guy about this—you like who you like. End. Of. Story."

"Please tell me we're talking about Zach's secret lover." Holden held his hands over the fire to warm them.

"Oh, no. There is no *we* in this conversation." I glared at my best friend before firing Charlie my best don't-you-fucking-dare look. They smiled as one and my gaze bounced between them. "Now you're just pissing me off."

"Everyone up to the table," Tom called.

I jumped to my feet. "Whoops. Look at that. Gotta go."

"Wait a minute." Holden put a hand on my arm.

Charlie looked between us and got to her feet. "Don't keep us waiting too long," she warned. "Alek will start chewing his arm off if he's not fed soon."

The second she was gone, Holden dropped his hand. "I just wanted to check in with you. You've been pretty quiet. It's not like you. Have, um, have things finished with this new guy?" He eyed me cautiously. "Is that why you've been such a prickly bastard?"

I couldn't, *wouldn't* respond, my throat thick and scratchy with emotion I wasn't prepared to show.

When I didn't answer, Holden sighed. "Okay, none of my business. All I'm going to say is that I haven't seen you smile as much as you have in the last couple of months for . . . well, for years. Including while we were doing *our* thing, which is a bit of a blow to the ego if I'm honest."

I snorted. "I'm sure you'll survive." Then I thought about what he said and added, "You think I've been smiling a lot?"

He snorted. "Hell, yeah. Like the cat who got the cream."

"Oh." Heat bloomed in my cheeks.

Holden laughed. "Yeah, exactly like that. Come on, let's eat." He threw an arm over my shoulder and steered me toward the table. We'd just finished loading our plates and grabbed a seat when the relentless brassy noise of a car horn echoed through the camp and up the river valley.

Heads spun as we all recognised the sound of Gil's ute, and Holden shot to his feet and started running. Seconds later the vehicle blasted through the gate into camp, kicking up stones and spraying water in a large arc off the back tyres. I ran to Holden's side, as did the rest of the team, my heart pumping. Gil's arrival like this meant nothing good, that was for sure.

The second he'd skidded to a stop, the driver's door flew open and Gil jumped out. To everyone's surprise but mostly mine, he bypassed Holden and made a beeline for me, blurting, "Your dad and Jules are missing somewhere up the top of Halifax beat above Yellow Tarn."

The air whooshed from my lungs. "What do you mean, missing?"

Gil shook his head, his expression bleak. "I'm not entirely sure, but apparently, your dad went up to check on a group of wethers he'd spotted from the Cessna yesterday. Jules insisted it could wait, that the cloud was too low. Everyone thought it was settled, but while they were busy in the woolshed, Paddy took Chip and headed off on his own. Just after lunch, he called your mum on the satphone to say he'd moved the wethers down and was on his way back. That's the last anyone's heard from him."

I shook my head in furious disbelief. "That idiot."

Gil nodded. "Jules took Hopper and went after him, but it's been three hours and still no word."

"Shit." I pinched the bridge of my nose.

"That's a steep bit of country." Holden sounded worried. "And the mountain fog is much worse out west."

I nodded, my mind spinning. "I have to go." I started toward the ute, then stopped. "I'll need the dogs." I veered toward the kennels, but Sam was already running.

"I'll get them," he called back.

"You can't go after them on your own, Zach," Holden protested. "I'm coming with you."

"No." Gil put a hand on Holden's arm. "Luke is bringing a chopper."

I blinked in shock. "Luke?"

Gil shrugged. "Your mum also rang Blue who gave the search team a head's up, including Wild Run. Apparently, as soon as Luke heard, he insisted on flying you there. It'll save you a ton of time."

"Does that mean they're going after them?"

Gil shook his head. "Your mum said the cloud's too low for a decent sweep of the area, and between the weather and the fact there's still time for them to walk out, no one's sanctioning an official search."

"If they could walk out, Jules would've found a way to do it or at least let us know," I argued, turning to Holden. "I know that beat like the back of my hand. With the right gear, I can safely leg it up there myself in half the time it would take a team." I braced for the inevitable pushback, and I wasn't disappointed.

Gil's tone flattened into his scary psychologist vibe that always made me feel like I was ten years old and caught lying about having my hand down Callum Roberts' trousers. "That's crazy talk, and you know it."

"It's not," I insisted. "You haven't lived in these mountains all your life like we have, Gil. We've all been caught on the hill during a storm at some point and in weather way worse than this, right?" I looked for support and there was a cautious nodding of heads that appeared to have zero impact on Gil.

His eyes darkened ominously, like he was setting up for a fight. "You can't—"

Holden stepped between us. "Those are entirely different circumstances, and you know it, Zach," he rightly pointed out. "More often than not there's a team with you in those instances, like muster, *and* a plan. It could take you a couple of hours to get above Yellow Tarn in this weather, maybe longer. By then it'll be nightfall and dangerous. Even if you find them, there's no way you'll be able to get back down again. You'll have to overnight, and the forecast is for freezing conditions."

"My point exactly." I glared at him. "And that's my brother *and* my father up there. If either of them is injured, they might not make it through the night." I swallowed around the ball of fear in my throat. "I can carry enough gear to get us all through one night. If there's even a chance that I can do it, then I'm their best hope, Holden. What would you do in my position? If that was Em or Sam?"

Holden returned a level stare, but I could see that steely reserve begin to falter until finally he sighed. "Fair enough. But you can't do it alone. I'm going with you."

Gil's eyes sparked. "Oh, hell no—"

"No, you're not." I stepped forward and took Holden's hands. "Thanks, but this is *my* area of expertise and *my* family. I won't risk you as well."

"I'll go." Charlie stepped forward, but I shook my head.

"No, for the same reasons. Plus, coming with me could screw up your chances with SAR. This is off the books. Besides, you're needed here to get that second mob down. I'll be okay. I'll have Jojo and Nina and the search team tomorrow. We don't know for sure there's even a problem yet."

Holden's jaw ticked and he looked anything but happy.

Then Gil squeezed his arm and surprised me by saying, "Let him go. Doug and Blue are already on their way to Lane's. They won't let him set foot out the door if it's too dangerous."

Which was why I had no intention of hanging around to ask. I'd be gone before anyone had a chance to stop me.

But Gil's words were enough to calm Holden down and eventually he nodded. "You'll keep us in the loop?"

"Of course."

"And you won't do anything stupid? If the weather is bad, you'll wait, right?"

"I'll be careful," I evaded, figuring there was a world of difference between my definition of stupid and his. If it was Gil up there, I knew exactly what he'd be doing. "Come on." I sidestepped Gil and headed for the ute. "We need to get moving. I'll have to pick up my gear from the cottage."

But Holden was at the driver's door before I could climb inside. "Not a chance, buster. *I'm* driving. I'm seeing you onto that chopper, and I want to be in cell phone coverage tonight for regular updates. *Regular*, understand me?"

"But—" I saw the set of his jaw and snapped my mouth closed. "Fine." I slid into the back seat, leaving Gil to ride shotgun.

Sam came running with Jojo and Nina in tow. He whipped them into their cages on the back of the ute and then slapped the roof. "Ready to go."

Holden slid into the driver's seat and started issuing muster instructions to Tom through the open window.

Tom scowled and waved him off. "I think I can remember what to do," he deadpanned. "Go. We've got this. We'll see you at Folly Hut tomorrow . . . or not . . . We'll be fine either way." Then he turned to me. "You do what you have to do, son, but be careful. You're a part of *our* family now, and we always look after our own. We don't want to lose you."

Tears welled unexpectedly in my eyes and all I could do was nod.

"Belt up, kids." Holden put the ute into gear. "This isn't going to be a comfortable ride."

I fumbled my seatbelt into place, took a deep breath, and tried to keep my stomach contents where they belonged as Holden hit the gas and we took off back toward the homestead.

CHAPTER TWENTY-TWO

Thirty minutes earlier

Luke

"You still here?" Gary paused on his way to the Wild Run office. "I thought you were done for the day."

"I should've been." I continued wiping the inside of the chopper door. "But the husband of the couple I took up this morning left most of his lunch on the floor in the back. I've cleaned it once, but it still stinks, so I'm giving it another go." The fact I was also sick to my eyeballs of doing nothing but thinking about Zach and moping around my house had absolutely nothing to do with it.

Gary poked his head inside and shuddered. "Jaysus, there's no arguing with that. But I'm not paying you overtime." He shot me a wink and kept walking.

"Did you hear me asking?" I grabbed the sudsy sponge from the bucket and let it fly at his back.

He lunged through his office door, and the sponge sailed past to land on the cake tin next to the coffee machine, sending it crashing to the floor.

Gary grinned and flipped me off through his office window. "Arse. And just so you know, I'm adding the cost of that to our contract. Mallowpuffs are my favourite."

I retrieved the sponge and checked the biscuits before walking the container into his office. "They're only broken. Perfectly edible."

He considered the sad array of cracked chocolate, dented marshmallow, and broken crumbs, and gave a weighty sigh. "It's a bleedin' massacre. The only decent thing left to do is put them out of their misery." He grabbed a couple of pieces and shoved them into his mouth, spraying crumbs across his desk.

I laughed and returned to my cleaning, leaving Gary to cope with his sugar coma all on his own. Under the gruff, straight-shooting exterior, he'd proved to be a bit of a cinnamon roll. After Zach had ditched me, Gary picked up on my flat mood almost immediately. He didn't ask any questions, which I was grateful for. He simply began checking in with me on a regular basis.

I'd be working somewhere in the hangar and he'd appear out of the blue with two coffees and proceed to drag me on a walk around the airfield. We'd talk about the business, about his family, and about how he missed Ireland. Eventually, he asked about Callie, and to my surprise, I found myself opening up. He never once tried to offer any solutions or suggestions. He simply listened.

The next day, I told him about Zach, and the same thing. He listened and said that life sucked sometimes and that he was sorry things hadn't worked out.

And wasn't that the truth?

Zach's flat-out refusal to even consider something more between us had hurt a lot more than I'd anticipated, expected or not, and I only had myself to blame. I'd done the stupidest thing possible under the circumstances.

I'd fallen in love with a man who wasn't ready for it, in a place I wasn't sure I was staying.

And I'd spent the following week berating myself for ever letting things get that far. Zach had been clear from the start. Hell, we both had. I'd practically chased the poor guy until he'd given in and then kept pushing for more. It wasn't Zach's fault that I'd fallen head over heels in love with him. It was mine. And it was hard to escape the irony in that.

Zach had walked away, and I couldn't blame him. And the fact I'd had no response to the text I'd sent kind of said it all.

He was done.

We were done.

I had to find a way to accept that and move on. Although how the hell I was supposed to do that while running into him every time I visited the station, I had zero idea. Wear my sunglasses . . . a lot. And maybe not be too available to help out for a while.

I'd toyed with simply heading back to Wellington, but I wouldn't do that to Gary, and in truth, I didn't want to. I hadn't been lying when I'd told Zach I'd been considering ways to stay longer in Oakwood. At the time, I'd told myself it was because of him. Because I wanted a chance of there being an *us*.

Turns out, I was wrong. I *liked* living in Oakwood. I liked the job and the people and the scenery. I liked Gary and the other pilots who worked for Wild Run. I liked meeting new people and flying over some of the most spectacular wilderness in the world. I liked the climate and I liked spending time on the station. I felt part of something new and exciting.

I might not be sharing that with Zach as I'd hoped, but I'd survived too much and lost too much to ignore the things that sparked any kind of fire in my belly. With or without Zach, I wasn't going anywhere. The contract had been drawn up and there was no going back. Oakwood was home for the foreseeable future, and that meant I had to find a way to deal with seeing Zach and knowing he wasn't mine.

I'd just finished wiping down the interior of the chopper and was about to power wash the outside when Gary hurtled out of his office waving his phone.

Zach and the others were waiting as I finalised my approach. The sight of him standing there did weird things to my heart, all the regret and yearning rising like bile in my throat. I swallowed hard. I couldn't afford to be distracted, not today.

The daylight and visibility were still decent at Miller Station, but a thick blanket of cloud hung over the sawtooth ranges to the west, and it was beginning to roll down the sides and into the valley in soft, pillowy grey folds. Lane Station sat in the next valley over, under all that cloud. I'd passed the southern end as I'd flown in, and just getting Zach safely to his family's home at the northern tip was going to mean tightly following the road rather than up and over the ranges as I would normally do. It was going to be a squeeze.

Dressed in full search and rescue winter gear, Zach appeared calm, but I knew better. His jaw had a steely set, his body poised and tense, those pretty green eyes daring anyone to get in his way. *Oh boy.* One look and I knew I had my work cut out for me. I set the skids down on the damp grass and took a deep breath. Keeping that man from putting his life at risk over the next few hours was going to be nigh on impossible.

He watched me land, hopping impatiently from foot to foot, his dogs harnessed, a huge pack leaning against his leg, not even bothering to turn away from the rotor wash like Gil and Holden did.

I knew that look. There was no way Zach was going to hang about waiting for Blue and Doug before he set out after his dad.

Just as well I had one or two ideas about that.

I glanced at my gear in the back and thanked Gary for having the foresight to insist I pack heavy. Every Wild Run pilot underwent basic alpine survival training, and our choppers carried an impressive emergency kit.

The second the rotors had slowed enough, Zach was at the door with Gil and Holden on his heels.

Holden stuck his head into the cockpit. "How's the cloud looking around Lane's?"

I shook my head. "Not great. And it's ten degrees and dropping."

"Please tell me you've got a satphone on you."

I patted my flight suit pocket.

He relaxed. "Zach's promised to keep us up to date. Call if you need us. Good luck."

"Don't need luck," Zach called from outside. "I'll find them."

Gil caught my eye and flicked his head toward Zach, mouthing the words, "Keep him safe."

I answered with my best you've-got-to-be-kidding look, because really? There was no question in my mind where this was headed. It wouldn't matter what the weather was like, Zach was headed up that mountain after his father and brother regardless. And no one was going to stop him.

Unaware of the exchange, Zach finished settling Jojo and Nina inside their carriers, then our eyes met briefly and he nodded. "Thanks for doing this, Luke. It means a lot."

I frowned at his words. "Jesus, Zach. What the hell else was I going to do? It's your dad and your brother. Now stop saying stupid shit and let's get you over there. Gary says he's a good mind to charge your dad for the nuisance value alone once we get the idiot back on safer ground."

"You'll have to get in line." Zach loaded his pack onto the back seat, surveyed my gear, and threw me a curious look. "And where exactly do you think you're going with all this?"

I levelled a look his way. "Wherever *you* are, so shut up and get in."

"Oh no, no, no." He shook his head. "You're not train—"

"Shut the fuck up and get into your seat. You're not the only one who can do shit. Do you think I'd just be winging it if this thing crashed up on a glacier? Or maybe you want to drive to your parents' place instead?"

He stared me down for a few seconds, then mumbled something under his breath that sounded like "Bossy fucker," and "We'll see about that," and clambered into the front seat.

Only then did I remember Gil and Holden still standing there, and when I looked up, sure enough, the two of them were giving us decidedly odd looks. *Well, shit.*

Gil caught my eye and one of those carefully manicured brows arched in unspoken enquiry. *Great.* Just what I needed. Waterboarding had nothing on those eyebrows. Holden said something into Gil's ear and Gil nodded, but I had zero time to worry about whatever they were thinking. I belted my harness, gave Zach's a tug to check it was secure, and then we were off.

It should've been a short fifteen-minute flight, a hop over the ranges and down into the next valley. But with the dense cloud hugging the peaks, I had to sweep back along the valley road toward Lake Tekapo and then turn north again to follow Lane Station's access road all the way back to their homestead.

For the first few minutes, the atmosphere inside the cockpit was thick enough to cut with a knife. With his gaze locked forward, his body rigid, and his hands clenched in his lap, Zach was practically vibrating.

Eventually, I couldn't stand it any longer. "For Chrissakes, sit on one and put the other hand under my thigh before you cut off the blood supply to your fingers"

Zach started and his gaze jerked sideways to meet mine, the fear in them enough to break my heart.

"Come on. If I can't hold your hand, that's the next best thing. Friends, right?"

Zac said nothing, but after a few seconds a hand slid under my thigh and a sigh escaped his lips. "Thanks." Then he faced forward again, peering through the windscreen to the mountains beyond.

"We'll find them," I reassured him softly.

He turned back to face me, misery turning those beautiful green eyes a muddy khaki. And when he spoke, his tone was bleak and unforgiving. "I might've sounded sure of myself back there, but I reckon I've got maybe an hour before those clouds completely engulf Yellow Tarn, making it a hellish climb. It'll be dark not long after and that's a big area to search, even with the dogs. There's a network of ravines, and if Dad or Jules—" He swallowed hard and the mic caught the sound. "If either of them took a tumble down one of those scree slopes—" He didn't finish, looking away to scan the hills as if his father and brother might suddenly materialise, but the thick grey cloak was creeping down fast and taking the temperature with it. "They could be anywhere."

The headset fell quiet, and as the homestead came into view at the end of the valley, I thought about our options. Zach was right. I'd flown over that area enough to know how rugged and treacherous the terrain could be. In the low clouds, finding Paddy and Jules would be needle-in-a-haystack material. The best chance Zach had was to make the best use of whatever daylight we had left.

I sighed inwardly. *Am I seriously thinking of doing this?*

Dammit, yes. Yes, I am. The groan of resignation *wasn't* meant for Zach's ears, but I'd forgotten the mic and he shot a questioning look. I held his worried gaze for a moment, then radioed Gary who was waiting for news back at the Wild Run hangar. It was his helicopter, after all.

I told him my idea and his response was, "Have you lost your damn mind, boyo?" Quickly followed by, "For fuck's sake, Luke." Which was then followed by, "Jaysus, you idiot. Okay, dammit. I'll call Norma and tell the others." And to finish up, "I'm adding the cost of therapy to the contract." His laughter sounded a little strained and I didn't blame him.

I signed off, aware of Zach's eyes burning two holes in the side of my face. "What the hell do you think you're doing?"

Considering he'd heard everything said, there was no need to explain, and so I didn't. "You want me to set down on the airstrip instead, just say the word. We can hoof it from there." I arched a brow and waited.

Zach's eyes held mine as his teeth worked the inside of his cheek until finally, he nodded. "Thank you, Luke."

My cheeks blew hot, but not as hot as my heart at the sound of my name on his lips. He continued to watch me for a long moment, his eyes gleaming in the fading light, but my gaze didn't linger. *Gratitude isn't love, dipshit.*

I took the chopper on a wide sweep over the homestead before heading up toward Yellow Tarn. As we passed over the sprawling red iron roof of the single-storey homestead—or the big house, as the station called it—Paddy's wife, Norma, and a couple of the station's shepherds ran out onto the front lawn and gave us a wave. Norma had her phone to her ear, and I could only guess she was talking to Gary.

I sucked in a deep breath, blew it out slowly, and flew the chopper straight for the steep range on the western side of the homestead and began to climb. I knew Yellow Tarn. I'd set down there a couple of times on tourist runs as it offered one of the best views over the valley and the Havelock River. But it was a tricky approach even in good weather, the tarn taking up most of the flat space, leaving a narrow strip on the western side—big enough for a chopper to land if you positioned it just right to avoid some gnarly boulders that shared the space, but a tight fit nonetheless. If we didn't get up there before the cloud swallowed the tarn completely, there was no way I'd risk a blind landing and Zach would just have to lump it.

As we drew closer, I breathed a sigh of relief. Ghostly wisps of cloud threaded across the murky surface of the pool, but I had a good enough view of the ground for a decent approach.

"I'm gonna need you to guide me on your side," I told Zach.

"Make sure that skid has plenty of clearance from the boggy edge of the tarn."

"Got it." Zach turned and slid sideways in his seat to get a better view. "Looking good so far." He circled his hand and I started to bring the chopper down whilst keeping a sharp eye out my own window and the front.

"Slowly, slowly." Zach pressed his cheek hard against the window to check behind. "Forward a little so you don't clip that boulder with your tail."

I did as he said—the view off the edge of the plateau both in front and beside me doing a number on my head. *Jesus, that was a long way down. Big breath, Luke.*

"Aaaaaand... okay, that's it. You're clear this side whenever you're ready."

Thank God. I was running out of room.

I eased her down the final few meters, and when the skids hit the ground and the chopper made a small groan, I let out the breath I'd been holding and shot Zach a grateful look.

He returned a quick smile. "Nice flying."

I returned the smile a little shakily, my heart still pounding from the adrenaline rush. "More like great teamwork."

Zach's cheeks brightened, so I quickly added, "If we find them quickly and get them back down tonight, the chopper will at least offer us some shelter."

He nodded, sending me another of those hard-to-read looks that I couldn't hold.

I glanced at the clock. Five fifteen. We had ninety minutes or so of daylight left, although how much actual visibility was an entirely different thing. The mountain fog was already swirling more thickly around the tarn.

"Right, let's get going." I opened my door and slid out. "We need to secure the blades and rope the body down before we leave. If the wind gets up, I'd prefer not to have to explain to Gary how his expensive machine was spun like a frisbee into the next valley."

"Got it." Zach followed me out and then freed the dogs before we safeguarded the chopper as best we could, the patchwork of boulders providing convenient anchor points for the ropes.

When we were done, I took another look at the dense cloud sinking around us and blew out a sigh. "Let's hope this lifts enough for us to fly out again tomorrow."

Zach followed my gaze and nodded grimly. Then we set about layering up and checking and strapping our packs. I grabbed the satphone from the chopper and put a call through to Gary, then handed it to Zach who checked in with his mother before updating Holden.

Gil's horrified protest was loud enough to be heard in the neighbouring valley. Zach held the phone out for me to take and stepped back with his hands in the air. A string of expletives about how fucking crazy I was, and how Gil was going to skin me alive echoed around the tarn. I grabbed Zach's wrist and slapped the phone back in his hand without saying a word to Gil. I wasn't going near that shitshow.

Zach grinned and held it out for us both to hear.

When the shouting died away, Holden came back on the line. "Gil is currently unavailable for further comment owing to the fact I shoved a tea towel in his mouth. I personally think it's a good idea. You saved yourselves a couple of hours. Keep in touch."

After I'd stowed the phone in my pack, Zach surprised me by reaching for my hands. It was hard to look into those beautiful eyes—so many memories.

"You're a good man, Luke," he said solemnly. "You didn't have to do any of this. Collect me. Land up here. Come with me. Any of it. I want you to know that I'm really fucking grateful, and to be honest, I'm glad I'm not doing this alone as well."

You don't ever have to do the hard stuff on your own. The words were on the tip of my tongue, but I swallowed them down and settled for a simple "You're welcome."

We held each other's gaze a moment longer, then Zach dropped my hands and studied the blanketed peaks. "It's getting colder by the minute."

I handed him his Swanndri, and he wriggled into the heavy bush shirt before adding his high-vis vest with its million and one pockets. That done, he sniffed the air like an old-timer and reached for his mustering stick. "Right, let's do this."

I almost smiled. I'd observed the shepherd version of Zach working many a time, but up there on the hill, on his family's land, in official SAR mode, he looked rugged, competent, determined, and so damn sexy.

"Here." He unstrapped a second shepherd's stick from the side of his pack and threw it my way. "You'll need it for keeping your footing in this pea soup. Once we start climbing, we won't be able to see shit. We're gonna be mostly relying on the dogs to find each other. I'll stop often so Nina can sound off. Her bark carries a long way. And watch your step. We'll be traversing a couple of razorbacks where it's straight down on either side for longer than you want to know. We stick together, got it? *Close* together."

I blew out a breath. "You're starting to worry me."

He locked eyes. "Then I'm doing my job because you *should* be fucking worried. I know this track like the back of my hand, but this isn't going to be a walk in the park. In this weather, at these temperatures, if you misjudge a step or take a tumble down a scree slope, you could be history. These mountains don't give a shit. They'll chew you up and spit you out and you'll never see it coming."

Well, all righty then. I managed a teasing smile. "So, you're saying I should be careful?"

He rolled his eyes and threw me my waterproof hiking jacket. "Fucking comedian. Get that on you before I make you wait in the chopper."

I snorted at that. "I'd like to see you try."

He shot me a grave look that gave me pause. "Luke, I'm deadly serious about this. Up here, *I'm* in charge, *not* you, and it's my job to keep you alive. You might be an ace pilot used to leading your crew, but these mountains are *my* territory, understood?"

I swallowed and nodded. "Understood."

Chain of command established, and with Zach's warning fresh in my mind, we shouldered our packs and headed up Halifax beat with the dogs launching ahead to lead the way.

CHAPTER TWENTY-THREE

Zach

Forty-five minutes in and we were down to a couple of metres of visibility through the dense grey curtain as we continued to slog our way up. More goat trail than track, the route was slick and treacherous underfoot. We'd both taken a slide or two, but so far, nothing serious.

The swirling cloud had an eerie quality to it, our voices swallowed into the hushed landscape as we kept climbing. Sweat dripped down my face, Luke's too, as he followed at my back, his lungs pumping hard. Even with all the stops for Nina to sound off, it was a tough and unforgiving climb—the thud of Luke's stick hitting the ground behind me, oddly reassuring.

He never once complained, and that was quite something, considering my own lungs burned and I'd done this shit for years. Hell, I'd done nothing *but* climb up and down those hills chasing merinos for almost my entire life.

Stones skidded behind me and Luke swore softly.

"You okay?" I checked without looking back.

"Fine," he grunted, and on we went.

One step at a time, ever higher, focused on the ground at our feet, on not making a mistake, and on listening for any sound of Jules or my father or their dogs. All the while, Nina and Jojo did this ping-pong dance of running ahead into the fog, circling back, and then running ahead again. With no way to see what they were heading into, I had to trust their surefootedness and instincts to keep them safe.

I called another stop, but Luke couldn't have heard because he walked straight into my back and almost sent me flying. I stumbled forward, the weight of my pack dragging me sideways. Luke grabbed me before I toppled over, pulling me back onto my feet and hard up against him. And just like that, even through the damp, odorous bush shirt that covered me from neck to knees, my body reacted like the last week had never happened. Like we'd never been apart. Every cell sizzled in awareness, and it took everything I had not to turn and kiss him.

"Shit. I'm sorry." He steadied me, and a shiver bubbled down my spine at the wash of his hot breath over my cheek. "I didn't hear you."

"I'm fine." I brushed myself off and realigned my pack. Then I turned to look for Nina, and instead met Luke's gaze, completely unprepared for what I saw. The flash of emotion in those bright blue eyes stole the air from my lungs. Pain, uncertainty, and something I wasn't prepared to name. A *lot* of that something.

My heart stuttered, and for the first time since that night I'd walked away, I took a couple of seconds to *really* study him. What I saw confused the hell out of me. Strain showed in a fine web of lines around his mouth and in the dark circles framing his eyes. He looked . . . dog-tired. He looked like I felt in those few times I let myself go there.

Shit. "Luke, I . . . I'm—"

"You better sound Nina off again." He broke eye contact and reached for his water bottle. "We're almost out of daylight."

He was right. Besides, this wasn't the time for . . . what? Nothing, that's what. I signalled Nina. And while she gave a series of booming howls that thundered up the ravines, Luke handed me one of the lights to strap on my head.

Jojo raced in circles around me, whimpering with excitement. Waiting for a reply from whatever dogs were up the mountain.

None came.

I laid a hand on Nina's head and she quieted, as did the mountains around us.

I fought a surge of disappointment and turned to find Luke looking a heartbeat away from gathering me in his arms. I doubt I would've stopped him. I almost crossed the distance between us myself. "Try the satphone again." My breath fogged between us, blurring his face for a second but not enough to hide the worry in his eyes. For Jules and my father, yes. But also for me.

The call rang unanswered, and my heart dropped into my boots with the ominous silence that filled the ravines. "This is the only way up or down, so either one or both of them are hurt and they've had to hole up somewhere."

Luke peered through the foggy cloud that clung to the track. "Best guess?"

I followed his gaze. "There's a rocky ledge with a good overhang about a hundred metres on. Beyond that, you're looking at an exposed mountain climb, which would be suicide in this weather and in the dark. But if we don't find them before that ledge, we're gonna need to overnight there ourselves."

Luke said nothing for a minute, his silence weighing heavily between us. I wanted to turn around, to see his face, to remind him that I still cared about him regardless of what I'd said that night, but I couldn't move.

His hand landed on my shoulder and squeezed. "Then that's what we'll do. We'll find them, Zach. One step at a time."

"I know." I didn't point out what we both knew, which was that finding them wasn't the issue. It was the fear of what we'd discover when we did. I placed my hand over his and drew on that strength he exuded by the bucketload. He was always so present, so large at my back, so . . . comforting. It was tempting to sink into all that reassurance and just disappear for a while.

A shudder ripped through my body.

Luke immediately pulled me into his arms and my hands slid around his neck, my face burying into the sticky damp of his coat. "What if . . . what if . . . ?"

"Shh." He stroked my hair. "Let's not what-if."

"Jesus, I'm sorry. I'm better than this." I tried to wriggle free, but he held on tight.

"Don't be sorry, baby. You don't have to keep it together all the time. This is me, remember?"

Baby? I doubted he even realised what he'd said, let alone had any idea of the power it wielded. Comfort buoyed my heart, his warm, steadfast presence giving me hope. And damn, I'd missed him. Missed him in a way that had been ripping me apart for over a week. In a way I hadn't been prepared to admit. I'd missed . . . this.

"They're your family, Zach." His hot breath washed over my ear and I wanted more. "So, we're gonna do this, you and me. We're gonna find your family and bring them home . . . one way or another." He leaned back to look at me. "Regardless of what happens, of what we find, *I'm* not going anywhere, understand? I'll be here for whatever you need." His gaze drilled into mine. "Nobody knows shit like this better than me."

I returned his stare, pulling every scrap of conviction from those midnight eyes and knowing he was right. Of all people, Luke understood my deepest fears better than most.

His thumb brushed under my eyes, and a smile caught the corners of his mouth. "Yeah, that's better. Now, let's keep moving. We can reassess our plan when we hit that ledge, right?"

We. Our. Despair gave way to possibility again, and I nodded.

He gave a quick smile. "How about you call in our position and tell them the plan? Just in case." Neither of us raised the matter of exactly what *just in case* referred to. There were a dozen ways the next hundred metres and the night beyond could turn to custard and talking about it wasn't going to change anything.

I made the call, whistled up the dogs, and we pressed on, visibility dropping along with my focus—my eyes glued to the ground and the next step ahead.

I instructed Luke to keep his hand on my shoulder and he complied without a word—a good indication he was as nervous as I was. The mountains ruled this land and shit happened. They were fickle and feisty and they didn't take kindly to intruders. One wrong step was all it took.

If my father and brother were holed up somewhere, they were in trouble. Even if Jules had found him, Dad would've been on his own for a bit and I'd worked enough SAR jobs to know the results of not having the right gear. Every small climb in altitude came with a corresponding drop in someone's chances of survival. I was trying not to dwell on that too hard when Nina's booming bark snapped my mind back to attention.

"Is that them?" Luke clamped down on my shoulder.

"Shh." I held up a hand and listened into the dark, but all that greeted me was silence.

Nina sounded off again and my head flicked from side to side, desperate for a miracle, but still, nothing.

Unless . . . I froze . . . was that . . . ?

I closed my eyes and focused. "There!" I exclaimed, catching a faint howl on the wind. "Did you hear that?" I spun to Luke, but he was frowning.

"No. I—" He broke off at the sound of Nina once again baying into the dark from somewhere on the trail ahead.

And in reply, a howl, higher pitched and faint, but growing louder.

Definitely louder.

"Holy shit." Luke's arm slipped around my waist. "Now, I definitely heard that!" He tugged me close at the exact same time as a howl emanated from the dense fog.

"It's Hopper!" I punched the air as a second bark rang through the cloud. "And that's Chip!" I grabbed Luke's face and planted a smacking kiss on his cold lips. "We found them, Luke. We fucking found them."

His wide eyes sparkled in my headlamp. "*You* found them," he corrected gently. And before I could pull away, he drew me back for another kiss. I didn't fight him, opening at the first touch of his lips and revelling in the taste of him once again on my tongue. I couldn't give a fuck that we weren't supposed to be whatever this was anymore, that it would only complicate things. I'd deal with that later. Right then, Luke's lips on mine meant every fucking thing in the world.

Nina sounded off again, and this time the reply was sharper, louder, moving toward us at pace. It broke the moment and I jerked out of Luke's arms. "They're coming." I caught the troubled look on his face and added, "I shouldn't have kissed you. I'm sorry."

He answered self-consciously, "Nah, heat of the moment, right? But in case you're wondering, I'm not sorry."

I hesitated, wanting to tell him that I wasn't sorry because I didn't want him anymore. The reason I shouldn't have kissed him was because it only made the ache in my heart a hundred times worse.

But there was Dad and Jules to find first.

I called Jojo and Nina to heel, not wanting an excited canine reunion to result in anyone going for an unexpected tumble. Seconds later, a black and white bundle of energy and a tan and gold monster of a huntaway launched themselves through the curtain of grey and into the dim light thrown by our headlamps.

I dropped to my knees and Jules' rangy huntaway raced up to start cleaning my face. "Hey there, Hopper. What a good boy. Is Jules up there, buddy? Is he okay?"

Desperate for some attention, Chip bounded over from where he'd been reacquainting himself with Jojo and Nina and pushed into my arms. Hopper gave way and moved on to Luke who did the decent thing and wrapped the dog in an almighty hug, telling him what a great dog he was.

I got to my feet, clapped my hands, and an eerie silence descended as four dogs froze and looked my way, awaiting instructions. I focused on Chip, since he was generally the brains of the operation as opposed to Hopper's loveable brawn. "Where's Paddy, boy?" I asked him. "Go seek. Show us the way."

The collie didn't need to be asked twice and immediately turned and bolted up the path, followed by the other three.

"Watch your feet," I reminded Luke as I loped up the path in pursuit.

"Watch *yours*," he shot back as the toe of my boot caught on a root and almost jettisoned me sideways.

As we drew close to the ledge and overhang, I'd been telling Luke about, I wondered whether I'd been right about them sheltering there after all. But before we got there, Chip and Hopper made a hard right and disappeared from view. The clacking and clattering of the tumbling scree shattered the hush of the foggy dark, and my heart sank. Dad or Jules or both were somewhere down there.

I called Jojo and Nina to heel before they followed the other dogs over, and with Luke puffing at my side, we stood on the edge and peered over, our headlamps lighting up the steep scree incline. The cloud was less dense on this side of the track, broken by a light breeze channelling through the river valley. Loose scree stretched as far down as the eye could see until it disappeared into the grey soup. But before it did, I caught sight of the one thing I needed to make my heart soar.

A familiar face.

Jules. Waving frantically up into the light.

Oh, thank God.

He stood precariously balanced on a rocky outcrop about ten metres down the slope, astride something that could only be our father, covered in a tarp and with a glint of silver thermal blanket poking up around his head. Water bottles and a pack sat to one side, along with the dogs who'd clearly been warned to keep their distance.

The good news? Jules appeared suitably kitted out for the weather, which had dropped from chilly and damp to super fucking cold. I could only hope my father had dressed the same. Freezing fog could easily be on the cards and would certainly provide the perfect curtain call to a shitshow of a day.

"Took you long enough, baby brother," Jules shouted up the slope and the teasing joke told me everything I needed to know. They were okay.

A sigh of relief whooshed from my lungs. The laugh that followed sounded slightly hysterical, but the comforting arm that found its way around my shoulder felt pretty damn perfect.

"I would've been here sooner, but you suck at leaving a trail," I shot back. "A few clues wouldn't have gone amiss, brother dear. As the sibling of a SAR legend, you're just damn embarrassing."

Jules chuckled and the warm sound of it had tears welling in my eyes. He apologised, adding, "I didn't think I'd need rescuing too. The satphone must've gone in the fall. There was no sign of it."

His words struck home, along with the realisation I'd come damn close to losing him, to losing them both. I sucked in a shaky breath and quashed the unnerving surge of panic in my chest.

"And that's another thing we're going to have words about when this is over," I grumbled. "You guys need more fucking satphones."

"I know. I know."

Luke's arm dropped to my waist to give a reassuring squeeze. "Time for that later, Zach. You found them. Now, let's finish the job and get them off this bloody hill."

I shot him a grateful smile and surveyed the scene. Getting them up the scree wasn't going to be easy. I shouted to Jules, "How's he looking?"

"Cold. We both are. I think he took a bang to the head on the way down. There's blood on that rock." Jules indicated a boulder about ten metres from where we stood. "He was unconscious when I got here and he's still a bit groggy and rambling. He said his legs gave way and that's why he fell. But the right side of his face isn't moving properly and I think he's had a stroke. I didn't fancy my chances of getting him back up in this shitty light without sending both of us to the bottom. I was about to evaluate my options when Hopper and Chip went crazy."

A stroke? The idea sent a wave of conflicting emotions through my chest. The old man might've been a bastard about me coming out, but hell if he wasn't still my father, and my heart flipped like a pancake at the thought of maybe losing him. It made zero sense under the circumstances, but the heart rarely made sense. I threw a glance Luke's way. Case in point.

"We'd have never seen you if it wasn't for the dogs," I agreed. "And FYI, you owe me a beer or fifty when this is over. Luke as well." I set my pack on the ground, freed the coils of rope from the side and looked for somewhere to anchor them. "The crazy guy landed next to Yellow Tarn. In this weather? Can you imagine?"

Jules smiled up at Luke. "Thanks for having his back."

Luke tugged on the rope and gave me a thumbs-up before answering, "No problem. It wasn't hard to figure out what he had planned and that there was zero chance of changing his mind."

Jules laughed and I flipped them both off before tossing a couple of ropes over the edge. "You can thank me later for saving *both* your sorry arses." I emphasised the point for my father's benefit. "We would've found two popsicles tomorrow and Mum wouldn't have been happy."

The smile drained from Jules' face. "I know, Zee." He glanced down at our father. "Believe me, I know."

"Good. Well, I hope *he* understands how close he came to royally fucking things up. Now get those ropes around you before one or both of you take a tumble. Do you think he can hold his balance?"

One of my father's hands lifted in the air as if to say he could manage.

"Not a chance," Jules corrected.

"Okay, then we'll do it the hard way. We'll rope him up like a sausage in the tarps—" I threw a second one down. "—and then haul him up."

Jules nodded. "Sounds like a plan."

It took a good thirty minutes before we had my father safely up the scree and onto the track. I checked him for broken bones and any other injuries that might impact my next decisions. He seemed okay other than the slackness to his features and zero strength on the entire right side of his body. As I worked, he shivered, a thin sheen of cool sweat covering his face, and although his pulse was regular, it was thin and thready. And when I laid a hand on his cheek, the cool draw of his clammy skin sang a warning. The adrenaline rush was crashing and shock was setting in.

"We should bunk down under the ledge tonight," Jules declared like it was a foregone conclusion and began gathering everything into his pack. "Let him rest and get him down tomorrow."

Dad grunted something that sounded like agreement, his dull grey eyes like deep pits in his ashen face. His right eyelid blinked sluggishly, the corner of his mouth loose and slick with saliva.

"No," I countered. "I don't like the look of him."

Jules frowned. "Exactly. It's too risky to be moving him down the track in the dark and in this weather."

"We'll do what Zach thinks is right." Luke met Jules' determined look with one of his own. "He's the expert here."

I cast a surprised glance Luke's way but all he did was shrug and say, "It's true."

Jules narrowed his gaze. "I know these hills as well as my brother." He eyed Luke like he was sizing up his options. On the station, Jules was used to issuing orders and only deferred to our father.

"I don't doubt that," Luke said calmly. "But Zach's trained for exactly these types of situations. You're not."

Jules' jaw worked like he was about to argue, but then his shoulders relaxed and he nodded. "You're right." He turned to me. "It's your call, Zee."

I blinked, not at being given the decision because I wasn't about to let Jules override me on that, regardless. I blinked because of Luke's clear spoken confidence in me—prepared to go toe to toe with my brother if necessary. No one had ever done that for me. Ever.

I put a hand on Jules' arm. "He's in shock and it's only going to get worse in these temperatures. If we get him back to the chopper, we can overnight there safely, and then we can get him all the way down tomorrow. If we stay here, we could lose him."

My father grunted but I shook my head at him. "No. You don't get a say in this. You might not respect who I am, but I know exactly what I'm doing, and my gay arse is the best chance you have tonight."

His eyes widened in a rare show of uncertainty, even fear.

I hated doing it to him, but it was the best way to make our case. "There's three of us, and we have lights, a stretcher, and plenty of gear. It'll be slow going, but we *can* do it."

Luke gripped my shoulder. "Then let's get it done."

Jules put the calls through to Holden and our mother while Luke and I got Dad onto the stretcher, wrapped him in thermal blankets and a tarp, and secured him with ropes.

"This is going to be like leg and arm day times a thousand," Luke observed wryly. "You doing okay there, hotshot?"

I gave a small smile and looped the rope back to him. "So far, so good."

He shot me a sly grin. "So . . . Zee?"

I groaned. "Jules has always called me that. Don't even think about it."

Luke snorted. "Personally, I prefer Charlie's Zebedee."

My eyes flared. "Don't you dare. I only let her call me that because I'm scared of her."

Ignoring the fact my father was watching, Luke reached across his outstretched body and gently cupped my cheek. "You did a great job today. I'm so fucking proud of you."

I froze at his words, at the tenderness in his tone, words failing me as my father lay between us. My father—watching another man, another *gay* man touch me in a way that couldn't be ignored for what it was. It was a surreal moment, and one I'd never imagined in my wildest dreams.

I waited for the panic to set in, for that familiar curl of uneasiness and even embarrassment at what my father would be thinking, but all I felt was . . . happy. So fucking happy.

"Thank you," I whispered hoarsely.

"You're so very welcome." Luke smiled and dropped his hand. "I'll go help Jules with the rest of the gear."

My father flailed his hand my way and I leaned down to catch him mumbling something that could've been, "Thank you." Then his eyes closed again and I wondered if I'd imagined it.

My gaze slid sideways to Luke and a smile crossed my face. It felt like a year, not just a week since I'd ended things between us. I wasn't sure I even knew the man who'd done that anymore. I also wasn't sure that I'd ever seen Luke as clearly as I did in that moment. I also wasn't sure what, if anything, I could or should do about it.

He fumbled a water bottle and cursed as it hit the ground. I scooped it up and handed it back to him. He thanked me and our gazes met and held. And with my father still lying at our feet, and because I'd sailed past giving a flying fuck hours before, I went up on my toes and pressed a single soft kiss to Luke's cheek.

"Thank you, for today." My fingers trailed over that rough stubble. "Without everything you've done, we wouldn't be here." I swallowed hard. "And considering what happened . . . with us . . . you didn't have to do any of it. But I'll always be grateful."

He smiled almost shyly, which looked all kinds of adorable on such a big man. Then he simply said, "Thank you. But you're wrong about one thing. I did what I did precisely *because* of everything that happened with us, Zach. We weren't just that one night. We were all the days and nights before that. And I want you to be happy, whatever that takes." He returned the kiss, his lips barely brushing my cheek, and then he went back to securing our packs like he said that kind of heart-breaking shit every day of his life.

Luke, who'd lost more in his life than most of us could survive. Luke, who had days when grief sucked him dry and laid him too low to do more than pull the bedcovers over his head. A man who still always found something to give, *a lot* to give. Most of which he'd given... to me.

A throat cleared and I turned to find Jules watching me with a small smile playing on his lips. My cheeks flushed hot and I grabbed the satphone from his hand. "Not. A. Word."

He didn't laugh as I expected. Instead, he drew me into a tight hug and whispered, "He's a good man, Zach. Stop punishing yourself. Or denying yourself, or whatever it is you're doing."

His words startled me and I wriggled free. "I'm not—" *Was I?*

He arched a brow and kept his voice low. "Living in the closet for thirty years can make it damned hard to trust your heart to another person, especially when the first man you gave it to handed it back. Don't give up, Zee."

My eyes narrowed at the unwelcome reminder. "How about you get back to me when you finally decide to risk your own heart, yeah?"

I watched the sting of my words hit home and instantly regretted them. "Shit. I'm sorry. That was a crappy thing to say."

He raised his hand. "Maybe, but you're not wrong. Still, we've got more important things to do right now than argue, yeah?"

Something we could agree on.

I called the dogs from where they'd been sleeping in a large, multi-legged furry ball, wrapped around each other to keep the cold at bay, and we started the long and precarious downward trek back to the helicopter.

CHAPTER TWENTY-FOUR

Luke

Making our way down through the pea-soup cloud with only our headlamps to guide the way took almost twice as long as it had to climb up. But we finally took those last few steps off Halifax beat onto the Yellow Tarn plateau and everyone breathed a sigh of relief, no one more so than me.

Zach's father had, thankfully, spent most of the seemingly endless descent asleep, or at least lying there with his eyes closed and his teeth gritted. Most likely the latter. Paddy Lane was made of piss, steel, and determination. I figured he'd have sooner bitten his arm off than complain, and for once, that stubborn, stalwart, crabby attitude was exactly what was needed.

The three of us had tag-teamed bearing the stretcher—the weight, the tricky descent, and the absolute concentration needed proved quickly exhausting. By the time we put the stretcher next to the chopper, every muscle and joint in my body was screaming, hot, and angry. The grimace on Jules' face and the set of Zach's jaw told me they were suffering just as much. It had been hell, but we were safely down, and as I looked up into the drizzling rain and thick dark night, I felt an immense sense of gratitude to the man who'd led us.

The thought of being stuck camped under a rocky ledge in the freezing cold, waiting for morning with no guarantee we'd have been able to get down any easier, was quite frankly, terrifying. I'd have rather landed an Airbus in a lightning storm than spend the night on that mountain. And judging by the grey pallid cast to Paddy's face, I wasn't at all sure Zach's father would've made it.

Jules grabbed his brother and pulled him into a bear hug. "We did it. *You* did it. I'm so fucking glad you didn't listen to me."

Zach slapped his brother's back. "Like that was ever gonna happen. I love you, bro, but you don't know everything, shocking as that must be to you. Now get off me."

While they settled Paddy onto the back seat of the chopper, I gave the machine a once-over and then updated a pissy, fretful Holden. God love the man, but he could be a right pain in the butt, but he promised to update Lane Station and then get back to me.

Five minutes later, he called back to let us know Blue and the team had arrived at Lane Station and were ready to make their way up at first light if the cloud cover didn't lift. But if it did and I could fly the chopper, my instructions were to get Paddy straight to Christchurch Hospital.

We were almost out of the woods. All we had to do was get Zach's father through the night.

Next on the list was Gary who, judging by his grumpy demeanour, had been up all night.

"The helicopter is fine," were the first words out of my mouth.

"Oh, super," he huffed with a distinct edge of sarcasm to that Irish lilt. "Because that's exactly what I've been worried out of my tree about, of course."

I couldn't help but smile. "Aw, so you *do* love me."

"In your dreams, boyo." But there was a smile in his voice.

I gave Gary a quick update on Paddy and the plan to get him off the hill since the final call on the use of the chopper was down to him. He agreed immediately, adding that he'd check whether the rescue chopper could maybe meet us at the station.

By the time I stowed the phone, Jules and Zach had managed to get a bottle of water and half an energy bar into their father—no easy feat with half his mouth not cooperating. They then helped him pee into an empty plastic bottle cut in half and then Zach checked him over once again.

When he was done, Zach joined the two of us standing by the tarn and handed out water bottles and more energy bars. "His heart rate's still too high for my liking," he said with an anxious look back to the chopper. "He looks like a ghost, his skin is clammy, and I'm sure he wasn't always with us on the way down. And I don't mean asleep. He's in shock, obviously, but who knows what else is going on."

I squeezed his shoulder. "Is there anything more we can do?"

Zach shook his head.

I cast an eye over Jules who looked equally worried. "Then I suggest we bunk down and try and get some sleep. One way or another, it's gonna be a big day tomorrow. Let's hope the weather plays ball because as far as I can tell, the best option is for me to fly us all to Christchurch, minus the dogs." I caught Zach's gaze and held it. "And since the flying bit is *my* area of expertise, I'll need a baton change on the decision-making regarding if and when it's safe to get us off here. Okay with you?"

Zach's cheeks pinked a little in my headlamp. "Of course."

Excellent news. The last thing we needed was a fight about whether it was safe to fly or not. "Then let's get the dogs sorted and then grab some shut-eye."

We used the tarps to form a shelter over the open equipment carriers so the dogs could sleep protected from the weather, and then Jules took the back floor of the chopper while Zach and I tried to get comfortable in the front. With the headlamps out, the cockpit was plunged into darkness.

Uncomfortable or not, it wasn't long before Jules' snores filled the cockpit.

Zach chuckled. "That man can sleep anywhere."

I found Zach's hand and gave it a friendly squeeze. I wasn't even going to pretend. I just needed to touch him. To my surprise, he responded immediately, squeezing back and sending my heart into its usual and ridiculous pitter-patter of hope. The memory of his elation when we found Jules and Paddy and the feel of his lips back on mine was stuck in my brain on an ever-repeating loop.

Overall, the day hadn't been at all good for my heart. Too many mixed messages. All except the one that had been accompanied by a look of regret that left no room for misinterpretation. *I shouldn't have kissed you. I'm sorry.*

"How are you doing?" I croaked out the words. "It's been a day."

I couldn't gauge his expression in the dark but his answer was . . . cautious. "Okay, I think. I'm not sure it's hit yet."

"Me neither."

And that was the sole measure of our conversation. Other than Jules' snoring, the cockpit remained as quiet as the hushed fog that blanketed it as we tried to fall asleep.

Yeah, not a chance in hell.

And when Zach's quiet breathing also failed to sink into sleep, I whispered, "Are you uncomfortable? Do you want to swap seats?"

He hesitated, then said, "No. I'm just . . . cold. Probably the adrenaline crash."

I swivelled on my seat and put my back to the chopper's door. Then, with one foot on the floor and the other leg pressed against the back of the seat, I opened my arms to him. "Come on. Shove that pack between the seats and try scooting back against me. Can't be any more uncomfortable than sitting upright in these things, and it'll keep us both a little warmer."

I sensed him weighing the pros and cons and totally got it. Having Zach curled in my arms wasn't going to help make things less awkward for either of us. Call me a masochist and be done with it. "Body heat, remember?"

More hesitation, but then with an obvious reticence that stung a little, he layered a couple of bags between the seats and gingerly perched on top of them before resting back against me. Neither of us could fully stretch our legs and we had to shuffle to find the least uncomfortable position, but eventually we settled, and damn, if Zach didn't fit like magic in my arms as he always did.

And if I had to bite my lips to stop from pressing a kiss to his head, that was nobody's business but my own. Over the next ten minutes, the stiffness in Zach's body slowly bled away and exhaustion claimed him. He grew heavy on my chest, his head lolling sideways against my jaw, his soft snores telling the rest of the story.

Sleep well, baby. You've earned it.

Rest didn't come quite as easily for me though—thoughts about the man in my arms tumbling through my brain like scree down those slopes. The scent of stale sweat, dog, damp mountain, lanolin, and all the crazy things I loved about Zach began to slowly unstitch all the good work I'd done on those wounds he'd left when he'd walked away.

I tightened my arms and he turned slightly and burrowed his face against the side of my neck, his warm breath giving life to memories of him sharing my bed. Memories I could well do without.

Still asleep, Zach's fingers hooked the green silicone wristband like they so often did, the feel of it making me smile. He seemed to like playing with it, spinning it around, or fingering the word *Poppa* when we were hot and sweaty after an epic round of sex. Sometimes he asked about Callie, sometimes he just played with it in silence, almost like the idea of it, of *me* as a father, more than simply the guy he was fucking was somehow fascinating, or maybe . . . unsettling.

Did it make it harder for him to keep me in that nice little box he'd put me in? I could only wonder.

What do you think? I asked Callie the question in my head. *Am I a fool to keep hoping?*

My head fell back against the side window and I stared out into the pitch of the night. *I wish you could've met him.*

Her answer when it came was no surprise. *I have.*

And somehow, I knew it was true. Not that it made the losing of him any easier.

And with that thought in my heart and Zach safely in my arms, I gave in to exhaustion and drifted into a restless sleep.

CHAPTER TWENTY-FIVE

Zach

It was the snore in my ear that woke me—reassuringly familiar and yet achingly tender at the same time. Then there was the heat at my back, the arms around my waist, and the unmistakeable scent of Luke's cologne rising from his skin amidst all the other aromas he'd accrued from the day before.

My eyes sprang open to the grey light of dawn flooding the interior of the cockpit. I lay quiet for a moment, revelling in Luke's hold while at the same time cataloguing the bone-deep ache that seemed to emanate from every square centimetre of my body. It protested like a tractor had run over it and then reversed just to make sure.

I glanced into the back seat to check on my father and blinked when my eyes landed on his, open and watching me in return, or maybe watching *us*. His expression was unreadable. I fought the urge to free myself of Luke's hold because . . . fuck my father. Without Luke, he'd still be on that hill and maybe not waking up at all. If he had a problem with what he was seeing, he could damn well keep it to himself.

"He's still groggy," Jules whispered, looking wide awake and sitting with his back against the door. "He knows where he is and most of what happened, but he still can't move his right leg and his speech is all over the place."

"You been awake long?"

He nodded. "Hardly the Hilton, right? I fed the dogs and gave them a run."

"Thanks." I eased myself out of Luke's arms, trying not to wake him, but his eyes sprang wide.

Blinking in the light, he dragged his hands down his face, grumbling, "Christ, what a night." He circled his shoulders and then turned gingerly in his seat, wincing at the protest from his muscles. "I'm gonna file an official complaint about this hotel."

I snorted and slid out the passenger door to stretch my cramping legs. Four dogs instantly appeared at my side in a boisterous welcome. After administering pats all around, I sent them back under the tarp to keep warm.

Inside the chopper, Luke popped the kinks from his neck and peered through the windshield. "It's still pretty murky out there, but I don't think it's as bad as last night. Whaddya think?" He directed the question to me. "Is there a breeze?"

I lifted my face to the sky and nodded. "More than yesterday, at least. And it's turned easterly. That should help."

The cloud still hung in wispy threads over the tarn, licking at its surface and swirling around the boulders, but that previous sense of a solid wall of grey was gone from the night before. In its place were occasional glimpses of mountains and the valley below. And looking up, I could even pick out a little of Halifax beat snaking up toward the peaks.

The helicopter door opened and closed, and a few seconds later Luke joined me at the edge of the small plateau. "Fuck, it's cold." He rubbed his arms and stared over the edge down into the misty valley with its tempting glimpses of the river. "If this wind keeps up, we'll be fine in a couple of hours." His shoulder nudged mine. "I just spoke to Gary about the rescue chopper idea, but since there's only one available and we can't give them a time for the pick-up, they suggested flying direct to Christchurch would be the quicker option. They can't clear us to land at the hospital, but if we call once we're on our way, an ambulance will meet us at the airport." He cupped my cheek. "Don't worry. We'll get him there safely. You can rescue me anytime, mister."

I snorted and elbowed him back. "Let's hope I never have to. And thanks . . . for last night. It couldn't have been comfortable for you."

He turned and our gazes caught for a moment. "I could never be uncomfortable with you in my arms."

My cheeks flushed hot and I quickly looked away. "I, um, better let Mum and the others know we're okay."

Luke nodded. "I left it on my seat."

I headed back to the helicopter for the satphone, aware of his eyes on me all the way. I had no answer for all those questioning looks or the troubling emotions that were surfacing inside me in response. His presence was a constant reminder of what I'd been missing, but more than that, of what I *wanted*.

Could I really risk my heart again? Was it as easy as that?

Charlie's words came to mind. *Who says you can't have all of it or at least some of it?*

I did. But I was beginning to wonder exactly where that certainty had come from. Or was it simply a warm blanket to keep me safe from another rejection, just like Charlie said?

Still thick around the peaks, the cloud had cleared enough from Yellow Tarn by eight thirty for Luke to give the green light, and once he'd let Gary know, we were off. Jules had intended to get off at Lane Station with the dogs and then drive Mum to Christchurch Hospital, three hours away. But we landed to find that Emily, Holden, and Gil had already picked her up after my earlier call that morning. She'd be there when Paddy arrived or soon after.

Considering the tension that existed between the stations, or more accurately, Dad and Miller Station, it was an incredibly kind thing to do, and I was reminded of Tom's comment that *I* was a part of Miller Station too and that they always looked after their own.

As promised, an ambulance was waiting at the airport when we landed and we handed Paddy over. Figuring Mum would need some kind of transport, Jules hired a car and then we followed to the hospital. Emily, Holden, Gil, and Mum were all waiting in the Emergency Department when we arrived, and my mother was first to grab me in a hug and thank me.

Startled, a jumble of emotions clawed at my chest—anger, disappointment, and just plain fucking hurt bubbled up inside, but it wasn't the time. And with Luke's presence looming over me like the biggest of shadows I couldn't seem to shake, I slid my arms around Mum's waist and returned the hug.

I was pretty sure I caught a grunt of approval from the big man at my back, and it almost brought a smile to my face. After that, Mum and I kind of retreated into our corners and I was okay with that. It allowed me the opportunity to lean against Luke's shoulder and snatch some sleep as we waited.

Once Dad finished a barrage of tests and was fully admitted, we followed him up to the ward where we waited again while another team looked him over, stinking up the visitors' room with our unwashed bodies. Mum, Jules, and Emily talked quietly at one end of the small room while we sat mostly in silence at the other. Looking to pass the time, I eventually excused myself to the accessible toilet and cleaned up as best I could with the scratchy paper towels and pump soap.

We'd been told Dad had indeed suffered a stroke—a big one, according to the physician who'd seen him in the ER. It had left him with a dense right-sided hemiplegia that was going to need months of rehabilitation and speech therapy. That he hadn't died on that mountain was down to Jules getting to him quickly and all of us getting him down to that helicopter to shelter.

He was still a bit hypothermic and his blood pressure was up and down, but he was stabilising. A night exposed on a mountain in near-freezing temperatures could easily have pushed him over the edge. How much mobility he'd get back, no one was prepared to guess at that early juncture. But I didn't need the details to know that whatever happened, my father's temperament would ensure it resulted in a massive pain in the neck for everyone on Lane Station. Paddy Lane unable to get around on his own, call the shots, or run his own land was going to make *Nightmare on Elm Street* look like a freaking fairy tale.

I caught my brother's eye and we shared a look. He was about to walk through the gates of hell, and judging by his expression, he already knew.

And then there was Luke. From the mountain to the hospital waiting room, he'd barely left my side. Every time I turned around, he was there, announcing his protective presence in big fucking neon capital letters. I thought about telling him to back off a little, and then decided, fuck it. I liked him there. I *needed* him there, and the admission wasn't lost on my stupid brain.

I knew we needed to talk. I just hadn't quite figured out the subject matter.

His towering and constant presence at my side hadn't gone unnoticed by the Miller crowd either, particularly Gil, who'd watched us with the curious amusement of someone who'd had his suspicions confirmed.

Holden mostly just stared, looking stunned, like the penny had only dropped. God bless the man's inability to see much beyond four legs and a woolly coat. Emily simply patted my arm, but the sparkle in her eyes was . . . disconcerting.

Goddamn station life and small towns.

Well, they could all think what they liked. I was beyond giving even the smallest of fucks. I was tired as hell, my stomach churned with bile from the lack of food coming its way, and my head pounded with the might of an entire percussion section on steroids. Gil's infamously arched brows, albeit expertly wielded, had lost all power over me, and if Holden's gaze didn't stop bouncing between Luke and me soon, he was going to break something.

"Here, get this in you." Luke sat down and handed me a sandwich and a bottle of water from the vending machine down the hall.

"I'm fi—"

"Eat it—" He glared. "—or so help me god, I'll feed it to you piece by piece until you choke."

I held that intense look for a few seconds, then grinned and took the sandwich. "Your bedside manner could do with a little work."

He huffed. "I've had no complaints so far."

I shot him a sideways glance but he'd already looked away.

Holden, sitting opposite, seemed to suddenly reach the end of his patience. He scooted forward on his plastic seat and beckoned me close. "Can we talk outside for a minute?" He flicked his head toward the foyer where the elevators were located.

Knowing full well he wanted to ask about me and Luke, I straightened in my seat and said, "No. Next question."

Gil snorted, and Holden rolled his eyes. Then he dropped his bottom lip in that cute-as-fuck pout that usually got him his way. "Please."

I was about to flip him off when Gil shot his boyfriend a look and groaned, "For fuck's sake, Holden. Leave the poor man alone." But then his gaze slid to Luke and a sly smile stole over his face. "But you, on the other hand—"

"Nope." Luke waggled the fingers on his left hand. "Oh, look at that. See? Not married to you anymore." And the cool look he levelled had Gil's eyes widening.

I swallowed a smug smile. *So, sue me.*

Gil considered Luke for a moment, then his smile broadened and he simply nodded. "Okay." And something passed between them in that look that sounded like a page turning.

Holden looked between them like he knew he'd missed something, but when Gil said nothing, he turned back to me. "Why didn't you say anything about . . . ?" His gaze flicked to Luke.

"Because it's none of your business, and because there really wasn't much to tell. Besides, it's finished." In my tiredness and my effort to shut Holden down, the whole thing came out far more dismissive of Luke and my . . . *relationship* than I'd intended. And it was too late to haul it back by the time I noticed Luke had gone quiet, too quiet, his expression shuttered.

After a few awkward seconds, he broke the silence to say, "What Zach said."

But I didn't miss the flash of hurt in Luke's eyes when they caught mine and I knew I needed to make that right. *Fucking fuck, fuck.* "Look," I began. "It wasn't quite—" But my apology was interrupted when the door opened and the charge nurse poked her head inside.

"The team will see you now. Only the family please." She beckoned the three of us forward. "They're waiting for you in Paddy's room."

My mother and Jules followed the nurse, but I hung back a moment, motioning for Luke to join me in the hall. He hesitated, then sighed and slipped through the door, closing it behind him.

"I didn't mean it to come out that way," I said, taking his hands. "I'm sorry. They're nosey fuckers and I only wanted to shut them down. I'm sick of people being worried about me."

He snorted. "Tell me about it."

I managed a smile, adding, "We both know what we had was a lot more than I made it sound."

His eyes softened. "Yeah, it was. Although I'm surprised to hear you acknowledge it."

"Zach, hurry up," my mother's voice rang from down the hall.

Luke pulled his hands free and made shooing motions at me. "Go. Be with your family. I'm a big boy, Zach. I'm fine. I understand."

I wasn't so sure about that, but I needed to go. "Can we talk later?"

"Zach!" my mother called again.

"Go." Luke waved me off without replying.

Gathered around my father's hospital bed, we listened to the medical team's verdict—the family on one side, the consultant and his team of three other doctors on the other, with the charge nurse at the end. It felt like a council of war, and I supposed in some ways it was.

My father's eyes remained locked on his primary physician like he was trying to read his mind. We all were. Right then, it was hard to feel anything but sympathy for Paddy Lane and the months of recovery he faced. He might not make life any easier for himself, but he wasn't too different from most of the station owners in the Mackenzie. You didn't succeed in farming the edge of the impossible by being a pushover. Dogged determination, strong leadership, grit, and a willingness to push everything to the limit was a trait shared by most. Admittedly, being a homophobic arsehole wasn't a pre-requisite, but there were a few of those as well.

We didn't learn anything new—it was more an opportunity for the medical team to expand a little on my father's plan of care over the next few weeks and for us to ask questions. I took a back seat, leaving it to Mum and Jules to lead the way. I wouldn't be taking point in Dad's care, not if he had any say in it, but I wasn't sure what it was going to mean *for me* in the wider scheme of things.

Because no matter how my father's recovery played out, things were about to go tits up on Lane Station. Paddy Lane was an ornery enough bastard on a good day with a tailwind and doing the work he loved with all his heart. How he was going to handle taking things slower, or worse yet, having to completely hand the reins over to Jules, who knew?

All I knew was that I wasn't up for any more fuckery going down in my family.

I'd be there for whatever Jules and my mum needed from me, but returning to work on the station wasn't high on my list of preferred ways to help out. As much as I loved my brother and mother, it wasn't *anywhere* on that list. I would never leave Jules hanging, but I had a plan in place for my future, my survival, and moving back to Lane Station wasn't part of it. Especially if I had to deal with my father's homophobic bullshit all over again. He might be grateful to me for getting him down off the hill, but I wasn't kidding myself that anything else had changed. If Jules needed my help at the station, it would only last until my father returned. There was no way I was ever going back to that bullshit again.

My mother's hand landed on my arm, breaking me out of my musings. "Zach? Is there anything you want to ask?" She looked . . . overwhelmed, and my heart broke at the sight.

I shook my head. "No, I think you guys covered it." Then I pulled her into my arms. "I'm so sorry, Mum." I wasn't even sure what I was sorry about. She loved my father for sure, so there was the pain and grief that came with seeing something like that happen to someone you love. But I think I was mostly sorry for all the responsibility that was about to land on her fragile shoulders, not least of all coping with her husband.

She pulled away and I caught the unguarded devastation on my father's face as he watched my mother and then turned to follow the medical team's departure. I'd never seen him anything but totally in control, and the vulnerability I saw jolted me.

So, no. It wasn't going to be easy for *any* of us, but especially the three of them.

My mother dragged a chair to my father's bedside, took his hand, and began to speak in hushed tones. He listened in silence, his gaze fixed on hers.

Jules came over and we embraced. Then he led me to the window and away from our parents.

"I'm here for whatever you need," I told him, meaning it. "Just say the word and I'll be there. The muster—"

"Holden's already offered." Jules' hand gripped tight on my shoulder. "And yes, a couple of extra bodies on the hill would be great." He glanced over his shoulder and lowered his voice. "But I want to make something clear."

My brows peaked.

"I don't want you to leave Miller Station and come back under some misplaced sense of loyalty. You went above and beyond the last twenty-four hours. You've got nothing left to prove." He squeezed my shoulder again. "You're a different man than the guy who left us last year. A better man. Stronger. Come and help out when we need it, sure. But I want you to live your life. I don't want you moving back. We'll be okay."

I couldn't deny the relief. It was so very Jules. Always looking out for me. "But what about you?" I shot back. "Are *you* living your life?"

He gave a slow blink. "This isn't about me."

"But—"

"Please, Zach. I can't deal with that right now."

I caught the sadness in his eyes and simply nodded. "Okay. But we're not done."

"I know." A small smile tugged at his mouth. "So, what about you and Luke? The past twenty-four hours, the two of you looked a combination of excruciatingly awkward and inexplicably cosy all at the same time. Hard to pull off, but you somehow managed it."

I groaned. "Don't start."

He considered me for a moment. "All right. One more thing and then I'll shut up."

I groaned and dropped my chin to my chest. "Fiiiine."

Jules waited until I looked up. "That man loves you, Zach."

I started at his words, but all he did was grin. "Like you didn't already know that, or at least suspect it," he said smugly. "It's obvious to anyone with eyes to see the way he looks at you. The question is, what are you going to do about it? The right person doesn't always come along at the right time, and I'm not sure we get so many opportunities that we can afford to simply throw them away."

My mother stirred and we both glanced over.

"He seems a good man, Zach." Her eyes remained steady on mine.

My heart jolted in my chest and I'm pretty sure I gaped. My gaze darted to my father, but his eyes remained closed. And after a couple of thunderous heartbeats, my mother looked the other way and lowered her forehead back to her husband's hand.

Jules wrapped a hand around my neck. "Nothing stays still, little brother." And with that, he returned to his seat on the other side of the bed, and I went back to studying the small vulnerable man in the hospital bed who couldn't possibly be my father.

I watched Paddy Lane for a long time. Watched his chest rising and falling. Watched his eyes flicker behind those closed lids. Watched and realised that even after everything that had happened, I still stupidly loved him. But loving Paddy Lane as my family, as my blood, as my father, didn't mean I had to like him, or listen to him, or look for his approval.

I watched and wondered what he was thinking behind those closed eyes. What he feared about the unexpected future he faced and the inescapable changes that were about to befall him and his precious station.

I watched, and for the first time in a year, maybe in forever, I didn't feel afraid of him anymore. Not of him, or what he thought of me, and not of a future that was still unformed in my head.

It might've taken me a long time to realise it, but I wasn't Paddy Lane's terrified and closeted gay kid anymore. And Jules was right. I wasn't the same guy who'd walked away from Lane Station the year before, either. Or the man who'd had his heart broken. Somewhere along the way I'd changed, and Luke had played no small part in that change.

Luke.

I grabbed my jacket and went to my mother. "If you don't need me, I'm gonna leave for a bit. I've got some things I need to sort out."

My mother gave a tired smile. "Go. No point everyone sitting around here, and you must be exhausted. This is going to be a marathon, not a sprint. We'll call you."

My father's eyes flickered open and his gaze landed on mine.

I gave him a curt nod. "I'll be back when I can." I couldn't read his expression and I didn't much care. If my father didn't want me to visit, he was gonna have to say the actual words because I was done with his bullshit.

Jules eyed me pointedly. "Are you going to talk to him?"

I muttered, "Maybe."

He grinned. "Then take as long as you need. Holden and Gil are driving me back tomorrow. We're gonna have to make some changes to muster. Emily is going to stay here with Mum until I can get back. Holden has the keys to the rental if you need it."

I all but ran to the visitors' room and burst through the door. Three sets of startled eyes jerked my way and Holden shot to his feet. "What's wrong?"

"Nothing. Where is he?" I scanned the room. "Where's Luke?"

Holden frowned. "He's taking the chopper back to Oakwood." He looked about to say something else when Gil interrupted.

"He's heading back to Wellington tomorrow." Gil ignored his boyfriend's puzzled look.

"He's got a—" Holden flinched liked he'd been pinched and shot Gil a scowl that I had no time to consider.

"Tomorrow?" My stomach dropped. "Why tomorrow?"

Gil shrugged and pulled Holden back into his seat while Emily watched on in silence. "You'll have to ask him that." He rolled his eyes and held up his left hand. "Not married anymore, remember?"

I narrowed my gaze. "What did you say to him?"

Gil's eyes popped. "Me? About what?"

He wasn't that ignorant. "You know damn well about what. About . . . us . . . him and me."

Holden frowned. "I thought there wasn't any him and you anymo—ow! Jesus!" He shot Gil a glare.

This time it was Emily who interrupted. "*No one* said anything to Luke about the two of you. You have my word."

I trusted Emily wouldn't lie to me, and yet there was something enigmatic in her expression.

Gil considered his nails. "Perhaps the real question is, what did *you* say?"

Holden stared at Gil like he'd dropped a grenade into the room.

"Or maybe, *didn't* say?" Gil was on a roll. "Because there's always that, right?"

And a pipe bomb joined the grenade.

I held my hand out and snapped my fingers at Holden. "Hand them over." It came out almost a growl.

Holden looked thoroughly confused. "Hand *what* over?"

"Here." Gil held out the rental car keys for me to take. "He gave them to me. And good luck."

I caught the last three words as I was bolting out the door, along with Holden's aggrieved, "Will someone please tell me what the fuck that was all about?"

CHAPTER TWENTY-SIX

Luke

THE WEATHER ON THE FLIGHT BACK TO OAKWOOD WAS stunning, because of course it bloody was. The cloud had burned off to leave bright, clear skies and picture-postcard views of the Southern Alps in all their glory. The mountains fanned west toward the Tasman Sea like a jagged, snow-capped carpet with not a wisp of cloud or mountain fog to be seen. From what I'd been told, that's how it rolled in early autumn in the Mackenzie. One day you were caught in freezing fog or the snowstorm from hell, the next could find you stripping off your shirt to wipe the sweat from your brow.

I touched my skids down outside the Wild Run hangar around five thirty, and Gary and Tommy rushed to meet me. Gary clasped me in a fierce hug and then manhandled me into his office where I was barraged with questions that all of Oakwood was apparently waiting on the answers to. Meals were already being organised for delivery out to the station, and the other station owners were organising a work rotation to help out during muster.

Not that Gary or Tommy were about to feed any information to the well-meaning gossip hounds. The two men were tighter than clams in that way, something I was grateful for. Still, I found the town's rallying behind the family kind of heart-warming. The upside of small-town life, I guessed.

Once I'd answered everything to Gary and Tommy's satisfaction, Gary sent me home, insisting that he and Tommy were quite capable of cleaning the chopper and putting it to bed. I wasn't about to say no, considering I was flying back to Wellington the next afternoon, which meant another trip to Christchurch airport.

It was almost nightfall by the time I opened the front door of the bungalow and threw my bag on the floor. Cleaning that sucker out could wait another day, but if I'd had to sit in my own stink any longer, I might've thrown up.

I got a fire going, not that it was really cold enough to need one, but I still felt chilled to the bone and craved the cosiness. Then I made a beeline for the shower and stood under the waterfall of blisteringly hot water until my skin wrinkled and the extractor fan threw in the towel, filling the bathroom with steam. I reached outside the shower and pushed open a window. Then I dialled back the water temperature and sank onto the tiled floor to let exhaustion do its thing.

The adrenaline crash had been a long day in the making, seemingly prepared to wait until I was in a safe place to tear down my defences and have its way with me. Top of the list, not the struggle up the mountain, or the freezing temperatures, or Paddy Lane's stroke, or the hairy flying conditions. No, it was Zach's summary to Gil and Holden of our 'relationship.'

There really wasn't much to tell. Besides, it's finished.

The latter was true, of course, but the former just plain hurt. Holden and Gil already knew about us, so even though Zach had apologised and partly taken it back, it was a reversal that was obviously meant only for my ears. And that spoke volumes. He wasn't reconsidering. I'd been an idiot . . . again. I'd let hope creep back in. I'd landed in Christchurch almost positive Zach was beginning to see me in a different light—maybe even rethinking his decision.

And that kiss up on the mountain? I swallowed hard at the memory. To have Zach's lips back on mine had meant every fucking thing. And it had been no mere polite thank-you peck on the lips. He'd kissed me back, hard. Caught up in the moment of finding Jules and his father, sure, but then he'd let me hold him that night as well, curled up in my arms to keep warm. That had to mean something, right?

Or was I grasping at straws because I wanted it so badly, and seeing him again after a week of radio silence had only made that ache a hundred times worse? I sat under the spray of water and counted all the ways I'd lost my freaking mind over this guy. Not since Gil had I felt anything close to this. And yeah, that one might not have had the fairy-tale ending but that wasn't because the love wasn't there. We just didn't look after it.

All that bullshit about love being all you needed was exactly that —bullshit. I'd learned the hard way that falling in love only gave you the raw ingredients. If you let them go stale, didn't mix them the right way, used the wrong proportions, cooked them at the wrong temperature, set the timer wrong, or any of a hundred other ways you could fuck up the process, love could slip through your fingers and fade into a pale shadow of what it might have been.

You had to pay attention. You had to watch and nurture each other. You had to keep things fresh, keep laughing, keep having fun. All the things I was going to do my best not to lose sight of ever again. All the things I'd hoped to have a chance to do with Zach.

I spun the green band on my wrist, thought of that stubborn look Callie got on her face when she was about to dig her toes in, and steeled my heart.

Fuck it.

I wasn't going to give up.

Zach was the man I wanted in my life, and I was damn well going to fight for the chance to be with him.

He may not see it as clearly as I did, but that didn't mean I was wrong to keep trying.

I could be a patient motherfucker if I wanted to be, and I believed in my heart that Zach wanted me too, if he would let himself believe in it. We may have started out as fireworks between the sheets, but we'd never been *only* that. We worked together, and somehow, I'd find a way to make him see that as well.

To see our potential.

To want more from me too.

If not, at least I'd know I gave it everything.

I fingered the word *Poppa* on the silicone band and smiled. "Okay, smart-arse. So maybe I'd hoped for a little less work on my part when I asked you for help, but I'll take it."

With no strength left in my legs, I sat on the tiles until the water ran cool. Then, feeling decidedly prune-like and with my eyeballs hanging out of my head, I dragged myself out of the shower. Avoiding my reflection in the mirror because . . . hell no to that shit . . . I scrubbed myself dry and pulled on some sweats and one of my favourite T-shirts.

Walking back into the lounge, I added a couple of logs to the dwindling flames in the fireplace and then padded into the kitchen to feed the gnawing pit in my stomach, which hadn't seen decent food for over a day. Gil's homemade mac and cheese leftovers stared back at me from the freezer. *Perfect.*

I threw a serving into the microwave, smiling at the knowledge he'd be horrified. Then I grabbed a light beer and headed wearily for the couch. But as I sank into the cushions, every joint and muscle in my body creaked and grumbled, and damn, I wasn't sure that I'd ever make it out of it again. I eased my long legs onto the coffee table and swallowed a guzzle of beer.

I was so frickin' tired.

Scooting my butt down on the cushion, I dropped my head onto the back of the couch and let my eyelids flutter closed. Somewhere in the background of my brain, I heard the microwave ding, but my body was past caring.

Just a few minutes' rest and then I'd eat.

I started awake, the bottle of beer dropping from my hand to the floor with an ominous thud.

"Shit." I whipped it off the rug before it emptied completely and set it on the local newspaper on top of the coffee table. The room glowed in warm autumn colours from the smouldering fire and I grabbed for my phone, blinking in disbelief at the numbers staring back at me: 9:32.

I'd slept for well over an hour. I sucked in a steadying breath and tried to clear my fuzzy head, the faint aroma of mac and cheese causing my stomach to growl. Groaning, I pushed to my feet and headed for the kitchen. If I didn't eat soon, my body would consume itself.

I hadn't taken more than a few steps when someone hammered on the front door and I almost jumped through the roof. It was oddly déjà vu, like maybe that's what had woken me up.

I switched direction and made my way down the hall toward the front door, my legs like limp spaghetti. No doubt Doug had come to interrogate me after hearing I was back. Before I reached the door, the pounding started up again.

"Hold on to your horses, for fuck's sake. And you better have food on you, that's all I'm gonna say."

The hammering stopped with my words, but there was no reply.

I opened the door and squinted into the harsh porch light. It took a second or two to register, because— "Zach?" I blinked and looked again. Nope, I'd been right the first time.

In reply, Zach's troubled green eyes narrowed. "You were expecting someone else? Because it sounded like maybe you were. I can, um . . . I can leave if you want?"

"What?" I tried to process the shock of Zach standing on my doorstep. "No. I assumed it was Doug coming to ask questions. Why aren't you still in Christchurch?"

"Doug?" Zach considered me for a long few seconds. "Why would Doug be here?"

There was something in the way he asked that gave me pause. *Huh.* Rather than answer, I replied, "Any reason Doug shouldn't be here? Because last time I looked, there wasn't."

Zach gnawed on his lower lip like he was thinking how to answer. Like whatever reason had brought him there, whatever he'd planned, had suddenly been turned on its head.

I sighed and put him out of his misery. "Doug is a friend, Zach. That's all he is. That's all he's ever been. The question is, why are *you* here? And come to think of it, *how* are you here?" I peered around him to discover the airport rental car sitting in my driveway and a worrying thought hit me. "Is it your dad? Is he okay?"

"He's fine. Mum and Jules are with him." He took a breath and swallowed hard. "I, ah, I came back on my own."

I considered that, put it alongside the nervous way he was hovering on my porch, and the intensity of those glittering green eyes, and yes, I had thoughts about why Zach might be standing on my doorstep. Maybe even hopes, as well.

But I needed to hear the words.

I needed Zach to say them before this went any further.

And so I asked again, "Why are you here, Zach?"

He looked to his feet and then back up. "I heard there was a position vacant."

I blinked. Not exactly what I'd been expecting, and I struggled to get my tired brain around his words. "A position?"

He gave me a sheepish look. "Yeah. I heard you might be looking for a . . . boyfriend?"

A boyfriend? Holy shit.

I froze and tried to steady my thundering heart. Failed that dismally and made a similar attempt to school my expression, which was about to go full-on gobsmacked. I perhaps did better with that because Zach looked about as nervous as I'd ever seen him, his eyes darting over my face, his breathing choppy.

I cleared my throat, leaned my shoulder against the doorframe, and gave him a casual once-over. "Boyfriend, huh?"

His lip twitched and some of the tension left his shoulders. "Yes. I'd like to submit my application if that's all right?"

"Your application." Because repeating his words back to him was clearly the super intelligent thing to do.

A tiny smile broke over his lips and he mimicked my posture against the porch upright. And even still dressed in that godawful rank Swanndri and jeans, he looked so fucking sexy it was all I could do not to drag him into the house and straight on into my bedroom, and to hell with the small talk.

Except I needed to understand exactly what he was saying before I offered my heart . . . again. That he and I were about a lot more than sex. But still . . .

"Yes, my application." His smile widened. "If that's all right?"

"I see." I folded my arms and studied his face. "You do realise that this is a long-term position? The last applicant left me high and dry, and I don't want to go through that again. I need someone who'll put their *heart* into it."

Apology filled his eyes. "That other guy must've been crazy to walk away. I promise I'll give it my very best."

Good enough for me. "Have you any job experience?"

He worried that lower lip for a moment, then answered, "Not *officially*, although I recently came close. But I'm an *enthusiastic* student." His hot gaze sent a thrill of goosebumps popping down my spine. "And I'm willing to put the work in. Whatever's necessary."

Holy hell. I fought a smile and cleared my throat. "Well, I'm sure that's all very interesting, but there's a strict interview protocol, and then an internship to complete, of course."

Zach's mouth curved up in a slow, sexy smile and my toes curled on the cool wooden floor. "Is that right?" He pushed off the upright and crowded me against the doorjamb, his breath washing hot over my lips. "Tell me about this . . . *internship.*" His lips brushed mine and all thought evaporated.

"Oh . . . um . . . well . . . you know," I flustered. "I'll need to see you in action . . . so to speak. Make sure you're up to all the . . . tasks I'll require you to complete."

Zach grinned and walked me backward, kicking the door shut with his foot before holding me against the wall and stepping between my legs, bringing us face to face and groin to groin.

"So, Mister Boss Man." He ran his nose up my neck to whisper in my ear, "Do I get a chance to redo anything that doesn't meet these exacting standards of yours?" He nibbled my earlobe, and I might've whined . . . just a little . . . or maybe a lot . . . it was hard to tell past the screaming in my head that went something like, *Hell fucking yes!*

"Ahhhh . . . I . . . um—" I fumbled as he drew down the neck of my T-shirt and nipped along the slope of my shoulder. "I'm sure we can arrange . . . oh *fuck*—"

He palmed my solid dick and gave it a squeeze. "We can arrange what?" His lips mouthed the base of my throat as he slowly stroked my cock through my loose sweats.

"I'm sure we can negotiate something that works for . . . *Jesus, fuck*—" I thrust into his hand as he stroked faster. "—both of us."

"Mmm, *both* of us." Zach kissed along my jaw. "I like the sound of that." And then finally, *finally,* his mouth was on mine and the world tipped back on its axis and slotted into orbit once again.

He mumbled against my lips, "Oh fuck, yeah. I've missed this." Then his tongue plunged inside and lodged somewhere south of my tonsils, and I didn't think anything, anywhere had ever felt so good, so right, so fucking miraculous.

He groaned and shoved me harder into the wall, his body plastered against mine as he ravaged my mouth, nipping and sucking and sliding his tongue in and out until all I wanted was his dick in my arse doing exactly the same thing and much, much more.

He kissed up my face and into my hair, rutting against my thigh as his hand worked my cock. "I've missed you so fucking much."

"Me too." I pressed my thigh more firmly between his legs and he groaned.

"Fuck me, you smell good." He stepped back, hungry for air, his pupils black as hell in the dim hall light. "Whereas I definitely don't."

I quirked an eyebrow. "This is true. Although not as bad as I expected."

He laughed and tore his sweatshirt over his head. "Thanks to a quick clean-up in the hospital restroom. Come on." He headed up the hall, discarding his T-shirt on the way, which left him in nothing but socks and jeans and acres of warm skin. I followed at a clip, but when we got to the lounge, he stopped and looked around. "Where're all the boxes?"

"Boxes?"

He looked confused. "Gil said you were moving back to Wellington tomorrow."

"Moving? No. I'm only flying back to meet with my lawyer."

Zach blinked. "Your lawyer? You mean you're not leaving Oakwood?"

I frowned. "Why would I leave Oakwood? I'm seeing my lawyer to go over a partnership contract with Gary. I'm hoping to use some of my money to invest in a second helicopter as my buy-in. Wild Run has more business than it can handle, but to expand, Gary needs investment and it's a great opportunity for me."

Zach squeezed his eyes shut and sighed. "I thought maybe . . . I didn't know if you—"

I smiled and drew him close. "You thought I was leaving because of you?"

He flushed. "Yes. No. Okay, maybe?"

I nuzzled his neck. "You thought I'd run with my tail between my legs because Zach Lane turned me down? No, baby. As irresistible as you might be, I'd decided to stay whether or not you saw a future for us. When you told me you didn't, I was gutted, and yes, I briefly considered canning the whole idea. But I don't give up easily, and I had a plan to woo you back. Besides, I like Oakwood. I love my work. I like the people. And I'm making friends, Doug included."

Zach pulled a face, which made me laugh. Then his eyes softened. "Just so you know, I would've done long-distance if that was the only option."

"So would I." I kissed him, my hands relishing the feel of all the warm pale skin of his bare back. "Just so *you* know, Gil was well aware of why I was going to Wellington."

Zach's eyes narrowed. "Why that little . . ." Then he huffed, "He was interfering again, wasn't he?"

"At a guess." I should've been pissed, but I wasn't, not if it had brought Zach running.

Zach thought about that then shrugged it off. "Whatever. Come on." He pulled me toward the bedroom. "After racing back to confess my feelings and stop you from leaving, I at least deserve an orgasm at the end of it."

"Whoa there." I tugged him to a stop outside the bedroom door and flicked on the hall light so I could see his face. "Confess your feelings?" I arched a brow.

He instantly flushed red. "Shit. You caught that, huh?"

I slid an arm around his waist and drew him close, brushing my lips over his. "Anything I should know?" I waited for his reply, our faces inches apart.

"Very likely." He bumped his nose to mine. "I . . . well. I . . . I guess I might be kind of—" He sighed. "I'm pretty sure I'm falling in love with you."

I couldn't hide the explosion of happiness in my heart, lifting him off the ground and spinning us both around with a whoop of delight.

He laughed and kissed the top of my head. "Put me down, you crazy man."

I dropped him back onto his feet and kissed him thoroughly, savouring the sweet taste of him on my tongue as he moaned into my mouth, demanding more. Pulling away, I cradled his face and stared into those bright green eyes. "Kind of, pretty sure, huh?"

He gave a pained groan. "Was it that bad?"

"Not at all." I walked him backward into my bedroom and pushed him onto the bed before following him down. "I love you, Zach." I cupped his cheek. "I've known it for a while. I love everything about you, the life you want to build for yourself, and I'm here for it all. But I get that this has been harder for you—deciding what you want, and who you want, and if the timing is right, especially with what's happened over the last year. I don't need to hear the words from you if you're not ready. Almost and pretty sure are just fine with me. That you have faith enough to give us a go tells me everything I need to know. I want all of you when you're ready."

He ran a finger down my nose and over my lips to my chin. Then he leaned in and kissed me. "Thank you."

I kissed him back. "No need to thank me. But we *are* gonna work on your prevarication."

His mouth curved up in a wicked grin. "If that's a fancy word for my dick, I am totally down with that."

"I'll inform Collins and Webster." I wriggled to my feet and then peeled his jeans and briefs from his legs, ignoring his socks as I kissed my way back up his body until I straddled his thighs. But when I lowered my lips to meet his, he held me back with a firm hand against my shoulder.

"I'm so fucking sorry I hurt you." His eyes shone with tears. "I'm sorry for what I said that night. I'm sorry for walking away. I was . . . scared, I guess? You were . . . so unexpected. The whole Gil and Holden thing, and then all the shit with my dad, it didn't seem something good like you and me could be real. I thought I was setting myself up for another fall."

I ran a thumb over his damp cheeks. "So, what changed?"

He took a deep breath and blew it out slowly. "I came to the realisation that I've lived most if not all of my life until the last year being scared of taking chances. You didn't with a father like ours. Life was pretty scripted if you wanted to keep out of trouble. He was a good enough dad in general, I suppose, but that homophobic thing was pretty fucking scary to grow up with as a gay kid. And then the two times I did take a chance and step outside the box—once with Holden and then coming out to Mum and Dad—they didn't exactly work out great for me."

"Neither of those were your fault." I traced the line of his jaw and he turned his head and kissed my fingers.

"I know, and I think I knew I'd made the worst mistake of my life as soon as I left you that night. But I needed a bit of time to understand why. And then the thing with Dad happened, and I finally got it. I looked at him lying in that bed today, and I realised how much I'd changed in a year. That I wasn't that scared kid anymore. That I didn't need anyone's approval for how I lived my life and the decisions I made. That I didn't care what people thought about us, even Holden and Gil. And that I wasn't going to settle for safe scraps any longer. Jules reminded me that there are too few people in the world who truly tick your boxes to walk away from one just because you're scared."

I chuckled. "Remind me to buy that man a drink." I cradled Zach's face. "So, I tick your boxes, huh?"

He leaned in and kissed me with such tenderness that it stole my breath. "Every one of them, baby. And probably a whole lot I don't even know I have."

"Mmm." I pulled him close and felt my cock thicken against his. "Good to know. And now I think we should get back to the giving you an orgasm part of the evening."

He laughed and wriggled his groin against mine. "Absolutely. Only if you have the energy, of course." He shot me a teasing look.

"I'm sure I can rally."

He grinned. "Excellent. Then I'm gonna ride you till your eyes pop. You sure you're ready?"

Not in the slightest, but I wiggled off him and onto my back, nonetheless.

Zach reached into the bedside drawer for supplies, then he straddled my hips and rolled a condom over my conveniently hard dick before slicking us both up, finishing by shoving a mountain of lube up his own arse.

"You know I could help with that," I said pointedly, watching him rock back and forth, groaning obscenely while my dick twitched in lonely anticipation.

"Nope," he whined, freeing his fingers with a pleasured sigh before wiping them on the sheet. "All done. Now hold still."

I steadied my cock as Zach rose up on his knees and wriggled into position. With my dick poised on his slack hole, he tweaked my nipple and winked. "Count that as your foreplay. I have about ten minutes of oomph left in me before my brain pulls the plug, and I'd hate to miss the good part."

I huffed out a laugh. "Such a romantic. I'm sure I'll cope. Did I tell you that I love you?"

He froze and a shy look crossed his face. His cheeks pinked and his expression grew flustered. "Um, yeah. I'm not about to forget anytime soon, but, you know, feel free to remind me."

I cupped his face and drew him down for a slow kiss. "I love you, Zacharia Lane. Take all the time you need. I'm not going anywhere."

His eyes grew serious. "I know you're not." And with that, Zach began to slowly sink down on my cock, one glorious centimetre at a time. Wet and hot and tight, and so fucking perfect that I wasn't sure I'd ever find the words.

I'd hoped to have him back.

Dreamed of it.

But never counted on it.

And the reality was sweeter than I'd thought possible.

Fully seated, Zach paused to let his body adjust, eyes closed, expression tight, his throat tense and corded. Then slowly that frown smoothed, his eyes fluttered open, and he shot me a warm, sexy smile. "Let's go for a ride."

I scrambled for purchase as he slid up my cock and almost off the end before plunging back down to shoot stars behind my eyes.

"Fucking hell," I grunted, fisting the sheets tighter.

He smiled and did it again, his eyes rolling back in his head. And then again. And again.

Fast, hard, and deep. Then shallow and quick. Then achingly slow. Changing angles. Grinding down.

On and on, until nothing existed in the world except Zach's body fused with mine and the mounting pleasure trailing fire through my blood.

He rose and fell above me like a dream, his body cast in a stripe of moonlight that painted the bed and left his auburn hair edged with silver—taking what he needed, what would always be his as long as he wanted. And then he dropped down, his hands on either side of my head, his face just inches away, his dick slapping against my stomach as he whispered, "Get me there."

My fucking pleasure. I wrapped a hand around his cock and stroked him hard, exactly how he liked it, struggling to keep a rhythm as he continued to slide up and down my cock. If he didn't come soon, I was gonna lose my shit regardless. "Come on, baby."

His eyelids fluttered closed and those auburn locks fell around his face. I ran my thumb over his slit on the upstroke and a string of expletives tumbled from his mouth.

I stroked harder. "Let me hear it."

"Oh, shit," he shouted, loud enough to wake the neighbours. "Jesus . . . almost . . . like that . . . ah, fuck!" He dropped down hard on my dick and froze, his back arched, his head thrown back, mouth open. "Holy fuck!" He repeated the slide twice more before grunting and spilling ribbons of come through my fingers onto my belly. A few more grunts, then a gasp and a long rumbling groan. Then his eyes peeled open. "All yours, baby."

I held his eyes. "Damn right, you are." And keeping our eyes locked, I thrust up into him once, twice, three times until the orgasm crashed through my body and Zach enfolded me in his arms and brought me home.

Sated and with bones like jelly, I cleaned us both up and he curled his body around mine, his big spoon to my little, his leg over the top of mine to keep me where he wanted me.

"Did I pass the interview?" His hot breath washed over my ear.

I snorted. "You certainly made the shortlist."

"Shortlist, huh?" He snuggled close. "I'll have to up my game."

I laughed. "I'm not sure I'd survive any improved version."

He chuckled, then fell quiet, and I sensed the mood taking a serious turn. "I want everything I said, Luke, don't get me wrong, but right now, my life is . . . complicated."

I stroked his cheek. "Then we take it slow. It's not like I don't have a few issues myself. *I'm* still a grieving mess more often than I'd like, and when I'm in that state, I can be curt and thoughtless and want nothing more than to shut the world out. I'll never mean to hurt you, baby, but I might. Not to mention the divorce isn't final yet, so there's that." I smiled wryly.

"Very true, although it's not as if I have any worries about the divorce, all things considered. But as to the other—" Zach hummed in thought. "Let's make a deal. You promise to keep talking and let me know when things get a bit much, and I'll protect your need for space when it happens and promise to tell you if I'm hurt." He hooked his chin over my shoulder. "But since we're putting our cards on the table, *you* should know that I'm not ready for moving in together or anything like that. Maybe not for a while . . . maybe even a year—"

I felt him watching me.

"Plus, I like living on the station, and I'll need to be close to the dogs."

I lifted a hand to stroke his cheek. "Then the station is where you should live. I'll wait as long as you need."

I felt his frown. "But what happens if and when we do decide to take that step? To be perfectly honest, I'm not sure I could live in town, especially not with a training business. The neighbours would hate me."

I chuckled, trying not to show how fucking delighted I was that he was even thinking that far ahead. "Then we talk about it. I don't need to live in Oakwood, Zach. Just within driving distance. Maybe we can find a compromise."

"Okay." Two beats of silence, then more softly, "You know, I've never dated before . . . ever."

The reminder squeezed at my heart, and I wriggled around in his arms to find him blushing. "Then that's something we should definitely do. Top of the list."

Zach chewed the inside of his cheek before finally smiling. "Yeah, I think I'd like that. And full disclosure, in case you missed the first part, there's a lot of dogs in my future. A. Lot."

I grinned. "As long as they're not sleeping in our bedroom, or at least our bed, I'm sure I'll cope."

A smile popped up on his face along with a thoughtful look. "*Our* bedroom." He rolled the words around in his mouth like he was trying them on for size. "I like the sound of that. But I'm going to be busy with the new business, and helping Jules, and shepherding as well. I won't have a lot of time. You might get sick of waiting around."

I nodded thoughtfully. "Mmm, I see your point. You might turn out to not be worth the effo—ow!"

He let my nipple go.

"Look." I took his hands in mine. "I'm gonna be busy with my new business, as well, and flying, and helping with whatever you and Jules need, too. We're both going to be busy. We're both going to have to work on it."

"You'll help us?" he almost squeaked. "But . . . Dad—"

"Will be out of action for a while. But even if he isn't, I'm not going anywhere. He's going to have to deal with you and me together, right? A team."

"A team. Right." Zach's eyes softened and a smile tugged at his lips like the idea of not dealing with his father alone anymore hadn't occurred to him.

"Any other questions?" I waited.

"A million. But only one that's important."

I ran the back of my knuckles down his cheek. "And what would that be?"

He leaned in and kissed me softly. "Do I get the job?"

I smiled and kissed him back. "It was always yours. The one and only candidate."

"Excellent." He rubbed his hands together. "Tell me it comes with a parking space."

I laughed. "Parking space, my arse."

He beamed. "That'll do nicely."

I laughed and I traced his mouth with my fingers.

He kissed my fingertips one at a time and then lifted my wrist to his lips. Keeping his eyes on mine, he pressed his lips to the green silicone band over the word *Poppa*. Then he flattened my hand over my heart and put his hand over top, the green band sandwiched between us. "Just so you know, I want all of you, too. Everything you were. Everything you are. Everything you're going to be."

His eyes held fiercely to mine, and everything I needed to know was right there. Every declaration I wanted to hear. Every hope. Every fledgling promise. Every feeling he was still unravelling.

I didn't need the words.

They'd come.

He frowned, then stroked my face. "Are you okay?"

I turned and pressed a kiss to his palm. "Never better."

EPILOGUE

Five months later

Zach

I blinked awake to the bright wash of dawn lighting up Luke's bedroom walls. I groaned and added a blackout curtain to the checklist growing in my head. Honestly, the man could sleep under a spotlight. If I didn't remember to close the damn things, it never happened.

I sighed and rolled onto my side, letting Luke's big body block the offending light.

Just a little longer.

A few seconds later, my eyelids snapped open.

Holy shit.

It was moving day.

My heart did a little flip-flop and I grinned against Luke's shoulder, a ripple of excitement rolling through my belly. I tucked my legs into the back of Luke's, spooning him from behind, my exhausted cock rallying for a second as it nudged his warm arse before quickly throwing in the towel. Luke had pretty much milked the poor thing dry the night before, not that I was complaining.

The memory brought another smile to my face as I settled my chest against his hot back and slid an arm around his waist.

Moving day.

Finally.

He murmured something I couldn't make out and then once again fell silent, his breathing calm, his heart beating steadily against the flat of my hand, his body like an anchor in my arms keeping me grounded, a solid touchstone, always present, always there if he was needed.

A six-foot-four, honest-to-God miracle in my life.

Funny thing, that whole love and moving-in-together conundrum I'd been so wary about. Turned out, it hadn't been such a conundrum after all.

I hadn't needed a year.

I hadn't even needed six months.

Five months and I was as sure as I needed to be.

Five months of dating. Five months of adjusting to the wonder of having a man plan his week and most of his life around me. *Me*. Of being made to feel that I was the most important person in someone else's life.

Five months of laughter and fun and spectacular sex. And of waking up to Luke more often than not and realising how fucking lucky I was.

Not that it had all been plain sailing.

Because it had been five months of me discovering how to be in a relationship for the first time as well. Five months of us working hard to hold on to that promise to keep talking things through, keep trying to listen, to adapt, to compromise. And it hadn't come without its curly moments.

Learning to trust that Luke was staying around was one of those. That particular concern was helped by his signing off on the partnership with Gary and watching the two men work so well together. Learning to believe in myself was another. That one was still a work in progress. The third big one—learning to protect and prioritise our relationship when the outside world pressed in.

Caught between wanting to help Jules, my shepherding job, building kennels, working with clients and their dogs, and trying to lay the foundations for a business—I'd been run ragged to the point of exhaustion and began blowing off dates with Luke. He'd called me out on my bullshit, sat me down, and helped me see what I was doing to myself... and to us. I realised I couldn't do it all. Go figure. And so we came up with a plan that saw him working with me to get some of it done, sharing the load. Fucking teamwork. Who'd have guessed?

But Luke was determined to avoid the same mistakes he'd made in his first marriage, and I was learning by watching his example, his readiness to apologise and change and do whatever it took to not go to bed angry with each other. We weren't always successful, but the percentages were on our side.

But most important of all, we were learning how to pilot our relationship through those shadowy times when Luke became cool and uncommunicative, staring off into the distance, lost in his grief. When it was hard for him to see beyond the hole in his life and soul that a bubbly ten-year-old girl had once filled.

Learning what to do when he was in that space hadn't been easy, and I'd had to dig deep and find a way to let him know that I wanted to be there for him in those times as well, that it was part of the deal, holding him or keeping guard from a distance—whatever he needed—but shutting me out wasn't an option. Never that.

We'd had some missteps along the way navigating my insecurities and his pain, but slowly, Luke began to open up about Callie and she became this real person to me, not a ghost locked in Luke's memory. He shared warm and funny stories. Sad stories. Hopeful stories. All the stories. And slowly over the five months, the time between those shadowy spaces stretched. Not gone. Never gone. The loss would always be there. But Callie was back in Luke's life in a different way. In a way that wasn't handcuffed to that singular horrific day.

Maybe the new life we were building together helped.

Maybe it was just Luke finding his way.

Luke said it was because of me.

But we both knew it was a lot more than that. It was another team effort.

All of us.

Luke, me, and Callie.

Because like Luke himself, Callie was never far from my thoughts. She was a third presence in our relationship, something I hadn't been sure I'd know how to deal with at the start. But I'd always known that Luke came as a package deal, and getting to know Callie through his eyes had turned out to be a real privilege. Hearing her voice for the first time on that message he so often played had almost broken me. But after a while, it had me smiling instead. She sounded like such a happy girl. A firecracker. I liked to think she and I might've gotten along pretty well.

Luke drew a deep breath, lifted my hand to his lips, and kissed my knuckles before mumbling something that sounded like, "Good morning."

I smiled and kissed his back. "Morning to you too. Go back to sleep. We don't need to get up yet."

"Good." He kissed my hand again and held it against his chest. "I love you."

Barely a morning went by that those words weren't the first or second thing out of his mouth and they still hit me in the heart every time. "I love you too. Now go back to sleep."

I love you.

Damn, those words hadn't come easily to me. The trust that Luke wouldn't run, that he wouldn't find me wanting, that he wouldn't suddenly decide he didn't love me after all or fall for someone else like Holden had. But I'd finally gotten there.

I loved this complicated man more than I'd ever believed possible, more than I thought I was capable of. And *finally*, two months after we started dating, I found the courage to tell him so.

We'd been snowed in at the station, my tiny couch pulled in front of a raging fire, Luke's feet in my lap, mine in his, the latest John Connelly novel in his hands, in mine a tablet open to a website listing of sheepdogs for sale. The moment seemed perfect. Then again, so had the dozen or so previous moments I'd thought about telling him only to totally chicken out.

And through it all, he'd never once pushed. Never done anything except tell me as often as he could just how much he loved me. That, and show me in every way it was possible to show someone that you loved them without saying the actual words.

In short, he'd dated the shit out of me. Turned up at the cottage with flowers, which I still hadn't lived down after Charlie ran into him in the driveway and spread the word. Then we'd both had to endure Gil's disbelief and good-natured teasing about the fact Luke had never brought *him* flowers. And if I'd happened to smile a little smugly at that fact, it was nobody's business but my own.

There were picnics bundled up in our winter woollies with the dogs for company. Surprise flights over the winter wonderland landscape of the Southern Alps in Luke's new chopper. A romantic weekend holed up in some luxury villa accommodation run by a gay couple just out of Queenstown, one who roasted the best coffee beans this side of the Tasman.

And finally, on that snowy night in the cottage, I'd crawled into Luke's lap, the heat of the fire prickling at my back, Luke's hands resting on my hips, his expression soft and warm as always. I'd cradled his face and stared into those beautiful blue eyes, and then I'd kissed him, long and slow, putting all my love into that single point of connection.

The sex, the lust, the craving of each other's bodies had always burned so brightly between us. But it was no longer enough. I wasn't sure it ever had been.

It was time, and I wanted Luke to know how I truly felt.

And so, I'd pulled back just enough to get the words out, our lips a heartbeat away. "There's something I need to say."

"Oh" was all he'd said, like he didn't dare hope.

And in the end, the words came so easily. "I love you, Luke Nichols. I love you so much I don't fucking know what to do with it all."

His breath whooshed out of his lungs. "You do?" He'd crushed me to him. "You really fucking do?"

I'd laughed. "Yes, I really fucking do." And then I'd bawled like a fucking baby against his neck.

My *declaration* had been quickly followed by the official meeting with Luke's family who flew down to Oakwood to meet me. No pressure, right? To say they'd been curious about the southern shepherd who'd stolen their son's heart was the understatement of the year. But that was relegated a distant second place to their wide-eyed astonishment when Holden and Gil hosted us all for lunch at the station. Reality TV had nothing on us. The meal wasn't without its awkward moments, but once Charlie offered up a toast to the ridiculous path of love and the miracle of second chances, there were nothing but smiles.

"Up and at 'em, boys!" The bedroom window rattled in its frame, and I shot bolt upright in bed. "Aw, there he is. Morning, sunshine."

Holden's voice registered in my brain, and I turned to shoot daggers at my best friend only to find Gil and Jules standing alongside, wriggling their fingers in greeting and wearing shit-eating grins that I wanted to wipe off their faces tout suite.

"Jesus Christ, I'm gonna kill them all." I flung back the sheet only to find myself held firmly in place by an arm wrapped around my waist.

"Whoa there, Tiger. In case you hadn't noticed, you're naked."

Gil was pointedly tapping his watch while Holden and Jules wore shit-eating grins.

"Oh, right." I pulled the covers back over my junk before flipping all three of them off. "But I'm still gonna kill them. Just as soon as I get some clothes on."

Luke chuckled. "My hero."

Holden held aloft a bag of pastries from Meg's café and pointed meaningfully toward the front door. "Let us in."

Luke leaned across and snapped the curtains shut, an act that only drew loud laughter from the men outside. Then he pulled me on top of him and kissed me soundly, adding a decent grope of my nether regions just for good measure. "Go on." He slapped my arse. "You take the shower and I'll get the coffee on."

"They weren't supposed to be here to help until nine," I grumbled, sticking my feet out of the covers before whipping them back under. "Fuck, it's cold out there."

Luke checked his phone and handed it to me before getting out of bed.

Eight forty? I blinked. "Damn, I must've gone back to sleep."

"Well, it *was* a tiring night." Luke circled the bed and pulled me up into his arms, nuzzling his way up my neck until he found my chattering teeth. "An extremely enjoyable but tiring night."

"Mmm." I wriggled my burgeoning semi against his. "Hmm. That feels promising." I wriggled again. "Wanna join me in the shower? Those bozos can look after themselves."

A loud pounding on the front door put paid to both our semis along with any hope of doing something with them.

Luke groaned. "Back to plan A. But remember, we have a new home to christen tonight. And a lifetime of days and nights after that to do whatever we want, whenever we want, however we want, and for as long as we want."

I brightened at the thought. "Excellent point. Still, do me a favour and put a spoonful of salt in Holden's coffee, will you? That fucker knew exactly what he was doing arriving this early."

By mid-afternoon, we had all our boxes moved and unpacked in our new cottage at the southern end of Miller Station, closer to Lake Tekapo. From there, I could be at the woolshed in under fifteen minutes, while Luke had a forty-minute commute to the airfield this side of Oakwood. Not ideal for him, but as he was quick to remind me, tons of city people had a much longer commute without the benefit of any spectacular scenery along the way.

It was Emily who'd come up with the suggestion of refitting the hunting cottage and renting it to us. She had offered us *her* cottage first since she and Harry had decided to move into Oakwood by the end of the year, but Luke and I had looked at each other, given the idea about five seconds of serious consideration, then answered with a flat no. As much as the two of us got on well with Holden and Gil, I wasn't about to live fifty metres from both our exes. That was *way* too close for comfort. And by the immediate relief visible in Gil's and Holden's expressions when we turned it down, it was clear they felt the same.

Originally built as a two-bedroom hunting and fishing retreat for the Miller clan, the hunting cottage had a cosy, rustic feel with a large sitting area, covered deck, and open-plan kitchen. But it hadn't been used in Holden's lifetime, and Luke and I had put in a fair amount of work over the previous few weeks to get it liveable. Nothing structural, just cleaning and repairs, some new plumbing, a few rugs, and a kitchen and appliance upgrade. The result was worth it. With Luke's furniture from Wellington and a few of my things from my old cottage back on Lane Station, which Jules had insisted I raid as needed, the place felt warm and inviting and completely and utterly ours.

Against our protests, Miller Station had fronted the costs of the basic repairs and upgrades since Gil insisted they'd be using it for guests once Luke and I eventually moved on to a place of our own in a couple of years. We'd talked about maybe building something on a small piece of land nearer to Oakwood. Room for my business and closer to town for Luke.

"Well, I think that's the last box emptied and flattened," Holden said, joining me on the deck with its view over the billowing tussock to Lake Tekapo in the distance. "We'll head off and leave you two love birds to settle in." He winked.

I shot him a sour look. "If by 'settle in' you mean inhale a reheated pizza on the sofa with a rerun of *The Bourne Identity* playing in the background to fall asleep to and absolutely zero chance of any sexy times happening, you'd be bang on."

Holden laughed. "Welcome to couple life."

"Hey, there's nothing wrong with a cosy night in front of the telly." Gil slid an arm around Holden's waist. "But seriously, the place looks great. And so convenient." He waggled his brows. "Just think, we'll be able to drop in to see you anytime we pass."

I narrowed my gaze and stabbed a finger toward the new bell by the front door. "If we don't answer, go away."

Luke's arm fell around my shoulder, pulling me close. "Yeah, what he said."

Gil laughed, and Holden kissed him on the side of the head. "I think that's our cue to leave, babe. We'll call in tomorrow for a housewarming beer if that's okay. And we'll drop off a couple of the new kennels."

"Perfect," Luke replied, weariness cutting deep lines into his handsome face. It had been a hectic few weeks. "We should be awake by, oh, let me think, around mid-afternoon should do it."

Holden laughed. "Point taken." He held up his hand and they high-fived.

"But no pizza," Gil called out as Holden tugged him toward the ute. "I left a few of your favourite meals in the fridge."

Oh, thank God. "You're the best."

Gil elbowed Holden. "See, I told you I'm the best. You never listen."

"Shut up and drive." Holden threw the keys over the roof of the vehicle.

Gil snagged them mid-air. "And I'm the best driver too."

"Oh my god, will no one save me?" Holden grumbled, adding a final wave before jumping into the passenger seat.

Jules appeared from inside the cottage. "I'll be on my way too. I've got some stuff to do in Oakwood before I head home. Congratulations on your new home." Jules pulled Luke into a hug and then did the same with me. "I'm happy for you both. Truly." He stepped back but held my gaze. "And in case I haven't said it enough, I couldn't have managed the last few months without your help. You both deserve this. Enjoy it, and thank you."

I took his hand. "It goes both ways. I'll always be here for you, you know that. It's not going to be easy when . . . well, you know."

He locked eyes. "I know. Please don't be a stranger when Dad gets home in a couple of weeks. Things are going to change, Zach, you have my word. After everything you've done, I won't be taking any of his bullshit."

I shot a tired glance to Luke and then squeezed Jules' hand. "I appreciate the intent, but we both know he's not likely to change."

"I don't care if he changes," Jules insisted. "As long as he keeps his mouth shut and his opinions to himself."

I let it go. My father knew Luke and I were together and that Luke had been helping at the station, but he'd never once mentioned Luke's name. And the hope that my father would keep his opinions to himself was the stuff of fairy tales, especially with his current frustrations. The hemiplegia had definitely improved with rehab, but he still needed a frame and supervision to walk, assistance with all his daily living tasks, and his speech was never going to be what it was. And no one could say how much or even *if* any more function would return. There was no way he could take the reins back on the station in the foreseeable future, which meant Paddy Lane was going to be hell to live with once he moved back home.

"There's one last thing before I go." Jules reached into his bag and pulled out a wrapped package. "This is from Mum. It's a housewarming gift."

My stomach swooped. "A gift?" I stared at the package, gobsmacked. Luke squeezed my shoulder and I leaned into him, swallowing around a sudden lump of emotion.

Jules nodded. "Go on, open it. It won't bite you."

I wasn't so sure, but I accepted the gift. Still staring at it, I thought back on all the times Luke had turned up at Lane Station to help with whatever needed doing. I considered those some of the most romantic gestures he'd ever made, especially knowing my father's views. On some of those visits, Luke had even encountered my mother, who came and went from Christchurch as needed. To her credit, she'd been nothing but gracious toward him, if somewhat curious, watching us together like she was trying to figure us out.

Then came the day that Luke, thinking we were alone in the big house, had shoved me up against the wall for a thorough kissing, only to pull away and discover my mother watching us from an open doorway. I'd braced, not sure how things would pan out, but Luke had simply slid his arm around my waist, and said, "Hi, Norma."

My mother had blushed, given both of us one of her warm smiles, and then left us alone. She and I had been finding our way back to each other ever since.

With trembling hands, I opened the package and dropped the paper to the deck. It took a second for what I was seeing to register in my brain, but when it did—*holy shit*. I stared in utter disbelief, recognising my mother's handiwork since something similar hung alongside the front door of Lane Station. I spun the small wooden plaque to better read the burned inscription and drew a sharp breath.

LOVE LIVES HERE.

It wasn't only the words, although holy fucking hell, they meant *everything*. My gaze shot up to Jules and I swallowed hard. "But she hasn't . . . in years . . . her hands?"

He gave a soft knowing smile. "She wanted to do this for you. For you both. And let's just say the arthritis meds got a good workout for a few days."

I studied the plaque again, reading all the unspoken things it represented, and letting them settle in my heart.

"Can I see?" Luke read over my shoulder and gave a soft grunt of surprise. "Well, good for her." He kissed my cheek and I turned and fell into his arms, a storm of emotions coursing through me.

I didn't even know why I was crying, or rather what in particular I was crying about. There were too many things at play, both good and bad, and I was so, so tired.

Jules' hand clasped my neck. "I'm going to leave you two alone and call tomorrow. Enjoy your first night."

He was halfway to his ute when I spun and called out, "Tell Mum I said thank you. Tell her I love it. Tell her it's going up beside the door tonight. Tell her—"

"I'll tell her," he assured me with a smile. "And I'll tell her, you'll call her . . . tomorrow."

I watched him leave with the reassuring warmth of Luke at my back, his arms around my waist, his lips on my neck.

"Alone at last." His hot breath brushed my ear, raising goosebumps down my spine. "So, are you ready to christen this place? Fuck on every flat surface?"

I almost choked on the speed that the words, "Absolutely not. Are you crazy?" burst off my tongue.

Luke laughed and squeezed me tight. "Thank God for that. Here I was thinking I was going to have to lie back and count merinos. How about a beer instead?"

I turned and snagged a kiss. "Hell yeah. You read my mind. But let's have it out here? With no fucking in our immediate future, it won't matter if we freeze our nuts off."

"I like the way you think." He steered me toward the large outdoor sofa that had arrived with his load of furniture, then ducked back into the cottage and returned with two heavy quilts and a couple of open beers.

We clinked bottles and then cosied up together to stare across the snow-capped clumps of tussock toward the lake, lying cool and flinty grey in the far distance, its surface like satin in the breathless air. The mass of wintered jagged peaks that cradled its top end stepped up and back in an endless staircase before disappearing into the pallid sky, the sun no more than a cream glow behind the curtain of high cloud.

We sat in silence for a long time, Luke's heart beating at my back, his hand resting over mine, his breath fogging in the cool air over my shoulder. My heart felt too full for words, the emotions too raw, too vast for my body to hold. It was enough to deliver them to the mountains, and to the rivers that cut through this country like braids of Rapunzel's hair. To the grey stone that girded the earth, the golden tussock that rolled endlessly over top, and the infinite sky that watched over it all.

That left only one thing that needed attending to.

"Do you remember that jeweller we visited in Queenstown? The guy who made my belt buckle?" I turned sideways to better see Luke's face.

He nodded, tucking a lock of my hair behind my ears. "Stef something. Married to the hot cowboy?"

I rolled my eyes. "Of course, you'd remember the damn husband."

Luke waggled his brows and then kissed me. "I have eyes only for you, my love. What about him?"

"Well . . ." I took a deep breath and blew it out slowly. "I might have done something."

His gaze narrowed. "As in?"

Okay. Here goes nothing. It had seemed a good idea at the time but you never knew. "Okay, so I might've called him once we got back, and then I might've asked him to make something for me . . . well actually, for *you*."

Luke said nothing, his eyes watchful, wary.

I replayed my words in my head and groaned. "Shit. Don't panic. It's not a ring or anything like that."

He swallowed a smile, his eyes soft on mine. "And why would I panic about that?"

What? My train of thought disappeared in a puff of astonishment. I hadn't expected that. "Nope. Nuh-uh." I wagged my finger at him. "You are not going to derail me." I eyed him up and down. "But I'll take a rain check on that topic later." I eyeballed him. "*Much* later."

He drew me close and kissed me. "Agreed. Now what have you been up to?"

"Oh, right." I winced, sent a silent prayer to Callie, and then dug into my pocket and drew out a small black velvet pouch tied with a blue bow. I handed it to Luke who gave me a puzzled look before taking it. "If you don't like it or want to change it, I want you to say so," I rushed. "I mean it made sense to me, but really, I have no idea about—" I stopped my rambling and sighed. "Just open it already. I can't stand the suspense and I might have to cry again."

Luke cradled my face and pressed the softest of kisses to my lips. "I already know I'm going to love it, whatever it is. Because it's come from you."

I drew a stuttered breath and wiped my leaking eyes. "Dammit. See, I'm crying already. Just open it."

He kissed me again and then opened the pouch, frowning at the loop of leather cord that immediately popped up. "Is that . . ." He shot me a crooked grin. "Why, you sneaky little fucker. So, that's where it got to. You know that I've been looking for this all week."

I shrugged. "Maybe."

He shook his head and hooked the cord with his finger, pulling until a flat circular pendant made out of grey polished stone came into view. He glanced up at me, eyes wide, and then set the pouch aside and turned the pendant in his hand, studying it.

I could still remember its smooth feel when I'd chosen it from the waters of the Havelock River, or rather, when it had chosen me, tumbling onto my toes.

Stef Hamilton had done a beautiful job. The design was clean and simple, the gorgeous layers in the polished stone left unadorned to speak for themselves, millennia in the making. The only addition was three words etched onto one side.

Forever and Always.

Luke's gaze jerked to mine, his throat working. "I—" He swallowed hard. "I don't know what to say. Is this . . . is this from—"

"The Havelock River?" I scooted closer and took the pendant from him. "Yes. Come here."

He leaned forward and I fixed the clasp around his neck.

He lifted the stone and stared at it again. "I can't believe you did this. It's so fucking beautiful. I love it."

Thank God. I ran my thumb under his damp eyes and rested my head on his shoulder. "I wanted you to have a memory of where she runs free. The heart that used to hang around your neck was for you and Gil and for bringing Callie home as a newborn. I wanted this one to be for you and me and also for bringing Callie home, but in a different way."

"Oh, Jesus, Zach." Luke's shoulders heaved. He cupped my face in his palm, and I leaned into his touch, his blue eyes glimmering, his expression soft with emotion. "You mean everything to me. I love you so much. And this—" He lifted the pendant. "This says everything about us. It's about you and me, and this land and its rivers, and Callie's memory, and our future." He sucked in a raw breath and clutched me fiercely against his chest, whispering, "It's all I need. It's all I'll ever need."

My hands slipped under his shirt and around the hot skin of his waist, the sense of coming home hitting me hard as it always did. We clung to each other with the silence of the vast Mackenzie Country as our witness, the only sound to break it, the soft whisper of my heart.

"I love you, too."

The End.

Want to keep up with all my news and releases, sign up to my newsletter HERE.

Follow me on Amazon HERE.
Follow me on BookBub HERE.
Follow me on Instagram HERE.
Follow me on TikTok HERE.
Join Hogan's Hangout HERE.

Don't miss the next book in the series

THE SCIENCE OF ATTRACTION

I am Mackenzie Country born and bred. Farming the high country runs in my blood, like my father, and his father, and his grandfather before him. My future has been mapped out for me since the day I was born. Or at least it was, until Liam Skelton walks onto Lane Station, lights a fire in my heart, and turns my whole world upside down.

Bossy, tatted, and out and proud, Liam is everything my father abhors.
And I want him.
Badly.

But having a chance with Liam means risking everything. My family. My future. And my life in these mountains that I love. Still, the heart wants what it wants, and mine wants Liam.

With so many things against us, maybe we don't have a chance.
Maybe we'll crash and burn.
Or maybe we'll find a way to have it all.

ALSO BY JAY HOGAN

SERIES

AUCKLAND MED SERIES

Book 1 First Impressions is free as a series starter at most retailers.

SOUTHERN LIGHTS SERIES

Book 1 Powder and Pavlova is free as a series starter at most retailers.

STYLE SERIES

PAINTED BAY SERIES

(Includes Off Balance — Recipient of the 2021 Romance Writers of NZ Romance Book of the Year Award)

MACKENZIE COUNTRY SERIES

(Includes The Art of Husbandry — 2024 Lambda Literary Finalist in Gay Romance)

STANDALONE BOOKS

FOXED

UNGUARDED

(Part of Sarina Bowen's Vino & Veritas Series)

DIGGING DEEP

(2020 Lambda Literary Finalist in Gay Romance)

AUDIOBOOKS

All of my audiobooks are available at a discounted price from my website HERE.

You can also find them at most audiobook retailers including

Spotify, Audible, Apple Books, Barnes & Noble, Chirp

and many others.

ABOUT THE AUTHOR

Jay is a two times Lambda Literary Award Finalist— 2020 DIGGING DEEP and 2024 THE ART OF HUSBANDRY.

Jay is also the recipient of The Romance Writers of New Zealand 2021 Romance Book Of The Year Award for OFF BALANCE.

I am a New Zealand author writing mm romance and romantic suspense primarily set in my home country. I write character driven romances with lots of humour, a good dose of reality, and a splash of angst. I've travelled extensively, lived in many countries, and in a past life I worked as a critical care nurse and a counsellor. I am owned by a huge Maine Coon cat and a gorgeous Cocker Spaniel.

Join my Facebook reader's group Jay Hogan's Hangout for updates, promotions, my current writing projects and special releases.

Sign up to my newsletter HERE.

Or visit my website HERE.